"Get out," she said flatly without shifting.

He laughed softly, that low musical laugh that never failed to make her skin heat with awareness. Ranelaw made her ache to fling aside dull morality and taste again the heady wine of passion.

But the wine of passion was deadly poison.

"I should have known you'd be too stalwart to scream at the sight of a man in your bedchamber. Although I'm sure you're shocked to the soles of your sensible shoes, Miss Smith."

"What do you want?"

"Would you believe me if I said you?"

"No, I wouldn't. At least I'm glad you chose the wrong bedroom. I'll make sure Cassie keeps her windows locked."

"I didn't choose the wrong bedroom," he said steadily, watching her with an unwavering stare.

Anger swelled above dread and reluctant desire. He didn't care that his actions could destroy her. He was such a selfish swine.

She blew out the candle and turned. Again, desperately, she sought some sign of moral turpitude. As ever, she found nothing but breathtakingly virile male.

By Anna Campbell

Anna Campbell

Midnight's Wild Passion

AVON

An Imprint of HarperCollinsPublishers

AVON BOOKS
An Imprint of HarperCollins*Publishers*
10 East 53rd Street
New York, New York 10022-5299

For my dear friend Annie West,
who turns the writing journey into a party!

Acknowledgments

So many people to thank! First I'd like to thank the wonderful team at Avon in New York who as ever has been a delight to work with. In particular, I'd like to thank May Chen, my editor; Amanda Bergeron; Pamela Spengler-Jaffee; Wendy Ho; and Christine Maddalena. I'd like to send a particular thanks to the brilliant art department—you've excelled yourselves with this gorgeous cover. I love it. Thanks too to the team at Avon/HarperCollins Australia, especially Anna Valdinger and Monica Svarc. I'd also like to thank my agent, Nancy Yost, for her continuing support.

As always, I'd like to thank the writing friends who enrich my life so immeasurably. My deepest gratitude to Annie West, Sharon Archer, Christine Wells, Vanessa Barneveld, Kandy Shepherd, Pamela Clare, Nancy Northcott, Anna Sugden, Jeanne Adams, Helen Bianchin, Pamela Palmer, Miranda Neville, Louisa Cornell, Tawny Weber, Jennifer Low, Sarah Mayberry, Kathleen O'Reilly, and Nicola Cornick. You're all wonderful! Special thanks to the multitalented Paula Roe, who looks after my Web site in between writing her own wonderful books.

My life wouldn't be the same without the rambunctious, irreverent, and funny Romance Bandits. My fellow Banditas, you always make me smile. I'd also like to thank the remarkable women at The Romance Dish: PJ Ausdenmore, Buffie Johnson, Gannon Carr, and Andrea Williamson.

I belong to a number of organizations that are a continual source of encouragement, information, and good old-fashioned fun. These include Romance Writers of Australia, Romance Writers of New Zealand, the Australian Romance Readers' Association, and Romance Writers of America.

I'd also like to thank the wonderful reader friends I've made since *Claiming the Courtesan* came out in 2007. I can't tell you how much your ongoing enthusiasm for my stories means to me.

Midnight's Wild Passion

Chapter One

ENEATH hooded eyelids, Nicholas Challoner, Marquess of Ranelaw, surveyed the whirling snowstorm of white dresses. A debutantes' ball was the last place the *ton* expected to encounter a rake of his appalling reputation. A rake of his appalling reputation should know better than to appear at any such respectable gathering.

With his arrival, the chatter faltered away to silence. Ranelaw was accustomed to causing a flutter. Neither curiosity nor disapproval distracted him. As the orchestra scratched a trite écossaise, he scanned the room for his prey.

Ah, yes. . .

His jaded gaze settled upon his mark.

The chit wore white. Of course. The color symbolized purity. It convinced buyers in this particular market that no human hand had sullied the merchandise.

For Miss Cassandra Demarest, he'd ensure that promise was a lie. Nothing much excited him these days, but as he contemplated his victim, satisfaction stirred in his gut.

After the brief, shocked silence, the room exploded into hubbub. Clearly Ranelaw wasn't the only person convinced he belonged elsewhere.

A fiery, subterranean elsewhere.

The guests were right to be perturbed. He carried mayhem in his soul.

A smile of wicked anticipation teased at his lips as he studied the girl. Until a caricature in black stepped between him and his object of interest, spoiling the view. He frowned, then turned when Viscount Thorpe spoke beside him.

"Sure you're ready for this, old man? The tabbies are giving you the cold eye and you haven't asked Miss Demarest to dance yet."

"A man reaches the age to set up his nursery, Thorpe." He glanced up again, seeking his quarry. The black barrier hindering his inspection resolved itself into a tall woman with a nondescript face. At least what he saw was nondescript, under tinted spectacles and a lace cap with ugly, dangling lappets.

Thorpe scoffed. "Miss Demarest won't give you the time of day, my good fellow."

Ranelaw's smile turned cynical. "I'm one of the richest men in England and my name goes back to the Conquest."

Thorpe released an unimpressed snort. "The name you've done your best to disgrace. Your courtship won't be the doddle you imagine, my fine friend. Miss Demarest has the kingdom's most fearsome chaperone. You might gull the filly, but the redoubtable Miss Smith will send you packing before you get your paws on the girl's fortune. Before you get so much as a whiff of it, I'll wager."

"I'm not interested in Miss Demarest's fortune," Ranelaw said with perfect honesty. "And surely you don't rely on some sparrow of a spinster to circumvent me. I eat chaperones for breakfast."

He ate courtesans and widows and other men's wives for lunch and dinner, with much more pleasurable result. He trusted very little in his life, but since his first heady experience of sex, he'd trusted the fleeting delight he found in a woman's body. He asked nothing more of his lovers, frequently to their chagrin.

Thorpe's eyes brightened with greed. "A hundred guineas say Miss Smith dismisses you with a flea in your ear when you make your bow."

"A hundred? A paltry risk for a sure thing. Make it five."

"Done."

Lady Wreston wove through the throng to greet the arrivals. Thorpe had made sure his aunt sent Ranelaw a card for the ball. Nonetheless she looked less than overjoyed to see him.

A pity. She'd looked overjoyed to see him yesterday afternoon in her summerhouse. She'd looked even more overjoyed half an hour later with her drawers around her ankles and a hectic flush heightening her famous complexion.

Devil take their delicious hides, but women were a capricious sex.

Ranelaw glanced past his comely hostess to where Cassandra Demarest shifted back into sight. He'd had the girl followed since her arrival in London a week ago and he'd observed her himself from a distance. She was a fetching little piece. Blond. A graceful figure. Ranelaw had never been close enough to read her expression with accuracy. Doubtless it would reveal the same vacuous sweetness that shone from the face of every maiden here.

If one excepted the chaperones.

His attention returned to the woman leaning over Miss Demarest like a sheltering tree over a ewe lamb. As if divining his thoughts, the chaperone stiffened. Her head jerked up and she focused on him.

Even across the room, even through her spectacles, her gaze burned. Severe, assessing, unwavering. Absolutely nothing fetching there, but he found himself unable to look away. Uncannily the surrounding cacophony faded to expectant hush.

As blatant as a tossed glove, she flung down a challenge.

Then she turned to answer something her charge said, Lady Wreston bustled up in all her plump glory, and the instant of hostile awareness splintered.

Unaccountably disconcerted by that wordless exchange of fire, Ranelaw bowed over his hostess's hand and asked to meet the Demarest heiress. Millicent, Lady Wreston, couldn't hide her flash of pique, but she knew what their world demanded. Girls were born to be wedded then bedded. Single men did the honors. Even single men who had sown a continent of wild oats required a legitimate heir.

The polite fiction of his interest in the marriage mart was convenient, although he rarely used respectability to cloak darker intentions. Hypocrisy counted among the rare sins he didn't commit on a regular basis. Nor did he indulge in willful self-deception. He knew that he'd roast in hell for what he plotted. Cassandra Demarest was an innocent who didn't deserve the fate he intended. But what he wrought was too important for him to ignore how perfectly the girl fitted his purposes. He couldn't allow scruples to discourage him.

Scruples and he had long been polite strangers.

He lingered to soothe his hostess's vanity, all the while watching Miss Demarest's every move. She'd accepted a dance, and her partner now returned her to the fearsome chaperone. The fearsome chaperone was a long Meg under that loose, rusty black gown at least five seasons out of date.

Then the Demarest chit spoke and the uninteresting Miss Smith smiled.

And became no longer quite so uninteresting.

Ranelaw felt winded, like someone had punched him in the belly.

Ridiculous, really, to be intrigued. So the crone possessed a lush mouth. Except now that he sauntered closer, he recognized Miss Smith wasn't a crone after all. Her skin was clear and unlined, with a soft flush of color like the pink of dawn. He found himself wondering about the eyes behind those unbecoming spectacles.

Good God, what was wrong with him?

The haggish chaperone demonstrated signs of desirability. Who the hell cared? He had other fish to fry. Young, unsuspecting fish trapped in a net of vengeance.

Lady Wreston performed introductions. "Lord Ranelaw, may I present Miss Cassandra Demarest, the daughter of Mr. Godfrey Demarest, of Bascombe Hailey in Somerset? This lady is her companion, Miss Smith."

Out of the corner of his eye, Ranelaw watched the chaperone straighten as if scenting danger. She was more awake than her charge, who blushed and dipped into a charming curtsy.

"Delighted, Miss Demarest," he murmured, bending over her gloved hand with a deference he knew the girl— and her dour companion—would note.

"My lord." Cassandra Demarest had long, childish eyelashes tipped with a gold darker than the luxuriant curls framing her piquant face. She inspected Ranelaw from under their shadow.

A natural coquette.

He wasn't surprised. Nor was he surprised to discover a beauty. She was as bright as a daffodil.

His skin prickled under the chaperone's glare. Curse the crowlike Miss Smith. He needed to concentrate on his goal, not some disapproving and insignificant old maid. Although with every second, he revised his estimate of the chaperone's age downward.

"May I have the pleasure of this dance?" A waltz struck up.

"I'd love—"

Miss Smith interrupted. "I'm sorry, Lord Ranelaw, but Miss Demarest's father strictly forbids the waltz. She has a country dance free after supper."

The dragon didn't sound sorry. Her husky voice was surprisingly resolute, considering she rebuked a man so far above her in rank.

"Toni, surely Papa wouldn't mind under these circumstances," Miss Demarest said in a winning tone.

Toni—an intriguingly pretty name for such a starched board—arched a blond eyebrow. "You know your father's rules."

Miss Demarest was clearly used to wheedling her own

way. Ranelaw prepared for a childish outburst, but the girl took denial in good spirit. Apparently he was mistaken in both women. Miss Demarest wasn't altogether a brainless flibbertigibbet. The black beetle showed unexpected promise.

How interesting. . .

More white-clad butterflies joined the group. Introductions were performed. The chaperone hovered protectively.

Wise chaperone.

Lady Wreston wandered away while Thorpe questioned Miss Demarest about mutual acquaintances in Somerset. Thorpe was related to half the nation and anyone he wasn't related to was apparently his dear acquaintance. The quizzing could continue into tomorrow. Taking advantage of the diverted attention, Ranelaw shifted nearer to the companion. She was even taller than he'd thought. In bed, she'd fit him perfectly.

What particular Gehenna spawned that thought?

"The chit won't take if you terrify all the eligible gentlemen, Miss Smith." Music and conversation restricted his taunting remark to her ears.

She started but didn't retreat. He found himself respecting her courage if not her sense of self-preservation. She kept her gaze fixed on Miss Demarest, who giggled at one of Thorpe's quips in a way Ranelaw found remarkably irritating. Would she giggle when he fucked her? He feared it likely.

"My lord, I hope you will permit me to be frank," Miss Smith said sternly.

He could imagine what the dragon wanted to say. She'd displayed only dismay when Lady Wreston introduced him to Miss Demarest. His reputation had preceded him. He counted on it as a weapon in his arsenal of seduction. Young girls found his wildness deplorably romantic.

Silly poppets.

"And if I said no?" he asked lazily.

"I'd still find myself compelled to speak."

"So I imagined," he said with a boredom that was completely feigned. Most people disapproved of him. Few had the backbone to tell him so to his face.

"Pray suffer no insult when I tell you I consider you neither eligible nor a gentleman, my lord. Miss Demarest can do considerably better than the Marquess of Ranelaw, even if your intentions are honorable, which I take leave to doubt."

He burst into laughter. His first unguarded response since entering this stuffy ballroom.

The woman had nerve. Damn him if she didn't. His interest, reluctantly aroused, became intent. He'd have the girl. No question. And before he was done, he'd have the chaperone as well.

He'd strip away that ugly gown. He'd unpin that wrenched-back hair—whatever color it was under that horrible cap—until it tumbled around her shoulders. He'd kiss those untouched breasts. He'd teach her to relish a man's caresses.

He reminded himself that the duenna was a side benefit of the main game. But his instincts didn't accept that. Right now, his instincts were pitched to hunting sharpness because of a desiccated maiden of uncertain age.

"You don't mince words, Miss Smith."

"No, I don't," she said calmly. Still, blast her, without moving away. Didn't she know he was dangerous?

He waved off a footman bearing a tray of orgeat. He despised that sickly sweet swill. Bugger it, he wanted a real drink. And he wanted to get his head screwed on right. For God's sake, he was accounted a connoisseur of the frail sex. He refused to let a prune-faced virgin divert him from his quest.

A prune-faced virgin who stood so close, he caught teasing hints of her scent. Something wholesome and clean. Something indicating innocence.

Of course it did.

"I make a difficult enemy," he said in a low voice.

She shrugged, still without looking at him. "Set your sights on another heiress, Lord Ranelaw."

"And that's a commandment from my lady disdain?"

At last she stared directly at him. The tinted glasses obscured her eyes, but he couldn't mistake her jaw's stubborn line. "You can't possibly consider this a challenge. A country miss and a harridan of a chaperone?"

He felt an unaccustomed urge to laugh again. He had the oddest conviction that she knew him better than anyone else here. "Why not?"

The primming of her mouth only drew his attention to its pink fullness. A spinster companion had no right to such kissable lips.

Now he'd actually met her, the prospect of bedding Cassandra Demarest flooded him with ennui. Whereas the idea of shutting Miss Smith's delectable but scolding mouth with passionate kisses, then thrusting hard between her spindly thighs made him vibrate with anticipation. Vinegar became his beverage of choice. He must have a maggot in his brain. He rarely found troublesome women appealing. Miss Smith had *troublesome* written all over her scrawny form.

Years of practice helped him conceal these unsettling reactions. Instead he tilted a knowing eyebrow and spoke in an indolent drawl that would irritate her to her undoubtedly thick and scratchy undergarments. "You know, for a woman little above a servant, you have a damned impudent manner."

Again she didn't back down. Her drawl almost matched his for self-confidence. Who *was* this woman? "Only impudent? How disappointing. When I strove for insolent, my lord."

This time a huff of laughter did escape. No female crossed swords with him, no matter how high born.

Miss Smith provided a refreshing change.

Perhaps that was why he found her so compelling. He couldn't possibly have developed a taste for hatchet-faced maypoles with sharp tongues and no dress sense.

"Miss Smith," he murmured in a silky voice, "if you seek to discourage, you're failing miserably. The prospect of besting you becomes irresistible."

Still she didn't take warning. Her chin tipped at a defiant angle. "Prove yourself a better man than the world believes and resist temptation, Lord Ranelaw."

A smile curled his lips. She was delicious. Tart like lemon curd. A sharp, fresh taste that wouldn't pall. Oh, he'd have her in his bed. She'd be his reward for ruining the poppet.

"Temptation is impossible to resist. That's what makes it temptation."

"You would know."

"Miss Smith, you'd be amazed at what I know," he said with as much salacious emphasis as he could manage. And a man with his experience could manage a great deal.

Through her spectacles, he felt her withering glance. Brava, Miss Smith. Seducing this woman would be like training a leopard to eat from his hand. She hissed and snarled now, but under a master's tutelage, she'd learn to purr.

"Lord Ranelaw . . ." she began, an edge to her voice.

The promise of a tongue-lashing was devilish exciting. What a pity he couldn't whisk her away and teach her to use that tongue for other purposes altogether.

The wench would have an apoplexy if she could read his mind.

Although something told him little disconcerted the stalwart Miss Smith. No wonder she was accounted the dragon of chaperones. Ranelaw rather liked casting himself as St. George. And this St. George would steal away both maiden and monster. Lucky fellow.

"Toni?"

Cassandra Demarest's uncertain question exploded into the tension bristling between him and the chaperone like a grenade tossed into an enemy line. With a reluctance he resented, Ranelaw wrenched his gaze from the outwardly uninteresting woman who so inexplicably aroused the strongest interest he'd felt in a donkey's age. He found himself and Miss Smith the cynosure of all eyes, and most of those eyes glinted with speculation and curiosity.

Hell, this was the last thing he wanted. His sudden decision to pursue the chaperone was purely a private matter, whereas he wanted his interest in the Demarest girl to become the talk of the *ton*.

Miss Smith's fine, pale skin reddened with humiliation. Her gloved hands strangled her plain black reticule. Ranelaw's lips twitched—he knew whom she really wanted to strangle.

A companion's employment relied on pristine reputation. An extended conversation with the notorious Marquess of Ranelaw would do Miss Smith no good. No wonder she looked furious enough to release a blast of dragon fire upon her tormenter.

Not that she glanced at him.

"Cassie, did you require something?" Ranelaw heard how hard she worked to steady her low voice.

Cassandra, to her credit, looked troubled rather than annoyed at her chaperone's lapse. "I was wondering if we received cards for the Bradhams' musicale."

Miss Smith's color heightened. In that moment as a blush warmed her creamy skin, Ranelaw's suspicion cemented into certainty. This was no aging spinster. The woman behind those tinted spectacles was young. Young and ripe for a man's picking.

His picking.

Chapter Two

URING the carriage ride home, Antonia Smith née Hilliard was still berating herself for her dangerous lapse. She knew better than to draw such attention to herself. Years of self-discipline, yet she'd made an utter fool of herself in public.

All for a blasted *rake*.

She was the biggest numbskull in Christendom.

Yes, Lord Ranelaw was handsome. Breathtakingly so, with a seductive manner that set her traitorous heart racing. She'd discovered in her disastrous acquaintance with the breed that rakes were almost invariably handsome. But good looks meant nothing when selfishness and debauchery blackened the spirit.

She knew that.

So why had she forgotten the carefully constructed fiction of Antonia Smith? Why had she responded with the élan she'd relinquished ten years ago, along with her virtue, her privileged place in the world, and her girlish hopes? She'd devoted a decade's service to creating a façade of irreproachable rectitude, of dull respectability. One glance from Lord Ranelaw's heavy-lidded eyes and she'd flung all that hard-won self-control aside. She must have lost her mind. Her security rested on her character remaining unsullied.

And it wasn't just Ranelaw's decorative shell that flustered her, may he roast in the hell designated for beautiful men with fetid souls.

No, he'd ambushed her as much with what he'd said as with his easy sexual confidence. She reminded herself that he used his sparking intelligence for sin. The knowledge couldn't quite snuff out the excitement of trading word for word with a man equal to the debate.

Foreboding oozed an icy path down her backbone. She didn't fool herself tonight would be her only encounter with the spectacular marquess. He was sniffing around Cassie.

With difficulty, Antonia had made it through the remainder of the ball. She'd resumed her role as perfect companion, invisible but watchful. Careful of her young cousin's reputation. Not that Cassie needed watching.

Or she never had before.

Right now Cassie sat in uncharacteristic silence on the bench opposite Antonia. When she did speak, the topic came as no surprise.

"I believe Lord Ranelaw is the handsomest man I've ever seen."

Oh, no. No, no, no.

Antonia's stomach cramped in denial. Surely Cassie hadn't succumbed so swiftly to the libertine's spell. She'd handled her dance with the marquess with equanimity and had seemed flattered but not unduly discomposed by his attentions. Through the rest of the evening, he'd studiously minded his manners. He'd cast Antonia only one mocking look from those fathomless dark eyes. A look she'd pretended not to notice.

"He's too old for you," Antonia said sharply, then was sorry when she watched Cassie's curiosity build.

"He can't be past his early thirties. A man in his prime. He made every other gentleman in that ballroom look callow or superannuated." Over the carriage's creak, Antonia heard the breathless admiration in the girl's voice.

"Cassie, your father would have a fit if he knew you encouraged scoundrels like Ranelaw."

"My father is in Paris and likely to stay there."

With his usual lack of forethought, her second cousin and employer, Godfrey Demarest, had decamped to France a month ago, set on immersing himself once again in the fleshpots. An occupation he took much more seriously than he ever took running his estate or raising his child.

He'd left Antonia responsible for his daughter, no matter how inadequate she felt to that task outside the bounds of his estate. In spite of the enormous gratitude she owed him, they'd verged on their first quarrel when he'd insisted that supervising Cassie's debut season presented few risks to Antonia.

Antonia had pointed out that someone from Northumberland might recognize her. Mr. Demarest retorted that her brother was the only likely candidate and he'd become a hermit since inheriting. Demarest also remarked—correctly so far, with the exception of that wily fox Ranelaw—that nobody looked closely at a companion. Even if they did, who would suspect dowdy Miss Smith was the renegade daughter of Lord Aveson? With his usual unbounded optimism, Mr. Demarest promised that if Antonia was safe from exposure in Somerset, she'd be safe in London.

After tonight, she didn't feel safe. One misstep and her identity would remain a secret no longer. With that revelation, scandal would rise to drown not just her, but her cousins, in a tide of disgrace. And she still had to convince Cassie that Ranelaw wasn't for her.

"There are regular mail deliveries, even to the wilds of Paris," she said dryly. "Don't imagine you're beyond reach of nasty gossip, my girl."

"Don't you think he's handsome?"

Knowing she fought a losing battle, Antonia tried to distract her. "Your father? Yes, he's a fine figure of a man."

Cassie smothered a belly laugh that would surprise the many admirers who praised her delicacy. "Not Papa. Lord Ranelaw. Toni, don't pretend you didn't notice. I saw you talking to him."

"I was warning him away from you," she said with perfect truth, if not with perfect completeness. Plenty else had gone on during that intense conversation in full view of the *ton*. Again she chided herself. How could she have been so reckless?

"I'll wager he's a wonderful kisser," Cassie said in a dreamy voice.

"That thought is unbecoming in a lady," Antonia said, even as she couldn't help picturing that long, lean body. She was a tall woman but he'd towered over her. Cassie was right. He'd turned every other man there tonight into a nonentity. That's what rakes did. She ought to know.

After her experiences, she'd imagined herself immune. She hadn't found a man attractive in ten years. Once bitten, forever shy.

So why did the old, insidious heat stir at the sight of the depraved Marquess of Ranelaw? A man who made the other rakes she'd met seem complete scarecrows. She should be repulsed by his self-confidence and blatant sexual games.

She hadn't been repulsed, curse her.

Now Cassie was starry eyed over the rogue. The headache that had threatened all night pounded in earnest at Antonia's temples.

"You haven't answered me." Cassie was a good, sensible girl, but stubborn. Something else that would surprise the numerous swains she'd gathered since her advent into society.

Antonia was firmly of the belief that a little stubbornness stood a girl in good stead. But sometimes she wished Cassie was the gorgeous, empty-headed doll the world considered her.

"His swarthy skin contrasts unattractively with his light hair."

You're such a liar, Antonia.

Ranelaw's unusual coloring was striking, drew the eye like his impressive height and lazy sensuality.

Damn him to hell.

Cassie gave another dismissive laugh. "Toni, what a fib. He's as handsome as Adonis and you know it."

"Forget what he looks like. He's a sewer rat." Her voice became urgent. "Cassie, for my sake, for your father's sake, for your own sake, don't set your cap at him. Men like that are heartbreakers."

She waited for the girl to object. Or perhaps worse, continue praising the marquess. To her surprise, Cassie took her hand. "I'm sorry, Toni. I'm not silly. I know what's at stake."

She was tactful enough not to say, *I know what a rake cost you.* But she might as well have. Once a future just as bright as Cassie's had extended before Antonia Hilliard. No longer.

Antonia returned Cassie's clasp and glanced out the window. They were nearly home. "He's not good husband material." She meant it to her toes.

"Perhaps not." Before Antonia could breathe a sigh of relief, she went on. "Although I'm sure he's an unforgettable lover. One look from under his eyelids and I get all shivery. When he took my hand for the dance, I vow I almost swooned."

"Cassie . . ."

"I know. He's dangerous. But I've never met anyone like him. He makes me think of stallions and lightning and the ocean and long gallops across the moors."

To her chagrin, Antonia knew exactly what Cassie meant. As a girl not much younger than Cassie, she'd experienced all those exciting urges and she'd let them ruin her life. The glittering life she'd been born to live was forever denied her because of her fatal weakness. No way would she permit that insanity to destroy this innocent girl she loved like a sister or the daughter she'd never have.

However handsome the wicked Lord Ranelaw was.

However powerfully her own recollections of stallions and storms and headlong gallops stirred when she met his knowing dark eyes.

* * *

Ranelaw returned to his London house poorer by five hundred guineas. As Thorpe gloatingly pointed out, Miss Smith had saved her charge from a scandalous waltz with a rake and therefore he'd won the bet. Ranelaw's encounter with the dragon had been so entertaining, it was almost worth losing a monkey to his friend.

Almost.

Smiling wryly at the surprising enjoyment he'd derived from the acid-tongued chaperone, he poured a generous measure of brandy from the decanter on the library sideboard. He downed the brandy, refilled his glass, and turned to the correspondence on his desk. He wasn't usually sober at this hour. Hell, he wasn't usually home at this hour. It was barely two. He should be carousing in some dive or losing himself in a woman's arms.

After Lady Wreston's ball, he could have continued the night's entertainment. A new opera dancer had caught his eye, and he'd intended to fix his interest with her. She was a luscious pigeon, small and titian-haired. Last night she'd exactly fitted his current tastes.

Somehow tonight, after the ball, she . . . didn't.

He swallowed a deep draft of brandy, the heat burning his throat. Setting the glass on the desk, he lifted the top packet from the pile.

He glanced through the reports from his land agents, decided nothing required immediate action, and turned his attention to the rest. Requests for parliamentary support, which he consigned to the fire. A perfumed plea from a discarded mistress who hadn't accepted her congé. That too fed the flames.

He held to few principles, but one was that he never lied to his lovers. When an affair began, he informed the lady that the liaison would last precisely as long as his interest did—generally not an extended period. He wasn't a good bet for faithful devotion. His family had schooled him early in the damage unrestrained passion caused. He hadn't seen anything since to change his mind. He was essentially solitary and glad to be so. Only his frequent sexual encounters reminded him, should he need such a reminder, of his continuing link to the rest of humanity.

Grim thoughts for the early hours. Perhaps he should have stayed out after all. A self-mocking smile twisted his lips and he selected another packet from the stack.

Finally one letter remained. His gut twisted into its accustomed mixture of sick guilt and regret when he recognized the neat, feminine hand on the seawater-stained missive. She wrote every week from Ireland, and every week he forced himself to read her letter and answer it.

He resisted the urge to top up his brandy before opening his half sister's letter. Instead he carried it across to the fire. He sank into an armchair, emptied his glass, and placed it with precision on the side table. Then with a violent gesture, he broke the seal and read Eloise's loving greeting.

For a long time, Ranelaw stared unseeingly at the flowing lines of words. Instead his vision filled with the heartbreaking events of twenty years ago. Helpless rage and regret pierced him as he relived those hellish days of Eloise's disgrace.

When he was eleven and his beloved half sister was eighteen, Godfrey Demarest had visited Keddon Hall. The late marquess and Demarest had linked up at some gaming hell or other. In his usual careless way, the marquess had invited the fellow to spend summer by the sea with the Challoner family. Any sensible man would pause before bringing a youth already hardened in vice into a house overflowing with pretty girls. Pretty girls who, thanks to parental neglect, roamed largely unsupervised. But then, nobody had ever accused the previous Marquess of Ranelaw of being a sensible man.

Throughout a sweltering June, Demarest doggedly pursued the most beautiful of the Challoner bastards. Naïve and lonely, Eloise swiftly fell victim to a rake's practiced wiles, sweetened with pretty compliments and false vows of devotion. Demarest plucked her as easily as he'd pluck a honeysuckle blossom.

Nicholas had been jealous of the attention his favorite sister paid the handsome visitor from Somerset. He should have foreseen disaster and pushed Demarest off a cliff before he ruined Eloise's life. After all, no child brought up in the harum-scarum Challoner household remained unaware of doings between men and women. But he'd stayed oblivious to the developing calamity.

By the time he knew, it was too late. Demarest swanned back to London, abandoning a bereft and pregnant Eloise. Clearly he'd considered the marquess's by-blow fair game and believed he owed her nothing in return for her virginity. For all his blustering, Ranelaw's father was too spineless to do more than beat Eloise and lock her in her room. The false lover never faced ultimatums from a furious papa. Instead Demarest blazed ahead to a carefree life and a rich marriage as if Eloise didn't exist.

Eloise had her share of pride and fire. She'd been stubborn and unwilling to accept rejection at face value. She'd broken out of her room and begged Ranelaw to take her to Demarest. The bitter memory of that journey still made Ranelaw cringe. Twenty years later. His hand clenched on her latest letter, crushing it.

They'd careered through the stormy night in a gig stolen from their father's stables, reaching Demarest's London lodgings before dawn. Eloise had leaped eagerly from the carriage, clutching her small bag. Nicholas waited in the gig as she dashed toward the imposing town house. He'd waited when a superior footman answered and left her standing while he went inside. Nicholas still waited when the footman returned, informed Eloise Mr. Demarest wasn't at home, and shut the door in her face.

His sister stood her ground, insisted her lover would see her. The footman left again.

She waited longer in the rain, her gay, new gown turning

wet and heavy. Even from a distance, Nicholas could see her shivering by the time the servant reappeared. The footman passed her a note and closed the door. Ranelaw never learned what was in that note. But his sister was pale as snow when she returned to the gig. The only words she spoke were a request to return to Hampshire. She looked as though she wanted to die. All the bright, vivid life—the bright, vivid life that had attracted that louse Demarest's interest, he realized now—was snuffed out. She was only eighteen but she looked older than the ages.

It was then Ranelaw swore one day he'd see that Demarest's life wasn't worth living. One day he'd destroy the weasel just as the weasel had destroyed Eloise.

The tragedy was that when Ranelaw made that furious vow, the most agonizing consequences of Eloise's folly still awaited.

He closed his eyes and tried to block the corrosive memories. Anger, pain, betrayal surged up from his belly, threatened to strangle him. He drew a shuddering breath and pinched his nose hard as he closed his eyes, praying to a God he didn't believe in for—

For what?

For a chance to change the past? For a chance to save Eloise? He wasn't stupid enough to believe either possible.

What was possible was this miraculous chance to repay the man who had ruined his sister. In the same currency Demarest had used to destroy a woman whose only fault was her open heart.

Over the years, Ranelaw had only occasionally encountered the cur. However disreputable Ranelaw might be, his rank gave him entrée to society's highest level. Demarest was almost equally disreputable, but his fortune stank of trade for all that he was distantly connected to the powerful Hilliard family.

Ranelaw had spent years waiting for the bastard to make the mistake that would bring him down. But Demarest, in spite of all his wild carousing, never did.

Then Demarest's only child, untouched by scandal, lovely and vulnerable as Eloise had been lovely and vulnerable, made her debut.

It was as though the devil served the perfect opportunity on a silver platter. Through Cassie, Ranelaw would finally requite Eloise's sufferings.

Then perhaps, *perhaps* Ranelaw would no longer feel he'd failed the only person who had ever loved him.

Chapter Three

*E*VADING Lord Ranelaw over the next week proved more difficult than Antonia had expected.

For a man with a reputation for avoiding respectable gatherings the way a healthy person avoided plague, he appeared at every ball, rout, and musicale Cassie attended. He always danced with Cassie and acknowledged Antonia with a nod but, thank heaven, no conversation. After that hostile exchange the night they met, Antonia was wary, but his dismissal also irked. She burned to give the bumptious marquess the dressing-down he deserved.

Invariably as they returned home in the small hours, Antonia berated Cassie for showing the reprobate marked favor. Cassie, however, had overnight turned into a headstrong miss who refused to heed counsel from older, wiser friends. With complete accuracy, she pointed out that Lord Ranelaw did nothing exceptionable and he never requested more than the acceptable two dances.

After days of battling to curtail the marquess's attentions to her charge, Antonia's patience dwindled. Her head ached with constant tension. Partly because of the marquess's unwanted presence during her evenings supervising Cassie. More because of his unwanted presence in her thoughts even when physically absent.

Every time she saw Ranelaw, she desperately searched

for something unappealing about him. Instead the list of his attractions lengthened. He was, as Cassandra continually and irritatingly reminded her, a remarkably handsome man with his gold hair and Gypsy-dark features.

Antonia was immune to mere good looks—or at least she'd believed so—but she was less immune to Ranelaw's dry humor. She wasn't at all immune to the sizzle in the air when he prowled into their little group like a panther into a hen coop.

Tonight she and Cassie attended the Bradhams' musicale, and of course the Marquess of Ranelaw was present. He inveigled a place beside Cassandra when the concert began. Antonia perched on Cassandra's other side, fuming and surreptitiously watching for the rogue to make some advance. Then found no satisfaction when he sat unmoving through some surprisingly adept performances. Antonia couldn't blame her burgeoning headache on the music—rare for a society musicale, where the entertainment was usually execrable.

When the first half of the concert ended, everyone trailed away to the supper room. It wasn't a huge crush and Cassandra remained under the watchful eye of Mrs. Merriweather, who also launched her daughter this season. Antonia sighed and struggled to relax tight shoulders. Surely a few minutes to herself wouldn't result in disaster.

She slipped onto the dark and mercifully empty terrace. It was too early in the year for people to seek the outdoors, but the cold night and solitude were exactly what she wanted.

Drawing her first unfettered breath in hours, she stepped forward to lean on the balustrade. She tugged off her spectacles and rubbed tired eyes. Lord Ranelaw didn't spoil only her untroubled relationship with her cousin. He spoiled her sleep as well. She prayed he quickly became bored with pursuing a young girl who was so manifestly unsuitable.

She didn't like her chances.

A distant hum drifted from inside but otherwise the night was blessedly quiet. Antonia inhaled again and felt her tension unwind.

The season had barely started. If only Cassie quickly fell in love with some eligible gentleman, bypassing all risk of disaster with the rakish marquess. Antonia would go insane if she had to devote the next months to keeping Ranelaw away from Cassandra. Between her prickling awareness, Ranelaw's lures, and the girl's rebelliousness, this London visit stretched ahead as an ordeal to try anyone's nerves.

"Careless shepherdess. Aren't you afraid I'll whisk your lamb away?"

Had her very thoughts conjured up Ranelaw? Her heartbeat a wayward gallop, she straightened and turned to face the open French doors. In the darkness on the edge of the balcony, the marquess lounged against the wall. His very stillness breathed danger.

Antonia was burningly aware they'd never been alone before. She was also burningly aware that if anyone caught them together, her reputation would be in tatters.

She fumbled to replace her glasses, although in this light, he wouldn't make out her features. "You admit your purposes are dishonorable?"

She should go inside. But something—perhaps the untamed spirit she'd never quite conquered, no matter how she tried—kept her leaning against the balustrade, studying the notorious rake who made her blood surge. And who reminded her of so much she'd struggled to forget through ten lonely, painful years.

He shifted, a patch of darker shadow in the shadows. She imagined the smile that curled his long mouth. He always acted as if he considered life a sardonic joke. His cynical amusement shouldn't be attractive, but it was.

Like everything else about him.

"Even if I denied that, you wouldn't believe me."

"No, I wouldn't."

He gave a soft, knowing laugh, already familiar. The sound brushed across her skin like thick velvet. Why, oh, why did sin always adopt such compelling guise? She knew to her bones what this man was, yet nothing stemmed the fascination.

Perhaps she could take advantage of this encounter to speak more plainly than she could in a crowded ballroom. "I want you to leave Cassandra alone."

He prowled forward, his movements smooth and lethal as the panther she'd compared him to earlier. The uncertain light from inside revealed that he wasn't smiling and that his gaze remained intent upon her.

Another frisson of awareness rippled through her. Thank heaven she was so far below his touch, in both rank and beauty. If he leveled those glinting eyes on her with any purpose other than subverting her duty, she'd be lost.

"Why should I care about your wishes, Miss Smith?"

Antonia spread her hands and decided on honesty. "Cassandra's too good for you."

Her eyes adjusted to the darkness and she saw him more clearly than she wanted. A ghost of a smile flickered. "She has better manners than her chaperone, I'll give her that."

"Let her find some decent young man to make her happy."

"Bore her stiff, you mean?"

"Decency isn't necessarily boring."

"Haven't you found it so?"

Without making any overt move, he was far too close. Looming above her so his head blocked the stars. The faint illumination from inside cast a sheen across his gold hair as if even the candlelight couldn't resist touching him.

Despair engulfed Antonia as her gaze clung hungrily to his lean, rangy body. It was wrong, wrong, wrong that he was so beautiful. It was wrong that she was so susceptible to his beauty. Beauty was an accident, a random arrangement of muscle and bone and coloring. It shouldn't have this power to cut to her heart.

"What . . . what are you doing?" she asked nervously,

abandoning her pretense at bravery. She backed away, to find herself trapped against the balustrade.

"Proving your expectations correct, of course," he murmured, bending nearer.

Curse that deep, musical voice. It always made her senses vibrate, even in a packed room. Here where there was only night and silence, that rich voice was as alluring as treasure to a miser.

His scent teased her nostrils. Soap. Healthy male. He should smell like fire and brimstone. Instead he smelled like everything clean and good. She resisted the urge to draw that delicious scent deep into her lungs. Good Lord, she was in enough trouble.

Although the movement brought them closer, Antonia straightened to full height. Once, she'd been a pliant reed in a rake's clutches. Never again. She was twenty-seven, not seventeen. She might imagine the air quivered with sensual awareness, but in truth, Ranelaw set out to manipulate her. Unless she demonstrated some backbone, he'd succeed, damn him.

She forced disdain into her voice. Miss Smith's voice, not Lady Antonia Hilliard's. "Come, Lord Ranelaw! If the gossips catch you flirting with an ape leader like me, your reputation will never recover. Let's take the lukewarm seduction as read and move on to discouraging your attentions to Miss Demarest."

Another soft laugh. "Miss Smith, you misjudge yourself— and my powers of observation."

Icy fear pierced the haze of attraction. She'd become so used to people taking her for granted, it hadn't occurred that a particularly perceptive pair of eyes might penetrate her disguise.

Don't be ridiculous, Antonia. Nobody's questioned your identity in ten years. This louche scoundrel is trying to frighten you into giving him access to Cassandra.

"Does crass flattery often gain your way?" Her voice was sharp. "I'm disappointed. I'd expected better."

He stroked her cheek. Inside he'd worn gloves. Somewhere since he'd taken them off. "Oh, I rarely disappoint." The shock of his bare skin on hers made her jerk away. She drew a shaky breath, then regretted it when Ranelaw's scent flooded her senses.

Good God, the man was a walking honeypot. No wonder he was so confident of his appeal. Even an old spinster like her longed to explore that hard chest, measure those broad shoulders, test the heat radiating from his long body.

"Do you imagine some unconvincing interest will magically dissolve my objections to your courtship? You overestimate your charms and underestimate my good sense."

"Never." He tapped her cheek softly as if in reproof. "And why should you find my interest unconvincing? On my honor, it's meant sincerely."

Her breath hitched at the casual caress, although it was over in an instant. She struggled for her usual barbed response to importunate gentlemen. Not that she'd dealt with many in the last ten years.

"Such an oath confirms your falsehood. You must be desperate for Cassandra or you'd scarcely waste time on such a fright as her chaperone."

It was strange though—without the evidence of her eyes, she'd guess his interest in Cassandra wasn't sexual. There was no crackle when they were together. Nothing approaching the sparking lightning that arced between him and Antonia now.

Stupid, stupid girl. That was a rake's skill, the ability to make any woman imagine herself his sole interest. Common sense, so far remarkably lacking, insisted he couldn't be attracted to Cassandra's forbidding duenna.

He used his formidable appeal to overwhelm her. She, silly goose, allowed him.

She felt him staring at her through the shadows. But she was safe. Her disguise had protected her for ten years. Lord Ranelaw just made her nervous.

It was as if he read her thoughts. "You know, your assumption of invincibility is damned challenging."

She shrugged. "Why would you bother? I'm well below your notice, my lord. Except in my role as Cassandra's guard dog. Be warned, I take that seriously. You're not a suitable match. Her father will never agree to a marriage if that's your hope. If you've anything other than marriage in mind, you're wasting your time. She's too sensible to allow herself to be ruined."

"Is that so?" he asked in a musing voice. "What about you?"

His nonchalance caught her on the raw. Anger rescued her from tumbling into beguilement. Anger she'd crammed deep inside for years. It was so easy for men like Ranelaw. No consequences. No dangers. Their swaggering left a bloody trail of broken hearts and lives, but what did they care as long as they satisfied their selfish desires?

For once Lord Ranelaw wasn't getting his own way.

She spoke with complete conviction. "Your attentions aren't welcome. Leave me alone. Leave Cassandra alone." She shoved hard at his chest. Her strength couldn't match his so she was surprised he stepped back. "Good night, my lord. I hope this is our last conversation."

"I would be devastated if that were so," he said in a silky voice that made her bristle.

"I'm sure you'll recover." She flicked her meager skirts and marched through the French doors.

She should feel triumphant she put the overweening Lord Ranelaw in his place. Sadly, she was aware she only escaped because he let her go.

This particular duel had hardly started.

Ranelaw watched the dragon flounce away. Unholy excitement bubbled in his blood. With every encounter, she became more intriguing, with her spirit and her resistance and her secrets, one of which he'd long ago guessed.

However much she wanted to hate him, she was far from immune to the heat surging between them.

An owl hooted from the undergrowth, reminding him he

wasn't here to satisfy his desires but to set his mark on the Demarest girl. With luck—and with women, he was always supremely lucky—he'd waylay her after supper.

Wishing he garnered more enthusiasm for the task, he grimly tugged on his gloves and strode inside.

He lurked in the gallery off the supper room and was delighted to see Cassie returning ahead of the crowd in company with another butterfly. Even better, gimlet-eyed Miss Smith was nowhere in evidence.

Perhaps his subtle threats daunted her.

Hell, he mused on the guardian and not the charge again. He needed to be careful. Cassie was innocent and easily flattered, but he couldn't become too blasé about seducing her. The prize in this game was too important for him to mar his chances with overconfidence.

"Miss Demarest, have you seen this beautiful Claude? Allow me to show you." He fastened a possessive hand around Cassie's arm. The girl started but made no attempt to escape.

Miss Demarest's companion burst into a peal of irritating giggles and blushed red as a tomato. Cassie cast him a skeptical glance that proved an unwelcome reminder of the way her chaperone had received his seductive overtures.

Cassie's voice emerged steadily. "Miss Smith and I admired the Claudes in the National Gallery last week. I should dearly love to see more of the artist's work."

"I'll find Mamma," the other girl twittered and darted back to the supper room in a rustle of white skirts.

"How kind of your friend to grant us privacy," Ranelaw murmured, staring at Cassie in his best rake manner and tightening his hold on her arm. "I've longed for a moment alone with you."

"We won't be alone for very long," the girl pointed out coolly.

"All the more reason to take advantage of our chance," he said, then added with complete honesty, "You're a devilish pretty girl, Miss Demarest."

"Thank you."

What the hell? He'd expected a little more reaction than that to his blatant interest. Blast the chit, she betrayed not one whit of nervousness. Instead she studied him with an utterly sexless curiosity.

When they'd been in public together, she'd seemed bedazzled by his attentions. Now, not so much. Briefly he wondered if his magic touch with women failed. Surely not. For all that she struggled to hide her reactions, he set Miss Smith quivering with excitement. The problem with Miss Smith was that she set him quivering with excitement in return.

He kept his voice low, persuasive. "I suppose a hundred men have told you that."

Amusement brightened her blue eyes. She really was a peach. What a fool he was, not to be more excited at the prospect of having her. "Oh, thousands."

He laughed softly. This particular game of advance and retreat was mightily familiar. He'd so often set himself to charm a woman hovering between uncertainty and surrender, and with far less reason than he had to seduce Cassandra Demarest. Surely it was only a passing humor that, much as he tried, he summoned so little interest in the chase. "Somerset must be awash in broken hearts now you've abandoned the country for London."

"You're teasing me, my lord." As he'd seen her do so many times before, she lowered her lashes coquettishly. "I'm not sure it's quite proper when we're on our own."

"I'm sure it's not." He let a wolfish grin curve his lips and he drew her closer but not so close that she'd take fright and run. "Miss Demarest, you make it impossible not to kiss you."

Her eyes flashed up to meet his. "If anyone sees, there will be a dreadful to-do."

The girl was either a hardened flirt or too stupid to guess his wicked intentions. At the very least, his improper declaration should make her blush. He was the notorious Marquess of Ranelaw. Mothers all over England used his name to frighten their virginal daughters into good behavior.

"Heaven forbid." His voice deepened to a purr. "It seems a pity to rush this . . . *conversation*. Let me take you somewhere we won't be interrupted."

On a giggling tide, the room flooded with a dozen debutantes, including Cassie's scarlet-faced friend. With a flash of irritation, Ranelaw realized his moment had passed.

"Not tonight, my lord," she said with a faint smile. She stepped away to turn, calm as you please, toward the painting behind them. Not a Claude.

His vengeance was no further advanced and it was his own bloody fault. He should have pursued the chit with more conviction. No wonder his wooing left her less than overwhelmed.

Damn Antonia Smith, if he spent less time thinking of her and more time luring his prey, he could be well on his way to achieving Miss Demarest's ruin.

As Ranelaw strolled away from the musicale, he yet again contemplated the prickly but increasingly appealing Miss Smith. Which didn't exactly please him. At last he had Cassie Demarest in his sights. He should concentrate on his overdue vengeance. Instead his mind veered toward the unwelcoming companion.

Except that while Miss Smith's lips spoke a continual no, her body whispered an alluring yes. The body he'd realized days ago was considerably more voluptuous than he'd first guessed. Those hideous dresses masked a wealth of promise.

The lady put up stout defenses. He didn't delude himself that piercing her thorny boundaries would be quick work. But he had an ally within the gate—the fact that she, however unwillingly, found him fascinating.

After years of easy conquests, wearing down Miss Smith's resistance proved a delightful game. A game whose outcome wasn't in doubt.

His jaded heart kicked against his ribs with unjaded excitement as he pictured her tumbling into his hands like a ripe apple. She'd taste just as sweet, with that tart edge he'd come to appreciate. He'd become bored with compliant women. His palate fancied something more complex.

Even better, her seduction would forward his revenge. Once he'd neutralized Miss Smith, he'd have open access to Cassandra.

How odd that he, who had silenced his conscience years ago, felt uncomfortable at the idea of blackmailing the dragon. Not that ethical qualms would stop him. He was a ruthless bastard and Miss Smith would rue the moment she entered his orbit.

He smothered a derisive laugh. Most men would consider him an idiot for preferring the subtle, almost invisible charms of the older woman to the younger's prettiness. But with every moment he spent in her company, he became more certain the enigmatic Miss Smith offered the discerning lover a rich banquet. Under that forbidding exterior, he'd caught hints of a wild, unforgettable beauty. He knew to his boots there was passion in Antonia Smith.

In comparison, tupping Cassandra Demarest would be like drowning in meringue.

Without making a conscious decision about his destination, he felt no real surprise when he stood outside the Demarests' Curzon Street residence. After the musicale, a crowd had formed for carriages, so neither Miss Demarest nor her companion would be home yet. A glow shone through the fanlight above the front door but the other windows were dark.

Clinging to shadows, he slunk around to the mews. Lights burned in the stables but nobody emerged to challenge him. When he tested the gate, he discovered it unlocked. Such carelessness in the city asked for trouble.

Trouble arrived in the person of the Marquess of Ranelaw.

Soundlessly he slipped into the garden and immediately imagined himself in the countryside. The scent of flowers and freshly turned earth overcame the pervasive London stink of coal dust and dank river. Even his debauched soul evinced a trace of spring's innocence.

He studied the rear of the house. He had a spy inside, one of the footmen, who had supplied him with a floor plan. The arrangement was so standard, he could have guessed Miss Demarest's room. What had surprised him was that Miss Smith occupied a chamber on the same floor as the family. Most companions were consigned rooms much closer to the servants' quarters.

Light streamed from Miss Demarest's window in the corner bedroom overlooking the garden. At the other end of the house, Miss Smith's darkened window opened onto a flowering cherry tree.

Ranelaw's whim solidified into determination. Now presented the perfect opportunity to woo the Demarest chit with a billet-doux on her pillow. But all night his thoughts had turned on the beguiling Miss Smith, not her simpering charge.

Grabbing a low branch on the cherry tree, he swung himself up.

Chapter Four

WITH a weary sigh, Antonia closed her bedroom door behind her. She loved Cassandra dearly but the girl was so overexcited by her social success that she invariably came home bubbling with an endless desire to relive the night's adventures. Tonight it had taken Antonia over an hour to settle her, and she suspected her cousin still lay awake counting the evening's triumphs.

Antonia regretted that, among those triumphs, Cassie included her flirtation with the Marquess of Ranelaw. After that disturbing encounter on the terrace, Ranelaw had shown Cassie special favor. It was as if Antonia's warning stirred a childish urge to flout her. Except that the marquess was disturbingly adult and his purposes contained no childish innocence. And he'd done it all in a manner that left Antonia helpless to reprimand either him or Cassie.

He was too damned clever for his own good, was the Marquess of Ranelaw. She wished him a speedy journey to Hades. Surely among the thousands of women he'd debauched, one must possess a jealous husband with a working set of pistols.

She quashed an unwelcome twinge of regret when she pictured all that glorious masculinity lying cold and still. Ranelaw was handsome but he was wicked. He meant trouble to Cassie.

And to her.

"What a ferocious scowl, my dear Miss Smith. Should I be nervous?"

She stiffened in disbelieving horror. With a shaking hand, she raised her candle to reveal what lay beyond the flickering firelight.

Surely not even Lord Ranelaw would break into her room. He couldn't be so bold.

He could indeed.

He slouched on the brocade window seat, the casement open behind him to the old cherry tree. The breeze shifted the parted curtains, filled the room with a faintly almond scent, ruffled his thick gold hair. He looked more delicious than a plate of roast beef to a starving man.

"Get out," she said flatly without shifting. Shock swamped anger.

He laughed softly, that low, musical laugh that never failed to tighten her skin with awareness. "Here I thought you'd fall victim to the vapors. Or a fit of hysterics."

"I never faint," she said, still in that hard voice.

Her brain worked feverishly at how to get rid of him. Dear God, the consequences of anyone finding him were unthinkable. As surprise ebbed, a tide of fear surged. Cassie and her father had sheltered her, allowed her to build a life that, for all its frustrations, meant she was fed and housed. If they thought she'd resorted to her bad old ways, she'd be out on her ear.

Ranelaw rose with a languorous grace that, even through her terror, made her blood pound hard and hot. Casually he brushed white petals from his broad shoulders. He still wore his elegant clothing from the musicale. For a rake, he had austere taste. His coats were always perfectly cut to his impressive physique and his waistcoats were masterpieces of simplicity.

Sweet heaven, he was temptation personified, for all the evil she knew of him. In comparison to Lord Ranelaw, handsome Johnny Benton, who had brought about her ruin, was a complete fright. Ranelaw made her ache to fling aside dull morality and taste again the heady wine of passion.

But the wine of passion was deadly poison.

"I should have known you'd be too stalwart to scream at the sight of a man in your bedchamber. Although I'm sure you're shocked to the soles of your sensible shoes, Miss Smith."

If she hadn't been so afraid of the consequences of his presence, she'd laugh. How ironic that this disreputable Adonis remained convinced he addressed an untouched virgin.

"What do you want?" Her room was isolated so she had no need to whisper.

"Would you believe me if I said you?"

This time she did laugh, a huff of disdain. She wouldn't give him the satisfaction of revealing her building alarm. She ventured closer because to hover near the door smacked of cowardice. "No. I wouldn't. At least I'm glad you chose the wrong bedroom. I'll make sure Cassie keeps her windows locked from now on."

"I didn't choose the wrong bedroom," he said steadily, regarding her with an unwavering stare as she lit the lamp on her dressing table.

"Of course you didn't." She made no attempt to hide her skepticism. He was yet to touch her. It did wonders for her wobbly confidence. "I assume you climbed the cherry tree. I'll have to ask the gardeners to chop it back."

"That's a prosaic response to a man daring convention to snatch a few moments alone with you, Miss Smith. Your maidenly heart should race with excitement."

She blew out the candle and turned. Again, desperately, she sought some outward sign of moral turpitude. As ever, she found nothing but breathtakingly virile male. Reviving anger swelled above dread and reluctant desire. He didn't care that his actions could destroy her. She mattered less to him than the dirt beneath his feet. He was such a selfish swine.

"Very romantic, I'm sure." She raised her eyebrows and leaned against the table, hooking her hands over the edge to mask their trembling. "You've made my vulnerability clear. I'm suitably warned. You can go."

He looked amused and far too sure of himself. "Miss Smith, you should show more respect to your betters."

"You're not my better," she snapped before she remembered with a pang just who she was. No longer the pampered daughter of Lord Aveson. No longer Lady Antonia Hilliard, with a brilliant match ahead of her.

He laughed again. "No, I doubt I am."

He paused, still staring. Wariness skittered through her veins. He wasn't just decorative, he was clever. She feared the cleverness more than she feared the beauty. As if to prove her right, he continued, his voice dispassionate. "Antonia's a damned incongruous name for a lowly domestic."

Fresh terror slithered down her backbone. A terror that he might discover just who drab Miss Smith was.

Never let your enemy see his advantage. Never let him think he'd won.

Hilliard pride injected a chill into her tone. "Lord Ranelaw, charming as I find this conversation, you must leave. If the servants hear a man in my room, or worse, see you, my reputation will be ashes."

He tilted one shoulder against the wall and folded his arms with a self-assurance that made her grind her teeth. "Nice try, my dear. But this room is a long way from the other bedrooms. Unless you scream, we're safe."

On unsteady legs, she stepped away from the dressing table. "My maid will arrive any moment."

"You look after yourself. My sources of information indicate you're an independent baggage."

"They indicate . . ." She faltered into appalled silence.

Nervously she pushed her glasses up her nose. Sweet heaven, she'd been wrong to disbelieve him earlier. He hadn't wanted Cassie's room. He'd wanted hers. He'd taken the trouble to discover she had no maid. The dissolute marquess had targeted her. Fear of scandal became a sharper, more primitive fear of the male. And of her female weakness.

"When I pursue a woman, I leave little to chance." He spoke as if he considered the admission unimportant.

She wouldn't cower. And she wouldn't surrender. Somehow he'd learned the household's secrets. Dear God, save him from learning her other secrets. Painful, destructive secrets that would put her in Lord Ranelaw's power.

Reminding herself she was a survivor, she tamped down alarm. If Ranelaw expected an easy conquest, he'd be disappointed. She stiffened her backbone and glared, fighting because fighting was all she knew. Once she'd been defenseless as a kitten. That was many hard years ago.

"Except you're using me to get to Cassie." Antonia's tone slashed like a razor. "You imagine if you scatter a few crumbs of attention my way, I'll become your cat's-paw."

His eyes traveled over her, from her feet—in their sensible shoes, curse him—to her unflattering cap. For the past ten years, she'd dressed like this, plainly, unappealingly, shabbily. Like someone a good thirty years older. Surely it was her imagination that those perspicacious eyes sliced through the unbecoming garb to the real woman.

In spite of her roiling resentment, that long, thorough survey was astonishingly arousing. Heat pooled between her thighs and her nipples peaked against her shift. Thank goodness thick wool hid how he affected her, although a rake would recognize she was far from indifferent. Perhaps he pursued her not only because of Cassie but because he scented her arousal. A man of his experience must also scent her loneliness, her desperation, her repressed passion. She loathed to think he read her most shameful desires and schemed to manipulate her through them.

"You're hard on yourself," he said in a musing tone.

"I'm realistic." Her heart cramped with regret, even if he was worthless and dangerous and would come to a bad end. It was ten years since a man had looked at her with desire.

Now that one did, he lied. She injected a taunting note. "I'd have credited you with a more subtle plan, my lord."

He shrugged, unabashed by her candor. "When the obvious promises success, why not use it?"

"If I'm awake to your plot, you have no chance of success." It shouldn't sting that now she challenged him, he no longer pretended interest. To her everlasting regret, Lord Aveson's vain, empty-headed daughter still lurked in her soul.

"I imagine the antelope knows the lion wants to devour it. That doesn't alter the outcome."

Her eyes narrowed. "I'm far from a defenseless deer."

"Perhaps. But you're no match for me."

She ground her teeth. What luck that he reminded her he was an arrogant ass. It helped combat this impossible physical attraction. "We shall see, my lord."

He flung his head back and laughed. She'd heard his unfettered laughter once or twice before. It was a free, joyous sound and seemed incongruous for such a world-weary rogue. The problem was the laugh was male and it echoed around her bedroom where no man had the right to be.

"My lord, I beg you . . ." Panic made her leap forward to silence him. As she raised her hand to his mouth, she realized who he was, who *she* was, and she hesitated.

His arm snaked around her waist, although he didn't bring her against his body. Through tinted spectacles, she met eyes as black as pitch. Eyes that glinted with predatory awareness.

"The noise . . ." she said, flustered. His grip felt immovable.

"I thought you meant to tumble me onto the bed," he murmured.

As he spoke, his breath drifted over her face with suggestive warmth. Antonia couldn't deny she'd thought about kissing that sensual, cynical mouth. Now, close enough to feel his heat, the impulse was nigh overwhelming.

"You flatter yourself," she retorted shakily, trying to pull away. Fear trickled through her veins like iced water. Fear of what he might do to her. Stronger fear of what *she* might do to him. "You can let me go."

"Why? I've got you where I want you—and you put yourself there, Miss Smith."

She struggled with more conviction. "I will scream," she hissed through her teeth.

He trailed his free hand down her cheek with a lingering softness she felt to her toes. "No, you won't."

No, she wouldn't scream. She couldn't risk anyone coming in and finding them. With her history, nobody would believe she was innocent of inviting him.

"Stop it." The protest emerged as a wisp of sound.

He traced the line of her jaw. No one, especially no man, had touched her with tenderness in years. The sweetness was a lie but her heart didn't recognize that. Her heart expanded in uncontrollable longing. Oh, she was such an idiot. She swallowed the tears that clogged her throat and jerked her face away.

"Can I take your glasses off?" he whispered, leaning forward to brush his cheek against hers.

She hadn't been this close to a man in years either. She was tinglingly aware how differently Ranelaw was made compared to her. The height. The strength. The leashed power. The stubble on his jaw.

Stupid little rabbit she was, she'd stopped struggling. Her heart banged so madly, every thud rocked her. Through her daze, she took a few seconds to register what he'd said. He already reached to unhook her spectacles.

"No!" She broke away, surprising him enough to force some space between them, although he didn't release her. "I told you to stop it."

"Don't you want to know what a kiss is like?" he murmured. "You strike me as a woman full of intelligent curiosity."

"You're utterly patronizing," she snapped back, straightening her glasses.

"And you're utterly beguiling."

Damn him, he sounded sincere. She reminded herself sincerity was a rake's trick. "Don't make me laugh."

He raised his hand to her face again, holding her when she tried to turn away. "Antonia, kiss me."

She struggled not to hear urgency. Rakes were never urgent. Rakes treated the world as one vast larder for their appetites. If one dish failed to satisfy, they indulged their cravings with another.

"You have no right to use my Christian name," she protested, sounding to her chagrin like a breathless virgin.

He smiled at her, smoothing a few stray tendrils of hair that escaped her cap. More sweetness. More hankering from her reckless heart. "Foolish girl."

His hold remained implacable. And if she was honest, the magic of his touch transfixed her.

Foolish girl indeed.

She tried to inject some force into her voice—and signally failed. "I won't betray Cassie for your beaux yeux."

He still stroked her temples. She wished he'd stop.

She wished he'd never stop.

"I don't know if you have beautiful eyes. In fact, I know so little about you. It's time that changed."

Even through the pleasure, that sounded ominous. She tried to escape but she was too late. He grabbed her lace cap and flung it to the floor.

"Curse you, Lord Ranelaw!" she said on a burst of anger, and this time she wrenched free.

She scrabbled for the cap. She hadn't realized quite how strongly she clung to the elements of her disguise until Ranelaw threatened to deprive her of them one by one.

She shook so badly it took her longer than it should to retrieve the scrap of lace. She rose, gripping it in both hands with a hold tight enough to tear.

"Go," she said in a low, throbbing voice. The tears that had threatened earlier surged closer to the surface. "Just . . . go."

She should have known he wouldn't obey. Instead he

stood stock-still. From their first meeting, his attention had been intense. Now his interest ratcheted up another notch. Almost reverently he touched her hair, his fingers as light as feathers. "Why do you cover it?"

"I'm a companion, not a courtesan," she snapped, and fumbled to restore her cap. And somehow in the process restore her sangfroid, her confidence, and her resistance to masculine wiles.

Against better instincts, she turned her back on Ranelaw to check that she covered her hair. She stopped aghast as she caught her reflection in the mirror. The hand clutching the cap dropped to dangle at her side. In spite of the ugly spectacles, she looked vivid and alive in a way she hadn't in years. The last time she'd looked like this, her life had collapsed around her in smoking ruins. She refused to let that happen again.

Her cheeks were flushed and her lips were red, begging for a man's kiss.

Not just any man.

Unfortunately the kisses she wanted belonged to the rapscallion who loomed behind her and put his hand on her shoulder with a gesture she read as possessive. Furious despair flooded her. Never, never would she allow another man to destroy her. She must scotch this insidious attraction. Loneliness was vastly superior to harlotry.

Ranelaw didn't shift his gaze from the pale braids coiled around her head. The severe style did little to conceal her hair's unusual color or its thickness.

"It's a sin to hide such beauty under that hideous rag." Ranelaw turned her to face him.

After a moment's resistance, she let him have his way. Angry bewilderment knotted her belly. How had they reached a point where he touched her with such authority, spoke to her with such intimacy? They were strangers. Antagonistic strangers at that.

He stared at her as if he'd never seen a woman.

So he liked her hair. That was no reason to glow with

pleasure. Johnny Benton had liked her hair too. He'd particularly loved to comb his fingers through it and drape it
over her bare breasts.

It hadn't stopped him seducing her away from her noble
family and leaving her alone to face the consequences.

She stared into Ranelaw's glittering black eyes and recognized that he entertained similar fantasies about her hair
draping her naked body. He grabbed her wrists in adamant
hands, stopping her from tugging the mangled lace over her
head.

"It's too late. I know."

"What . . . what do you know?" Dread snaked through
her, almost killing the desire.

Desire was an old enemy. She knew to her cost that nothing killed it once it stirred. It had stirred the minute she'd
seen this beautiful, dissolute man.

Only the damage awaiting kept her from surrender. That
and the truth that he didn't really want her, much as his
eyes sparked hunger and his big, strong hands warmed her
skin. The knowledge that he initiated this elaborate charade
merely to smooth his path to Cassie made her straighten and
glare at him. He took her for a henwit if he imagined his
feigned desire duped her. He didn't desire her. He couldn't.

But it was hard to believe the seduction halfhearted when
she met his arrested expression. He frowned at her scared
little question but his answer allayed her worst fears. "I
know what beauty you hide under those rags."

"Don't be a fool, Ranelaw," she snapped, anger defeating
momentary vulnerability.

"Oh, I'm a fool, all right," he muttered and tugged her
into his body, his arms lashing her against him.

A chaos of impressions, familiar and unfamiliar, overwhelmed Antonia. She knew how a man's embrace felt. But
the fierceness of this hold, the hard strength of this body, the
clean, fresh smell, these were all Ranelaw.

She flung her head up to deliver the scolding he deserved,
then forgot everything when she met the blazing excitement

in his eyes. A blazing excitement echoed in her pounding heart and rushing blood.

"No . . ." she whispered, but he didn't seem to hear.

He bent his head and kissed her hard, using his tongue like a weapon to part her lips and give him access to her mouth. He was ruthless. He was insatiable. He gave no consideration to her unwillingness or her lack of preparation or what he believed was her inexperience.

Shock rather than anything as commendable as virtue kept her unmoving under his mouth. Even as molten heat flooded her and a deep trembling set up in the base of her belly.

With a muttered exclamation of frustration, he raised his head. He seized her shoulders in an adamant grip and stared down at her. "You can do better than that."

Anger flashed through her. The famous lover had kissed her with all the finesse of a navvy breaking ground for a new canal. "So can you," she snapped.

Immediately she realized her mistake when challenge sharpened his black gaze.

"N-no," she stammered, at last making some attempt to sidle away. So far she'd stood in his embrace like a quiescent doll. She needed to start thinking about self-preservation before it was too late.

It was too late.

"Ah, but how can any red-blooded man ignore a demand from a lovely lady?" he said silkily.

"Believe me, you should ignore it." Her voice was as uncertain as her attempt to escape.

"Chivalry forbids." His lips twitched with the humor that never failed to transfix her. She was so utterly brainless when it came to Ranelaw. He turned her common sense to sawdust. Before she could summon a crushing retort, his touch softened to seduction and a calculating light entered his eyes.

Run, Antonia, run. . .

Her feet didn't heed her mind's panicked message. Instead she waited in tremulous silence for his mouth to claim hers.

At the touch of his lips, she made a muffled sound in her throat. She clenched her hands in his coat, ready to push him away. Until he began to ravish her mouth and her knees turned to water. The salty, spicy taste of Ranelaw flooded her senses.

Briefly everything but pleasure receded. With a sigh, she sagged into his arms. Impossibly she felt him hesitate, as though her abrupt surrender disconcerted him. Before she could take advantage of the fleeting reprieve, his mouth moved in unmistakable demand. Everything dissolved into heat. Her mouth opened wide, her tongue curled over his in welcome, her arms circled his powerful body, drawing him closer.

Antonia shut her eyes and drowned in hot, black delight. Deep in the recesses of her mind, she admitted this was what she wanted from him. Had always wanted. It was wrong, but his kiss made her feel more alive than anything else in the past ten years.

"You taste so sweet, Antonia . . ." he murmured against her neck. He bit down on the tendons until she trembled.

He returned to her lips, kissing her so violently that she staggered. As she stumbled, he caught her and dragged her tighter against him. She felt the nip of his teeth, the rough velvet of his tongue against hers.

Through the symphony of desire, discordant bells clanged warning. She must end this shattering pleasure. Before she was lost.

Weakly she pushed at his chest even as she stretched upward to seek more delicious torment. Her body arched shamelessly into his, relishing the heavy weight of his rod against her belly. She wanted to touch him there. She wanted to hold him in her hand. She wanted him to push that hard length inside her until this restless, throbbing need ignited in a climax to eclipse anything she'd known with Johnny Benton.

Stop.

Don't stop. . .

Her attempt to hold Ranelaw away turned into a feverish exploration of his chest. He was as hot as a big open fire. She wanted his waistcoat and his fine linen shirt gone. She wanted his skin against hers.

She wanted . . . him.

His hands moved up and down her back in rhythm with the movement of his lips. She drifted into a fog of sensation. A place that held only Ranelaw and his rich scent. Still he pressed her, giving no quarter. She felt dizzy, off-balance, bewitched.

Incapable of protest.

Until one hard hand closed over her breast. Her nipple tightened, and sharp pleasure slashed through her bedazzlement like lightning through a cloudy sky.

She realized what she did. He kissed her and she let him. Worse, she encouraged him to pursue this encounter to its end.

Where only misery lurked.

For the sake of fickle pleasure, she'd once sacrificed everything. She'd never do it again, no matter how intoxicating Ranelaw's kisses.

She ripped her lips from his and forced out the word she must say. "No."

The denial nearly killed her. Wild, unleashed Antonia, reveling in her first freedom in years, screamed in protest. Wild, unleashed Antonia demanded more of Lord Ranelaw, the way a drunkard craved gin.

He returned to kissing her neck, shooting arrows of heat straight to her belly. His hand opened and closed on her breast, making her shake with arousal. She sucked breath into lungs starved of air. She gripped his arms. Pride insisted the action was intended to control any further incursions. Brutal honesty made her admit she just wanted to touch him.

"Ranelaw, no." This time her denial emerged with some

conviction. She backed toward the hearth. Eventually she'd run out of space, then what would happen?

Sadly, she knew exactly what would happen.

"You don't mean that," he said unsteadily, lifting his head to survey her from under sensually heavy eyelids.

"I do," she said, then gasped as he began to flick open the buttons that fastened her modest bodice. "Stop that." She brushed his hand aside.

"I want to see you." His low voice was a seduction in itself. But she'd come back to herself enough to be horrified at how close she verged to disaster.

"You're not getting what you want."

Her dress gaped, revealing plain white cotton stays and shift. He must have seen women in the scantiest, most enticing of underclothing, but even so, she couldn't mistake how his attention sharpened on her cleavage.

"I promise I'll just look."

She sent him a quelling look. "Yes, I believe that. Of course I do."

His arm firmed around her waist. "I like you better when I'm kissing you."

"I won't fall victim to your shabby charm."

She tried to fasten her dress but her fingers shook so violently, she couldn't unite even one button with its buttonhole. Furious misery closed her throat. Damn Ranelaw. His charm might be shabby, but she couldn't resist it. The glint in his eyes told her the devil knew it.

"How can such pretty lips say such nasty things?" His mouth twitched with amusement.

The hint of humor made her burn to kiss him again. She silenced Wild Antonia and lifted her chin. "Get out, Ranelaw."

He looked breathtakingly handsome with his hair mussed. To her shame, she knew how those thick golden waves became so tousled. She'd buried her fingers in his hair while he pleasured her mouth.

God help her, why was she so weak? She knew what she

risked, but one touch from Ranelaw's skillful hands and she forgot everything else.

He grabbed her chin. His face was alight with a mixture of blatant sexual interest and laughter. "Oh, no, sweeting. This encounter is too interesting to abandon at this critical point."

Inevitably he'd kiss her again. Determination tautened his angular jaw and arrogance sparked in his eyes. He believed her opposition merely token.

Why shouldn't he when she'd kissed him as if he showed her the gateway to heaven?

"No," she said staunchly, stiffening without managing to pull away.

"Yes." He tilted her face up.

His mouth covered hers. She braced for another assault on her senses, but this time, he wooed her with a gentleness as ruthless as his passion. For one lost moment, she succumbed to delight.

He grabbed her arms, his kiss deepening. On unsteady feet, she retreated. Heat on the back of her legs told her she neared the fire but the only really dangerous flames in the room were those Lord Ranelaw ignited in her soul.

He slid one hand under her bodice. At last he touched her naked breast. A blast of arousal shuddered through her. As his thumb brushed her beaded nipple, she gasped into his open mouth. Her muscles loosened, resistance faded to a whisper in the far reaches of her clouded mind.

Desperate, knowing she had seconds before she begged him to do whatever he wished—and what he wished was no mystery at all—she fumbled behind her with one hand.

Damn it, where was it?

At last her hand closed over what she wanted. Her grip firmed, she summoned the faltering shreds of will.

And clouted him as hard as she could with the fire iron.

Chapter Five

MERCIFUL heaven, she'd killed him.

Antonia stared aghast at Lord Ranelaw's loose-limbed form sprawled across the red and blue Turkish rug. The poker she'd swung at his head dropped from nerveless fingers to hit the carpet with a muffled thud.

Bile soured her mouth. Vaguely she realized she should feel remorse, but terror was paramount. A terror that cramped her throat shut and set her swaying with dizziness.

Explaining a live Lord Ranelaw in her bedroom would be difficult enough. How to excuse a dead one? She had no way of hiding the body. She'd have trouble even shifting him.

The blood flowing copiously from his temple stained the rug, she'd never get the betraying marks out. Her heart racing, she whirled toward the washstand. Before she reached it, someone knocked on the door. Antonia's stomach twisted with nausea as she remembered it wasn't locked. If anyone came in, her goose was well and truly cooked. In fact, her goose was completely incinerated.

"Miss Smith, are you all right?" It was Bella, Cassie's middle-aged maid, who slept in the dressing room next to her mistress. "I heard the most almighty thump."

"Bella . . ." Oh, dear Lord, could this get any worse? She struggled for a cheerful note. She hoped it sounded more convincing to Bella than in her own ears. "I tripped over a chair. Nothing to worry about."

"Are you sure you're not hurt?" The maid, jealous of Antonia's influence on Cassie, would luxuriate in any fall from grace. No way could Antonia ever enlist Bella's sympathies to keep this incident secret. "Would you like me to come in?"

Sweet God, no!

"No." Then because her sharp answer might rouse curiosity, she continued more carefully. "No, thank you. No damage done. Go to bed, Bella. You must be tired after these late nights."

There was a fraught pause. An iron band of suspense tightened around Antonia's chest as she braced for the door to swing open. Then what on earth could she do? She had no money to buy the woman's discretion. And she'd never bring herself to silence Bella permanently with the poker.

Lord Ranelaw was one murder too many.

Her breath hissed in relief when Bella eventually spoke. "If you say so, miss. Good night to you."

"Good night, Bella."

Antonia poised in quivering stillness as she listened to the maid make her way up the corridor to her room. Then, wishing herself anywhere but here, she stared at the disaster lying motionless at her feet.

She'd killed a peer. She could claim self-defense, but who would believe a woman with her history? Given the scandal that threatened, the hangman's noose almost offered blessed escape.

Please don't be dead.

She'd caught him across the face as well as the temple. A long graze marked one slanted cheekbone. Blood dripped sullenly from his wound onto the carpet. Her paralysis shattered. She dashed over to splash water into a bowl and grab a washcloth. Breathlessly she dropped to her knees beside Ranelaw.

So desperately she'd wished to banish him from her

world where he caused nothing but chaos. Now it looked likely she'd never hear another of his sardonic responses or shiver with unwilling awareness when he laughed.

She struggled against suffocating panic. She hadn't hit him that hard. But when she was a girl, a branch had struck the temple of a workman in Blaydon Park's orchard and he'd died instantly.

Ranelaw's face was pale, severe. The provoking glint in his eyes usually distracted attention from his elegant bone structure. Unconscious, he looked surprisingly ascetic. Like a knight carved on a monument, not a man whose name was a byword for vice.

Please, don't let him need a monument anytime soon.

The dreadful truth hammered at her heart. She didn't want him lying dead. He made her life difficult, he threatened disaster to Cassie. But the world, *her world*, would be poorer without him.

She wet the cloth and pressed it to his wound. Her hands shook uncontrollably and she sank her teeth into her bottom lip to stave off frightened tears. His skin was warm. Surely if he was dead, he'd be cold as stone.

Don't die.

She wasn't aware she spoke the words over and over like a litany until he groaned and stirred, and she faltered into silence.

He became terrifyingly still once more. Had she imagined that brief sign of life? His thick black lashes lay unmoving on his cheeks. At least her agitation had exaggerated the blood. It was only a sluggish dribble. She raised one hand to brush moisture from her cheeks.

"Ranelaw? Speak to me."

Nothing.

She injected a stronger note into her voice and his Christian name slipped out before she realized. "Nicholas? Nicholas, please, please wake up."

His face was white as paper, apart from the shocking red weal. She bit her lip so hard she tasted blood. She wouldn't let him be dead. And not just because his demise made him as troublesome deceased as he ever was alive.

Coherent thought gradually seeped into her numb mind. A pulse. She should check for a pulse.

What the devil was wrong with her? That was the first thing she should have done. Usually she was coolheaded in a crisis, but Ranelaw's kisses had turned her into a hysterical fool.

She fumbled at his cuff until she pressed her fingers to his powerful wrist. Immediately her stomach clenched with sick relief. The hard, strong beat confirmed she hadn't killed him.

Tumbled prayers of gratitude filled her head.

Surely she could revive him, send him on his way, forget tonight. One thing was for sure. After this, he'd never want to come near her again.

Which should make her happy.

But in this quiet room, she admitted something she'd never admit to another living soul—something heinous but starkly true. After so many dull, chaste years, she'd relished tasting a man's desire again.

And from such a man. Strong. Virile. Beautiful.

She was irredeemably wicked. Ranelaw tugged at her senses the way a magnet drew a rusty nail. With steely determination, she mashed the unwelcome perception deep down in her soul, into the darkness where it would never rise to the light. Once, ten years ago, she'd stared into an abyss where whoring herself had loomed as the inescapable future. She'd never let herself sink so low again.

She had to get him on his feet and send him on his way. Fast. She wiped again at the blood.

"Wake up. *Please.*" Below the pooling redness, a long scratch extended. It didn't look serious, but she wasn't qualified to say with certainty. "Ranelaw, I beg of you, wake up."

"You called me Nicholas before," he murmured, without opening his eyes.

Her ministrations paused while thankfulness vied with aggravation. As so often when she was in Ranelaw's presence, aggravation emerged triumphant. "You're alive," she said flatly.

"Of course I'm alive." He didn't open his eyes. "It requires more than a slip of a girl to send me to my heavenly reward."

In spite of the giddy relief stewing in her belly, she gave a dismissive grunt. "There will be nothing heavenly about your final reward. Why didn't you say something earlier? I've been sick with worry."

"You deserve to be. That was one hell of a whack."

"You wouldn't stop," she said, even as her conscience pricked her. She'd never before struck anyone in violence. Ranelaw brought out the absolute worst in her.

At last he looked at her. Or at least he opened one eye. The side she'd hit was swelling. By tomorrow he'd have an impressive black eye. "You didn't want me to."

Beating back another twinge of remorse, she pressed more forcefully on his injury. "You're such a vain coxcomb."

He winced. "No need to try and kill me again."

"I'm cleaning up the blood," she snapped. How could she have regretted trying to murder the clodpole? He deserved clouting with a poker. He deserved clouting with a ship's mast.

His lips quirked with familiar amusement. "Can't you kiss it better?"

"No, I can't." She wrung the cloth over the bowl. Despite her irritation, her gorge rose when blood stained the water bright red.

He struggled into a sitting position. "You look a little pale there, Miss Smith."

Violently she wrung the cloth again. "It's late. I'm tired. It would serve you right if I had killed you."

"If I died kissing you, I'd die a happy man."

She arched her eyebrows in disbelief and dabbed again at his wound. The bleeding almost stopped but the bruising became more spectacular by the second. He'd bear the memento of her assault for a few days.

"Do you get results with lines like that?"

He laughed, then winced, raising one long-fingered hand to press her palm to his head. "You'd be surprised."

She twisted her hand from under his and leaned back on her knees. She didn't want him touching her. That was where the problem had started. Except of course that wasn't true. The problem started the moment she'd met his eyes across that crowded ballroom.

God rot him for being as addictive as opium. She could still taste his kisses, and Wild Antonia wanted more. She ignored Wild Antonia and injected a practical note into her voice. "I've done all I can. You need a physician and perhaps a stitch or two. You should put ice on that swelling."

He smiled at her as if she were the birthday present he'd begged for all year. "You're a remarkable woman, Antonia."

Clearly, if he was well enough to flirt, he'd survive without her attentions. She dipped the cloth into the bowl and lifted it out sopping. She started to scrub at the blood on the rug. Fortunately it was nothing like the lake she'd imagined in the first, horrible moments after hitting him.

She felt him watching but refused to look up. He'd uncovered too many secrets tonight. She needed to restore the distance between them. Difficult when her lips tingled from his kisses and her heart pounded with a stormy mixture of fear and desire.

"Will you help me up?"

She didn't look at him. "Will you go home?"

He laughed, and despite everything, her resistance melted at that soft, deep sound. "You're not exactly the kindest of nurses, are you?"

With an irritated gesture, she plopped the cloth into the dirty water. She rose to carry the bowl toward the washstand. "You shouldn't be here. You should never have been here."

He still smiled. His ruined beauty made the smile more precious. When he attended society events, he was almost too perfectly turned out. The disheveled, bruised man lounging at her fireside set her heart cartwheeling with helpless yearning.

Helpless yearning? She needed to get rid of him before she lost her mind completely.

"Should, should, should. The woman who kissed me wasn't such a martinet."

"No, she was insane," Antonia said in a discouraging voice. "And a gentleman would never refer to a lady's lapse in judgment."

He laughed again. "You told me I was no gentleman."

Amazement stifled her retort. Even after tonight, she hadn't imagined that plain Miss Smith had left an indelible mark on his attention. Yet he remembered exactly what she'd said the night they met.

"Antonia?" He extended a hand, and for once didn't sound mocking or superior. Instead he sounded something she'd never heard before. Vulnerable. "Will you help me?"

She was a thousand times an idiot, but she responded to the sincere appeal in his beautiful black eyes. "Here."

"Thank you."

He gripped her hand and staggered as he stood. She realized with a lurch of sick guilt that he wasn't as whole as he strove to appear. She rushed to put her shoulder under his arm. "Can you make it to the bed?"

"Miss Smith, I thought you'd never ask."

"Don't be a rattlepate," she said without venom.

He was heavy and his height made him awkward to support, even for a tall woman like her. With shuffling and grunting and a good deal of ungentle pushing, she managed to get him to the bed.

He collapsed with a groan. Sitting on the floor, he'd seemed a little more like himself. Now he was pale and blood oozed from his temple. Reclining against the headboard with a nonchalance that didn't conceal his pain, he looked cursedly romantic, like an injured hero from a Minerva Press novel.

"Do you have any brandy?" He sounded exhausted.

"Of course I don't have any brandy." Her sharpness wasn't totally to keep him in line. Alarm streaked through her at his waning stamina. She retrieved the cloth and knelt on the mattress to wipe the fresh blood from his face.

"Pity. You look like you need it."

She rose and poured him a glass of water. "You can't stay."

He accepted the glass with an unsteady hand and took a long drink. "I can't climb down the tree. I'm dizzy on my own two feet, let alone a dozen yards up in the air."

"You can't go through the house. Mr. Demarest left strict orders to post a man at the door every night."

"Well, the only other exit is up the chimney."

She hoped his hint of asperity indicated returning strength. For all her wish to have him gone, right now he wasn't fit to negotiate the tree. "Rest awhile. But you have to go."

"Soon." With visible discomfort, Ranelaw stretched out and gingerly settled his head on her pillow. He looked big and dangerous against her white sheets.

How odd to have a man in her bed. An alien presence in this eternally feminine domain. But there was no shifting him and she knew for all his bravado, he wasn't pretending weakness. She'd knocked him unconscious, for heaven's sake. She was lucky she hadn't killed him.

Antonia didn't want him dead. She just wanted him out of her life. Although she hadn't spent such an *interesting* evening in years. She frowned and struggled against the impulse to smooth the thick golden hair from Ranelaw's forehead. He wasn't a helpless child. Anything but. "You need a doctor."

His eyes closed and he looked remarkably at home, damn him. "Unless you intend to summon one, the sawbones must wait."

Frowning, she drew the blankets up around his chest. He didn't stir as she extinguished the lamp, leaving the fire to light the room. She shut the window, took another blanket, and curled up in the padded chair near the grate, determined to watch over him.

Distant thunder disturbed Ranelaw's restless dreams. He blinked into gold-tinged darkness and wondered where he was.

He was accustomed to waking in unfamiliar rooms, but rarely alone and never in a bed that smelled fresh and clean. He turned his head, only to close his eyes as a legion of demons clashed cymbals inside his skull.

He remembered.

He'd climbed a cherry tree then kissed that termagant Antonia Smith. And she'd walloped him with a poker.

Huzzah, Antonia.

The fearsome dragon was asleep in an armchair beside the fire. Carefully, partly because of his pounding head and partly because he didn't want to wake her and her defenses, he rose. He fought back a wave of dizziness.

The redoubtable Antonia didn't look like a fearsome dragon right now. She looked young and heart-wrenchingly beautiful.

He edged nearer and only then realized what was different. Somehow through all the chaos, she'd kept those disfiguring spectacles in place, but she'd removed them before sleeping. Her exertions had loosened her lovely hair. The plaits sagged and loose tendrils of silver formed a firelit halo. One long strand trailed over her shoulder toward her lush breasts. His hand curled as if it still cupped that breast, stroked the budded nipple.

Who would imagine that under her spinster armor, such spectacular curves lurked? He was delighted she hadn't fastened her dress. She'd been too terrified she'd murdered him to notice, he guessed. He'd heard her fear when she'd begged him to live. Manipulative bastard he was, he'd pretended unconsciousness long after returning to alertness.

Her breasts sloped above that ugly corset. If he was responsible for dressing her, he'd burn every garment she owned. He'd deck her in black lace. Or scarlet. Something to set off her skin's creamy purity.

He reached out to grab the mantel. He wasn't as sure on his feet as he'd prefer and his head ached like the very devil. His gaze didn't shift from the sleeping woman who had proven such an unexpectedly luscious armful.

Why did such a gorgeous creature hide her bounteous attractions? Why did a filly like her settle for such a restricted existence?

His temperamental mother had employed a string of companions, none of whom lasted more than a few months. To Ranelaw, the life had always seemed a thankless one. At someone's beck and call. A tiny wage in return for a modicum of respectability and a roof over one's head. He guessed the Demarests treated Miss Smith with more consideration than his foolish, flighty mother had ever treated her companions. But in essence, there was little difference between Miss Smith and those faceless women.

Surely Antonia had a choice in the matter. Thousands of men would gladly trade their fortunes for a wife so lovely. She'd have her own house, her own life, children, a husband to warm her chaste bed.

Except she'd shocked him, he who claimed to be unshockable. Antonia Smith didn't kiss like a virgin. She kissed like a woman who thrived upon a man's touch. He'd meant to coax her inch by inch into revealing her delights. But after the slightest hesitation, she'd responded with a fervor that had nearly blown his head off.

Absently he scooped the spectacles from the side table where she'd left them. He twirled them idly, then lifted them, wondering how shortsighted she was.

The lenses were plain tinted glass with no magnification.

Well, well.

Miss Smith became more intriguing by the moment.

After tonight's revelations, he wanted her more than ever. She wouldn't fight him if he seized her now. Or she might fight at first, but she'd yield soon enough.

So why was he standing mooning after her like damned Romeo instead of demonstrating how explosive sex would be? It made no sense.

It also made no sense that he found pleasure in merely looking at her. Even asleep, her face was full of character and a vivid, womanly beauty.

Why had no other man seen what he had? Her disguise was rudimentary. Hair scraped up under that cap, glasses, the unflattering wardrobe.

Forcing back the banging drums in his head, he bent over her. She couldn't sleep in that chair all night. With a gentleness he refused to categorize as care, he slid his arms under her and lifted her high against his chest.

She was tall, but slender. Normally carrying her would take little effort. His head swam and the room whirled around him. Briefly he wondered if they'd both end up toppling to the rug. Since she'd knocked him out, he wasn't up to carrying slumbering dragons.

She murmured something incomprehensible that might have been his name—he was sure it couldn't be—and curled into his body. His hold tightened and something shafted through him that in another man he might call possessiveness. He stood still, relishing her warm weight for all that his knees threatened to give out under him.

Her familiar scent teased his nostrils. He still couldn't place it, although it made him think of everything that had no place in his life. Innocence. Joy. The open beauty of the countryside. Spring flowers. Rain. As if to confirm the thought, rain dashed against the windowpane, rattling the frame.

He stared down at her, transfixed by how lovely she was. In this moment, Antonia seemed as young as Cassie Demarest and much more vulnerable. If he had any drop of pity, he'd let her go. He'd only end up destroying her.

It was too late. He wanted her and he'd have her. She wanted him too, although he couldn't imagine her admitting that this side of Hades.

The short distance to the bed felt like miles, but strangely it never occurred to him to wake her and make her walk. Carefully he laid her upon the sheets so when the maid arrived in the morning, Antonia would be where she was supposed to be. Just for tonight, he didn't want her suffering for his reckless invasion. He'd already caused her trouble. He didn't miss the signs of sleeplessness and strain on her face, even in repose.

He should take her gown off. But he didn't trust good intentions that far. She'd have to invent some excuse about dropping off half dressed.

Reluctant to release her, but knowing he must, if only because the urge to hold her was so strong, he slid his arms free. She settled upon the mattress with another of those damned arousing sighs.

He must go. The servants would be about soon. Already he'd have to take care not to alert the stable hands to his presence. And he still had to accomplish a climb in the rain with a head that ached fit to explode.

She sighed again and her eyelids fluttered open. Her eyes were ice blue like the sky on a clear January morning.

He shouldn't be shocked. From her pale, silvery hair to her white, white skin, hers was a wintry beauty. But the purity of that unaware glance cut like a knife. His hands clenched at his sides.

"Nicholas . . ." A drowsy smile curved her mouth.

He knew she still drifted in slumber. But he couldn't stop himself leaning down and whispering. "Sleep, Antonia."

She turned her head and pressed her lips to his briefly. The sweetness pierced him to the bone. He endured the kiss without deepening it, although his gut lurched at the silent invitation.

"I'm dreaming, aren't I?"

"Yes," he forced from a constricted throat. Unable to

resist one last taste, he brushed his mouth over hers in a kiss hardly less innocent.

If he didn't go now, he wouldn't go at all. He hoped to hell he made it down the tree. After the wet night, it would be as slippery as a greased pig. If he fell on his arse, Miss Smith would still have explanations to make, however he'd tried to protect her reputation.

Slowly he straightened and cast her one last, lingering look. He wanted to imprint *this* Antonia on his memory, to hold against next time he saw her decked out like a damned scarecrow.

He turned and prowled toward the window.

Antonia opened her eyes to a sunny morning. She lay in her black bombazine dress on top of her bed. There was no disorientation. She remembered exactly what had happened, although details toward the end turned fuzzy. Strangest of all, she had a vague memory of Lord Ranelaw kissing her tenderly before leaving.

She must have conjured that from her imagination. Even if every other unbelievable event was real.

Groggily she sat up and pushed tangled hair away from her face. Exhaustion weighted her limbs. A cup of chocolate sat congealing on the bedside table. She'd been so deeply asleep, she hadn't heard the maid. An unusual occurrence for Miss Smith, who usually bustled around the house well before breakfast.

A soft knock before Cassie dashed in, wearing a muslin dress the color of sunshine. "Toni, you slugabed. I've been up for hours."

Antonia placed her feet on the floor and struggled to force her tired mind to function. "Good morning, Cassie."

Antonia's focus remained on last night. Was Ranelaw all right? She hoped the poker hadn't done serious damage. What did he make of her this morning? She wasn't optimistic enough to imagine he'd disregard what he'd learned. He was too clever for that, blast him.

"And you didn't even get undressed." A frown crossed Cassie's pretty face. "Am I working you too hard? You never sleep in."

Antonia started to shake her head, then decided weariness might excuse her uncharacteristic behavior. "I'm unused to so many late nights. I'm not a young sprig like you."

Cassie gave one of her snorts. "Yes, at twenty-seven, you're in your dotage. Are you up for the trip to Surrey?"

"Surrey?"

Cassie caught her hand and squeezed it. "We're going to the Humphreys' for a fortnight. Had you forgotten?"

The Humphreys. . .

Two weeks in Surrey. Two weeks away from London's temptations and distractions. Two weeks away from one fascinating rake in particular.

Antonia's gaze wandered to the window, skittering over the snowy white petals littering the floor. Nicholas Challoner was dangerous and becoming more dangerous every day. If heaven had mercy, by the time they returned, he'd be bored with his absent prey and hunting new quarry.

Fate rescued her from further nocturnal invasions. What a wicked, wicked girl she was. Right now, she didn't feel especially grateful.

Chapter Six

FTER several days in the country, Antonia had finally beaten her brief madness into submission. The steady, unexciting routine that had sustained her for ten years resumed, for all that she was in a different house with different people. Cassie too returned to her cheerful self. The feverish edge that marked her activities in London receded.

The house party was composed largely of people Cassie's age and their families. It was more like the entertainments at Bascombe Hailey. Rural. Innocent. Unsophisticated. Horses. Dogs. Country walks. Games in the evening, then an early bed.

No sizzling threat of danger.

No fiendishly handsome rakes lurking to lure an unwary lady. Or an unwary lady's wary companion.

Pelham Place was in a pretty corner of Surrey. Wilder than most of this cultivated county, with woods and a river and a wilderness that could almost pass as a moor.

Antonia devoted enjoyable hours to exploring the grounds. Hours when she convinced herself it was acceptable to spare an occasional thought for the disreputable Marquess of Ranelaw and his kisses.

For one brilliant, incendiary moment, she'd been Lady Antonia Hilliard again. With every day that passed, she remembered Lady Antonia was no more, destroyed by her wanton passions. In her place was Miss Smith with too much at stake to gamble her future on a rake's smile.

Particularly a rake who pursued her merely to facilitate his flirtation with another woman.

Although no matter how she insisted he wanted Cassie, the deepest part of her couldn't accept that was true.

Surely that was vanity speaking. Vanity and oak-headed foolishness. Cassie was pretty and far from a featherbrain. Any man would be proud to claim her for his own.

Five days after their arrival, she and Cassie crossed the rolling lawns toward Pelham Place. They'd taken a long afternoon walk by the river. The uncertain weather that plagued their London stay had transformed into perfect spring. Antonia had been glad of her chip bonnet, however ugly it was, and she'd scolded Cassie to keep her own, much more attractive hat on. Cassie was inclined to freckle, something Antonia thought charming but which would incur disapproval from the arbiters of fashion.

A group on the terrace turned to observe their approach. Lady Humphrey often served tea outside so the gathering didn't immediately alert Antonia.

About twenty guests stayed in the house. As she neared the terrace, she realized their numbers had been augmented—and she was familiar with the newcomers, or at least one of them.

"Lord Ranelaw!" Cassie cried breathlessly, swiftly mounting the shallow steps to the terrace.

When Ranelaw swept off his hat to greet Cassie, Antonia saw his face still bore marks of assault. There was bruising around his eye and the graze had healed to an annoyingly dashing slash along one high cheekbone. The injuries only emphasized his attractions.

"Miss Demarest." Ranelaw took her hand and bent over it. When he glanced at Antonia, standing dismayed behind Cassie, the lids lowered over his eyes. Nothing so crass as a wink.

Horror ripped through her, leaving her giddy. Her hands clenched at her sides and she glared at the reprobate.

God in heaven, help her.

She'd thought she was safe. She was in more danger than ever.

So was Cassie.

Antonia had moved to wrench her overjoyed cousin away from him before she remembered where she was. She bobbed into a brief curtsy edged with insult.

Lady Humphrey stepped forward. "Lord Thorpe has invited some additional gentlemen to join our revels, Miss Demarest. Our quiet evenings should become rather lively."

Too lively, Antonia thought sourly. She glanced at Cassie and wasn't surprised the girl showed no astonishment at Ranelaw's arrival. She understood now why her charge had submitted to rustication with such good grace. She wanted to blast Cassie for being a naïve little fool but most of her rage was targeted at the cocksure marquess.

Ranelaw stared at Cassie in flagrant appreciation. Why not? The girl looked charming with her cheeks pink from exercise and excitement brightening her blue eyes.

Oh, Cassie, you're so easy to read.

Antonia could do little to quash her cousin's pleasure. She'd like to think Ranelaw would tire of the girl's blatant admiration, but experience indicated men never wearied of flattery. Cassie's bedazzlement would only feed his interest. No wonder he was such an arrogant scoundrel.

Through a red haze of temper, Antonia barely heard Lady Humphrey introduce the four arrivals. Lord Thorpe turned out to be the lady's nephew. The fellow wasn't just her bugbear's fast friend, he seemed to be related to half the *ton.*

She emerged from fuming to hear one of the gentlemen quizzing Ranelaw about his face. His eyes rested mockingly upon her, but she refused to give him the satisfaction of embarrassment.

"Would you believe a tiger attacked me?"

"A tiger?" Cassie raised a hand to her chest in a flirtatious gesture Antonia had never seen her use. Ranelaw exercised a detrimental effect on her cousin who until now had been delightfully free from artifice.

"Don't be a henwit," Antonia snapped under her breath.

Ranelaw laughed. "Perhaps I should say a tigress."

Thorpe clapped him on the shoulder. "Watch for those wild beasts on Piccadilly, old man!"

General laughter followed, and this time, Antonia couldn't resist meeting that sly black gaze. His faint smile woke the demons inside her that she'd hoped country air had banished.

His invasion of her thoughts had been penance enough. Now she'd find no escape from him. He'd infect the next fortnight with fear, anger, and unwelcome desire. This house party promised to become the definition of purgatory.

Damn and blast Ranelaw. Was she never to get a moment's peace?

Cassie, understandably, made every attempt to avoid a private conversation with Antonia. In spite of her dishevelment, she lingered outside for tea and the flirtation that the gentlemen's arrival engendered in what until now had been a pleasantly easy party.

Lord Ranelaw and Cassie joined the merriment, without, Antonia was relieved to note, concentrating solely on each other. But then, she thought sourly, why rush to express their preferences? They had days to make mischief and a vast estate to do it in.

Not for the first time, she cursed Godfrey Demarest for leaving her alone to shepherd Cassie safely through her first season. Just for once, surely he could have put his daughter ahead of his worldly pleasures.

Her headache returned with a vengeance and eventually she excused herself on a murmur of apology. With so many eyes observing, Cassie wasn't likely to sneak away with her suitor.

Nobody watched Antonia leave. Apart from Ranelaw. He did a marvelous impression of involvement in the conversation, but Antonia knew his attention hadn't shifted from her for a second.

He had no intention of letting her forget their unfinished business.

Antonia retreated to the small, dark room off Cassie's that had been assigned to her. The chamber was appropriate for a superior servant. Away from home, she couldn't be treated as a family member without undue comment.

To calm the mad rush of her pulse, she splashed cold water on her flushed face. She lifted a threadbare towel and told herself for the hundredth time to get used to her shabby accommodations.

By the end of this season, it was highly likely Cassie would be betrothed. Dear God, let it not be to Ranelaw, although he wasn't really a candidate for Cassie's hand. Mr. Demarest would never give permission for his only daughter to marry such an unrepentant rake, even if the marquess did the pretty and proposed. Being an unrepentant rake himself, Demarest was most insistent that his daughter stay far away from the breed.

Once Cassie wed, she'd have no further use for a chaperone. Her cousin had long said she planned to take Antonia with her to her new home, but few young men newly married would approve that plan.

No, the most likely future for Antonia Smith was employment in another household. As she surveyed her unappealing room, she muffled a depressed sigh at the prospect of a lifetime of such surroundings.

Cassandra came up late to change for dinner, breezing into her room with a smile. The smile faltered when she saw Antonia waiting in the chair beside the lit fire. The day had been warm but evenings still drew in with a chill.

"Toni . . ." Cassie blushed and looked away guiltily as she laid her hat upon the bed. "Aren't you changing?"

"I can change in five minutes and you know it," Antonia said repressively. "You deceived me."

"I . . . I don't know what you mean." The girl didn't meet her eyes. She wandered to the dressing table with an unconvincing show of carelessness and began to unpin her hair. "Bella will be here soon."

"Bella's appearance may delay what I have to say. It won't save you from hearing it."

Cassie turned, her chin at an angle that Antonia recognized. Cassie rarely dug her heels in, but when she did, she was as stubborn as her father. "If I'd told you Lord Ranelaw came to Surrey, you'd have found some excuse to stay in London."

"At least you admit the scheme."

Cassie had the grace to look shamefaced. "It wasn't a scheme."

Antonia arched a skeptical eyebrow. "No?"

Cassie fiddled with the pink ribbon at her bodice. "Lord Ranelaw asked if I attended the Scanlan ball. I told him we left Town for two weeks. It's not my fault he followed us."

Us? Oh, no. Not *us.* The disreputable Ranelaw pursued her charge, and if Antonia wasn't careful, he'd get her. "Cassie, he's handsome, he's charming, his attentions would turn any lady's head. Even a lady as sensible as you."

Cassie still looked mulish. "You're treating me like a child."

Antonia shook her head. "No. But I more than most know what you risk."

"His intentions are honorable."

Antonia's heart sank. She told herself it was because she hadn't realized things reached such a pass. Honesty compelled her to admit some of her dismay stemmed from wanting Lord Ranelaw herself, for all the good it did her. "Has he said so?"

The girl shrugged and began to brush her hair with the heavy silver hairbrush her father had given her for her twelfth birthday. Cassie was good-hearted and far from stupid, but Antonia couldn't forget she was also impossibly spoiled. If this became an issue of her will versus Cassie's, trouble loomed. For years, she'd been Cassie's confidante and companion. Most of that time, the task had been ridiculously easy.

Clearly Antonia made up for that now.

"Cassie?" When the girl didn't answer, she deliberately kept her voice level. "Has Lord Ranelaw mentioned marriage?"

During the fraught pause, her mind flooded with mad, passionate memories of Ranelaw kissing her. Once she'd been green enough to believe a man who kissed a woman so desperately could have no interest in other conquests.

Eventually Cassie reluctantly shook her head. "No, it's too early." She continued in a strident tone as if convincing herself as much as Antonia. "He's behaving as a respectable man does when courting a woman. If his intentions aren't aboveboard, he wouldn't be so public."

"Cassie, he's too old for you. He's too experienced. Even if he plans marriage, I can't see you happy with him. A man like that doesn't know the meaning of fidelity."

The girl tossed her head. "Don't you think I'm woman enough to keep him in line?"

"Cassie . . ." Antonia paused, at a loss for words. The problem was she did mean that. She wasn't sure anyone was woman enough to curb Ranelaw's roving eye. She fell back on something she'd said before. "I don't want you hurt."

Her response angered rather than mollified Cassie. "Just because you lost your head over a pretty face doesn't mean every other girl will."

Antonia stiffened, wounded by Cassie's sneering tone. Cassie had never been spiteful, but she'd noticed changes in the girl in London. Such general admiration would overset anyone. Until now, Antonia hadn't realized how far the damage extended.

She told herself Cassie didn't mean to be hurtful. But as

she read the angry defiance in the girl's face, she couldn't quite convince herself that was true.

"I know you think I'm overly careful, but . . ."

"I'm not a wide-eyed innocent," she said resentfully then flounced away. "I know more than you think."

Antonia felt a twinge of guilty fear. Was her charge aware of the prickly sexual awareness between her and Ranelaw?

Surely not. In public, Ranelaw was careful to conceal his interest in Antonia.

Dear God, save her from this nonsense. There was nothing to conceal. His interest wasn't real.

"Cassie . . ." she began just as Bella bustled in. Again surely it was her guilty conscience and nothing concrete that Bella's glance seemed sharper than usual.

"Are you ready to dress, miss?" The maid immediately picked up the troubled atmosphere, and her gaze darted between Antonia and Cassie with avid curiosity.

"Yes. I'll wear the lavender silk." Antonia heard relief in Cassie's answer.

Antonia smothered a sigh. It was best she stopped. Any more and she risked their first serious quarrel. Over a rogue like Lord Ranelaw.

Without looking at Cassie, Antonia stood and straightened her skirts. The jibe about youthful foolishness had hurt. It hurt even more that Cassie seemed unaware how cutting her comment was.

"I'll see you downstairs, Cassie," she said quietly.

"As you wish," Cassie said sullenly. Then with a spark of spirit, "I believe Lord Ranelaw is placed next to me for dinner. He asked Lady Humphrey specially."

Antonia didn't answer. What point nagging Cassie right now? For the thousandth time since she'd met him, she consigned Lord Ranelaw to Hades.

After a restless night plagued with anxiety about Cassie and Ranelaw's open flirtation, Antonia rose early. Soon she wouldn't need a disguise to play the hag. When she checked the mirror, she looked so tired and distraught, it was a relief to hide behind her spectacles.

The sun wasn't long over the horizon. The guests wouldn't stir for hours. This was her favorite time of day here. Before she left the house, she peeked into the room beside hers to see Cassie asleep and looking the perfect angel she certainly wasn't when awake.

In the stables, the grooms had her usual chestnut gelding saddled. The horse greeted her with a soft whicker.

"Hello, my beauty," she murmured, extending her palm with a piece of apple.

She'd eaten the rest of the apple on her walk across the dew-laden grass. The world seemed made anew. Her turmoil receded. Evil couldn't prevail on this pristine morning.

She wasn't fool enough to believe her contentment would endure, but carefree moments were so rare lately, she snatched at this one. Carefree moments when she was alone and unobserved. That was one reason she treasured these rides in the quiet dawn. At first she'd expected the more vigorous gentlemen to be about, but the lure of the port bottle and the smoking room past midnight proved too strong.

Her first two mornings, she'd dutifully asked a groom to accompany her. Now she knew the estate, she rode alone. For one brief hour, she tasted freedom. Fleetingly she became Lady Antonia Hilliard, not dour Miss Smith.

Once out of sight of the house, she slid her spectacles off and slipped them into her pocket. Immediately colors sprang to life. Drawing a deep breath of fragrant air, she urged her horse to a canter down a wide forest path.

She should have guessed her contentment would prove short-lived.

She rounded a bend and before her, on a large gray, waited the devil who blighted her existence. He was dressed for the country in a buff brown jacket, breeches, and black boots polished to a mirror shine. Her belly knotting with a queasy mixture of irritation and excitement, she drew her horse to a stop a few yards away.

"Miss Smith, what a delightful surprise." That mocking smile twisted his mouth as he doffed his hat. Sunlight glanced across his gilded hair, vied with the glitter in his black eyes.

His eyes devouring her as if she was the woman he wanted, he replaced his hat at a jaunty angle. Resentfully she stared back.

He'd spent all last night making up to Cassie, through dinner and later during an uproarious game of forfeits that had caused general notice. Clearly Antonia's cautionary lecture had only incited Cassie to demonstrate she wouldn't be guided on Ranelaw's courtship. Antonia should have left well enough alone.

Of course jealousy stabbed her when she witnessed him flirting with her cousin. She wouldn't be human if it didn't. But her overriding reaction was concern for Cassie's happiness. At her deepest level, Antonia was convinced Ranelaw meant the girl no good.

"Lord Ranelaw," she said in a repressive voice. "You followed me."

"Of course I didn't follow you," her nemesis said calmly.

She realized she wasn't wearing her spectacles. Her heart pounding with trepidation, she fumbled in her pocket. "Don't treat me like a fool."

He watched her with that same predatory glint she'd seen in London. A few days in Surrey had made her forget its devastating effect. "I didn't follow you for the good reason that I knew exactly where you'd be. One of the grooms and I had a long chat about your morning rides yesterday. To his profit."

He made his scheming sound like the actions of a reasonable man. "Surely bribing servants becomes tiresome," she said acidly, still trying to find her glasses.

"The rewards are worth it." He focused on what she did. "It's too late to worry about hiding from me, Antonia."

Just like that, she was back in his arms in London. It was as immediate as if he kissed her with his hot, voracious mouth and pressed her against his long, lean body. She froze with humiliation, and a prickling tide of color flooded her face.

"Why are you here, Ranelaw?" she said in a hard tone, as she withdrew her trembling hand from her pocket and curled it around the reins. The chestnut sensed her disquiet and shifted with an uneasy snort.

Ranelaw looked around, his face alight with amusement. "It's a lovely morning for a ride."

She noticed the emphasis he placed on *ride* but ignored it. As so often when she was with Ranelaw, uncertainty receded under anger. Neither was as potent as her stirring physical awareness of his presence. "Stop playing games."

His black gaze centered on her, bright with curiosity and a sensual appreciation that made her pulses race. Since yesterday the bruising had faded but it still added a rakish danger to his features. She didn't want to respond to his manifold attractions, but she suspected while she lived, she had no choice.

"You're playing games too, Antonia."

"No . . ." she breathed in horror before she realized he couldn't have discovered her identity. He knew more than he should, mostly through her fault. But he couldn't know everything.

"What else would you call this masquerade? You're a beautiful young woman, yet you dress like a damned grand-mother."

He guided his horse closer, so her chestnut sidled nervously once more. "You act like you've never known a man's touch, yet you come alive in my arms. Who's been kissing you, Antonia? I'll swear I'm not the first man who has."

She feared her face would go up in flames, it was so hot. Somewhere she found the will to fight. So far, he'd had everything his own way. "It was a natural reaction to your tawdry skills."

He laughed softly. "Oh, cruel."

"I want you to go back to London." She knew she wasted her time. She'd told him to go away before and it hadn't done her a morsel of good.

"If wishes were horses, beggars would ride." His tone turned silky. "I must say your charge is considerably nicer to me than you are. She positively glowed when she saw me yesterday. A man has his vanity. Perhaps I'm better devoting my attentions to Miss Demarest than her duenna."

Her hands bunched on the reins, causing the horse to shift again. "Don't threaten me, Ranelaw."

He still smiled lazily at her. "Or you'll what? Biff me with the poker again?"

"Not if I've got a pistol handy."

His lids lowered so his dark lashes shadowed his cheekbones. "You know, for another kiss, the risk might be worth it."

"Touch me again and I'll kill you," she said in a low, throbbing voice. She was angry at him and angry at herself that no matter how she tried, she couldn't wean herself of this perilous weakness for him.

Devil take him, he laughed once more. "Just how do you intend to fulfill that threat, my sweet? I don't recall you fighting too hard last time."

To her bitter shame, he spoke the truth. She could see he awaited some coy denial that only confirmed her susceptibility. Well, he'd wait until Hades froze over.

"You're spoiling my morning, Lord Ranelaw," she said coldly, and spurred her horse into a bounding gallop along the path. She bent low over her mount's neck and let the wind whip away her scalding tears.

Chapter Seven

*H*IS hunting instincts alert, Ranelaw watched Miss Smith career headlong through the trees. The surprisingly expensive and diabolically becoming riding habit fitted more closely than her usual clothing. He had no trouble discerning the magnificent body his hands had explored—too briefly—during those turbulent moments last week.

Since that revelatory evening in her bedroom, she'd gathered her defenses. Perhaps he should have fucked her. She wouldn't be so insolent then.

He mightn't be quite so frustrated either.

She'd left him wanting her, and somehow wanting her made every other woman unappealing. They all seemed absurdly . . . uncomplicated and docile.

Whereas with each meeting, Miss Smith proved more interesting. Who would guess the dowdy chaperone was a spectacular horsewoman? The chestnut was temperamental, yet she controlled the animal with hardly a thought, and she'd galloped away as sure in the saddle as a young Amazon.

He should let the baggage go. He'd made his point, asserted his advantage, confirmed the fragility of her barriers against him. Strategy insisted he leave her to stew on his intentions. Strategy insisted he return to Pelham Place and further last night's progress with the Demarest chit. She'd been considerably more forthcoming than in London. If he pressed his interest, he'd have her on her back before she left Surrey. Perhaps even by week's end.

By riding helter-skelter into the thick woodland, Miss Smith left her chick unprotected. This was exactly the moment to pursue Cassandra Demarest.

Thick woodland. . .

His revenge must wait. He mightn't get another chance to corner the intriguing Antonia away from prying eyes.

With a heady surge of anticipation, he spurred his horse into a gallop.

Ranelaw easily caught up with Miss Smith. His horse was bigger and swifter and he wasn't riding sidesaddle.

She shot him a glance like blue lightning from under her stylish beaver hat and urged her mount to a faster pace. As they thundered into a clearing, he lunged over to grab her horse's bridle and drag the beast to a heaving stop. He wanted to seduce Antonia but he had no intention of chasing her to Timbuctoo for the privilege. He spoke softly to her horse, calming it. With animals and women, he always had a magical touch. Although so far, this particular woman resisted his fabled charm.

Most of the time. . .

"Let me go, damn you," she gasped, raising her crop.

She was incandescent with fury. Nobody who saw her would ever again consider Miss Smith mousy. She looked like a queen decreeing a fractious subject's execution.

Ranelaw laughed, excitement fizzing in his veins like champagne. He'd never before felt this extravagant hunger to push a woman to her limits, to take her until she screamed.

"Don't hit me, Antonia."

"Why?" she snarled. "Because I might hurt you?"

He snickered. She had such an inflated opinion of her ability to withstand him. It was one of the things he found delightful about confounding her. How delicious when she finally lay under him, panting with unconditional surrender.

"No, because this time I bloody well will tell anyone who asks exactly where I got my bruises."

Her eyes flashed azure with temper. Yet again, he marveled at their beauty, usually concealed behind her spectacles. Large, clear, and slightly slanted. Thick lashes darker than her pale hair. He noticed with a stab of unwelcome remorse that the lashes were matted with drying tears.

However upset she might be, the gaze she leveled on him held no softness. Only anger and something that in a less complex woman he'd read as desire.

"I'm willing to take the risk," she sniped.

"I'm not." He snatched the riding crop from her gloved hands. "You're a violent wench, aren't you?"

There was an enchanting flush of pink high on her cheeks. How could he ever have considered this woman plain? Even under her disguise, he should have recognized her splendor. As he stared in admiration, something about her coloring struck him as familiar. The fleeting thought drifted away before he could catch it.

"Only when goaded." She tried to jerk her horse free but he kept a firm hold. All she achieved was a restive sidle from her mount.

"Such passion, Antonia." With a deliberately dismissive gesture, he dropped the crop to the ground. "It makes a man hunger to seize you in his arms. You'd go up like fire."

The light dimmed in her ice blue eyes and her mouth flattened with what he recognized as shame. Sour anger stirred in Ranelaw's gut. Someone somewhere had taught her to loathe the thrilling woman she was.

Her gaze flickered away from him. "Please let me go," she said in a dull voice.

He'd set out to cow her, to gain the upper hand. Now that he couldn't mistake the slump of her shoulders, he realized he wanted her spirit, not her dejected submission. He wanted her fighting.

Who the hell was he trying to gull? He wanted her any way he could get her. Every minute with her honed his craving.

He wasn't by nature a gentle man, but he knew how to feign gentleness to get what he wanted. He released his grip on her reins and lowered his voice to the coaxing tone that never failed to lure a woman to ruin. "The morning's too fine to quarrel. Walk with me, Antonia."

She stiffened and sent him a nervous glance. "I need to get back."

"Nonsense. It's still early."

She tilted her chin with familiar defiance, but to his regret, the shadow of shame remained. "If I stay, will you promise to leave Cassie alone?"

Brave little bird. She thought to bargain with the devil. When surely she knew the devil couldn't be trusted.

"Today."

"For the rest of the visit."

"For such a concession, you'll have to surrender your virtue."

He waited for her to bite back, but instead her lips twitched. "No."

"Worth a try."

"I'm sure." With every second, she looked more like the strong woman he knew. He felt an uncharacteristic impulse to plant his fist into the face of the man who had undermined her confidence.

Inevitably it was a man.

Was it the same man who had taught her how to kiss?

The fellow had made a good job of that at least. Although Ranelaw suspected Antonia demonstrated natural talent.

His horse shifted. Perhaps at the long delay. Perhaps at the tension building in his rider. Ranelaw injected all the charm he could summon into his smile. "Will you walk?"

Antonia didn't smile back. "Will you behave?"

"Of course."

She studied him with an assessing light in her eyes, then relented with a sigh. "For a moment."

A moment was all he needed. He hid his triumphant grin and swung out of the saddle. "Let me help you."

She still looked as though she ventured into the den of a hungry bear. But she reached for his shoulders and only flinched slightly when his hands circled her waist.

As he lifted her, she was stiff, expecting him to pull some trick. Wise dragon. He wasn't yet ready to make his move. His hands didn't linger when he set her on the ground, much as having her close made him itch to kiss her senseless.

"There's a brook not far away," she said with unconvincing calm. She looped the reins over her arm and bent to collect her crop from the grass.

"Of course you've had days to explore the estate."

To his surprise, she answered readily. "I miss the country. London's so crowded and dirty."

While she didn't sound at ease, her voice wasn't edged with the usual hostility. He wasn't sure what prompted her to stay, but he refused to question the fortunate turn in his scheming.

As they followed a faint trail through the trees, he fell into step beside her. The leaf litter muffled the clop of their horses' hooves to a soothing rhythm. Even under the trees, the morning became uncomfortably warm. He shucked off his jacket and slung it over one shoulder. She cast him a sharp glance. He waited for a protest at this breach in decorum, but she remained silent.

The path was so narrow, his arm occasionally brushed hers. The first time it happened, she jumped like a scalded cat, but when he pursued no further liberties, eventually she relaxed.

Ranelaw took advantage of her uncharacteristically confiding manner. He wanted her in his bed. But with that never-ending desire came gnawing curiosity about her seemingly inexplicable choices. "You grew up in the country?"

She nodded, swishing her crop at the long grass edging the path. In the capital's ballrooms, she bottled up her natural energy. Here she revealed more of her true self every second, did she but know it.

"Yes. But in a much wilder place than this."

She was at home on this estate, and the groom had commented on her aplomb when handling a difficult horse. From the first, Ranelaw's title hadn't struck her with particular awe.

Unusual in a paid companion.

Everything pointed to a woman from Ranelaw's level of society.

If that was so, why did she play the stultifying role of companion to a spoiled flibbertigibbet like Cassandra Demarest? Even Cassie's father wasn't top drawer. The man was second or third cousin to the Earl of Aveson, a link too tenuous to sweeten the whiff of trade that clung to the Demarest fortune.

Hoping to encourage her to continue, Ranelaw found himself confiding in turn. "So did I. In Hampshire. Near the sea. In a tumbledown manor house infested with ungovernable children and even more ungovernable adults."

He rarely spoke of his childhood. The subject stirred few happy memories.

In his opinion, his upbringing provided an infallible argument against marriage as an institution. His parents had loathed each other. He'd hated his father more with every year and once he was old enough to form an independent opinion, he'd felt little but contempt for his shallow, self-indulgent mother.

The house had brimmed with a continually shifting tide of unruly humanity, children, mistresses, servants, various relatives and toadies. Political intrigue that wouldn't have disgraced an Ottoman court had poisoned his boyhood. Until he was eleven, Eloise's affection had provided his one constant, but then his father had banished her forever.

No, he was more than happy to relinquish the dubious joys of family life to people whose optimism outstripped grim reality.

Wary curiosity laced the glance she cast at him. "That wasn't what I imagined."

He'd known she must think of him in his absence—if

only to consign him to perdition. But her admission filled him with pleasure. If he took up residence in her thoughts, he'd soon take up residence in her bed. "What did you imagine?"

Her lips curved with wry humor. "That you were spawned fully formed as Satan's minion."

With every second, her tension seeped away. She reached up to grab a dangling leaf. This time when her arm brushed his, she hardly jumped at all.

Even through his shirtsleeve, her heat seared. Desire surged. Still he bit back the impulse to seize her.

Not yet. . .

He released a soft gust of laughter, not at all offended. "I was a child like any other."

"I doubt that." She slipped her crop under her arm and absently tore at the leaf, scattering the fragments on the path at her feet. "I've always considered you a lone wolf. Now I discover you have a bevy of brothers and sisters."

He shrugged. If she wanted, he was willing to talk about his background. He knew this seemingly harmless discussion allayed her lingering fears.

"I *am* a lone wolf. It was the only way I kept sane in that chaos. From my father's three marriages, I have six legitimate siblings. My mother whelped two bastards to different lovers before she died in a carriage accident when I was eight. My father acknowledged another five bastards of his own. There were rumors of more. In the local village, the family coloring certainly proliferates. My first stepmother brought two sons to the marriage and my second stepmother brought three girls. Keddon Hall is a barn, big enough to billet an army, but the Challoners en masse threaten to burst it at the seams. It was a relief to leave for Eton and escape the pandemonium."

She paused to stare at him with an odd expression. Not the familiar suspicion. And unfortunately not the melting surrender he connived to see.

A kind of hard, speculative curiosity.

He too stopped so his horse's nose nudged him in the shoulder. "What?"

"You speak of your family like strangers."

He shrugged. "With such a crowd, it was like living in a menagerie. Most of them are strangers."

Most. Not all. Which was why he was here now.

The reminder provided a fillip to his determination for revenge. He berated himself for allowing Antonia to divert him. But when he met her vividly interested gaze, the admonition faded to a distant whisper.

"Where are they now?"

"My father was careless where he sired children, but once he had them, he saw the girls were dowered and the boys found suitable employment. The youngest children are still in school. My other sisters, mostly, are married. A few brothers went into the army, some into the church, some into the law."

"Do you see them often?"

"Some of them." He paused. "Sometimes. You'll be shocked they all ended up respectable members of society. I'm definitely the family black sheep, if you discount my parents."

She laughed, the sound too warm and enchanting for his comfort. "I am shocked."

"What about you?" He didn't need to feign his curiosity. "Do you have brothers and sisters?"

The ease drained from her manner. Again he had the odd perception that his question trespassed on private sorrow. He braced for her to tell him to mind his own business, but eventually she answered. "I have nobody."

"An orphan?"

It made sense, especially if she was a woman of good family who had come down in the world. Increasingly that's what he believed she must be.

Her lips tightened and she stared straight ahead as she preceded him, leading her horse. The silence bristled with unspoken regret.

"I have . . . *had* a brother."

He couldn't see her face, but her tone's flatness indicated longstanding pain. He caught up with her. "Older or younger?"

"Three years older." Thick underbrush forced her to veer closer. Again he resisted the urge to grab her.

They emerged from the bushes onto the bank of a sparkling stream. Antonia stopped and faced him. He couldn't mistake her strain, however hard she strove to hide it.

"I told you the brook was pretty." Her tone indicated she'd reveal nothing more of her mysterious past today.

His gaze swept their surroundings. The spot was indeed pretty. And isolated. He was astounded he'd coaxed her to this secluded location with so little effort. She'd always been awake to his stratagems before.

He stretched out a gloved hand. "Let me tie the horses."

Unsuspectingly she cooperated. Holding both sets of reins in one hand, he grabbed her crop and poked it through her horse's saddle leathers. No need to court danger when he finally touched her.

Once he'd secured their horses, he stripped off his gloves and shoved them in his coat pocket. He wanted to feel her skin against his. Anticipation rising like an approaching storm, he carelessly tossed his jacket over his saddle.

He turned. Antonia stood on the edge of the stream. Under her hat, her face was in profile. Hungrily his eyes traced the high forehead, the imperious nose, the lush lips, the determined chin. For a long moment he stared, wondering why she exerted this peculiar power over him.

Of course, once he'd had her, she'd lose her fascination. They all did. But he had to admit she'd made this chase interesting.

Now at last he had her alone. And the chase would end with his victory as had been ordained from the first. He was desperate to tumble her.

Because desperation was a rare sensation in his life of easy pleasures, he lingered to savor it.

With a graceful gesture, she removed her hat and set it on the ground. He appreciated seeing her out of her usual dusty black. The dark green riding habit emphasized her sumptuous curves and sunlight gleamed on her blond hair, swept up into a chignon. A few loose tendrils softened the severity. Her pale hair and the gold light should remind him of angels and halos, but Miss Smith—surely not her real name—wasn't nearly so ethereal. She was earthy and real and he could scarcely wait to show her what a man could do to her body.

His attention returned to her face. She looked pensive and her lips turned down at the corners. He should have been more careful of his conversation. He shouldn't have mentioned her family. Next time he'd know better.

Would there be a next time? He'd imagined having her would be enough. Once to satisfy his itch and gain the power that he'd use to attain his real goal, the Demarest chit.

Now the prize was within reach, he wasn't so sure.

If this house party was like every other he'd attended, the guests would scatter across the estate and nobody would consider either his absence or Miss Smith's significant. He had several hours to enjoy her before they needed to return.

Glorious prospect.

His booted feet soundless on the thick grass, he prowled up behind her and slid his arms around her waist. He drew her into his chest.

"Ranelaw!" she gasped, stiffening. For a brief throbbing moment, her buttocks rested against his thickening cock, then she ripped herself free and whirled to face him. "What are you doing?"

More seduction was required, clearly. He supposed it was overly optimistic to expect a virtuous woman to topple into his arms just for the asking. A pity. He enjoyed these games but with every second, he burned hotter for her.

Still, he didn't want to spook her into running. He resisted the urge to grab her again. "Don't pretend ignorance of what awaited."

She frowned, looking adorably confused and much younger than he'd ever seen her, except for those sweet and damnably frustrating moments when he'd watched her sleep. "But you promised."

He released a dismissive laugh. "Don't take me for a sapskull. You brought me here to make love to you."

Antonia straightened to her full height, resistance tightening her expression. "No."

"Yes," he said implacably, stepping closer. "I'm more than willing. I'm even willing to go through the motions of pretending to suborn a woman of unshakable chastity if that makes your conscience sit more easily."

She looked devastated again. He wished she didn't. He hated her vulnerability. It set up an odd, uncomfortable twinge in his chest that he couldn't quite identify.

"You think I led you on?" she asked in a whisper. She edged back a pace. "Truly I didn't mean to."

Oh, no, now she felt guilty. He scowled as he contemplated the unimaginable prospect of failure, of not spending the next hours entwined in her arms.

Devil take that idea.

"Of course you did."

Her stricken gaze clung to his face. "You swore you'd act the gentleman."

He took another step toward her. "You've always known I'm a liar. What made you believe me this morning?"

She shook her head helplessly and shifted back. "I don't know. I'm so stupid."

"You must know your cooperation indicated consent."

"No." She retreated again.

"Watch out." He grabbed her forearms and hauled her away from the crumbly bank before she ended up in the drink. She trembled in his hold. Whether from her near fall or from his proximity, he wasn't sure.

"Take me back," she said on a whisper, without trying to break free.

"After I've worked so hard to get you alone? I don't think so."

The eyes she raised to his were stark blue. Nervously she licked her lips, and the sight of the pink tip of her tongue blasted heat through him. "You won't get what you want."

He couldn't help laughing, stepping back and drawing her with him. "We both know I can have you on your back in ten minutes. Five if I really try."

Arrogance was the wrong approach. He realized it the instant temper flashed in her eyes. At least anger dissipated the vulnerability that left him so uncomfortable.

Her body became as rigid as a ruler. "Only if you intend to coerce me."

She tried to awaken his better self. Little did she know his better self had given up the ghost years ago. "Brave words."

She tilted her chin and glared at him. "True words."

"We'll see."

"You're so sure of yourself. It's not attractive."

Ranelaw smiled. He loved that she fought him. He'd love it more if she stopped. "So why are you still in my arms?"

"Because you won't release me."

He raised his hands palm upward with a mock apologetic gesture. "You're free, madam."

Her eyes darkened with tempestuous emotion. Anger? Desire? Then her lashes swept down and her mouth lengthened with determination.

Would she stay?

Would she run?

Suspense tightened every muscle as he awaited her decision. After a breathless second, she whipped her skirts to the side with haughtiness worthy of a duchess. Her head high, she marched toward her chestnut, peacefully cropping at the rich grass.

Damn it. By now, he should know better than to challenge her.

Chapter Eight

*A*NTONIA staggered as a strong, masculine hand curled over her shoulder and whipped her around.

"Oh, no, my lovely," Ranelaw bit out.

She glared at him, panting with outrage. And, much as she wished otherwise, excitement. She'd known he wouldn't let her go. The promise he would was just another game on this fine morning that suddenly bristled with danger.

Why in heaven's name was she here? She'd had a hundred opportunities to turn back. But Ranelaw had lured her with the one bait she couldn't resist. The overwhelming temptation to find out more about him. In spite of gossip, she knew virtually nothing of the real man.

"You understood what would happen if you came with me."

Had she? She'd never imagined she was at real risk of losing her nonexistent virtue. But the purposeful light in his eyes and the hard line of his jaw indicated he intended to tumble her on this verdant stream bank.

"I want to go back to the house," she said in a flinty voice, meeting his determined glare with a determined glare of her own.

"No, you don't."

The grip on her shoulder became a caress. Even through layers of clothing, the warmth reached her skin. Damn her weakness, she couldn't gather will to struggle, although he no longer constrained her.

"You think you know me better than I know myself," she snapped.

"In some things, I believe I do." He trailed one long finger down her cheek. She read tenderness in the gesture. But of course they both knew he was a liar.

"Stop it." She jerked stumbling from his grip. "I'm not some silly chit ripe for cheap seduction."

His smile held more than a hint of ruthlessness. "Yet here you are and not trying too hard to escape. Cheap seduction seems to be working."

"You deceive yourself, my lord," she said sharply, and without a backward glance, dashed for her horse.

Again he was too quick. For a man of such lazy charm, he moved faster than a striking adder when he wanted.

With a steely efficiency that made her heart pound with fright and more of that insidious excitement, he grabbed her waist and backed her against an oak. He braced his arms on either side, trapping her.

He panted, not with exertion but with arousal. His body radiated heat, and this close, the clean, musky fragrance of his skin intoxicated her.

Frantically Antonia cast around for a weapon. Nothing was within reach. He slid his hands closer, hemming her in. She told herself she dreaded the prospect of those hands on her. The truth was nowhere near so simple. Nor so flattering to her rectitude.

"No poker. No riding crop. Not even a fallen branch to beat me with." She struggled not to respond to the laughter in his deep voice. He took none of this seriously, whereas it was vitally important to her. "You're not going anywhere, my enchanting Miss Smith."

She angled her chin up to meet his eyes. Far up. He carried himself so easily, she only remembered how tall he was at moments like this when he was breathtakingly close.

He studied her with a fixed attention that shivered sensual awareness across her skin.

He leaned in and breathed deeply as though taking her scent into his lungs. The action was astonishingly stirring.

For ten barren years, she'd trodden virtue's path. Lord Ranelaw awoke her wildness. She was as incapable of resisting him as her virginal seventeen-year-old self had been of resisting lying, charming Johnny Benton.

If she fell again, she deserved everything she got.

"I won't cooperate," she said coldly, even as her pulse drummed erratically in her ears and her skin tightened with arousal.

"Of course you won't," Ranelaw murmured, in the same tone he'd used to calm her horse. However much she resented the fact, the low, velvety voice soothed her just as it had soothed the restless animal.

She strove for another sharp retort. As long as the battle of words continued, she held out hope of safety. But his nearness, his heat, his unabashed hunger banished her ability to summon something witty and cutting. Instead a low, almost keening sound emerged from her throat.

A triumphant smile kicked up the corners of his lips and he bent his head. Last time he'd kissed her, he'd demanded surrender. At least at first. She braced for another assault, but the kiss was as fresh as the spring morning around them.

Antonia shut her eyes, neither encouraging nor impeding him. His mouth's soft, satiny exploration demanded no more than she wanted to give. The moment was piercingly sweet, suspended in a golden prism, separate from anything before or after, untainted by wickedness.

In a great wave, her tension ebbed and she sagged against the tree, her knees trembling. She grabbed his shoulders, feeling the leashed power under the fine linen of his shirt.

Although she shouldn't, she'd loved his kisses in London. Those kisses had been marvelous, heady, intoxicating.

This kiss was unlike anything she'd ever experienced.

A rake's kiss as pure and innocent as the brush of an angel's wing.

Too soon, it was over. He raised his head slowly and studied her. His black eyes were unguarded and held an expression she'd never seen. A shock echoing hers. Appreciation. Something that could almost be tenderness.

"Ranelaw . . ." His name emerged as a husky whisper.

What could she say after that kiss? Words seemed blasphemy compared to what he'd communicated without speech in those magical seconds.

She swallowed and battled to return to reality. A grim, perilous reality where the Marquess of Ranelaw was the personification of sin, not a man who kissed her as if afraid he'd bruise her if he pressed too hard. A man whose lips touched hers as softly as the stroke of a flower petal.

As she battled to form a demand to release her, she watched his face change. The softness ebbed, all trace of vulnerability evaporated. She knew him well enough to understand that the emotional truth of that kiss would displease him mightily. Ranelaw didn't readily reveal his heart to anyone, yet that kiss had hinted at a deeper, sweeter connection between them than mere lust.

A deeper, sweeter connection that clearly he had no intention of acknowledging.

This time the intent in his face wouldn't be gainsaid. His lips parted hers and he slid his tongue inside. She gave a stifled denial and pushed at his shoulders. He was taut and unyielding under her hands. It was like trying to move a great, sun-warmed monolith.

Horror swamped her as she realized she might have missed her chance to save herself. If she kept fighting, he'd stop. She doubted he'd force her. He wasn't a complete brute.

Even now when Ranelaw displayed a single-minded determination that should appall her, her blood pulsed hot and hard. His unbridled passion filled her with forbidden excitement. Some perfidious voice in her head whispered that if she let him take her, it wouldn't be her fault. He'd made it impossible to escape.

She muffled that wicked, wicked voice and shoved him again. But never had Ranelaw seemed so large, so invincible. He leaned closer, no matter how she squirmed to create some space. He crushed her against the tree trunk until she could hardly breathe. Or perhaps desire constricted her lungs.

She felt herself toppling toward surrender.

Her tongue tangled with his, stroked the soft underside, the rougher upper surface. She explored the hard edges of his teeth, the cushion of his lips. He had wonderful lips, firm and full and sensual. He could seduce her with his mouth alone.

Through the mist of arousal, she realized he did exactly that. His hands remained braced beside her.

With a groan, he raised his head. His hunger for her was unconcealed, but she'd swear other, more complex reactions lurked behind the wall she saw in his eyes.

"What is it?" she asked shakily. Her heart constricted with fear and distress. "What's wrong?"

"Nothing's wrong." A muscle jerked in his cheek as he surveyed her under heavy eyelids. His hard, glittering eyes and bruised face conveyed a satanic air for all that his voice descended to a seductive purr. "Stop fighting me. We both want the same thing."

She flinched as though he'd hit her. For a bewildered, devastated moment, she stared at him. "Why are you angry? What have I done?"

"That's the first time you've sounded like a silly virgin, Antonia. The games have been enjoyable but time has come to pay your forfeit."

"Never," she vowed, curling her fingers into claws and aiming for his face. Trapped between his body and the tree, she didn't have room to slap him although she'd dearly love to.

His soft laugh whispered along her veins like a drug. Like it always did. He caught her hand before it made contact. She wriggled to bring up her knee, but he easily maneuvered her into powerlessness. "No, sweeting. You've done enough damage."

"Obviously not," she hissed through her teeth, hating her helplessness. "I wish I'd killed you when I had the chance."

Crammed so close, she felt the pulsing power of his erection against her belly. Once she'd doubted that he felt genuine interest in her. She doubted no longer.

Although she tried to resist, he lowered her hand to her side and, pinning her with his weight, curled his other hand over her breast. His touch was skillful, quickening her desire. To her humiliation, her nipple hardened against his palm. She bit back a whimper of shamed enjoyment.

"Give it up, Antonia. You know you can't win."

She growled and strove again to wriggle free. No use. He raised her skirt and she felt cool air on her stockinged leg, then on the bare thigh.

Blank unreality paralyzed her.

This couldn't be happening. Lord Ranelaw wasn't about to take her without ceremony against a tree. She wasn't standing acquiescent, letting him tug at her clothing.

"Stop," she gasped, stretching down with a shaking hand to prevent him lifting her skirt higher. "For pity's sake, stop."

"You don't mean that," he murmured, easily evading her. He stroked her leg before slipping his hand between her thighs.

She gasped with shock and unwilling pleasure when those clever fingers penetrated the slit in her drawers and found her wet heat. He released a deep sound of satisfaction, feral in its intensity. Now they both knew she was aroused, however she protested.

She moaned as he stroked her, unerringly finding her center. Sensation shuddered through her and her hands formed fists in his shirt.

"Yes." He spoke the word in a drawn-out hiss of appreciation.

Swirling response rose when he pressed again. She closed her eyes and panted while her faltering sense of survival screamed that she must flee. Now. Before he had her flat on her back and begging.

He rubbed his palm against her breast. Despite everything she knew about him and about what this reckless act would cost her, she nudged her hips closer to his seeking fingers.

Again he kissed her. Eager kisses that demolished resistance. Kisses that weighted her belly with impossible longing. Kisses that seemed designed to wipe out any memory of the betraying kiss that had so angered him. For a fleeting moment, he'd treated her like the one woman in a million. Now he was completely the rake, interested merely in losing himself in hot female flesh for an instant's pleasure he'd forget just as quickly.

Even recognizing that, she couldn't stop herself responding to his mouth. Kissing him back with a passion so scorching, flames ignited behind her closed eyes. The merciless onslaught of desire left her giddy and disoriented. She'd never wanted a man the way she wanted Ranelaw. Her body wept to have him inside her, filling the emptiness.

She felt like she was falling and only realized he edged her toward the ground when her back met cushioning grass. He straddled her and tore at her bodice with urgent hands. The ruthless efficiency of his actions pierced her daze.

She grabbed his hand. "Ranelaw, we can't."

He bent to nuzzle the side of her neck. "Of course we can."

"This won't help you get to Cassie," she forced herself to say. Speaking her cousin's name seemed sacrilege when Antonia sprawled beneath him.

He released a gasp of laughter. "Cassie who?"

"Ranelaw . . ."

"Nicholas."

What point pretending any formality existed between them? "Nicholas."

"Now say, 'Yes, Nicholas.'" He stroked her throat, lingering where her pulse fluttered against her skin. His touch was hot and stoked her need.

"No, Nicholas."

He rose on his arms and stared at her. He'd never looked so handsome. His golden hair was ruffled and one lock tumbled across his high forehead, softening features that could seem austere for all their beauty. His eyes gleamed under heavy eyelids and his nostrils flared as if he lived by her scent.

She studied his face, seeking some hint of the man who had kissed her so sweetly. None existed. Appetite gripped him. And beneath the arousal, he was still angry. She felt it in his hands and his mouth, even through the pleasure, even through the seductive words.

He wanted her. But he also set out to prove something. Something that required her debasement while he maintained his distance.

Was he troubled beneath that perfect façade? Was she mistaken to imagine a better man wandered lost in the murk of Lord Ranelaw's soul? Or did she romanticize him the way Cassie romanticized him? The way she'd romanticized hopelessly weak Johnny Benton?

Nonetheless as she stared into his blazing eyes, her heart contracted with longing. She sensed Ranelaw needed her. Beyond the gratification of a sexual itch, he demanded something essential and profound from her. Something even he didn't recognize.

Stop it, Antonia. You know a rake's tricks. Yet you fall for them as easily now as you did ten years ago.

"Admit it, Antonia. You've lost the battle."

"Have I really?" She couldn't resist smoothing the wayward lock that flopped across his forehead.

"Yes," he snapped, the seductive mask shattering. Like that, the quivering moment that promised more than mere physical satisfaction vanished.

He jerked his head away from her soothing touch as if she burned him. For all the hostility bristling between them, his rejection stung. This time, his mouth was hard when he kissed her. He ripped at her jacket and roughly cupped her breast through the thin shirt.

"Wait," she gasped, shoving at his shoulders.

To her surprise, he heard. He raised his head and stared unseeing at her. Before the unemotional shell descended, she caught something in the black eyes that might have been shame.

"I don't want to wait." He jerked his hips against hers to emphasize his readiness.

The moisture dried from her mouth as she imagined that powerful weight thrusting into her. Even in his current temper, she ached to feel him inside her.

"Let me go." She struggled for words to persuade him to stop. "It shouldn't be like this."

He bared his teeth in a snarl and for the first time, she realized his anger went far beyond a momentary impatience or irritation. It stemmed from deep within. "How the hell should it be?"

With love . . .

Dear God, she hadn't really thought that, had she? What existed between her and Lord Ranelaw was animal lust. She was a fool if she imagined anything else.

"Get up, Ranelaw," she said in a decisive voice. "This isn't going to happen."

For a moment, Ranelaw poised above her, his legs trapping hers. She couldn't read his expression although threat was implicit in his vibrating tension. Her muscles tautened as she waited for him to assail her again. This time, she was grimly aware that he'd win.

Then with a grunt indicating endless masculine irritation, he rolled away. He sat with his back to her, his head bowed over his raised knees.

Shocked that this final appeal worked, bewildered that it had, Antonia remained lying where she was, sucking air into starved lungs. She struggled to calm the primitive surge of her blood.

The sullen hunch of Ranelaw's shoulders, the silence charged with so much she didn't comprehend, pierced her. Usually he seemed impervious to human vulnerability. Right now he looked like the loneliest man in England.

Perhaps he was.

He'd sounded so cold when he delivered that terse, unadorned description of his childhood. His parents clearly hadn't known the meaning of fidelity and he'd apparently formed no close attachment to any of his many siblings. His impassive recounting had touched her, stirred reluctant compassion. All those people. Yet somehow Ranelaw struck her as completely isolated in the center.

"Ranelaw, look at me," she whispered, wondering why she cared after the way he'd treated her.

In a wordless gesture of comfort, she laid a trembling hand between his shoulder blades. Something told her he was utterly desolate.

He flinched away from her reluctant tenderness as he'd flinched when she stroked his hair.

All right. She might be slow to learn, but now she understood. Humiliation was a bitter taste in her mouth. She jerked her hand away. He wanted raw passion from her. Nothing else.

Perhaps after this morning, he didn't even want that.

She bit her lip and told herself it was ridiculous to let him upset her. He was a worthless, wicked rake. If he ignored her, that was to her benefit. She should be grateful he'd sampled her charms and decided she wasn't worth pursuing.

As her heart cramped with misery, that's not how it felt.

"Go away, Antonia," he said in a low voice, still without glancing at her.

"Ranelaw . . ." She sat up and slid back to lean against the tree. She felt shaky, on the verge of tears.

His shoulders tensed until they were as rigid as planks. Still he wouldn't look at her. "For God's sake, take your reprieve and go." He sounded savage, like a man at the limit of his endurance.

Confused, afraid, dizzy with unsatisfied desire, Antonia scrambled to her feet. Her legs were still frighteningly unsteady. Her hair tumbled around her shoulders. She glanced down at herself, and horror squeezed her lungs. Her neck cloth was gone, her jacket hung open, half the buttons were missing. Her shirt was crushed and tugged out of line.

Anyone seeing her would know exactly what she'd been doing. Would imagine more had happened than actually had. She could hardly believe more hadn't happened. Given her foolishness, she should be flat on her back with Lord Ranelaw's seed inside her.

On a tremulous inhalation, she scooped up her hat and stumbled to her horse. With difficulty, she dragged herself into the saddle. Ranelaw still didn't turn to look at her.

On an inarticulate cry, she urged the horse into an ungainly gallop through the trees.

Chapter Nine

*R*ANELAW remained still while Antonia rose and paused. Although she didn't speak, the confused babble of her questions was loud as thunder. Then as if his sullen silence provided an answer, she scuttled across the clearing and rode away.

Still he didn't move. Only when the pounding hoofbeats faded to nothing and he was finally alone did he drop his head into his hands and release a deep groan.

Bloody, bloody, bloody, misbegotten, thrice-cursed idiot.

He dug his fingers into his skull so hard, it hurt. Nothing stanched his self-disgust.

What the hell was wrong with him?

He'd schemed assiduously to suborn Antonia Smith. He'd bribed servants. He'd climbed a damned cherry tree to seduce her. He'd braved assault by fire iron. He'd pursued her to Surrey.

He'd manipulated and maneuvered to get her on her own. He'd kissed her into breathless malleability. Success had loomed so close. The possession of her body, leverage to promote the Demarest chit's ruin, a short-lived but memorable pleasure.

Nothing terrifically complicated.

Then she'd stared at him with those radiant blue eyes and asked him to let her go.

And bugger, bugger, bugger, he'd suddenly imagined he was sodding Sir Galahad.

He hadn't felt pity for a woman since he was a boy. The women he fucked were perfectly willing when he took them, however much they might repent their behavior later. Yet he'd pitied Antonia Smith. Although pity seemed too weak a description for the emotion that had closed his throat and made him suddenly long to be an honorable man.

He'd grieved to think he disappointed her.

Hurt her.

He was a rake. Hurting and disappointing women were the mainstays of his existence.

That kiss had been a bedamned mistake.

Not the kisses that commanded her response. That other kiss. The poignant, heartbreaking one.

The kiss that had flung him into a different world, that had promised a clean start. Salvation. Kindness. Something beyond the forgettable parade of women.

He already knew Antonia Smith wouldn't join that parade. He'd remember her forever.

Blast her to Hades.

How dare she remind him. . .

Remind him of what? His essential solitude? His lack of direction, beyond this quest for revenge, which ended any day now? His longing for something better than he deserved?

His longing for a woman like Antonia Smith?

If he'd had any breakfast, he'd be casting it up over his boots. What inspired this sentimental pap?

Just in case she misunderstood exactly who he was, he'd set out to frighten her, convince her he was a heartless beast. He'd never treated a lover so. Shame was a foreign emotion, but he recognized shame as he remembered those rough kisses he'd forced upon her.

Kisses she'd repaid with a piercing tenderness that made him sick to the gut at the bastard he was.

He'd stared into her eyes, dark with confusion and unwilling passion, and for one stark, horrible instant, he'd wished to be that different man. He'd wished to be worthy of her.

Hell, no. He was perfectly happy with who he was. He had more freedom than anyone he knew. He took what he wanted and discarded it when he'd had his fill. His world held no limits.

In his arms, Antonia had verged on surrender. Would have surrendered if he'd persisted after that astonishing kiss that sent his brains a-begging. He could right now be pounding into her.

Instead he'd let her go.

He'd let her go.

Never again.

Twice she'd escaped. And twice, for God's sake, he'd released her. He couldn't even pretend she'd evaded his pursuit.

With a purposeful surge, he rose. Antonia Smith had had her amnesty. The game between them became as important as life and death. The man he believed himself to be, the scoundrel he wanted to be, wouldn't permit compassion to sway him next time.

The dragon would be his. Compassion be damned.

Antonia sneaked into her room without anyone except the stable hands seeing her. She didn't deceive herself they had the slightest doubt what she'd been up to. Even without Lord Ranelaw bribing them for information about her, her rumpled appearance betrayed her. She'd left dressed like a respectable woman. She returned looking like she'd been dragged through a hedgerow. It didn't take much to guess the reason why.

She could weather a little gossip below stairs as long as it didn't reach the houseguests. Dear heaven, let the gossip not spread.

Curse Ranelaw, he turned her life topsy-turvy. If anyone should be furious, it was she, not he.

She remembered how he'd looked when she'd left. Not angry, although there had been anger in his touch.

He'd looked utterly devastated.

The ache in her heart sharpened. Stupid to want to heal him, redeem him. Especially when he intended her nothing but ill.

As she crept past, Cassie's door was shut. It was still early. Hard to believe, after all she'd been through this morning. Luckily the gentlemen were shooting rabbits in one of the estate's far corners and the ladies hadn't emerged yet.

Antonia was pinning her hair and telling herself she'd had a fortunate escape, when Bella rapped on the door and barreled in without invitation.

"You must come," she said breathlessly, for once not subjecting Antonia to a critical inspection. Thank heaven. Antonia had already changed out of her stained and torn riding habit, but even a cursory glance would reveal Miss Smith was unusually flushed and dewy eyed.

Antonia set down the brush and turned to the maid. "What is it? Is it Cassie?"

Bella nodded. "Yes, miss. She's awful sick."

Sick? Guilt choked Antonia. While she'd been in Ranelaw's arms, Cassie had fallen ill. It was illogical, but she couldn't help connecting the two facts and blaming herself for her absence. "When I checked on her, she was sleeping peacefully."

"Well, she's not sleeping peacefully now." A hint of waspishness crept into Bella's voice. "You didn't check on her too well, did you?"

The maid's jockeying for position was too familiar for Antonia to pay attention. Instead she swept through the door into Cassie's room, her heart racing with trepidation.

The curtains were drawn and the room was dark. Antonia took a few moments to distinguish Cassie huddled in the chair by the blazing fire. The girl had wrapped a shawl around her white cambric nightdress but even sitting so close to the hearth, she shivered.

"Cassie, darling," Antonia said softly, moving closer and peering through the gloom. "What's the matter?"

"Antonia, I feel awful," she said, and burst into tears. Antonia dropped to her knees and drew Cassie's quivering body into her arms.

"You're burning up," she said in dismay, glancing at Bella, who looked as bewildered as Antonia felt.

"But I'm c-cold," Cassie stammered, her teeth chattering. "So cold."

"Let's get you into bed." Carefully she helped her cousin to rise before turning to Bella. "Bella, get the maids to bring towels and water. We need to bathe Cassie and lower her temperature."

For all her dislike of Antonia, Bella looked relieved that someone took control. As Antonia supported a failing Cassie back to her tumbled bed, she worried that the maid's confidence was misplaced. This illness had come on so quickly and seemed so virulent, she felt helpless against it.

The next days blurred into sickroom duties. As Cassie's illness worsened, Antonia snatched what little sleep she could, leaving her charge under Bella's watchful eyes. Otherwise she was at the girl's bedside, cooling her fever, forcing liquid into her dehydrated frame, supporting her when she retched, talking to her with soft encouragement when she could do nothing else.

Around her, the household disintegrated into chaos. Whatever ailed Cassie was contagious. Most of the guests were confined to their rooms, and the few healthy staff were run off their feet. It was fortunate Antonia and Bella remained well enough to nurse Cassie.

The local doctor visited on a regular basis and every time, pronounced the illness a pernicious fever. Which meant precisely nothing. Antonia did learn, however, that a large number of local people had also been struck down.

Through wrenching anxiety—an anxiety that verged on panic when Antonia heard from a maid that three people in the village had died and more hovered at death's door—and weariness, she spared an occasional thought for Lord Ranelaw. Was he sick too? He seemed too invulnerable to succumb, but what did she know?

She plucked up courage to inquire of a maid how the other guests fared, hoping to garner news of him. But the girl was distracted, doing the work of several servants, and only informed her most of the household was sick, something Antonia already knew.

Perhaps Ranelaw had left. Any unaffected visitors had departed once the disaster's scale became obvious.

Perhaps she wouldn't see him again. If Cassie's recovery was slow, or—dear God, make it not so—if she didn't recover at all, Antonia had no reason to return to London and Ranelaw's wicked temptations.

She should be relieved to banish him from her life. It was a sad reflection on her character that her reaction wasn't so uncomplicated.

Because she operated in a haze of exhaustion, her days occupied with Cassie's care, those torrid moments by the stream receded, became like a dream. As if they happened to someone else or she'd witnessed them in a play. Compared to her struggle to save her cousin, even the passion and regret of that encounter lost their sting.

However Antonia slaved and fretted, Cassie's grip on life eased with every faint breath. How could such a young, vital woman sink so fast? This mysterious, seemingly invincible illness flooded Antonia with futile, acrid rage. Her rage was all that bolstered her strength as day trudged into day and Cassie became weaker and weaker.

Antonia was in an agony of indecision whether to send for Mr. Demarest. In the end, she decided if the fever took a fatal turn, Cassie would be dead long before her father arrived. Far better to struggle on with Bella's assistance and hope Cassie's vigor and youth brought her through.

All the time, she prayed. She prayed until words lost meaning.

Please, God, don't let Cassie die. Please, God, don't let Cassie die.

In spite of Antonia's tirade to heaven, Cassie's strength continued to ebb. Antonia could only assume that the Deity refused to heed entreaties from a miserable sinner like her.

Ranelaw strode toward Pelham Place from the stables. He entered through the servants' quarters. It was more convenient and he wasn't a man who stood on ceremony when ceremony served no purpose.

During his ramshackle childhood, the servants had seemed on the same social level as the family. In fact, the more superior servants had considered themselves several steps above the disreputable Challoners. Of course superior servants tended not to linger at Keddon Hall. The disorderly crowd of children and dogs and dependents, including his father's mistresses, didn't constitute a well-run household.

In contrast, as he tracked through the dim hallway toward the back stairs, Pelham Place was eerily quiet. It was five days since the majority of residents, upstairs and down, had succumbed to fever. The healthy had fled, leaving the household to the sick, those paid to look after them—and the Marquess of Ranelaw, who continued to enjoy the pink of health.

Clearly the devil looked after his own.

Two days ago, his valet had become unable to continue his duties. Again thanks to his unconventional upbringing, Ranelaw was more than capable of shifting for himself until the fellow was back on his feet. Although his idea of shifting for himself differed from Morecombe's. He glanced at his dull boots, usually polished to a shine, and a rueful smile curled his lips. Morecombe would have a fit if he could see him in his dirty boots, with his shirt open and no coat.

Ranelaw had tried to nurse the man, but Morecombe had been so horrified at the prospect, he'd suffered a relapse. So Ranelaw had retreated to what outdoor amusements he could find. He'd just enjoyed a brisk ride through the woods and now he headed upstairs to wash the dust away.

His hostess was well, but fully occupied with the afflicted, including several family members. Occasionally he encountered her, fluttering with distraction. She'd made it abundantly clear that she'd prefer he left, so the staff needn't worry about someone capable of taking himself elsewhere.

Ranelaw pretended not to notice.

Although good sense indicated he should cut his losses and return to London. From what he'd heard, the Demarest chit probably wouldn't survive to be ruined.

Now there was fate taking a drastic step to protect innocence.

It said something about his hopeless state that not seeing Antonia seemed considerably more important than his faltering quest for retribution. All very well to decide he'd seduce Miss Smith without compunction. He couldn't do it while she remained day and night at her charge's bedside.

As if to prove him wrong, he heard someone emerge from the scullery behind him. When he turned, he saw Antonia, carrying two pails of water.

"Antonia . . ." he said, for once in his life stuck for words.

"Lord Ranelaw."

She looked equally shocked to see him. She took a shaky step back, and water sloshed from the pails onto the dusty flagstones. She didn't just look shocked, she looked pale and weary to the point of collapse. That odd twinge in his chest made itself felt again.

Automatically he stepped forward to take her burden. "The maids should carry these."

His comment made her mouth firm in displeasure. "The maids are nearly all sick. I'm surprised you hadn't noticed." She cast a jaundiced eye over him. Clearly she'd had time since their last meeting to remind herself he was an irredeemable villain. "What are you doing here?"

Her sarcasm couldn't dampen his happiness at seeing her. He'd missed her, even her censure. "I've just come from the stables."

"No, why haven't you left? You must be the only able-bodied person who doesn't have to stay."

He shrugged. "You're here."

To his chagrin, the answer was nothing less than the truth. If he expected his admission to soften her attitude, he was disappointed.

"You should go back to London," she said flatly. "You're in the way and the servants have enough to do."

He laughed softly. If he was a vain man—he had many faults, but vanity didn't count among them—she'd wound him. "At this precise moment, I'm devilish useful. Shall I carry these upstairs?"

He saw her consider insisting she could manage. Then common sense kicked in. She gave a brief nod. "Thank you."

"You're welcome," he said with a hint of irony. He turned and carried the buckets along the corridor to the servants' staircase.

"You know your way around." Her tone implied criticism.

"So do you." He stepped aside to allow her to precede him up the uncarpeted wooden stairs.

"I'm a servant." He sought but didn't find resentment in the statement. Her voice sharpened and she cast him a disapproving glance under her lashes. "I hope you're not down here chasing the maids when they're so busy."

He burst out laughing then had to juggle the pails to stop them spilling. "You really don't like me much, do you?"

For once, he couldn't read her expression. "No, I don't."

He didn't bother pointing out that her claim sounded less than convincing. He knew she found him attractive.

The feeling was mutual.

Even now when she looked tired enough to fall over.

When they reached the first landing, he set down the buckets with a thud and caught her arm. He expected her to pull free. After all, their last encounter had ended on a sour note and he couldn't blame her for considering him both a brute and a lunatic. He'd had five days to regret his actions beside the stream and because of this damned epidemic, no chance to ameliorate the barbarous impression he'd left.

"You're running yourself ragged." He sounded angry instead of concerned. Not that he was concerned. He just didn't like to see her looking so tired.

"Of course I am," she snapped, staring up at him out of blue eyes dull with weariness.

He suddenly realized what was different. She wasn't wearing her spectacles. She must have decided anyone who might penetrate her disguise wasn't likely to be wandering about this charnel house.

She wore a brown dress of some coarse stuff with a stained pinafore over the top. Somehow the costume only emphasized her natural distinction. Again his instincts screamed there was more to Miss Antonia Smith than Miss Antonia Smith let on.

"Doesn't Cassie have a maid for the heavy work?" He didn't want to identify the sensation in his gut as rage on Antonia's behalf, but he couldn't attribute the response to anything else.

Antonia still stared at him as though he were mad. "Yes, *Miss Demarest* does. Bella works as hard as I do."

He didn't miss her emphasis on formal address but he ignored it. He was only interested in Antonia. "You'll get sick yourself if you don't rest. You look terrible."

"Thank you," she said dryly, moving forward to lift one of the pails. "I can manage from here."

He sighed and wondered where the hell his famous charm had buggered off to. Usually he could woo a woman using words alone. With Antonia, all he seemed to do was put his foot in it.

Easily he angled her out of the way and picked up the second pail. "You know what I mean." She relinquished the other pail without resistance. Her docility was yet another sign of exhaustion.

She cast him a sharp glance. "I do believe you're attempting in your ham-fisted way to express concern, Lord Ranelaw. How astonishing."

He was hellishly grateful to see her spirit return. For a moment there, she'd looked as though life held neither hope nor happiness. He hated seeing her crushed and defeated.

"Of course I'm bloody concerned," he admitted roughly, stamping up the stairs. "I'm not a complete savage."

He knew without looking that she followed. "I'm touched."

"I want you alive and well so I can roger you," he growled. "And don't tell me to be quiet. There's nobody to listen in this mausoleum and even if they could, they've got better things to do than worry about what you and I get up to."

"I wasn't going to," she said calmly. "Although you had the chance to seduce me and let it pass."

Astonishment blasted him. He could hardly credit she brought up those fraught moments with such a casual air. They hadn't felt casual to him. Damn the chit. He didn't understand her.

"Sheer madness," he muttered, shouldering his way through a plain door to the corridor outside Cassandra's bedroom. "I can't believe you're holding that against me. Believe me, madam, you won't escape next time."

He waited for some deflating remark about never letting it happen again. But she kept silent. She really wasn't herself. Once more that sharp little twinge.

"Where do you want these?" His voice was still rough. "Your room or Cassie's?"

"How do you . . ." She stopped and stepped forward to open the door to her room. "I suppose you bribed the servants again. It's a good thing you're one of the richest men in the kingdom and you can afford all this chicanery."

She didn't sound outraged. She sounded as though she expected nothing better of him. She almost sounded . . . fond.

Silly girl. One shouldn't be fond of a hungry tiger. One should be terrified.

Right now, he didn't feel like a tiger. He felt like a man

incapable of offering aid to the woman he . . . desired. He felt left out and bereft and furious that the brief moment of her company was almost over.

Her company? Good God, get him a gun. He needed to shoot himself before he started writing poetry praising the arch of the wench's eyebrow.

He trailed her inside and set the pails on the bare floorboards. The air was redolent of Antonia's scent, reminding him of holding her in his arms. The room was tiny, with one mean little window high over the bed. Compared to her luxurious London bedchamber, this was a hovel. Small and stuffy. Shabby and spartan.

Mess was everywhere. But of course she'd had her hands full the last five days nursing Cassie. This disorder was mute testament to how frantic she'd been.

She'd tossed clothes willy-nilly across the narrow bed. He noticed a virginal white night rail among the browns, grays, and rusty blacks. Ridiculous really, but the sight of her nightwear made his heart beat faster.

He'd sworn to show no hesitation when he got her to himself. He had her to himself now, but grimly recognized this was neither time nor place. Even in a house turned upside down, if he was caught in Antonia's bedroom, there would be hell to pay.

And she, given the world they lived in, would pay it.

"Thank you," she said in a low voice, staring at him with a blankness he found discomfiting.

Hell, don't let her cry. He couldn't bear it if she cried.

"Oh, for God's sake, sit down," he growled, folding his arms and glaring at her. He kept his voice low, aware they could be overheard. "You're safe enough."

She was too dispirited to argue. Instead she slumped onto the bed amid the drab chaos of what looked like her complete wardrobe.

Frustration swirled in his belly, along with the desire and curiosity and unwelcome admiration that Antonia always aroused. He guessed she meant to race in to check on Cassie the minute he left. He wanted to demand she seize a moment's respite, but he couldn't find the heart to say it. The misery and anxiety in her expression were indications that she loved the girl. A woman of her stubborn nature would fight to the death to save anyone she loved.

Lucky Cassie. . .

He smothered the thought before it stuck its claws into him. Love was a tiresome emotion. He wanted none of it. He never had. His experience indicated that any profession of love masked a million selfish demands. But even so, Antonia's unstinting devotion to her charge touched something deep inside him.

The moment extended. Became uncomfortable.

"I should go." He turned toward the door but didn't take the two steps across the room.

"Yes." She bent her head and stared down at the hands she twined in her lap.

Chapter Ten

RANELAW had every intention of leaving. This was no place for a heartless devil like him. With Cassie next door, he couldn't seduce Antonia. Anyway, even desperate as he was, he rebelled at taking her for the first time on that narrow cot.

His feet seemed nailed to the floor.

Antonia looked fragile. A word he'd never before associated with the gallant Miss Smith. His eyes dwelled on the graceful droop of her slender neck under what seemed an impossible weight of silvery hair. She'd caught it up in a loose style Miss Smith would usually disdain but which was infernally becoming. Her shoulders rounded and the graceful hands twisting in her lap were distressingly thin.

Clearly she hadn't been eating. Clearly she'd hardly slept. Even before Cassie fell ill, Ranelaw had tormented her nights. Cur that he was, he'd been proud of his ability to disturb her peace. He didn't feel proud now.

He should go. She was tired and distracted. She wanted to be alone.

He shifted. And ended up sitting beside her.

"Ranelaw?" she whispered, shooting him a nervous glance.

She seemed so young, not at all the dragon chaperone from Millicent Wreston's ballroom. Ridiculous now to think her disguise had fooled him even briefly.

"Shh," he said softly, feeling awkward himself.

He wasn't used to entering a lady's bedroom with any purpose other than fornication. Right now, he had no intention of dragging her under him, much as he desired her.

He'd be dead before he stopped desiring her.

She tensed at his nearness. She probably suspected him of some wicked purpose. Who could blame her?

Hesitantly, and he hadn't been hesitant with a woman since his earliest youth, he extended one arm and curled it around her shoulders. Her muscles tightened and wariness shadowed her expression.

"What do you want?" Her sharpness lacked its usual bite.

Oh, Antonia, you're so strong. Too strong. Bend a little or you'll break.

"We're in my bedroom, Cassie's only a few feet away. She's sick, not deaf," she said in a dark tone. "If you think I'll let you have your way here, you're a fool."

"Miss Smith, your suspicions wound me," he said with a smile. He drew her, stiff and unwilling, against his side. Immediately her warmth seeped into his veins. He'd known he'd missed her, but only now did he realize how much. "I mean no harm."

"You lie."

"Often," he agreed amiably, feeling the resistance leaching from her. "Not this time."

"I'm in no fit state to fight you," she muttered, curving into him as if created to fit his body.

"I know," he acknowledged ruefully, wondering why of all the women in the world, she was the only one who ignited any glimmer of chivalry in his soul. "But it's no fun when you just give in. I'll wait until you're up for another bout."

She hid her face in his shoulder. She inhaled on a shudder, as if she hadn't taken a full breath in days. "You're an evil devil, Ranelaw."

"Absolutely," he said softly, firming his hold as she shifted, not away as she should, but closer.

He waited for her to continue her excoriations on his character but she remained quiet. Nor did she attempt to break free.

The room had no fireplace, but the day was mild for early May. Antonia was soft and warm in his hold. She smelled of fields of flowers and a trace of sweat. The combination was unaccountably evocative.

He turned his head and rested his chin on the soft cushion of hair. He'd never touched a woman intending only to comfort her. Unless he counted Eloise when he was a child.

"Are you crying?" he whispered after a long, surprisingly peaceful interval.

"No," she said in a choked voice, burying her face deeper into his shirt. One arm snaked around his waist almost like she expected him to pull away. As if he would.

Women's tears never affected him. He'd witnessed too many, going back to his mother, who used emotional blackmail more effectively than any female he'd known since. And he'd encountered virtuosi at the art.

Antonia's reluctant tears made him want to punch something.

He tried to reawaken his cynical self. Remind himself that before he finished with her, Antonia Smith would be crying in earnest.

His cynical self scorned to enter this untidy room.

He placed a hand beneath her chin. She resisted as he tilted her face. "Now who's lying?"

"It's . . . it's just tiredness," she said unsteadily. "I'm fine. Truly."

Still she kept fighting. He couldn't help but respect her for it. Although she must recognize she neared the limit of her endurance. He felt it in her boneless weight. He read it in her drawn, pale face drenched in tears.

"I can see that." He frowned. "Is Cassie really so sick?"

"Yes." She dashed the tears from her cheeks. More fell to take their place.

He didn't want to feel sorry for Miss Demarest. He'd

rather she stayed a stranger, for all that he meant to bed her. If he started to think of Cassie as more than just an instrument of revenge, his ruthlessness mightn't hold.

But it was impossible to remain unmoved by Antonia's suffering. He didn't bother spouting platitudes about Cassie being young and healthy and surviving this crisis. Antonia was too smart for such drivel.

"I'm sorry."

"I'll get her through this, I will." Her fist clenched in his shirt. "She's not going to die."

He'd been right about her determination to save the people she loved. He wondered with a sudden pang he couldn't identify how it would feel having someone like Antonia on his side.

He bent and placed a gentle, chaste kiss on the corner of her mouth. She tasted salty, she tasted like tears. "If anyone can get her through, you can. Rest for a moment. Then go in and win the battle."

He smoothed loose tendrils of hair away from her hot face. She looked an absolute fright with red eyes and a pink nose. Yet another revelation—he, the connoisseur of diamonds of the first water, hardly cared.

"She's like my sister," Antonia said thickly. "I couldn't bear to lose her. I've lost . . . I've lost too many people."

It was almost a confidence. Somewhere in the distant reaches of his brain, a voice insisted this was the time to pry open her secrets. The voice urged him to seduce her now, when her defenses crumbled, the rest of the household be damned. Nobody had seen him come in, and silence from the next room indicated interruptions were unlikely.

He ignored the voice. With more ease than he expected.

He was a rotter through and through. Even the world's worst rotter wouldn't take advantage of a woman in this state.

"She's lucky to have you." He meant it.

"Why are you being kind to me?" Familiar, watchful Antonia returned.

"Haven't a clue," he replied with perfect honesty. Sincerity felt like a luxury, which spoke reams for his relationships.

Her choked laugh ended on a broken sob. "That makes two of us."

He kept stroking her hair back from her sticky face. Tears clumped her eyelashes together and her mouth was full and swollen. He resisted the urge to kiss her.

Something inside him shifted as he looked at her. The sensation was astonishing enough to check his usual rakish impulses. And to stir the need to restore the light in her eyes. He struggled for words to cheer her.

"Cassie will be leading you a grand chase through the ballrooms of London before you know it," he said, with absolutely no basis for his claim.

Antonia's lush mouth quirked as if she too recognized the flimsy logic behind his assertion. "With your encouragement." Her face crumpled and she drew a quavering breath. "I hope you're right, Nicholas. I hope to heaven you're right."

Shock held him motionless as she crushed her face into his chest, clutching his shirt in shaking hands. She'd only once before used his Christian name without his prompting, when it slipped out after she thought she'd killed him. Hard to equate that avenging angel of chastity with this broken woman.

Except the inner core of strength remained. Even as she lay in his arms, crying her heart out, he recognized her essential valor. He suspected she hadn't permitted herself the relief of a good cry since Cassie fell ill.

He felt hot moisture against his skin. Some instinct made him place his hand behind her head and press her closer. The same instinct that made him murmur foolish reassurance.

He had no idea if he helped. He had no idea if his words penetrated her fog of misery. She just huddled against him, weeping with a heartbroken desperation that made him want to hit someone.

Eventually she calmed.

He'd always loved how she fought him. He loved the crackle and spark of her wit. Now he discovered he also loved the way she lay against him in what felt like perfect trust.

He knew there was no such thing and like most people, she'd betray him eventually. If only by disappointing him after she incited such anticipation.

Right now he couldn't bring himself to believe it.

Antonia was a tall, vital woman, no shrinking miss. Now she felt brittle and vulnerable. He tightened his hold and told himself the surge of protectiveness meant nothing.

Again he couldn't quite believe it.

He brushed his cheek against her disheveled hair. He was surprised she remained in his arms. After all, she knew exactly what he was. She'd always known. It was a sign of the tribulations of these last days that her usual spiky barriers were absent.

Take advantage, the voice insisted.

Next time, he assured the voice, wondering why he delayed.

It couldn't be consideration for Antonia. The only person he considered when he wanted something was himself.

Still he held her without forcing the encounter. Still his embrace offered comfort and nothing else.

When she sat up, he recognized how reluctantly he released her. With unsteady hands, she brushed the last tears from her cheeks. The action was childish, charming.

"Thank you. You've been so kind."

He drew away and scowled. "I'm not a kind man."

"Nevertheless, that's what you were today." Her lips twitched into one of her wry smiles. "Don't worry. I won't tell anyone. I doubt anyone would credit it anyway. The rakish Lord Ranelaw in a lady's bedroom for an entire hour without undoing a single button? Incredible."

"You're in better spirits," he said dryly.

"I am." She sounded surprised, although whether at his

circumspection or at the fact that tears had done her good, he couldn't say. She definitely seemed less wound up than when he'd met her downstairs.

He must be losing his touch. With the Marquess of Ranelaw in her bedroom, she should be as nervous as a cat in a shooting gallery.

But she'd only rarely been frightened of him, even before she'd stirred his rusty protective instincts. She'd never reacted with the proper trepidation when he expressed an interest in her.

Foolish woman.

She sniffed delicately and fumbled in her pocket. He sighed and passed her his handkerchief. "Here."

"Thank you." Amusement still lingered in her face, contrasting oddly with the drying tears. "Another kindness. You'll have to polish your halo soon, Ranelaw."

"Don't get used to it. You know what I want."

The look she sent him under her straight blond brows was penetrating. "I thought I did."

He, famous for his eloquence, wasn't sure what to say. Insisting he was as unprincipled and callous as ever seemed a little desperate. And unconvincing in light of his recent behavior.

He stood, yet again feeling awkward. And he was a man who never felt ill at ease. He never cared enough to worry what impression he made.

"I should check on Cassie." She still watched him.

"Yes."

Again he couldn't force himself to leave. Although it was obvious, had always been obvious if he was honest with himself, that he wasn't going to fuck her today. He wanted her to come to him with spirit and passion intact. He didn't want to take her while she struggled against defeat and wretchedness.

"Let me check the corridor," she said, rising.

"The corridor. Yes."

He felt disoriented. Perhaps he came down with the mystery illness after all. Something was seriously wrong. This wasn't how he acted with a woman he targeted.

She slipped past, her faded cotton skirts brushing his legs with a seductive whisper. In a room this small, some physical contact was inevitable when two people crowded inside.

Desire had simmered beneath the surface. Now he hardened and his hands itched to grab her. Not to comfort but as a man seized a woman he wanted.

Carefully she opened the door and peeked out, then closed it and turned. "There's nobody there."

He needed more from her. He needed a promise to take away with him. Hunger gripped him like a fever. Perhaps it was a fever. He felt alarmingly light-headed.

"Meet me tonight," he said urgently, snatching her hand and carrying it to his lips. He pressed a passionate kiss to her palm and felt her tremble.

She frowned, looking delightfully confused. He saw that with every second, yielding Antonia submerged into the woman who persistently fended him off.

The hellish dilemma was he found both versions of her breathtakingly appealing.

"You know I can't." Her voice was husky. Perhaps from tears. Perhaps because her desire stirred too.

"I know you can." His grip on her hand tightened as if he tried to convince her through touch alone. "With the mess in the house, nobody's paying attention to you. Or to me for once in my life. What harm can it do?"

She tugged her hand free and cast him an unimpressed glance. Hard to believe only moments ago she'd rested in his arms as supine as a dozing kitten. "Don't be deliberately naïve, Ranelaw. You know exactly the harm it could do. You mean to cause harm."

Yes, Dragon Antonia revived. But he'd had a heart-stopping glimpse of a softer, more malleable woman. He suspected if he got her alone, he could revive that pliant creature.

"Be brave, Antonia. We share a powerful desire."

He expected denial. As so often, she surprised him. "I'd be absurdly self-destructive to act upon it."

He paused to digest how readily she owned what she felt. It left him giddy. "There's a summerhouse on the other side of the lake. Do you know it?"

"Yes, I know it."

"Come to me there once the household is asleep."

She shook her head and he read no uncertainty. "I have to stay with Cassie."

"Let her maid sit with her tonight."

She retreated, bumping against the bed. This room really was no bigger than a rabbit hutch. Something in him resented her poor surroundings. She was a woman born for silks and diamonds and marble halls. If he seduced her, would she agree to become his mistress? The prospect set excitement blazing through him.

She shook her head again and her hands clenched at her sides. "I won't meet you."

He took the single step to corner her and slid his hand behind her head. Since he'd released her, he'd missed touching her. Soft hair tickled his fingers. He stared hard into her eyes, searching for the concessions he knew she wanted to make, common sense be damned. "Tonight, Antonia."

Again he expected her to evade him but she stood quiveringly still. He leaned forward and kissed her, a kiss rich with promise. Her lips moved softly in silent consent.

When he raised his head, he caught a longing in her face that made his blood thunder with anticipation. Yes, she wanted him. Perhaps almost as much as he wanted her, although in her inexperience, she probably didn't recognize that.

He turned on his heel and left.

Chapter Eleven

"*T*ONI, stop fussing." With a peevish gesture, Cassie flinched away from Antonia's attempts to bathe her.

The girl had started to improve the night after that astonishing hour Antonia spent with Lord Ranelaw in her room. She still couldn't believe that he'd had her in his arms on a bed and hadn't taken advantage. She still couldn't believe he'd been so kind.

Kindness was a word she'd never linked to Lord Ranelaw. Although perhaps she should. He'd had her at his mercy in her bedroom in London. He'd had her at his mercy by the river. And again here in the manor. All three times, she'd escaped. Purely thanks to his good graces. Honesty forced her to admit her principles had provided no defense at all.

That hour had been three days ago. Three days offering Antonia a chance to be glad she'd resisted the temptation to meet him. It was always easier to be sensible when she wasn't actually with Ranelaw.

Of course she hadn't gone to the summerhouse. She wasn't a complete fool, much as the marquess scrambled her brain when he kissed her. Ah, his kisses. If she closed her eyes, she still felt his mouth hard and demanding against her hand, then sweet upon her lips.

Ranelaw was such a contradictory mixture. No wonder he left her so befuddled.

Away from him, though, she saw her path clearly. She couldn't risk breaking society's rules again. For all that she often felt strangled as Antonia Smith, at least she was safe.

Cassie's sudden improvement rescued her from having to decide. Antonia smiled to recall her astounded gratitude when Cassie had turned to her and enunciated a complete sentence. Nothing profound. A request for water. But the first coherent words the girl had spoken in two days, since she'd descended into sweat-soaked fever.

After that, Antonia had watched Cassie sleep without pain for the first time in five days. She'd sent up a joyous prayer of thanks when her cousin woke clear-eyed and clearheaded, if exhausted.

Three days later, Cassie was strong enough to resent her confinement. She couldn't yet fend for herself, but she was well enough to complain. Over and over. Antonia was ready to scream. Even devoted Bella lost patience with the girl's pettishness.

"I want to go downstairs," Cassie said for the hundredth time in the last hour, then proved herself incapable of leaving her bed by breaking into a prolonged fit of coughing.

With an irritated gesture, Antonia plopped the flannel into the bowl of warm water. "You tried to stand this morning when we weren't looking and I had to pick you up, remember?"

"I'm feeling better now," Cassie said sullenly, tugging her night rail over her head.

"Maybe you can go downstairs tomorrow." Antonia had said the same thing yesterday.

With a heavy sigh, she turned away. She was deathly tired. Most of the household were still incapacitated so she and Bella continued full-time nursing. Although with every hour, a relapse in Cassie's health seemed more unlikely. Antonia began to think the greatest threat to Cassie's recovery was the possibility that her faithful companion Miss Smith would throttle her with a curtain rope.

"I want to go downstairs now."

"Nobody is around. The people who weren't sick have left and everybody else is in their rooms, ill or recovering. You'll be as bored downstairs as you are up here."

Thankfully, apart from an unlucky housemaid, there had been no deaths at Pelham Place. The village hadn't fared as well but even there, the epidemic receded.

"I'm bored altogether." Cassie flopped against the bed and stared discontentedly at the ceiling. "When are we going back to London? I'm sorry we came. Did Lord Ranelaw get sick?"

Antonia hid another sigh. It was the first time Cassie had mentioned her rakish suitor since she'd fallen ill.

"No."

Cassie still eyed the ceiling. "I suppose he went back to London."

"I don't know," Antonia said with perfect honesty, turning her back to tidy the gear from Cassie's bed bath. She didn't dare meet Cassie's eyes in case she betrayed that she and Ranelaw were no longer hostile strangers. Although for the life of her, she couldn't say just what they were instead.

"I'm sick of the country," Cassie said fretfully, plucking at the sheet beneath her.

"If you're better tomorrow, we'll go. You're up to traveling in short stages and I'm sure Lady Humphrey is weary of having her house turned into a hospital."

Cassie looked brighter. "That would be wonderful, Toni."

Antonia dared to mention something she knew wouldn't meet with approval. "Perhaps we should go back to Bascombe Hailey. You've been dreadfully sick, Cassie. I thought you were dying. I can't remember being so worried."

With an irritated gesture, Cassie brushed Antonia's concern aside. "Of course I wasn't dying. I'm going to dazzle the *ton.*"

"You'll need to get considerably better than you are now before you start dancing yourself into a stupor," Antonia said repressively.

As expected, Cassie didn't take that well. "Go away, Toni. Bella will be here soon and I'm sick of your scolding."

"I was going to read to you. It will pass the time."

Cassie looked away with a pout. "I can read for myself."

Yesterday, even this morning, Antonia would have ignored Cassie's spoiled behavior. But she couldn't help feeling that if Cassie was well enough to be surly, she was well enough to manage with Bella's sole attention for a few hours.

Cassie wasn't the only one bored with the room. Although at least this chamber was airy and light and furnished with every luxury, unlike the tiny cupboard assigned to Antonia.

Briefly she closed her eyes as the image rose of Lord Ranelaw's powerful body making her room seem even smaller. She'd tried not to dwell upon that encounter, but it was impossible. Especially since Cassie started to recover and nursing no longer occupied Antonia's every thought.

One thing was clear. Ranelaw wasn't quite the evil reprobate she'd once judged him.

Of course he wasn't. His complexity was part of his fascination.

Her attraction to Ranelaw made her girlish infatuation with Johnny seem a fickle fancy. That fickle fancy had destroyed her life. What disaster, then, did her interest in Ranelaw threaten?

"Toni, I said go away," Cassie repeated when Antonia didn't immediately respond. "I want to be alone. Between you and Bella, I haven't had a minute's privacy."

"If we'd left you alone when you were sick, you mightn't have lived to see another day," Antonia said with a hint of acid. "You could express a little gratitude. Poor Bella left in tears yesterday."

Cassie, to her credit, looked uncomfortable. "She fidgets like an old woman."

"She loves you."

"I know." Cassie sent her a guilt-ridden glance. The resentment drained from her voice. "I'm so tired of being stuck in bed. Honestly, some time on my own would do me good."

"As you wish." Antonia poured a fresh glass of water and placed it on the nightstand. "Don't be mean to Bella. She hardly slept while you were ill."

Cassie grabbed Antonia's hand. "I'm a witch."

Antonia's lips flattened on a fervent agreement. Instead she answered less contentiously. "We're all stretched to our limits."

Cassie's hold tightened. "I don't deserve you."

Antonia met her cousin's eyes and spoke nothing less than the truth. "I owe you and your father a debt I can never repay. But I look after you because I love you. I know you want some entertainment. I can't blame you. But it's neither my fault nor Bella's that your strength hasn't returned yet."

Cassie flushed and glanced away. "I know. I'm sorry."

"Thank you," Antonia said quietly.

Cassie looked at Antonia. "But seriously, Toni, don't you want to get out of this room too? Leave me be for the evening. Bella will bring up my supper, then I'll sleep."

"You need rest." She injected a lighter note. "Especially if you soon mean to dance the night away."

"I hope so." Cassie lifted the glass and sipped. "I was having such a marvelous time. I'd hate to think it ended."

Antonia wandered toward the open window. Cassie's room overlooked the formal gardens to the side of the house. No summerhouse in the distance to remind her of Lord Ranelaw. She glanced up at the evening star in the moonless sky, shining alone in the deepening blue. The view was beautiful, serene, calming, and suddenly, yes, Antonia did want to breathe air untainted by illness and pique.

Cassie was right. She fussed. Antonia turned and caught an assessing look in her cousin's face. She was puzzled, then decided she must mistake the expression in those limpid blue eyes.

She headed toward the door. "I'll be walking in the grounds if you need me."

"I won't need you," Cassie said with unflattering confidence. "If anything happens, Bella's here."

Antonia slipped onto the terrace where she'd encountered Lord Ranelaw the day he arrived. She wore one of the few dresses remaining from her life as Lord Aveson's daughter. She'd made numerous alterations to the blue muslin gown, but no new braiding or fresh buttons could hide the woefully outmoded style. Or that it was an extravagant garment utterly beyond a humble companion's means.

In spite of her crushing weariness, she was edgy and restless. She needed to get outside, move about. And for a moment, reclaim Antonia Hilliard from the unending drudgery of playing Miss Smith.

She glanced into the clear sky. After a beautiful day that she'd seen only through Cassie's windows, it was that magical hour before full darkness. A nightingale trilled from the thick shrubbery beside the terrace. Otherwise the world was hushed.

She felt trembling, expectant, like anything could happen.

Inevitably Antonia's feet led her toward the summerhouse on the far side of the lake. She'd discovered the building early in her visit when she'd still enjoyed the luxury of long walks.

Twilight deepened into night as she traced the faint path under the trees to the small building glimmering white ahead of her. A bizarre mixture of Egyptian and Greek taste set back from the water and perfectly private.

For a rendezvous, Lord Ranelaw couldn't have chosen better.

Or worse, if one took a moral standpoint.

She smiled faintly. Morality never impinged on Ranelaw's considerations.

When she rounded the side of the building, she glanced across the silent lake. Stars shimmered on the still blackness, turning it into an inverted sky.

"Good evening, Antonia."

She wasn't surprised to look back at the summerhouse and see Lord Ranelaw watching from the shallow flight of steps. His presence seemed part of the enchantment. Or perhaps she was so tired, she drifted in a blur where nothing seemed quite real.

"Lord Ranelaw," she said softly. A breeze across the lake ruffled her loosely arranged hair.

"Nicholas," he said equally softly. He leaned against one of the four Corinthian columns that supported the portico and folded his arms.

"Nicholas." His name signaled a concession they both recognized.

Starlight glimmered on his white shirt—did the man never go decently dressed in coat and neck cloth?—but she discerned few other details. She didn't need to see him. His image was etched on her heart. Handsome, careless, wicked. *Precious. . .*

"I knew you'd come." He sounded calm, sure.

The darkness sharpened senses other than sight. She heard the rustle of the trees, smelled the slight dankness of the lake behind her, felt the evening breeze cool against her skin. Skin flushed with awareness.

"You waited three days."

"I can be patient," he responded steadily.

She bit her lip. Had she expected to see him? Did her presence mean they'd make love? Somewhere she'd already said yes.

"Are you going to run?" he asked in a casual voice, as if consent or refusal were all the same to him. But even in the shadows, she saw he tautened with anticipation.

"I should."

He straightened and prowled down to the bottom step. She knew he waited for her to flee like a frightened bird. Like a woman with an ounce of self-preservation.

He became preternaturally still. His voice was low, coaxing, thick and deep as velvet. "What's it to be, Antonia?"

"Don't bully me, Ranelaw," she said sharply.

"Are you pretending you're just out for an evening walk?" That's what she'd told herself. Not even she believed it.

She'd left the house, wandered toward the summerhouse, because she knew Ranelaw waited. She admitted that to herself. She wasn't quite ready to admit it to him. "I didn't realize you'd be here."

Her eyes had adjusted enough to see the glint of his teeth as he smiled. "Yes, you did."

What use struggling to preserve her pride? He'd soon know she was helpless to resist him. He knew already.

"Yes, I did," she answered almost soundlessly.

The words lay between them like a challenge.

She poised in breathless suspense for him to sweep her into his arms. Across the several yards separating them, she couldn't mistake his urgency. The silence developed a vibrating quality. Even the breeze dropped in expectation.

Why hadn't he touched her yet? They both knew she wouldn't fight.

He turned his face to the glittering sky then he stared directly at her. Through darkness, that regard burned.

"Why?" The question cut through the night like a blade.

She released a disbelieving gasp of laughter. "I can't believe you're havering. You've schemed to get me on my back since we met."

She heard the scrape of his boots as he shifted. Still without coming closer. "And you've fought with all the determination you could muster."

"Not always," she said with reluctant honesty.

"What you've yielded, you've yielded against better judgment."

"I'm here against better judgment." She clenched her hands in the skirts of the dress she'd chosen because in the recesses of her mind, she'd hoped to meet Ranelaw. A dress that belonged to Antonia Hilliard not Antonia Smith. He'd never know her identity, but tonight he'd make love to her true self.

"I'm sure you are."

Something discomfiting shivered through her. Something that felt like chagrin. "You've changed your mind?"

"No. My mind has always been set on you."

He sounded like he meant it. She wished she could believe him. "At least that's what you'd like me to think," she said resentfully.

"My hunger is real enough."

She stepped closer. "Don't you want to kiss me?" she asked with an edge of desperation. "I'm here. We're alone. There's nobody to stop us."

"You think I'm out of my head."

"Yes."

He laughed softly. "Perhaps I am at that. Why are you here?"

The impulse was to offer some nonsense to content him so he stopped talking and kissed her. Instead she replied with complete sincerity. "It's Cassie."

"Cassie?" She heard curiosity.

She paused, wondering how to make him understand. Wondering why it mattered that he should understand. "She almost died."

"I know." She waited for more, but he remained silent, luring her to spill her secrets. This intimacy was dangerous, but she couldn't summon the will to shatter it.

"Cassie's illness reminded me life is short and I should snatch what I want while I can."

"Does that mean you want me?"

Ah, she saw his strategy. He meant to strip her pride. Or any illusion that she ceded under anyone's auspices but her own.

Defiantly she raised her chin. She sprang from one of the greatest lines in the land. Stretching back to the Dark Ages, the blood of warriors flowed in her veins. Still, for all her bravado, her stomach cramped with nerves. "Yes, I want you."

"At last," he breathed, so softly she scarcely heard.

She stood in tense silence, while he leaped down the last step to stand before her. With a slowness she felt in every beat of her yearning heart, he slid his hand behind her head and tilted her face toward his.

"You're trembling," he said softly.

"Of course I'm trembling. I'm scared to death. But desire is stronger than fear."

The deceptive starlight lent his smile a tenderness she knew not to trust. Even as she consented to become his lover, she wasn't gulled about his essential nature. He was a predator. If she forgot that, she was lost.

"I'm glad."

Any instant now, he'd press that beautiful, passionate mouth to hers and reason would vanish. She gathered the last shreds of sanity. "Before . . . before we start . . ."

She stopped and licked her lips with nervousness. Had she been this awkward with Johnny? She didn't think so. She'd been too intoxicated with the vision of sacrificing everything for love.

She wasn't so foolish now.

"Rules, beautiful Antonia?" he murmured, nuzzling her neck and threatening what little common sense she retained. She shivered. It was hard enough keeping two thoughts in her head when he wasn't touching her.

"Y-yes," she said on a husky sigh.

She tried without great conviction to establish some space between them. He'd only held her three times before. Why was his touch more familiar than her own skin?

"Let me guess." He brushed his face against the side of hers. "This must remain a secret."

The glancing touches should feel innocent. Of course they weren't. They readied her for him, made her wet, beguiled her into a state of hazy arousal where she'd let him do whatever he wished. She wasn't far from that state now. But she wasn't yet ready to throw over ten years of circumspection without a safeguard or two.

"Yes."

"Do you trust me to follow your rules?" The question was a whisper across her collarbone and she realized he'd pushed aside her sleeve so he could taste her shoulder. Another of those sensual shivers. Another welling of moisture between her legs. He drove her to the edge of madness. She should have started this conversation when he was ten feet away, not when he touched her and turned her mind to custard.

"I have to trust you," she said grimly even as the needy ache in her sex intensified. "What choice do I have?"

"Poor Joan of Arc, so bravely going to the stake." The hint of laughter shot another jolt of awareness through her.

She bolstered her failing determination. "You'll never use me against Cassie, even if you publish my brazenness to the world."

"What a nasty opinion you have of me, sweet Miss Smith. Do you consider me so manipulative?"

"Yes," she admitted on a sigh as he bit down gently on a nerve in her neck. She rubbed her thighs together to ease the emptiness but the soft friction only built her craving. If she didn't set her conditions quickly, she'd swoon in his arms.

"Wise woman." He kissed the place he'd bitten. "Yet still you're here." He ran his hands up and down her ribs, stopping breathtakingly short of her breasts. Even through clothing, his touch trailed fire.

"I'm not wise." She gathered her thoughts, difficult when her sex was molten with heat and her breasts ached for his hands.

"You have my word this is unrelated to my pursuit of Cassie."

"Thank you," she whispered, but he hadn't finished speaking.

"However, nothing will deflect my interest from Miss Demarest."

She stiffened. Where was her pride? She should march away when he refused to relinquish his pursuit of another woman. Pathetically she'd come too far for will to prevail over hunger. "I won't let you hurt her."

"You'll do your best." His hard tone contrasted with his languorous touch so near her swelling breasts. "Is that everything?"

Was that everything? She dredged elusive thought from the sea of sensual pleasure. "You have to protect me from conceiving a child."

He drew back and his teasing caresses stilled. She felt him studying her through the darkness. "Yes."

"That's all?" Astonishment pierced the mists in her mind. "Just yes?"

"Well, I'll do my best. Nothing is foolproof." His hands tightened on her waist. The air prickled with anticipation. "More conditions? Perhaps you want assurances in writing?"

"This is such a game to you," she said bitterly, gripping his forearms. She didn't deceive herself that this man held to anything as inconvenient as a principle. At this blazing moment, she didn't care.

His voice was ragged as he closed the distance between them. "This stopped being a game a long time ago."

Chapter Twelve

*R*ANELAW gripped Antonia's hips hard through the filmy dress and dragged her into his body. The scent of her arousal made his head swim. Ruthlessly he pressed against her belly, letting her feel how he wanted her, how she was in his power and he wasn't letting her go.

She made a muffled protest when he crashed his mouth into hers. Her fingers formed talons on his forearms, digging into his skin through his thin cambric shirt. The sting fed the storm of passion inside him.

Ruthlessly he forced her lips apart, plundered the interior of her mouth with his tongue. Bit and licked and tasted. He treated her like the most experienced courtesan.

A voice inside his head shouted for him to stop. She was an innocent. He should woo, coax, lure. But his hunger attained such a pitch, he, who prided himself on his control, couldn't rein in his desire.

She stood stiff, trembling and unyielding, for all that she claimed to want him. His grip tightened. She'd stepped into this particular lion's den of her own will. If he devoured her, she had only herself to blame.

Even unresponsive, she was delicious. The most delicious woman he'd ever kissed. The voice at the back of his mind screamed that she was untouched, a virgin, deserving of care. He'd frighten her.

To his shame, he frightened her now.

For the first time in his life, he didn't know if he could restrain himself. He wanted her so much. Flattening her breasts against his chest, he tugged her closer. Clothes became an unbearable barrier.

He must stop. He must stop.

With shocking suddenness, her arms snaked around his neck. She released a strangled whimper and kissed him back with frenzied passion. Her tongue stabbed into his mouth, danced with his in dizzying fervor. He growled with masculine satisfaction and dropped his hands to her buttocks, pulling her into his erection. The sensation, even through her skirts, nearly blew off the top of his head.

Their earlier kisses had been powerful. This . . . this was like being crushed in an earthquake, whirled away in a flooded river, blasted into the sky. He'd always known she was extraordinary. But what flared now promised to fling him, the famous debauchee, into a universe beyond his experience.

Reluctantly he wrenched his lips from hers. Some minuscule trace of reason yet remained. He was mad for her, but he couldn't take her here on the ground. Not her first time. He swung her into his arms and swiftly mounted the steps. She was restless, touching him, kissing his neck, shaking and gasping with the desire that crackled between them.

It was darker inside the summerhouse. He felt a momentary yen for light. He longed to look into her eyes at this moment and know her lost to passion. As was he.

Next time. . .

His arms firmed around her and he kissed her again. His heart thundered so fast, his senses were so crammed with her scent and taste, he wasn't sure he'd survive the night. This was what he'd perceived in her from the start. This voracious goddess. A woman who matched his passion ounce for ounce.

More by luck than calculation—calculation was beyond his ken—he bumped into the cushioned bench circling the room. With roughness born of urgency, he lowered Antonia and came down over her, shoving up her skirts as he straddled her.

The voice that insisted he take care shrieked in protest.

He was deaf to its cries. The roar in his blood swamped everything, caution, plots, even this squeak from his long disregarded conscience. He'd waited so long for Antonia. It felt like an eon. He'd have her and he'd have her now.

She didn't lie quiescent under him. Her hands tugged and tore at his clothing, rubbed his flanks, curved around to press into his buttocks.

His hand unsteady, he stroked up her thigh to the sleek, silky cleft. To his wondering astonishment, his fingers encountered nothing all the way but hot, bare skin. Reckless Miss Smith wasn't wearing drawers. Thank the Lord Almighty. She must have guessed hindering undergarments would end up shredded on the floor.

Reckless indeed. With breathtaking eagerness, she curled her legs around his hips. A hot drift of her musky scent made him crazy. Her body breathed its longing for him. His nostrils flared to draw her female essence deep into his lungs.

"Wait . . ." he grunted, trying to wrench his shirt over his head.

"No," she panted, angling up toward him. "No waiting."

She seized his shirt and ripped it down the front. Her palms flattened against his heaving chest. She pressed her mouth across his torso in biting kisses that shot his arousal higher. Her teeth scraped his nipple and he released a hoarse groan.

Hell's bells, she really would kill him.

He stroked her deeply, thrusting a finger into creamy heat. She was so tight. The searing prospect of that snug passage closing hard around his cock made him shake. On a strangled cry of pleasure, she pushed into his hand, demanding more, demanding everything.

Slowly, testing her, he eased a second finger inside, the

first knuckle, then pressing up to the second knuckle. Her passage clenched and a flood of hot desire drenched his hand.

Again he struggled to slow down. Vaguely he remained aware of the need to coax her into climax, to prepare her with his hand before he thrust inside. But he'd moved past the point where he could wait. Her womanly scent intoxicated him, made him drunk till next Sunday. Her body tensed around his fingers. Her incoherent litany as she scattered eager kisses across his chest indicated she wanted him now.

"Stop me," he groaned, hardly aware of what he said. "Stop me before I hurt you."

"No," she moaned, wriggling closer to his hand with shuddering impatience. His fingers curled in a subtle caress that made her buck. "Never."

She tangled her hands in his hair and dragged him down for another agitated kiss. He'd never witnessed such passion in a woman. Every breath emerged from her throat as a sob. Her need fed his, made it unbearable.

He stroked her once more, relishing the succulent tug of her muscles, then withdrew. She deserved better from him, but he could resist no longer. With unsteady hands, he tore at his breeches, desperate to free himself.

For God's sake, man, go easy. She's a virgin. You'll split her in two if you don't control yourself.

He was past heeding anything beyond arousal. She sank her teeth hard into his shoulder, inflicting real pain that stoked the blaze of desire. Blackness filled his head. He must have her. He tightened his buttocks, sucked a rattling breath through his clenched teeth, and thrust hard between her slender thighs.

He went deep on a perfect, smooth slide. She closed tight around him and arched on a guttural cry. He shut his eyes, the wonder of finally being inside her drowning his over-loaded senses in honey.

Heat. Desire. Completion. She held him inside her as if she never wanted to let him go. Time, the world, everything he'd been before, everything he promised to become disappeared into one radiant moment of sublime communion.

She was perfect. She was everything he'd dreamed she'd be. She was his. At last.

Reluctantly he opened his eyes. In the darkness, he discerned only the faintest details of her face. But her scent filled his head, drugging him with Antonia. Her body squeezed him as she curled her arms around his back. She sighed luxuriantly, shifting so he slid further into her.

Into paradise.

She shifted again and raised her knees, cradling him. He had to cling to this instant.

He had to move or go mad.

On a jagged breath, he slowly withdrew, loving the powerful slide of his cock in her satiny wetness. He paused on a panting instant of suspense, then thrust deep once more.

Again that ineffable feeling of welcome.

She sighed as if she too measured the boundaries of pleasure. With a natural acceptance that made his heart slam against his ribs, she tilted her hips to take more of him.

The world exploded into light. Everything turned physical. Fierce heat sizzling through his veins. The pull and release of his body moving in hers. Her breathy moans of encouragement. He wanted her to come more than he wanted the promise of heaven.

She was close. So close. He felt the sweet change in the grip of her inner muscles. He rose on his arms to watch her although her face was only a pale shape in the gloom.

His change in position made her gasp and push up against him. Her desperate search for consummation made him burn to satisfy her. His balls tightened in agony, but he beat back the savage urge to lose himself.

Not yet. Not yet.

He felt the ripples start inside her. It wasn't enough. He wanted her to shatter into a million pieces. He wanted to create her anew so she'd never forget him. He wanted her to admit she was helpless under the dominion of this magic.

Changing the rhythm, he penetrated as deep as he could, then held still at the end of each stroke.

Still she didn't give him what he wanted.

He drove into her hard, sliding her up the bench. She moaned and clutched at his shoulders. The ripples intensified, tormenting him into a frenzy. Still she didn't break.

Ruthlessly he touched her between the legs. She released a hoarse cry and liquid heat doused him. He stroked again and felt her shudder. Her every move threatened to send him over. Holding back promised to destroy him. His jaw ached with clenching. Hunger blasted him like cannon fire.

Except in the end, he couldn't sustain the power games. He wanted her too damned much.

With a groan that expressed defeat as much as need, he plunged into her, spiraling higher and higher.

Nearer and nearer.

Her sobbing breath was a storm in his ear. He didn't know whether she quivered with rapture or pain. He was past stopping. His blood pounded the fevered necessity for release.

Just as he neared his peak, she began to convulse. Her moans broke on a sharp cry. For a moment, as he poised on the edge, he recalled his promise. He burned to pour himself inside her, to mark her in the most primitive way.

But she'd trusted him.

Grinding his teeth with painful force, he held back the swelling release, the agonized need to answer her quivering rapture with a flood of his seed. When her wildness receded, he wrenched free and spilled himself on her tumbled skirts.

Ranelaw collapsed on his back beside Antonia, his chest heaving in exhaustion. Gradually his body quieted. Satisfaction throbbed through him. The air was sharp with sex, mixed with the lake's muddy smell and dust from the neglected summerhouse.

His mind was pleasantly blank. For the moment, all his

sensations were animal. That mighty release left him drifting in a glorious ocean.

He didn't resist oblivion. It seemed a gift. Just as the coruscating rapture seemed a gift.

Slowly he coasted back from the outer reaches of experience. His mind stirred.

As if she too emerged from another world, he heard Antonia exhale on a shaky breath. He waited for her to speak. He heartily wished she wouldn't. Not yet. Their union had been so perfect, he didn't want words.

Words inevitably meant argument.

He didn't want to argue. He wanted to remember how it had felt to move inside her magnificent body and know she was irrevocably his. He wanted to remember her wholehearted participation. Never had he known a woman who sought her delight with such openness.

Above all, he wanted to contemplate doing it all again.

She shifted gingerly and a faint whimper escaped her. A needle of guilt pierced his well-being. She must be uncomfortable. He'd hammered into her like a battering ram at the end. He should be bloody ashamed. Instead he felt like he owned the world.

As though his arm weighed a hundredweight, he lifted it and laid it across her naked belly. Her skirts bunched beneath her breasts. He hadn't even bothered to undress her, he was such a barbarian.

A very happy barbarian. She'd drained him to the lees. No woman had ever done that. He loved sex but a niggling dissatisfaction had always remained.

As if there should be more.

It took defiant, difficult spinster Antonia Smith to show him more.

God bless her.

Under his arm, he felt her uneven breathing. Awe wouldn't silence her long. Not his spirited Antonia.

He closed his eyes and rested his forehead against her shoulder. He drew a great breath, filling his lungs with her.

He adored the way she smelled. That fresh scent, combined with musky essence of pleasured woman.

If only life was always like this.

She touched his hair with a hesitant caress, then lifted her hand. When he made an inarticulate sound of encouragement, she stroked his hair again. He was a fool, but the caress seemed to convey more about what had happened tonight than words ever could.

For an immeasurably long time, they lay unmoving. Ranelaw's mind settled into a drowsy dream. At his side, Antonia slid her hand to his nape. The gesture felt absurdly protective. Nobody had protected him since Eloise.

Lying here was utterly delicious. Peace was too rare in his life to sacrifice it precipitately. How odd that of all the gifts Antonia offered, including spectacular pleasure, this peace was the sweetest.

He let himself float. Savoring the woman's quiet nearness.

And realized something that pleasure had blanked from awareness.

Defiant, difficult spinster Antonia Smith hadn't been a virgin.

The fact was so astounding, he hardly credited it.

Another man had possessed her. He guessed some time ago. For all her passion, her unpracticed response indicated she wasn't used to lying under a lover.

Not a virgin. . .

When he looked at Antonia, he'd prided himself on seeing more than anyone else. His arrogance had been misplaced.

He wasn't sure what he felt. Shock, certainly. He'd always known she concealed secrets upon secrets. Layers remained hidden, perhaps would always remain hidden.

He'd wondered if possessing Antonia would shatter her mystery. Whether once she opened her legs to him, she'd become like every other woman. He'd hoped she would. He resented the way she affected his decisions, kept him awake at night, made him desperate to have her.

Sampling her lush, beautiful body only made him crazy for more. He wanted to strip her naked. He wanted to watch her when he slid into her. He wanted to touch every inch of her. He wanted to pleasure her in all the ways he knew.

Her lack of innocence made her more intriguing.

If tonight was supposed to break her spell, it had proven a rank failure. The last hour just meshed him deeper in enchantment.

Still without speaking, she slid her hand from his neck. Pulling her skirts down, she shifted to sit with her elbow bent on the windowsill. He couldn't help but feel her movement as absence.

Neither he nor Antonia was created for tranquil communion. He couldn't bask in recollected bliss forever. Still, only with the greatest reluctance did he lift himself up to lean against the wall at his back.

The stars through the summerhouse windows showed Antonia with the sky as her background. She raised her knees and linked her hands around them. Her moonlight hair hung loose around her shoulders, shadowy and soft in the darkness.

He couldn't remember unpinning it. He'd been so eager, he didn't remember much apart from the exquisite delight of taking her. He really had been a savage.

"That was . . . that was . . ." Her husky voice petered out.

He closed his eyes and remembered the moment of delicious resistance as he penetrated her body. "Yes, it was."

"No wonder you're the toast of London's ladies." He heard a sardonic and unwelcome hint of Miss Smith.

He didn't want to talk about his other lovers. Damn it, he didn't want to talk at all. He wanted her under him again. After that gasping release, he'd believed himself exhausted, but she already had him hardening. He hadn't been this hot for a woman since adolescence. Whatever magic she possessed, it was powerful.

"Come here," he said lazily. "You're too far away."

She turned to stare at the trees and starlight sculpted her

profile, the high forehead, the straight nose, the delicate, stubborn jaw. Again a fleeting wisp of memory troubled him. He'd seen those features or something very like before. But right now he was too distracted to pursue the faint recollection.

He noticed her lips turned down. Why? He knew she'd found her pleasure.

"Antonia?" he asked when she didn't immediately answer.

He didn't like to think her sad. Which was absurd. He'd make her bitterly sad before he was done. Even apart from Cassie's ruin, he wasn't a man who offered happy endings.

She turned and studied him through the darkness. She didn't move any closer, devil take her. "They'll miss me if I'm away much longer."

What? He felt disoriented. He wanted more than one tumble, breathtaking as it had been.

He straightened and grabbed her hand. "We haven't finished."

"Yes, we have," she said with an implacability he couldn't mistake. She jerked her hand free and slipped along the bench away from him.

He'd been so sure she'd want to explore the glittering universe of desire. Again his arrogance led to assumptions. He should know by now any assumptions about Antonia were likely wrong. He never pleaded with a woman. He found himself pleading now. "There's no danger of discovery. Stay."

The low-voiced request hovered in the air for a fraught second. It was as though he asked more than the next hour. As though he asked for forever.

Damn it. He never asked for forever.

This was the first time he'd regretted that grim reality.

Hell, fucking her was supposed to simplify everything, scratch his itch, send him off with a few fine memories and a sigh of relief that the madness ended.

Instead the sex left him floundering like a drowning

man. The joy he'd discovered only promised more and greater joy. His mind was roiling confusion. All he knew was he didn't want Antonia to leave.

Passion clouded his thoughts. Away from her, he'd be free. The hell of it was he didn't want to be away from her.

"Nicholas . . ."

She paused, giving him time to savor how readily she used his Christian name. He wanted her crying out his name when he drove into her. He wanted to obliterate all memory of previous lovers. She'd think only of him.

He was a selfish bastard, he knew. She could leave now and remain relatively unscathed. But he loathed the idea of her treating him as a fleeting fancy.

"Stay," he repeated softly. Into that one low word, he injected all the persuasion he'd learned through years of debauchery.

All his persuasion did him no good. "I can't."

Hell, surely he could change her mind. The impulse surged to grab her but he wanted her consent first.

"I treated you roughly." Hoarse sincerity edged his voice. Just because he set out to subvert her will didn't mean everything he said was a lie. "My behavior was inexcusable. My only explanation is you've driven me insane. I'll be kinder next time."

He'd thought pleading was difficult. Any moment now he'd be apologizing. He *never* apologized.

Her short laugh contained no amusement. "Don't be a fool, Nicholas. You didn't do anything I didn't want you to."

Shaming relief flooded his veins. Usually he was too sure of himself to require reassurance. Nothing with Antonia Smith was *usual*.

She paused and her voice frayed with bitterness. "What happened at least had the virtue of honesty. Tenderness would be a falsehood."

He bit back the lunatic urge to disagree. Beneath tumultuous desire lurked respect and liking and, yes, tenderness. Those moments afterward when she'd touched his hair with a softness that scored his obsidian heart? Those moments were tender. When he'd taken her, passion was paramount. It didn't mean passion was all they had.

"Don't rush away. It's still early." He reached across the distance between them and cupped her jaw in his hand.

She trembled, not nearly so controlled as she wanted to appear. He continued in that coaxing tone. "Let me show you I'm more than a rapacious beast."

"I rather like the rapacious beast," she admitted on a sigh that almost, but not quite, sounded like capitulation. "You're usually so controlled."

He smiled, partly because she made no move to escape. Under his hand, her cheek was smooth and soft, like warm satin. Almost unconsciously, he stroked it. "Not when you're around."

"That's what I like," she whispered.

"Good." He leaned toward her. "Because you're going to see a lot more of it."

"Nicholas . . ."

"Hush, Antonia."

He knew she intended to say something sensible, something about retreating to the house and her duties. Perhaps, heaven forbid, something about never seeing him again.

He didn't want to argue. He wanted to kiss her. Then he wanted to see her naked. Then he wanted to revisit the hot depths of her glorious body.

He was a man who invariably got what he wanted.

He'd start with the kiss.

The problem was kissing her drove him out of his mind. So hard to calculate seduction when he was afire for her. Did she know what she did to him, the unprecedented effect she created with her mere existence?

So far she hadn't set out to seduce him. God help him if she did. The greatest rake in the kingdom would be helpless against her.

He pressed his lips to hers in a sweet kiss reminiscent of the kiss that had so overset him by the stream. Unfamiliar emotion shivered its way into his heart. He fought the urge to be rough, commanding. Vulnerability never ambushed him when he overwhelmed her with passion.

He'd used her so carelessly tonight. He'd loved it. She claimed it was what she'd wanted. But something in him ached to cherish her. Last time was like diving headfirst into a blazing building. Now he wanted to take his time.

Her lips trembled, then opened like a flower blooming to the sun. He swept his tongue along her lower lip, then dipped inside to taste the interior. She sighed so softly, he wouldn't have heard if he hadn't been this close.

Her mouth opened wider and her tongue brushed his with shy invitation. How incongruous her hesitancy when she'd just flung him up to heaven.

Ardor rose with adamant insistence. He struggled against the need to ravish her, push her against the wall, shove her legs apart.

Reluctantly he retreated. He panted with arousal. So did she. Her hand rested upon his shoulder.

"I'm trying to be gentle," he said gruffly.

He caught the glimmer of her smile. This night seduction was beguiling, but next time, he wanted to see her. "I know."

Then astonishingly she kissed him. The chaste, undemanding kiss blasted him with shock. She rarely touched him without his incitement.

"I have to go, Nicholas."

He was so astounded by her kiss that it took a moment to understand. He snatched after her hand but she'd risen and moved to the center of the room.

"Antonia . . ."

"Please don't make it more difficult."

He caught something in her voice that sounded like tears. That twinge in his chest stabbed once more.

"Meet me tomorrow," he said urgently, standing but not approaching. He realized his breeches flapped open. Fumbling he fastened them. Something in her vibrating tension told him the instant when she might have surrendered had passed. "I'll be here."

His fists closed at his sides as he struggled against compelling her to stay. He wanted more than she'd given, but the promise of tomorrow would tide him over.

Ranelaw, you are in a bad, bad way.

It was another sign of his bad, bad way that he didn't experience his usual yen to flee difficulties or complications. Even though Antonia Smith with her thorny, barricaded soul was the personification of difficulty and complication.

"I can't." Already she backed away. He had a horrible, eerie feeling that if he let her go, he wouldn't find her again. "Don't ask me."

"I have to." He swallowed and told himself he couldn't steal her like so much contraband and rush off somewhere they'd never be disturbed. Such places only existed in fairy tales. "I'll wait for you."

She shook her head. "Don't. Please don't." Her voice cracked. He wasn't mistaken about the tears.

"We have so much more to discover."

Was this really he? Notorious, heartless Ranelaw? He didn't deserve either description right now. He felt miserable and starved for some sign that Antonia wasn't leaving him forever.

Even worse for his amour propre, he starved for some sign that what had happened meant something to her. She was upset, but he needed to know she felt more than regret.

"Good night, Nicholas," she whispered, and turned in a swirl of pale skirts.

He could chase her. If he caught her, she wouldn't fight.

Nonetheless he let her go. As he listened to the rapid patter of her feet along the path, he slumped onto the bench that had witnessed such incomparable passion.

Chapter Thirteen

ANTONIA managed to slip unnoticed into her darkened room.

Trembling she sagged against the closed door. She was a mass of bruises. Physical satisfaction throbbed hot and slow in her blood. Ranelaw's musky scent was all over her. Between her legs, she ached. Every movement was an uncomfortable reminder that tonight she'd done something she hadn't done in a long time.

What on earth had she been thinking?

The problem was she hadn't thought. Pure instinct had overwhelmed her. Her body still hummed from the astonishing climax. Her skin yearned for Ranelaw's caresses. Low in her belly gaped an emptiness that only he could fill as he'd filled her tonight. In those burning, blinding moments, she'd become a different woman.

Yes, a sour voice remarked, she'd become like every other woman Ranelaw had seduced.

A poisonous mixture of confusion, desire, and self-castigation threatened to choke her. She bit her lip and told herself she wouldn't cry. Crying hadn't helped last time she was ruined. It wouldn't help now.

One searing tear squeezed its way beneath her eyelid and trickled down her cheek. A cheek that still tingled from Ranelaw's tender touch.

Ranelaw's lying, tender touch.

He was a large man, much larger than Johnny. She'd always remember how she'd stretched to accommodate him. He'd seated himself deep, then paused as if staking possession. For one quaking, brilliant instant, he forged a connection stronger than steel. She'd believed nothing would sunder them.

That odd conviction of union had persisted, enriching every detail of their lovemaking. And after.

Tonight he'd sounded sincere, almost yearning. It was a trick. She was just another body sacrificed at the altar of his appetites. Yet when he joined his body with hers, he'd felt like her other half, the man she'd sought all her life.

Stupid, stupid, stupid sentimental rot.

Dangerous sentimental rot.

At the height of his passion, she'd braced for him to pour his seed into her. In that incendiary moment, she'd wanted him to claim her as his.

But he'd kept her safe.

Hardly the act of a selfish beast.

Nor had he forced her to stay, although she knew he was primed to take her again. On a preternatural level, she'd always been aware of his reactions. After tonight, that awareness approached the uncanny.

With a muttered curse, she straightened and took a few halting steps. As she moved, she ripped the gown from her body. Later she'd carry the ruined, stained dress downstairs and burn it.

Finally she stood naked and panting by the nightstand. With unsteady hands, she lit a candle, then poured water into a bowl. She trembled so hard, water splashed the bare floorboards. She was desperate to wash Ranelaw off her skin.

Nothing would wash the blemish from her soul.

Ranelaw was adamant that he wouldn't loiter after Antonia like a lovesick sapskull. But following a night troubled by frustrated desire—good God, wanting her was worse now he'd had her—he headed for the summerhouse.

In the bright morning light, the place was no longer a mysterious temple of sensual delight. Instead it held an abandoned air that darkness had concealed. He climbed the steps and walked inside, recalling how he'd carried Antonia. His pulses raced with anticipation, no matter that it was too early to expect her.

He couldn't escape her phantom presence. The breeze lifted his hair, reminding him of Antonia's touch. Did he imagine a trace of her scent? Footprints showed on the dusty marble floor. Absently he scuffed one boot across the marks.

Lighting a cheroot, he wandered to the bench. A small stain discolored the seat. The heat between them should have left a few scorch marks, at the very least. But as he drew on his cheroot and glanced around, nothing here indicated the world had changed.

No, the changes were inside him, blast Antonia Smith to Hades.

With a weary sigh, he slumped down, stretching his legs across the floor and tipping his head back against the window frame. It was another sunny day, warm for May. Perhaps later he could coax Antonia to swim in the lake.

His blood eddied with desire as he imagined her magnificent body gleaming with water. He still hadn't seen that magnificent body unclothed. Last night he'd been in too much of a rush, God forgive him.

Something in Antonia melted his cold, hard core, ate into his proud self-sufficiency. He knew he invited trouble. The pleasure had been so extraordinary, right now he couldn't bring himself to mind too much.

He finished his cheroot. Smoked another. The sun filled him with languor, quieted the clamor of need to a gentle hum instead of a screaming demand. He closed his eyes, promising himself a nap. After all, he'd hardly slept last night and his exertions beforehand had been noteworthy.

When he opened his eyes, shadow bathed him. He glanced out, astonished to see the morning had become late afternoon. His belly grumbled, reminding him he hadn't eaten since a snatched breakfast. He'd been too eager to see Antonia to linger over the meal.

Antonia, who was still absent. Even asleep, he'd know the moment she turned up. His senses were so attuned to her, he felt her breathing when she was near.

Clearly she hadn't been able to postpone her duties.

Tonight?

The surge of expectation should dismay him.

He should head to the house, forage something, perhaps steal a few delicacies to sustain him and Antonia later. Once she arrived, she was staying until he'd taken his fill.

Which might require the next six months, the way he felt right now.

Ignoring the dull protest of tired muscles, he rose and stretched. He set off for the house at a lazy run.

The kitchens were more crowded than usual. The household returned to its routine. For all his selfishness, Ranelaw didn't wish fatal illness on anyone. But he regretted that the interval drew to a close when Antonia was free to meet him with minimal risk of discovery.

The maids were inured to his presence. At first they'd treated him as an interloper for all their politeness to someone of superior station. But he'd kept his hands to himself even as he'd flirted outrageously. Odd that he wasn't tempted to tumble one or two. There were some pretty girls belowstairs and a few had indicated willingness. But he had more than enough seductions to deal with already.

"Here you are, my lord. Some of last night's roast beef and a wedge of the estate's cheddar." Mary, his favorite among the maids, slid a pewter platter before him, piled with bread and fruit as well as meat and cheese. "And some ale to wash it down."

"Thank you, Mary. I'm famished." Under the girl's approving regard, he tucked in.

"I do like a man with a big appetite."

Usually he'd pursue the heavy sexual hint. Not today. Today he had more important things on his mind. Like where in bloody blazes Antonia was.

For discretion's sake, he couldn't ask outright about Miss Demarest's dour companion, so he took the roundabout way. He inquired after ill family members. Then ill guests. And gradually worked around to Cassie.

All this beating around the bush made him nostalgic for open dealing with an honest whore. For all that, he wouldn't shame Antonia more than he already had when he'd bribed the grooms. It was odd, her reputation was more precious now he'd had her than when he'd lusted from afar.

To his regret, today he still lusted from afar.

He downed a deep draft of ale and glanced at Mary. "What about pretty little Miss Demarest? Is she better today?"

"Must be, my lord." Jean, another maid, piped up from where she kneaded the bread. "Up and left first thing without stopping for so much as a crust for breakfast. Didn't half cause a flurry below stairs. But that companion of hers, that nice Miss Smith, she wouldn't delay even an hour to say good-bye to Lady Humphrey. Not that Lady Humphrey will mind having more of her visitors gone. It's been a rum sort of house party, it has."

A bristling silence descended. Ranelaw realized he stared at Jean in furious shock. He forced himself to pick up the ale and drink, although he tasted nothing.

The birds had flown. . .

When he put down the tankard, he struggled to keep his voice even. "I thought the chit was at death's door."

"She's been improving, although I must say the poor mite looked peaky when they bundled her into the carriage. Nigel carried her down the staircase. She couldn't walk on her own."

"Aye, and a sweet armful she was too, beggin' your pardon, my lord," Nigel remarked from the corner where he polished a silver food cover.

"She's a diamond." Ranelaw raised his tankard in a toast to Miss Demarest. And to Miss Smith, who escaped him.

Damn her.

"I suppose they're bound for London?" he asked with forced idleness. To his own ears, his comments sounded too interested to be casual. None of the servants seemed to notice.

"Not sure, my lord." Nigel critically regarded his reflection in the silver. "I imagine so. Or perhaps they're taking the lady home to the country."

Double damn.

If they'd slunk back to Bascombe Hailey, his plans—for both women—must wait. Perhaps until next year.

He should be fuming that Cassie escaped. All he saw through a fog of blistering temper was Antonia staring up at him, her eyes pools of shining mystery as he pounded into her.

She had no right to run. She knew they weren't finished. The lying—

Then with a jolt of grim awareness, he recalled she hadn't agreed to meet him.

He'd been so certain of her. Yet again arrogance led him wrong. He bit back burgeoning rage. "It's time I left too."

More than time. Morecombe still wasn't himself but he'd resumed his duties yesterday. His valet could travel with the luggage while Ranelaw rode to make extra speed. First he'd try London, then worry about Somerset.

Burning to overtake the women, he left the kitchen and mounted the steps to his room two at a time. His heart raced with the thrill of the chase.

If Antonia thought her dawn departure left him flat, she had an unpleasant surprise ahead.

Chapter Fourteen

*W*ITH a curse, Ranelaw dismounted outside the prosperous inn. The summery weather had deteriorated into a cold, blustery night more like February than May. He had a sudden sour recollection of his thwarted plans to take Antonia swimming.

Grimly he passed the reins to the shivering groom and strode into the taproom, rubbing his gloved hands together to restore circulation. Only sheer stubbornness kept him on the road. Common sense insisted he rest, shelter from the storm. Especially as he could be on the wildest of wild goose chases. He had no idea if Antonia made for London. Even if she did, he couldn't confront her in the middle of the night. He knew she'd take measures to stop him climbing into her room again.

These days common sense was woefully absent.

As it was, he'd put off stopping as long as he could. But he was cold and hungry and his horse was exhausted. The beast needed a little warmth and a feed before Ranelaw pushed him the last fifteen miles to London.

The inn wasn't crowded. It was late and the night banished the locals to their own hearths. Only desperate lunatics like Ranelaw traveled in such weather.

Dropping onto a bench near the fire, he ordered sirloin with potatoes and a tankard of ale. He was grateful none of the scattered patrons paid him a moment's attention. When the plump tavern maid sent him a meaningful glance, he ignored her.

He had enough woman trouble.

The beer arrived quickly. Ranelaw took a deep draft to wash the dust from his throat and tilted his head back against the dark wooden paneling behind him. He wished to hell his thoughts didn't immediately run to Antonia.

After last night, how could she leave? If she'd attained such a pitch of desire that she gave herself to him, surely she was as much victim to this attraction as he. He'd considered the act a beginning. She obviously believed it was an ending.

Well, he had news for her.

He'd taken his time so far, given her leeway to choose without undue compulsion. By bolting, she changed the game. That and the incomparable pleasure he'd found in her arms.

He'd have her again. Soon.

He opened his eyes and found himself staring at a man slumped over a table across the room. A well-dressed traveler, like Ranelaw, drinking alone.

Something about the shape of his head and his dark curls struck Ranelaw as familiar. The last thing he wanted was a coze with some acquaintance. He was about to glance away when it was too late. The man turned his head and stared straight at Ranelaw.

Johnny Benton. . .

Good God, what a turn-up for the books. He couldn't recall the last time he'd heard even a whisper about the coxcomb.

During his short career at Eton, Benton had been a year below him. The season Ranelaw came down from Oxford, Benton had been the toast of the *ton*. He'd fancied himself a poet. More beautiful than Byron, although sadly nothing like as talented, Benton had broken hearts all over Town and probably beyond. He'd been considered the handsomest man in England. Potteries had struck medallions of his profile. A portrait at the Royal Academy had set off riots. Ranelaw vaguely remembered the fellow hying for the Continent in the footsteps of Byron and Shelley.

Pretending he didn't recognize the puppy, Ranelaw stared down into his ale. Unfortunately his distinctive coloring meant nobody could mistake his identity.

"Gresham? It is you, isn't it? By Jove, I don't believe my eyes."

With a sinking sensation in his gut, Ranelaw found Benton hovering at his elbow, clutching a brandy and eager as a hound welcoming its master home.

"It's Ranelaw now," he said coldly. At school, he'd been known as the Earl of Gresham, one of his father's junior titles. Calling him Gresham proved how out of touch Benton was.

Benton frowned. "The pater passed on, did he? My condolences."

"Eight years ago," Ranelaw said with a lack of emotion he didn't have to feign.

"I've been in Italy." Without invitation, Benton sat opposite Ranelaw. "Only back a week ago."

He'd clearly left his manners in Tuscany or wherever he'd been skulking. Ranelaw leaned back, took a mouthful of ale, and observed the fellow.

He seemed . . . less.

He was still too pretty for a man, with his ruffled black locks and Roman profile. But there was a soft edge to his features as if over the years, he'd enjoyed too much food and wine and easy Italian living. The flashing dark eyes, celebrated by society papers and not a few poetesses, were dull and sunken.

Ranelaw wondered briefly if the man fell victim to opium or drink. It must be a good decade since he'd encountered the milksop, but Benton seemed to have aged at least twenty years.

"Going home, are you?" Ranelaw frowned. "Your people are in Devon, aren't they?"

"Yes. I'm on my way south now." With an unreadable expression, Benton brooded into his brandy. Fleetingly he looked like the poetical swain who had conquered society ten years ago. "I had . . . business in Northumberland."

A difficult silence fell. What the devil was the matter with the blockhead? He acted as if his dog had just died.

"Do you want another drink?" Ranelaw asked reluctantly as the maid slid a full plate in front of him.

Benton continued to contemplate his empty glass. "Bring the bottle."

The girl sent Benton the same flirtatious glance she'd cast Ranelaw. But Benton didn't even look up as he spoke. She flounced off and returned to slam a full bottle of brandy on the table. Benton refilled his glass with a shaking hand. In his hurry, he slopped some on the table.

Feeling distinctly uncomfortable, Ranelaw began to eat. The sooner he got out of here, the better. Benton showed no sign of moving on and was proving even worse company than anticipated. The fellow emptied his glass and filled it again, still with that prodigal clumsiness.

"You're drunk, man," Ranelaw said softly.

Benton shook his head and to Ranelaw's horror, a tear oozed down his cheek. "Not yet. But I will be." Before Ranelaw could think of anything to say, Benton fixed a bleary gaze on him. "Do you believe in the one?"

Ranelaw emptied his tankard and wondered how the hell to get rid of Benton. "The one what? God? King? Pope? The fucking Archbishop of Canterbury?"

Benton didn't react to the angry sarcasm. "The one woman. The girl who owns your heart forever. True love. Soul mates. You know, *the one*."

"No," Ranelaw said shortly.

He was trapped in hell. Was he hungry enough to make staying worthwhile?

"I do, damn it all." Benton drained his glass in a single swallow and filled it again with more finesse.

"I take it congratulations are due." Although if the bugger

contemplated marriage, he didn't seem particularly jolly at the prospect.

"Bloody hell." Benton's hand clenched around the glass before he flung it into the grate. The crash made heads turn with unwelcome curiosity.

Ranelaw gritted his teeth. Much more of this and he'd tell the numbskull to sod off. It was the kind of flamboyant gesture that had made Ranelaw despise Johnny Benton when they were younger. For all that, he couldn't mistake that under the flashy dramatics, the man was genuinely distraught.

"Wouldn't she have you?" Benton's seething despair demanded some response, even from a heartless bastard like Ranelaw.

Benton focused burning eyes upon him. "She's dead."

Good God.

Ranelaw wasn't sure what to say. He hadn't been a chum of Benton's. But it seemed cruel to abandon the man to his sorrow. "I'm sorry," Ranelaw said, knowing his words were inadequate.

Benton's eyes swam with tears, which damned well embarrassed Ranelaw even if they didn't embarrass him. "She's the one I'll never forget. She's written her name in my heart. Has that ever happened to you?"

"Hell, no," Ranelaw said with sincere horror, while that inconvenient voice reminded him of his astonishingly profound emotions when he'd thrust inside Antonia. He gave the taunting voice the cut direct.

"Then I feel sorry for you." Benton filled his glass again but didn't lift it.

Ranelaw bit back a heated retort. How dare a broken-down wreck like Benton pity the magnificent marquess? He took a vicious swipe at his sirloin and heartily wished he'd ridden on to London.

Benton addressed his glass. "Through ten years of exile, I couldn't forget her. I did wrong by her and now I'm back to remedy my evil. I prayed she was still free, that she'd marry me, in spite of what I'd done."

Ranelaw refrained from asking what Benton had done. Frankly he didn't much care. The story sounded banal in the extreme. All this lachrymose emotion put him off his dinner. With a grunt, he shoved his half-full plate away.

The fribble still maundered on. "I rode up to that gloomy pile in Northumberland and asked for her. Her brother saw me. More than I deserved. Her father would have chased me off with a shotgun. When I stated my honorable intentions, he informed me the lady died shortly after our last meeting."

He looked up with such misery, Ranelaw, who grew increasingly impatient, couldn't bring himself to up and leave. Much as he wanted to. He struggled to think of something to stem the man's torrent of confidences, but weariness and turmoil over his own chaotic love life kept him mute.

Benton went on, his voice raw with desperation. "How can my heart's darling be dead a decade without me knowing? How can I make peace with her after wronging her so egregiously?"

Ranelaw winced at the word *egregiously*, even when slurred with drink. Couldn't the scoundrel talk like a real person? "Buck up, old man."

Benton's mouth quivered and he stared down at the table. Ranelaw had no doubt the fellow fought more tears.

"You don't understand. Only someone who has loved as I have would understand."

"I'm sure."

Benton was too upset to notice his audience's lack of enthusiastic support. "Gresham, if you could have seen her. She was seventeen when we met and there's never been a woman to match her. Tall, hair a perfect silver blond, eyes the blue of the sky at dawn, skin like a white rose, lips like soft pink petals, a form Venus herself would envy. A low, sweet voice like the music of a cello. Clever and wise and witty. A brave, proud spirit. Rode a horse like an Amazon. And she loved me, she risked everything for me, for all that I deceived her."

It couldn't be . . .

Shock rocketed through Ranelaw, settled like a lead weight in his empty belly. This description sounded nauseatingly familiar.

He must be mistaken. He was obsessed with Antonia Smith. Benton couldn't be talking about her. That was too much of a coincidence.

Anyway, the chit Benton sniveled over was dead. Had been dead ten years.

And yet. . .

Still difficult to credit, but Antonia hadn't been a virgin when Ranelaw took her. At least one lover lurked in her past. Disbelief warred with the impossible suspicion that Antonia's previous lover must be this lugubrious weasel.

How many women had eyes that particular shade of blue, which, curse Benton, he could picture immediately? Eyes of that unusual blue and hair like moonlight? Benton couldn't have described her more accurately if Antonia had stood before them in all her splendor.

No, it was absurd. She preyed on his mind and inspired him to ridiculous fancy.

But he couldn't leave it alone. If he added up the years Benton mentioned, she was the right age. Fear of a scandal might explain why she bundled herself in those god-awful rags, hid behind tinted spectacles, and played a humble companion when anyone with eyes could tell blue blood ran in her veins.

Then there was her anomalous treatment from the Demarests. Her bedroom was suitable for an aristocratic lady. However fond Cassie was of her companion, this seemed generous provision for someone little above a servant.

Antonia, Benton's lover? Ranelaw couldn't believe it. He refused to believe it. She was a thousand times too good for the worm.

Benton sucked in a shuddering breath, then to Ranelaw's absolute disgust, lowered his head to the table and burst into theatrical sobs. The maid rushed to his side, bleating comfort, but Benton was beyond consolation.

Ranelaw scowled at the rogue's heaving shoulders while his brain worked busily at what he'd learned. Could Antonia be Benton's lost love?

Surely not. After all, Benton mentioned a brother and Antonia had no family. There must be other women in England who could carve a rift in a man's heart so deep that it never knitted. Other women who were tall and blond and had eyes the color of the sky.

Striving to rein in his rioting imagination, he shifted his gaze from the overwrought Benton to the congealing remains of his meal. His gut insisted that Antonia was Benton's mysterious beloved. His brain insisted she couldn't be.

The Antonia he knew wouldn't have a bar of this man's overweening vanity. She was too shrewd, too suspicious, and she had a jaded view of humanity, or at least the male half.

What if that jaded view resulted from her affair with Benton?

Because Ranelaw couldn't mistake the source of Benton's guilt. Ten years ago, Benton had been breathtakingly handsome. Antonia at seventeen would have seen considerably less of the world than she'd seen since. She wouldn't be the first female to fall for a pretty face with no character behind it.

Had this bastard ruined her?

Ranelaw clenched his hands on the table. The yen for violence was a rusty taste in his mouth. He burned to beat the slug to a bloody pulp.

Steady, man, you don't even know he's talking about Antonia. You leap to conclusions faster than a hungry trout leaps after a fly.

Nonetheless his gut assured him he was right. His gut was never wrong.

The mongrel deserved to roast in the lowest circle of hell. What right had he to place his hands on Antonia?

Ranelaw closed his eyes as fury surged, bathing him in stinging acid. Benton had known Antonia. Benton had heard those husky moans she made in the throes of climax. Benton had felt her passage tighten around him.

Ranelaw couldn't contain his anger when he pictured her in Benton's arms. Innocent, unprotected, and brought down by this man's selfish passion.

Benton needed to die slowly and in excruciating pain. And Ranelaw wanted the pleasure of killing the spineless son of a whore.

But as he glowered at the sobbing craven, he couldn't summon the stomach to challenge him.

Ranelaw needed to know for sure yet he couldn't bandy Antonia's name around a common tavern. And who could say the name would be familiar? Long ago he'd decided Smith was an alias.

"Oh, my love, my darling," Benton was moaning into his folded arms.

Ranelaw closed his ears to more of the same while he tried to calm the chaos of questions bubbling in his head. Antonia as Benton's paramour? Imagination, surely.

"Sweet, sweet Antonia . . ."

Antonia?

What the blazes? Surely he'd misheard.

Even if he had, it wasn't as if no other woman was called Antonia, especially in society's upper echelons. This still wasn't unassailable proof, even while his gut obstinately insisted that of course Benton was talking about *his* Antonia.

His Antonia who perhaps had once been Benton's Antonia, God rot the bastard.

He felt suddenly trapped, suffocated. He needed to get out of here. Before he did something rash like murder this mongrel. Assuming Antonia was Benton's long-lost and supposedly dead lover was crazy. He couldn't breathe without thinking of her. She made him mad. Fresh air might clear his head.

Abruptly he rose and scattered a handful of coins across the table. They landed with a rattle, but Benton didn't look up. He was too sunk in self-pity.

His belly churning with frustrated bloodlust and his mind buzzing with a thousand angry questions, Ranelaw strode into the freezing night and curtly ordered his horse.

Chapter Fifteen

𝒻OR a fortnight after returning to London, Antonia managed to restrict Cassie to quiet strolls in the park and a few small gatherings at the house. The girl's strength hadn't fully returned, but her determination to rejoin the social whirl was so powerful, that scarcely mattered. Antonia tried again and again to convince Cassie to return to Somerset to convalesce, but she became so upset at missing her first season that it seemed less injurious to her health to remain in Town.

Eventually Antonia reluctantly consented to accompany Cassie to the Merriweather ball. But only after extracting the strictest promise that if Cassie felt ill, they left.

Antonia was well aware it wasn't just Cassie's well-being that made her desperate to escape London. She'd be a hypocrite of the first rank if she pretended it was.

She'd hoped giving herself to Ranelaw would cool the heat in her blood. Instead it only stirred demons she thought she'd conquered ten years ago. Demons that now tormented her, broke her sleep, made her unusually intolerant of everyone around her.

Tonight she'd see Ranelaw. He had at least one spy in the household so he'd know their plans. She'd considered dismissing the entire staff, but that seemed unfair to the honest servants. Anyway, she had a healthy respect for Ranelaw's charm, not to mention his ready coin. She might as well stick to people familiar with the domestic routine.

Since their visit to Surrey, neither she nor Cassie had mentioned the disreputable marquess. He'd sent flowers and a note wishing Cassie a quick recovery, but Antonia hadn't remarked upon his bouquet among the hundreds Cassie received.

When they entered the crowded Merriweather ballroom, Antonia immediately scanned the throng, seeking a tall man with guinea gold hair. She told herself it was for Cassie's sake. She knew that for a lie.

The pressure around her chest eased when she realized Ranelaw wasn't present. He was such a striking man, she couldn't miss him.

Perhaps fate granted her one boon by keeping Lord Ranelaw away for the evening. Wild Antonia burned to see him, but her saner self had had time since that shattering encounter in the summerhouse to recognize the risks she took.

She turned to Cassie with her first genuine smile all night. "It's quite a crush."

Cassie looked ethereal and breathtakingly lovely in white silk, like a visitor from celestial realms. Antonia already noticed masculine heads turning in their direction. If she could divert Cassie's attention from Lord Ranelaw, a number of men here would make her cousin a suitable husband.

"It's going to be a wonderful ball." Cassie returned Antonia's smile.

Briefly Antonia forgot everything but the excitement in the girl's eyes. How wonderful to be so full of life and hope. She said a silent but fervent prayer that Cassie kept this joyful spirit, that nobody crushed her girlish dreams the way Antonia's had been crushed.

"Are you all right, Toni?"

Antonia realized she blinked back tears. Dear God, she needed to get a grip on her emotions or she'd make an utter spectacle of herself. She'd been on edge ever since leaving Surrey.

"Of course I am." She heard the betraying huskiness. If she wasn't careful, Cassie would suspect something momentous had happened at Pelham Place. "I'm just thinking how pretty you look."

Cassie thanked her very sweetly just before her coterie surrounded her. Most of her friends had called at the house during the fortnight—although thankfully not the Marquess of Ranelaw, which she knew irked Cassie.

Antonia lagged behind as her cousin glided through the crowd like a beautiful white swan. She'd never had a season, she'd broken all the rules before she entered the marriage mart. She wouldn't be human if occasionally she didn't envy these glowing, laughing young people.

You made your bed, my girl. Now you have to sleep on it.

She raised her chin, told herself to stop being a henwit, and made her sedate way to where she belonged, the chairs grouped in the corner. For one brief starlit moment, she'd become a woman who pursued what she wanted. That moment had passed.

The other duennas raised their heads and greeted her more warmly than she'd expected, although she soon realized they hankered after gossip about the house party. A chaperone's life was stultifying. Scandal was the only spice permitted these women.

She closed her eyes and let her mind drift with the lilting music. In her imagination, a man's arms enfolded her as they whirled around the room. Surely nobody could chide her if her fantasy man possessed Ranelaw's features.

When she opened her eyes, it was inevitable she saw Lord Ranelaw bowing over his hostess's hand and making her blush and giggle like a debutante. Antonia's heart crashed against her ribs and her breath jammed in her throat.

For one forbidden moment, Antonia drank in his sheer physical magnificence. The powerful body, the gleaming gold hair, the perfect profile as precise as if carved from marble. If she had to fall, at least she'd fallen to a man who made the stars stand still with breathless admiration. His was a harder, more ruthless beauty than Johnny's, and all the more compelling for that.

As if sensing her attention, he glanced up and unerringly caught her eye. Her heart, which had just begun to beat again, slammed to another stop. Across the distance, that obsidian gaze seared her. He claimed her with his eyes and she, poor, gullible fool, couldn't deny his unspoken demand.

She bit her lip and hot color flushed her cheeks. Thank goodness, nobody spared a moment's attention for a drab companion. To break that silent intensity, she stared down at her hands twining in her lap. She prayed the desire settling hot and heavy in her belly wasn't apparent on her face.

She very much feared it was. At least to someone as finely tuned to her reactions as Ranelaw.

After a breathless pause, she chanced another glance and caught a flicker of a self-satisfied smile. Oh, yes, he guessed the torrid images flooding her mind.

Damn him.

Cassie danced with Lord Soames but her gaze was fixed on the doorway. She sent Ranelaw a brilliant smile over her partner's shoulder. Ranelaw bowed with a depth that indicated interest.

Antonia's heart plummeted. Cassie's fascination with this notorious rake hadn't faded. How could it? Ranelaw was an intrinsically fascinating man. Who knew better than she?

She'd forgotten how her stomach coiled with dismay at every flirtatious glance between Cassie and Lord Ranelaw. Why in heaven's name had she become involved with him? She was such a stupid jade.

Then he cast her a taunting glance brimming with heated promise, and she answered that question. With one look, he transported her back to Pelham Place and the blazing sexual need that had propelled her into his arms beyond sense, beyond will, beyond self-preservation.

She'd become involved with him because she couldn't resist.

She was grimly aware she joined a long line of women

who embraced disaster for the sake of his lazy smile. A long line of women would come after her.

But nothing controlled the hard thump of her heart or the surge in her blood now she was in the same room as this depraved roué. Nothing stopped her skin aching for his touch. She'd wanted him from the moment she first saw him. Now, having known his possession, desire threatened to incinerate her where she sat.

The quadrille ended and Soames escorted Cassie back to her friends, lingering to talk to her. Antonia's glance sharpened as she observed the young earl. Soames was an eligible *parti*. He was in his twenties and she'd heard no vicious gossip about him. Compared to Ranelaw, he looked a callow boy. Unfortunately that was true for most of the men in this room.

Her mind buzzing, Antonia recalled entertainments they'd attended. Had Cassie shown any preference for the earl? She'd been too preoccupied with Ranelaw's courtship of Cassie—and his pursuit of her—to notice.

A waltz struck up. Ranelaw had respected Mr. Demarest's ban on the dance. Antonia watched him prowl the ballroom and couldn't help craning her neck to see which lady he favored.

Prior to their visit to Surrey, he'd made a point of dancing only with Cassie. Perhaps things had changed. Remarkably, he hadn't yet spoken to the girl.

Had his interest focused on some other woman? Was his flirtation with Cassie over? It seemed too good to be true.

Through her confusion, she watched him cut through the crowd like a shark slicing through deep water.

As he veered nearer, she noticed details she couldn't discern at a distance. Impossible to insist she wouldn't look. She was hungry for the sight of him. Had been since she'd fled the summerhouse.

His bright hair was longer and slightly disheveled, as though he'd run his hand through it. He looked tired, for all that he bristled with energy and determination.

She tried to stifle the instinctive impulse to comfort him. He didn't need comforting. Sharks were nothing but conscienceless predators, and God help any small fish swimming into their range.

She waited for him to select a partner yet still he advanced. Antonia devoted a bewildered moment to wondering what he was doing. Did he mean to slip onto the terrace?

All that lay in his path now was the gaggle of women who observed the festivities without partaking of them.

Oh, no. . .

Shocked denial pierced her as he strode nearer. Every step communicated his implacable determination.

He couldn't. Surely he couldn't.

He knew he couldn't single her out and expect her to emerge unscathed. He might be rash and selfish, but he was neither stupid nor spiteful.

She glanced to either side but none of the other chaperones noticed Ranelaw's approach. If he went through with this crazy plan, they would. So would every other person in this crowded ballroom. From this ballroom, the news would spread across polite society, branding Antonia a leper. Making people ask questions about Cassandra Demarest's chaperone. Perhaps even strip away her disguise to discern her true identity.

This was a catastrophe in the making.

Her heart drumming with terror, she lurched to her feet, ready to flee.

She was too late.

Ranelaw sent her a sly look under heavy eyelids and bowed deeply. As if she was an aristocratic guest and not merely the hired help.

"Miss Smith, may I request the honor of this waltz?"

Chapter Sixteen

*A*s Ranelaw loomed nearer, he watched horror dawn on Antonia's beautiful face. She wore her dowdy disguise, but these days, he couldn't regard her as anything other than spectacular.

"Go away," she growled under her breath. Behind her ugly spectacles, her eyes darted from side to side as if she sought some way of fending Ranelaw off without attracting notice.

"Miss Smith?" He didn't lower his voice. Challenging Antonia was always exhilarating.

"Stop it. I won't listen," she hissed, trying to sidestep.

He hemmed her in, easy when surrounded by so many chairs, most occupied. The old kitties finally noted the small drama. He read surprise and prurient curiosity in their faces.

"You'll generate considerably less interest if you agree to dance with me," he said in a low voice, seizing her arm in a grip that brooked no resistance.

For two weeks he'd wanted her, with a craving so painful and persistent it was like an illness. Touching her kicked his heart into a gallop. Through several layers of fabric, he felt her power and vigor. The same power and vigor that made possessing her such a world-shaking experience.

Even for a rake like him.

"You'll generate less interest if you go away," she muttered through her teeth. He saw her consider struggling, then decide, sensibly, that physical confrontation would only bolster gossip.

Smart girl.

"But I'm not going away," he said equably, striding toward the couples forming in the center of the room. To prevent him dragging her unceremoniously after him, Antonia was forced to follow.

Her hand covered his where it lay on her arm and she dug her fingernails in hard. Black lace gloves shielded her claws. Heat shuddered through him as he remembered her hands bunching in his shirt. She'd have drawn blood that night if he'd had the finesse to undress before tumbling her.

"I hate you," she said viciously.

"No, you don't." With a commanding movement, he swung her around to face him. "Now dance with me like a sweet little poppet or set tongues wagging."

"I hope you rot in hell." Under his hands, she vibrated with outrage. He'd intended the poppet remark to raise her hackles.

"That outcome is beyond argument, sweet Antonia." His devil-may-care smile was sure to stir any hackles *poppet* left undisturbed.

The waltz started and he swept her into a twirl. Excitement buzzed in his veins. Around them, curiosity rose to a cacophony.

"They know you're mocking me," she said without inflection, performing a perfect waltz step. She followed him with a lightness that made his heart dip with admiration. He'd known she'd dance like an angel.

"Let them think what they like."

He whirled her into a dizzying turn that had her hand clutching at his shoulder. Another memory shuddered through him, of her hands digging into his shoulders as he pressed his way inside her body. Since she'd deserted him, he'd relived every detail of that fierce encounter again and again. With her now, the vividness of the recollections left him shaking with desire.

He'd been unhappy, restless, irritable since leaving Surrey. He'd lived on memories of her. Her absence slowly strangled him. The instant he took Antonia in his arms, he breathed again.

"I'd rather they thought me the butt of a joke than guessed the truth," she sniped back.

"What is the truth, my lady mystery?" he asked silkily, performing another breathtaking turn.

For all her hostility, she moved smoothly. However they argued, physically they were in complete accord. His arm was firm and possessive around her lissome waist and their bodies were so close, her heat curled out to lure him. Her fresh scent teased. He drew it into his lungs and his curious sense of rightness crescendoed with the music.

"What are you up to, Ranelaw?" She glanced around fretfully.

All eyes fixed on them. Laughter, much of it cruel, lit the watching faces. Futile rage ripped at his gut. Antonia was worth a million of these self-satisfied fribbles. Hell, Antonia was worth a million of the Marquess of Ranelaw.

He'd walked into the room and immediately seen her in her frumpish costume. Something in him had mutinied. Society wits talked about diamonds of the first water, but for Ranelaw, Antonia was the one true gem among all these paste imitations.

By God, he'd make her shine before he was done.

"You shouldn't be sitting with the old tabbies."

She flushed with annoyance and her back was ramrod straight. Under the spectacles, she looked flustered and annoyed and poignantly young. "Yes, I should," she retorted through tight lips.

He fought a nigh irresistible urge to press his mouth to those lips until they parted and begged for more. Even for a libertine, publicly kissing a respectable woman was beyond the pale.

"You should be draped in silk and rubies, commanding the room with one flash from those ice blue eyes."

Before she could snap him down, he executed a series of turns that left her clinging just to stay upright. She drew a shuddering breath and the stiffness eased from her spine. Out of the corner of his eye, he caught Cassie staring with unguarded interest.

He shot her a triumphant grin—he felt triumphant, he danced with the woman he desired. To his shock, she grinned back. Not the polite, consciously appealing smile she usually awarded him, but a full-blooded grin.

"Please stop." Antonia clutched his shoulder as they circled the room. "You're making me a laughingstock."

"I want to dance with you," he said stubbornly, although he couldn't mistake the throbbing misery in her voice. His hand tightened, feeling the warmth of her skin through their gloves.

"I don't want to dance with you," she said with renewed defiance. Behind those distracting glasses, he caught the sparkle of anger. She didn't act like a servant. She acted like a lady playing at fancy dress.

"I can't dance with you, but you'll give yourself to me?" he asked slyly.

The blood drained from her face and she cast a horrified glance around the watching crowd. "We can't talk about that," she insisted in a frantic whisper. "Not here."

He blithely ignored her. They were far enough away from the other couples for privacy. "I want to do it again."

Aghast she stared at him. "No . . ."

He smiled at her. Surely she couldn't be surprised. He'd had her once, too briefly. Even so, it was the most intense sex he'd ever enjoyed. "Yes."

The prospect of another encounter was so intoxicating, he missed a step. She stumbled and for one breathless moment, her breasts slammed against his chest. Automatically his arm hooked around her back, crushing her. His heart battered his ribs.

"Ranelaw!" she gasped, struggling for balance. As she fought to straighten, she brushed against him. Her head jerked up and she stared appalled into his face.

She'd discovered how aroused he was. He'd wanted her the moment he saw her. After all this physical contact, he was as hard as an iron bar.

He glanced longingly at the open French doors. Through them waited a garden with dark walkways and hidden arbors. Two or three gliding steps and he'd whisk her into the night.

Two steps . . .

A soft breeze wafted through the doors, begging him to heed the impulse. Steal Antonia away to unbridled pleasure.

For all the lure of the forbidden, he didn't make that final move. Hell, now he was stuck having to restore himself to decency. He couldn't shame her by announcing to the world that she made him as randy as an untried boy.

Quickly she found her feet, forcing a small gap between them. He burned to snatch her against him. The bloody agony of it was that he couldn't. Not here.

This was death by desire.

She glanced down to his rampant cock and bit her lip. Sweet, fugitive color seeped under her skin. "You shouldn't have started this." For once, animosity was absent.

A rueful laugh escaped. "I couldn't help myself." Nothing less than the truth. "You're utterly irresistible." Again the truth.

"Stop it, Ranelaw," she snapped, her eyes lifting to clash with his.

"In Surrey you called me Nicholas."

"I'll call you lots of things before I'm done," she said sharply. "Take me back to the chaperones. You've made your point."

"What point is that, I wonder?"

Her lips flattened in disapproval and she glanced around the room again. Avid eyes fixed on them and derisive titters rose above the music. "That I'm completely susceptible to your machinations."

He frowned, firming his grip on her waist as he swung her around and around. "That's not true."

"Yes, it is." She lifted her chin with a pride that triggered the now familiar ache in his chest.

To his piercing regret, the waltz drew to a close. He'd managed to restore some control to his unruly body. The music's coda heralded the end of touching her. For tonight at least. Pussyfooting around social conventions was a bloody nuisance. He couldn't hope to get away with another dance. Even one was dangerous.

"I want you to myself." Much as he strove to sound the assured man of the world, ragged emotion edged the words. Every moment she moved so beautifully in his arms made him ache to get her alone. His hand trailed down her back in a surreptitious caress.

"Ranelaw . . ."

She paused and swallowed and for one searing instant, her hand clenched on his as if she too regretted parting. Her voice was so low, he had to bend to hear. Another drift of that clean, fiendishly enticing scent filled his head. He was sober as a judge, yet he felt drunk on finest brandy.

She spoke with difficulty. "Nicholas, we had . . . we had our occasion. I can't . . . I can't be sorry. But it can't be repeated."

"I refuse to accept that."

"You could so easily destroy me." Antonia's stare was a burning brand. "If anyone discovered what we did in Surrey, I'd be on the streets."

"You wouldn't be on the streets," he said in a harsh voice. "You'd be in my bed."

"For how long?" she asked dully.

Something in him wanted to insist he wouldn't use then discard her the way he used and discarded every woman he seduced. Innate honesty stifled easy promises.

She didn't wait for his answer. "I can only appeal to your

black heart. Please, if you possess an ounce of goodness, leave me alone. Leave Cassie alone."

Shame stirred in his gut. He hated it. And he hated Antonia Smith for making him acknowledge the bottomless abyss of selfishness within him.

Even hating her, he couldn't let her go.

"I can't leave you alone." He whirled her around for the waltz's last few bars, loathing that within seconds, he must release her.

"Please . . ."

Antonia Smith was a woman born to command, not to plead. Another sour punch of shame in his gut. She'd consign him to the lowest corner of Hades before they were done.

"You should save your scolding for a better man," he said with genuine regret.

Her lips turned down in cynical disapproval. Even under the hideous disguise, she looked like an angry goddess. "It's easy to be a better man, Nicholas. You just decide to do the right thing."

As the music descended to its final cadence, he burned to argue with her uncompromising statement. Instead he remained silent. She'd stared unflinching into his heart, and the barrenness there aroused only her contempt.

The waltz ended and Ranelaw released Antonia with a reluctance she felt in her blood. She hoped his lingering withdrawal wasn't as obvious to their audience. The room still buzzed with sniggering curiosity. All attention focused on Ranelaw and his drab partner.

Ranelaw extended his arm with a sardonic smile. Antonia curled her fingers around his elbow and raised her chin to hide her turmoil. What choice had she but to pass this off in high style? If she displayed embarrassment, the *ton*'s cats would shred her.

After ten unexceptional years, every move in the last few weeks set her teetering on the brink of disaster. The abrupt change left her giddy.

To her surprise and relief, Ranelaw didn't return her to the duennas but escorted her to Cassie and her friends. She wondered what Cassie made of Antonia dancing with Ranelaw. She wondered what Cassie made of Antonia dancing at all.

She hadn't danced since rare gatherings at Blaydon Park during her girlhood. After her elopement, opportunities for dancing became nonexistent. She'd forgotten how much she loved it. Furious as she was with Ranelaw for making a blatant show of her, joy had unfurled inside her to waltz in a swirl of music and color.

"Toni, I've never seen you dance." Cassie's voice was warm.

Half a dozen pairs of eyes settled on Antonia with malicious interest. She forced a smile although she felt shaken and edgy after touching Nicholas for the first time since making love. She released him and shifted to create some distance between them. Terrifying how difficult it was to relinquish the privilege of touching him. The link they'd forged in the summerhouse seemed to strengthen by the minute.

"Lord Ranelaw bet a crony that he'd get the fiercest of the chaperones to dance with him," she said, grateful the words emerged with dry amusement. A note of tolerant laughter that boys will be boys.

The look he cast her spoke volumes. She braced for him to contradict her.

"I wouldn't dream of employing such an unflattering description, Miss Smith." He bowed over her hand. Through her glove, her skin tautened with longing for the brush of his lips. To his credit and her grudging regret, he didn't make contact.

She breathed a surreptitious sigh of relief. He meant to cooperate. His hand briefly tightened and his black eyes glinted, brilliant with desire.

He turned to Cassie. "Miss Demarest, are you quite well again? I'm sorry illness marred your visit to Surrey."

He bowed over Cassie's hand with the same elegance he'd

directed at Antonia. Was she a fool to imagine his manner less engaged?

She was indeed a fool.

Cassie and Ranelaw started their usual flirtation. Antonia should curtail the encounter. She was so overset by the dance, she couldn't summon the will. Her heart pounded and her knees felt unsteady. Not because of the notice she'd attracted but because a notorious rake deigned to touch her. She sank deeper and deeper into the mire of sexual hunger. Nothing she'd felt with Johnny had prepared her for this gnawing, eternal craving for Ranelaw.

When she gave herself to him, she'd felt unfettered and reckless, as though she made a last throw of the dice. But after the game, gamblers went home with their winnings. She hadn't gauged how she'd react to his continued presence, to pretending nothing existed between them apart from the gulf separating their stations.

It was impossible to stand beside him without remembering how he'd ravished her. Nor to listen to the deep timbre of his voice without hearing his hoarse groans of release. Her senses flooded with his scent. As though he'd marked her that night the way an animal marked its mate.

Before Surrey, dealing with Lord Ranelaw had been difficult. Now they'd become lovers, it threatened to defeat her.

At least his public ease within Cassie's circle made the waltz seem less shocking, less a declaration of predatory intentions. Not that anyone imagined the high stickler Ranelaw could ever be moved to pursue a hag like her.

Of course his interest could make people look more closely at her. If he penetrated her disguise, so could other sharp eyes. Nervously she surveyed the ballroom, but people no longer paid her any attention. The hiss of scandalized whispers ebbed as it became clear this was a prank to put a too scrupulous chaperone at a disadvantage. The joke was on Antonia. But the joke was also on Ranelaw for partnering such a fright.

Ranelaw danced with Cassie, then excused himself after a volley of pretty compliments. He hardly cast Antonia another glance. But she knew, *she knew*, that he noted her every move.

Cassie went into supper with Lord Soames. Antonia took the opportunity to slip away. Cassie was safe with her friends. And this evening Nicholas had been uncharacteristically discreet about his interest in the girl.

The retiring room was down a long corridor on the floor above the ballroom. With everyone at supper, Antonia had it to herself. She made her way back when strong arms twined around her waist from behind.

"Let me go!" she gasped as her assailant dragged her into a side room and slammed the door behind them.

"Antonia, I need to see you."

"Nicholas, you've already caused too much talk tonight," she said repressively, even as her pulses leaped with forbidden excitement.

Of course it was Ranelaw. Nobody else would evince a moment's interest in dour Miss Smith. His touch had become so familiar, she'd know it blindfolded.

She tried to back away but only bumped the door behind her. They were in the library. A single lamp on an imposing Boulle desk provided illumination, leaving most of the room in shadow.

He traced her jaw with one finger and a faint smile lifted his sensual mouth. Traitorous warmth oozed through her veins. Her heart skipped a beat as she recognized again how his male beauty sliced away resistance. It was so unfair.

"My purpose isn't seduction."

She arched a skeptical eyebrow. "Really?"

She should have expected this. She'd recognized his hunger when they danced. But he must know they couldn't make love in the Merriweathers' elegant library in the middle of the famous annual ball.

Even Ranelaw couldn't be so foolhardy.

"Really." The smile faded and he stared hard into her face. She had the odd impression he struggled with what he wanted to say.

Nervousness stirred. A nervousness unconnected to the possibility of scandal. Her hands settled on his forearms with a naturalness she hardly noticed. He kept a firm hold of her waist.

"What is it?"

She stared into his dark face. Something was definitely wrong. A muscle jerked in his lean cheek and his voice was harsh.

"John Benton just arrived."

Chapter Seventeen

*R*ANELAW'S hands tightened as Antonia staggered. Until this moment, he still hadn't been completely sure Benton had been her lover. He was sure now. She made a choked sound of distress in her throat and her face turned paper white. Even her lips turned pale.

For one fraught moment, he wondered whether she'd faint.

She was stronger than that. After a moment's horrified silence, her chin tilted with false bravado. But nothing stopped her voice emerging in an unsteady whisper. "You know."

It wasn't a question.

"I guessed." His chest constricted with rage and a helpless ache to take away her pain.

Under his hands, she felt as fragile as a blade of grass. He had a sudden piercing memory of their first meeting, when he'd vowed to humble her haughtiness. Now he watched her pride crumble to dust, and he counted himself the lowest creature in existence. Her naked suffering made him want to flay Benton alive.

She continued to stare at him through those ugly spectacles. For once, he was glad they obscured her eyes.

"How?" She sounded as if forcing out even one word tested her.

"I met Benton in an inn. He spoke of you."

"Oh, God." She shuddered and sagged at the waist as if she suffered a blow. "Did you know before . . ."

"No," he said quickly. "No, not then."

"Of course you knew afterward," she said almost soundlessly, straightening with a jerk. Her lips were still that frightening color and there was no blood in her face at all. "A man of your experience would know he wasn't making love to a virgin."

"Antonia, stop it." He abhorred her desolation and the corroding shame beneath it. With sudden violence, he ripped off her spectacles and flung them onto the desk. "I don't care that you've had a lover."

"If that's true, you're the only person in Creation who doesn't," she said bitterly. Her eyes were glazed with betrayal and misery. "Now Johnny's tossing my name around a common tavern."

He grabbed her shoulders and fought the urge to shake some spirit back into her. Dear God, why couldn't she be angry? He couldn't endure this biting sorrow. "I met him when I rode back from Surrey. Nobody except me would recognize you from the description. And that he said you were unforgettable."

"How cozy." Her sarcasm did nothing to mask her crushing humiliation. "I imagine you compared notes. His recollections, of course, are ten years out of date, but you could offer something more recent."

He didn't bother gracing that with a rebuttal. "Antonia, he thinks you're dead."

"The woman he knows *is* dead." She stared at Ranelaw as if he was a stranger. Under his hands, she remained as pliant as a cloth doll. He loathed this. Loathed it more than he'd loathed anything since watching Eloise's life disintegrate when he was eleven.

"No, she's not dead," he said sharply, desperate to spark a response other than this terrifying blankness. "She's more alive than anyone I've ever met."

She hardly seemed to hear. "Do you know everything?" She closed her eyes and sucked in a quivering breath. "How you must have laughed."

His hands dug into her shoulders. She felt so brittle, he was afraid she'd shatter. "Not everything. I don't know who you are."

At last, the unnatural control cracked. Her mouth trembled and when she opened her eyes, they glittered with tears. "What does it matter? You know the most important fact. That I'm a whore."

"Antonia, my darling," he groaned, and dragged her against him, lifting one hand to press her head into his shoulder. His gut coiled with crippling grief. Her suffering shredded him to ribbons. The protectiveness he'd always refused to acknowledge surged like a boiling wave. He'd rather cut off his own arm than hear her denigrate herself. "Don't do this."

Briefly she resisted his embrace. Then she slumped on a shuddering exhalation. She threaded her arms around his waist, muffling her broken sobs in his coat.

As if his strength alone could keep the ravening world at bay, he wrapped her tight in his arms. Yearning to take her pain on himself. Yearning to shield her.

Of course he couldn't. He'd flirted with damnation too often to pose as anyone's savior.

Within too short a time, she withdrew, dashing at her eyes with unsteady hands. "If Johnny sees me here, everything is lost." Shakily she stepped back to lean against the desk. "He must continue to believe I'm dead."

She was right. She had to leave this house. Before encountering Benton. Before anyone saw her so obviously distraught. This at least Ranelaw could do for her.

His mind clicked into practicalities. "I'll fetch Cassie and have your carriage brought around the back."

"Won't that cause speculation?" Her voice was dull and her gaze skittered away from his.

"Even if your absence is noted, everyone knows Cassie's been ill."

Her face was still drawn although she wasn't crying anymore. He almost wished she would. Tears might be an improvement on her trembling desolation.

She raised her chin with a resurgence of the pride that had always struck him as completely unsuitable in a woman of her station. Whereas he discovered that the pride wasn't unsuitable, it was the station. He swore that before much longer, he'd find out exactly who she was.

"My lord, I'm grateful for your trouble. There's no reason you should aid me."

He laughed shortly and with a hint of grimness. Surely she knew by now that they were in this together. "Don't be a complete goose, Antonia."

He strode behind the desk and rifled through the drawers until he found what he wanted. He dipped a pen in the inkwell and passed it across, sliding a sheet of paper before her.

"Ask Cassie to meet you in the retiring room. It's the one place you're safe. Although Benton's such a milksop, he probably uses the ladies' facilities."

To his surprise, she released a choked laugh. "Poor Johnny. He never was a tower of strength." Then she sobered. "I hoped I wouldn't see him again."

If Ranelaw had his way, she *wouldn't* see the bastard again. Even if she wanted to. He extended the pen. "Write. We'll work out a strategy tomorrow."

She arched an eyebrow, reminding him of the woman who had fought him every step. He sent up hosannas of gratitude. He wanted her strong. Her wretchedness made him want to kill someone.

"We?" She took the pen and bent over the paper. She had slashing, quite masculine handwriting, he noticed.

"Yes. You and me." He waited for her to sign the note and seal it. His voice lowered into urgency. The need to be with her was a rushing torrent in his blood. He had an absurd fancy that he could keep her safe. Absurd when safety was the last thing a rapscallion like him could offer her. "Will you meet me tomorrow?"

A faint line between her blond brows, she stared at him. "Nicholas . . ."

She sounded uncertain rather than hostile. She must feel like her world disintegrated, leaving nowhere to hide.

"I can't bear to think of you facing all this alone. I want to help you."

"You want more than that," she said with a return of familiar wariness.

Just what did he want? The answer became more complicated by the day. He began to believe nothing less than all of her would satisfy him. God help her.

"Yes, I do. And so do you." He caught her arm with a gentleness that acknowledged her vulnerability. She stiffened but didn't pull free. "Antonia, don't come because you're afraid. Come because you want to. Come because you can't stay away."

Her eyes were troubled. "You think I'm too weak right now to say no."

Cupping her cheek, he fought the urge to kiss her within an inch of her life, until she forgot Benton and the threat of scandal. He ached to snatch her in his arms and steal her away to a place where gossip and old pain couldn't reach her. "I'll meet you at noon in the mews behind the house."

Already she shook her head. "Someone will see. And what will I tell Cassie?"

"You'll think of something." Suddenly he found himself smiling at her. Even with her cheeks sticky with tears and her beautiful eyes red and swollen, she was utterly glorious. "The woman who invented that story about a wager for a waltz can concoct a tale to satisfy a silly chit like Cassie."

"She's not a silly chit," Antonia said automatically. She paused, biting her lower lip. Her face was pale and set, as though she contemplated a death sentence instead of untold rapture. Suspense bunched his belly into knots until she nodded briefly. "It will have to be later. I'll meet you at six in the churchyard of St. Hilda's. It's near—"

His heart leaped with triumph. "I know it."

"If I can't be there . . ."

"You'll be there."

"Yes."

He swept her up in a hard, passionate kiss. She kissed him back without hesitation. She tasted of tears and desire. She tasted like everything he'd ever wanted.

Before the kiss took fire, he dragged himself away. The effort nearly killed him. He hated that they parted now, although he knew there was no choice.

Then tomorrow. . .

He raised her hand to his lips in a final kiss. "Go to the retiring room and wait for Cassie."

She nodded and slipped out without a backward glance. Ranelaw left the library and located a footman, pressing the note and a coin into his hand and requesting that he find Miss Cassandra Demarest. He sent another footman to arrange for the carriage to wait at the back gate.

How bizarre for such a disreputable rogue as he to protect a woman's honor.

Don't get used to it, man. You'll be her ruin before you're done.

The churchyard was empty when Antonia slipped through the gate, wearing a black hooded cape that turned her into just another anonymous female figure on the crowded streets. The evening was gray and cold, discouraging anyone from dawdling in the tumbledown graveyard. Even the weather conspired to grant her one last glimpse of ecstasy. She felt like a thief, stealing this single night of rapture before she returned to life as Antonia Smith.

After tonight, she'd go back to Bascombe Hailey and stay for as long as Mr. Demarest cared to employ her. Once he no longer had a use for her, she'd endeavor to find a position as companion to some reclusive old lady in the provinces or a middle-class family with aspirations to gentility. Somewhere that promised no contact with high society, including the decadent marquess.

She'd spent last night tossing in her bed, tortured by how quickly her restricted but safe little world unraveled. Tortured by whether she could risk meeting Nicholas. Now when Johnny's return made the possibility of her unmasking loom ominously close.

Eventually, weary of chasing grimmer and grimmer forecasts around her troubled mind, she'd risen to write to Cassie's father about Johnny's arrival. Once Mr. Demarest sent instructions for Cassie, Antonia would leave London. If she didn't hear quickly, she'd make arrangements on her own.

She'd devote the rest of her life to being good. Tonight she would be wicked.

Perhaps that was why she'd succumbed so swiftly to Nicholas's blandishments in the library. Or perhaps it was that he'd rushed to her rescue with a chivalry she still found difficult to credit.

When she realized he knew about Johnny, she'd wanted to crawl into a ditch and hide forever. His personal connection with her seducer made her stomach heave. She'd braced for Nicholas's contempt, but he hadn't played the hypocrite. Her heart had fisted with emotion when he'd so immediately taken her part. That heart had finally broken when he'd drawn her into his arms and held her while she cried for all the vile mistakes she'd made.

For a brief interval, he'd made her believe she was no longer alone against the world. That she had a stalwart and formidable ally in the Marquess of Ranelaw.

The memory of his strength shoring up her weakness had fundamentally changed the way she thought about him. And made it impossible to deny him—or herself. He'd made her believe that her reputation was secure with him. Not just hers, Cassie's too.

She was here now because Nicholas had kept her safe, because he'd been kind.

Don't lie, Antonia. You're here now because you want him and you always have.

She was half an hour early, which was dangerous. The longer she remained in public, the more likelihood of someone noticing her, remembering her. But she couldn't bear to loiter around the house any longer, awaiting the fateful hour.

Seeking the peace she usually found here, she glanced across the unkempt churchyard. She often took the short walk from the Demarest house to this haven of greenery. More often since she'd become entangled with Lord Ranelaw.

She missed Somerset's rural quiet. This hidden corner of London behind the beautiful little Christopher Wren church had become a refuge. She rarely encountered anyone. Even on a Sunday, the small, mainly artisan congregation wasn't inclined to linger among the memorials. Now she met Nicholas here, this wilderness would no longer offer sanctuary. Hardly important when she left for the country so soon.

Antonia wandered across to sit on a stone bench under a cherry tree. Inevitably she remembered the night Nicholas climbed through her window. She'd never understood why he hadn't seduced her then. Her resistance had been as flimsy as rice paper, they'd both known that. His abstinence made her wonder yet again if he was a better man than he admitted.

The lie a woman always told herself when she surrendered to a Lothario.

"Antonia."

The low rumble of Nicholas's voice behind her made her start. She turned around. He leaned against the tree trunk, watching her under lowered lids with a concentrated regard that shivered awareness across her skin.

"You sound surprised." She rose on unsteady legs.

"*You* sound nervous."

She realized she twisted her gloved hands. On a shaky breath, she lowered her hands to her sides. "I am."

Beneath the staccato conversation, attraction swirled and eddied. Luring Antonia to hurl herself at him and beg him to show her heaven. She'd long ago recognized something was wrong with her. Safe, good, sensible men never roused her interest. Only dangerous men made her heart beat faster.

Her soul was black with sin.

Sin had never looked so beautiful as it did in the person of Nicholas Challoner, Marquess of Ranelaw. The curling golden hair so striking against his dark skin. The remarkable face that concealed as much as it revealed. The black eyes sparkling with challenge and wickedness. And self-deprecating humor that might just prove his salvation.

He folded his arms across his chest. The curling brim of his hat shadowed his features and he wore a greatcoat that reached his ankles. "You're early."

She nodded jerkily. The continuing distance between them fed her disquiet. She'd imagined he'd lash his arms around her and save her from thinking. When he touched her, she could forget she broke every rule of propriety and morality. And common sense.

"So are you."

A sardonic smile tilted his long mouth. "Blame my eagerness."

He didn't sound eager. He sounded watchful, predatory. She'd taken an uncertain step back before she realized it betrayed her turmoil. The smile deepened, developed an unsettling element of seduction.

"I'm not going to eat you," he murmured. "Or at least not until I get you into bed."

She blushed. Unlike most unmarried women of her class, she knew exactly what he meant. Another of those shivers, half excitement, half terror, rippled through her. She raised a trembling hand to her chest, where her heart drummed so hard, it was as if it wanted to escape her body.

She felt drunk on a heady brew of desire and uncertainty.

He loomed closer, sliding his hands behind her head. Her skin heated under that fiery touch. "No spectacles today?"

Her body yearned toward him. "You know what I look like."

He stared at her as if he'd never seen her. "I know you're beautiful."

"Nicholas . . ." she whispered, helpless against the possessive light in his eyes. She strained up against his hold, wanting to kiss him more than she wanted to live. "Don't mock me."

"You take my breath away."

"I wish you'd take my breath away," she said with a hint of pique. He was supposed to be crazy for her. Yet he treated her as though she was spun glass.

The fascinating lines beside his eyes deepened with amusement. "You've become very demanding."

She made an irritated sound and stretched to press her mouth to his. For one giddy moment, she tasted the moist warmth of his breath, the satiny firmness of his lips. His tongue flicked out to touch hers. She sighed and leaned into him. Then, incredibly, he withdrew.

She frowned. "I don't understand."

With a wry laugh, he tugged her behind a moss-covered mausoleum, cracked and neglected like most of the monuments. She stumbled as he backed her against the cold, damp marble.

"God damn you, Antonia, I'm trying to act the civilized man."

"Why?" she whispered, curling her hand around one powerful shoulder.

He snatched her hand, bared the pale skin at her wrist, and kissed it. The brush of his mouth made her quiver with need. He spoke in a low, urgent tone. As if someone might overhear. "We're not safe. I've got a carriage waiting. How long can you stay?"

The word *stay* blazed through her like lightning. Because even if he asked her, she couldn't stay with him. This was one night snatched from the jaws of time.

Her voice shook. "Cassie's staying with the Merriweathers so she can attend Lady Northam's musicale tonight and the Parrys' Venetian breakfast tomorrow." Luckily Cassie had become fast friends with Suzannah Merriweather. Mrs. Merriweather had agreed to supervise Cassie's outings when Antonia claimed illness prevented her from fulfilling her duties.

"The servants?"

"Cassie's maid went with her. I gave the others the evening off. They're used to me fending for myself." She knew she took a crazy risk, that an overzealous maid might still check on her or some emergency with Cassie could require her presence. But even after weighing the dangers, the lure of one final taste of Nicholas's magic was too strong to resist.

His lips curved in a delighted smile. "So I have you until tomorrow?"

Banked fire lit his eyes. Antonia battled to cling to reality. She told herself this affair meant nothing to him, beyond transitory hunger. And perhaps the urge to dominate a woman who defied him. She was nothing special.

Her stupid, foolish heart refused to believe it.

Her stupid, foolish heart believed the next hours were as significant for him as for her. When he'd saved her from disaster at the ball, every barrier against him splintered. She hated her defenselessness even as she yielded. Because along with ruin, he promised limitless sensual satisfaction.

She wanted him as she'd never wanted another man. She was fatalistically aware that she'd never want another man this way again. Tonight would scar her soul. More deeply than her childish capitulation to Johnny's flattery and good looks. More deeply even than that titanic encounter at Pelham Place.

"Antonia?" His thumb stroked the back of her gloved hand with a rhythmic insistence that made her restless. "If you've changed your mind, I'll let you go. I shouldn't have pushed you last night."

His eyes were soft as they studied her face. She bit back

a surge of shame at what this man knew of her. But she read no condemnation in his expression, only concern for the woman who had cried in his arms. Concern and desire.

She was free to go, free to stay. Doubt and self-hatred receded. They'd return to savage her, she knew, but she wouldn't allow them to spoil her last night with Nicholas.

"You aren't forcing me to anything," she said softly.

He shot her a glittering, obsidian glance. "So I don't have to carry you away like a demon stealing your soul?"

She didn't smile. "Would you?"

He shook his head, suddenly somber. "No. I've had you willing. I want you willing again."

"I'm willing." She tried to sound teasing, amused. But it was impossible. Every breath she drew spelled the end of the world.

"Thank God," he said equally softly and pressed his mouth to hers again. She tasted yearning and arousal. He paused, and another shadow crossed his face. She tried to interpret the expression but it vanished too fast. "You ran away in Surrey."

With anyone except Nicholas, she'd imagine her precipitate departure from the summerhouse had hurt him. But of course no woman could hurt the Marquess of Ranelaw. Even so, she touched his angular jaw. "I ran like a startled rabbit. I was frightened."

He lifted one hand to press her palm against his face. "Not you. Nothing frightens you."

She gave a hollow laugh. "Everything frightens me." She swallowed and risked honesty. "You most of all."

He frowned. "I don't want you afraid of me."

"I'm afraid of what you make me feel. I'm a woman with better reasons than most to tread the straight and narrow."

"You're a woman made for love." For an electric moment, his final word hovered between them like a drawn sword.

"I'm a woman made for ruin," she said bitterly.

When they'd met, she'd believed him a man without a shred of empathy. Now she couldn't mistake the compassion darkening his face. "Oh, my dear," he said softly. "Your sin wasn't so great."

"You don't know," she whispered.

"Actually I think I do." He leaned forward to brush a piercingly sweet kiss across her lips. "We must go."

He released her and arranged her hood to shadow her face. The action conveyed a care that made her heart constrict.

She didn't deceive herself. He'd never place another person's needs above his own. She doubted he'd ever loved anyone. He certainly hadn't revealed any affection when speaking of his family. Were her occasional glimpses of a better man the result of her wishes outstripping her common sense?

Catching her hand, he led her toward the gate through the tangle of cow parsley and buttercups choking the graves. In the alley a nondescript carriage waited. She credited Nicholas's discretion. Again she struggled for an ounce of detachment. She reminded herself he was the veteran of years of intrigues, and discretion was second nature. Poignant emotion stifled the cynical thought.

It was like her lover was two separate men. The notorious rake Ranelaw. And Nicholas, who paused to adjust her hood so she wasn't exposed as the wanton she was.

Still without speaking, he opened the door for her to step inside. Her heart crashed against her chest as she climbed into the carriage. She entered Nicholas's dominion. She'd emerge a different woman. Already she knew that.

He followed and knocked on the ceiling. The carriage rolled into motion as he joined her on the cushioned bench. The seat was cramped and his thigh brushed hers. A wave of arousal made her head swim.

She waited for him to seize her.

He didn't move.

Eventually she slid back her hood and turned to him. He studied her with an unreadable expression. It wasn't his usual lazy sensuality or even the rapacious light she'd seen in the summerhouse.

For a long, breathless moment, they stared at each other. As if they sized up an enemy.

She didn't consciously move and she didn't notice him shift. Suddenly they clung to each other and his mouth crashed down on hers with a passion so powerful, it rattled the doors of heaven.

Chapter Eighteen

*R*AIN beat down, pounding on the roof with a thunder that vied with the thunder in Ranelaw's heart. The world shrank to the shadowy, lurching carriage and the hunger raging between him and this remarkable woman. Moments flowed into a shimmering continuity. He struggled to linger but it was impossible. Time slipped from his eager hands even as he entered eternity.

Eventually, reluctantly, he raised his head and stared at Antonia. In the dimness, she was flushed and her lips were red and full. Breathless tension twisted between them.

Very slowly she opened her eyes. She looked as dazed as he felt. As if that kiss swept her into a new world.

His breathing ragged, he shoved her cape aside and slipped his hand inside her bodice. She wore something wispy and pale with a blessedly low-cut bodice. Undressing her would be like opening a wonderful present. As his hand curled around her breast, she released a constricted moan.

His thumb flicked her beaded nipple. Her eyelids fluttered and her lips parted, giving him a glimpse of white teeth and the honeyed darkness within.

"I want you," he whispered, his voice barely audible over the vehicle's creak.

He firmed his hold on her breast and nipped at her lips, teasing her with his tongue. She growled and grabbed his head with an abandon that knocked his hat into the well between the seats. He dived into another devouring kiss, then pressed feverish kisses to her neck.

Clumsily she pushed aside his greatcoat and tugged at his clothes. Pleasure shuddered through him as she stroked his bare back. She must have removed her gloves after entering the carriage. In his urgency, he hadn't noticed.

Groaning, he grabbed her wandering hand and pressed it to the front of his trousers. As his cock swelled hard and greedy against her palm, she gasped. Closing his eyes, he drowned in hot sensation. Since Surrey, every cell had ached for her. Tonight finally he'd sate that excruciating craving.

"Yes," he hissed as her fingers curled to caress him.

He hooked one hand under her buttocks, squeezing her through her skirts. It was torture to venture so close to her center, but he recognized the limits of his control. If he touched her sex, he'd take her here, now, in this carriage.

After last time, he'd sworn he wouldn't fall on her like a starving lion. He'd explore paradise inch by inch, not in one headlong rush. Everything in Surrey had been so mad and passionate, he couldn't separate details from the explosive whole. Tonight he wanted to store away each shining second.

"Nicholas," she whispered, trailing her lips down his throat. She stroked his cock, building the pressure. His resolution faded.

"Mmm?"

She kissed along his jaw and up to his ear. Butterfly kisses. He'd insist she kissed him properly, if the phantom touch of her mouth wasn't so incendiary.

"Nicholas, we have to stop." Her words held a lovely hint of laughter. "The carriage isn't moving."

"I'm in no fit state to pay attention to carriages," he growled, grabbing her by the waist and tipping her against the bench.

She watched him with a sweet confusion that made his blood swirl with desire. "If your coachman opens the door, he'll blush."

"He knows better than to open the door." Ranelaw nuzzled her throat. She was delectable, rich and female, with that fresh scent he'd never identified. Except as essence of Antonia. "What's that perfume you're wearing?"

"I like it when you do that." She arched like a cat seeking a petting. He had a sudden vivid memory of the dragon chaperone. Who knew this wealth of sensuality lay concealed under that starchy exterior?

"Perfume?"

"I'm not wearing perfume." She insinuated her hands under his shirt once more and ran them up and down his back.

"Don't be absurd. You always wear it."

She released a breathless laugh. "Soap? Surely lavender is too prosaic to get you excited." She bumped her hips against his to confirm his excitement.

He smothered a groan. She obviously didn't realize how *excited* he was or she wouldn't tease. "Miss Smith, stop distracting me. We've reached our destination."

"Let me up. I want to see where we are," she said breathlessly.

"No great mystery. We're in the mews behind my house."

Her beguiling languor leached away. She stared up in horror. "I can't come to your house, Nicholas. I thought you understood."

He sat, drawing her upright even as he felt her resistance. "It's the safest place."

"Apart from the servants," she said acidly. "Who presumably possess eyes and ears and tongues."

He smoothed the pale hair that framed her flushed face. She looked thoroughly kissed and thoroughly annoyed. It made an enchanting mixture. A tide of emotion choked him. Something not altogether comfortable, something composed of protectiveness and admiration and a huge dollop of desire.

He welcomed overwhelming desire. After all, this attraction promised pleasure beyond his wildest dreams. But what he felt now went beyond mere attraction, set him teetering above a bottomless abyss.

"I've sent the servants away until tomorrow. Bob coachman knows I've brought a lady but he has no idea who you are. Anyway, he's as closemouthed as an oyster."

Praise heaven, the tension drained from her expression. "Thank you," she said in a low voice.

He leaned past her to raise the blinds. The world was awash with silvery sheets of rain. He could barely see the garden gate a few feet away. "We'll have to make a dash for it."

"Perhaps we should stay here."

He shot her a quick smile. "My plans require more space, beautiful girl."

He caught a flash of curiosity before she lowered her eyes. "Goodness gracious," she breathed.

Ranelaw retrieved his hat and placed it on his head. Antonia, looking enticingly rumpled, made an ineffectual attempt to order her clothing.

Gently he shifted her hands and hitched her bodice into decorum. The actions took longer than they should. Antonia wasn't the only one shaking with desire. He fastened the elaborate silver toggle on her cloak. It was a noblewoman's garment, not a companion's workaday covering. He beat back his curiosity. Questions could wait. Physical need couldn't.

Finally he pulled up the hood. "Ready?"

"Yes."

He read heat in her eyes. She wasn't merely consenting to a run through the rain. With that assent, she offered him surrender. The knowledge set his heart galloping like a wild horse.

He opened the door, kicked down the step and plunged into the storm. The water was frigid on his neck and face, pelting down with stinging force.

He laughed with the sheer joy of having the woman he wanted with him at last. Turning, he extended his arms. "Jump!"

* * *

Antonia hovered in the carriage doorway and stared at the tall man holding out his hands. Rain slicked over his fashionable hat, probably ruined it forever, and down the capes of his black greatcoat. He stood in a puddle, drenching his once-gleaming half boots in muddy water.

"Antonia! I'll catch you."

He sounded so strong, so steadfast. He didn't sound like the scoundrel who would shatter her heart. Although of course he would.

She had the strangest feeling that despite everything that had passed, this was the deciding moment. This was when she cast her fate to the winds.

Nicholas waited patiently, although he wasn't at heart a patient man. His eyes were steady, although he wasn't at heart a steady man either.

She smiled through the downpour. He smiled back with a devil-may-care insouciance that made her feel young and brave. She hadn't felt young and brave for ten long years.

Whispering a silent prayer, she drew a breath that tasted like rain and flung herself into Nicholas's arms.

Nicholas's arms closed hard and sure around Antonia and he swung her up against him. He wrapped the front of his greatcoat around her to shield her from the weather. Desperately she struggled against lapsing into a romantic stupor at this strong, handsome man carrying her. It was impossible. Her life had been devoid of girlish dreams since girlish dreams had nearly destroyed her. It seemed girlish dreams weren't so easily vanquished.

"I caught a mermaid," he said with a carefree laugh, striding toward the gate. The coachman splashed ahead to open it. She heard it shut behind them, enclosing her in a private world with Nicholas.

"A drowning mermaid." Antonia curled her arms around his neck and turned her face into his chest.

He'd told her she smelled like paradise. She couldn't

smell half as wonderful as he did. Clean male with a hint of laundry soap. And fresh, fresh rain. Rain that she prayed would wash away her sins.

Today, slung high in Nicholas's arms as he headed through a dripping garden to a large white house, she felt virginal. As if he drew her out of the storm and into a haven of safety and peace. As if he carried her over the threshold like a bride.

The bride she'd never be.

Her arms tightened around his neck and she pressed closer. The rain's icy bite made her shiver. In contrast, Nicholas was endlessly warm. A shelter against the weather. A shelter against unwelcome qualms.

She'd promised herself one night of passion. One night without future or past before she returned to Somerset and a life of perfect and stultifying virtue. Nothing would steal this away. Nothing. Not God. Not the devil. Not society. Not even her vulnerable heart.

With unmistakable purpose, Nicholas marched inside. Anticipation ripped through her. On this gloomy evening, the house was dim and mysterious. Antonia gathered a vague impression of a black and white tiled corridor lined with closed doors, then an imposing entrance hall in white marble that reflected the torrential rain falling against the windows.

Nicholas climbed a curved staircase flanked by huge, dark landscapes. As promised, she saw no servants.

"Welcome to my lair," he murmured, shouldering open a door.

It was a joke, but she couldn't contain a premonitory shiver. The room was shadowy, chilly. The candles offered little defense against the darkness.

"Damn me for a thoughtless dog," he said gruffly. "You're cold. I should have waited, got Bob to fetch an umbrella."

"No, I'm all right," she said huskily. Nicholas had taken much the worst of the weather. Her cloak was damp but underneath, she was relatively dry.

He carried her to the huge four-poster bed and after whipping her cloak away, laid her down with heart-stopping gentleness. The thick mattress sagged beneath her weight and the pillows were soft beneath her head.

He shucked the sodden greatcoat and joined her. As he knelt above her, he looked serious and intense. She'd arrived expecting blazing passion that would incinerate all her qualms. His care made her yearn hopelessly for more than just this one night.

"That's a pretty dress," he murmured, his eyes skimming her with glittering approval. Everywhere he glanced, her skin took fire.

"It's old."

The soft rose gown was hopelessly out of date. She hadn't worn it before although she'd packed it for her elopement with Johnny. She'd often wondered why she kept it. Except that it was pretty and expensive and it indicated dour Miss Smith hadn't completely subsumed Antonia Hilliard.

When she dressed to meet Ranelaw, her hand had automatically fallen on the garment. It belonged neither to Johnny Benton's adolescent lover nor to Cassie's frumpy companion. It was a dress without history—today she wanted to be a woman without history.

A ghost of a smile flickered. "It's from before you were Antonia Smith."

Startled, she met his gaze, although he must know or guess her entire sorry story by now. "Yes."

His voice deepened into rawness. "I need to see you."

For a fraught moment, emotion vibrated in the air. What she felt was strong enough to shift mountains. "Then undress me, Nicholas," she whispered.

His Christian name emerged perfectly naturally. She stroked the side of his face with a gesture that conveyed the tenderness blossoming inside her.

He kissed her softly. It wasn't a passionate claiming. Instead it was like the kiss he'd given her by the brook in Surrey, the kiss that had nearly broken her heart. This was the kiss a man gave the woman he loved. She blinked back stinging tears. She tried so hard to armor herself against him, but he put her completely at his mercy.

He undressed her with a dispatch that would disturb her if she hadn't noticed how his hands shook with desire. She emerged from her trance when only her filmy chemise remained. It was white silk embroidered with pink roses, another relic of reckless Lady Antonia Hilliard. Her hair tumbled around her shoulders in brazen disarray.

"Wait," she said in a thready voice she barely recognized. When she placed her palm on his chest, she felt his ragged breathing.

"Dear God, Antonia, don't torment me," he bit out.

"I need to see you too," she murmured, bunching his shirt in her hand and hauling him closer. "You're dressed for a duchess's garden party."

He laughed with the hint of self-deprecation that always beguiled. He caught her hand, pressing it again to the front of his trousers. "I'd shock the duchess."

"Any duchess worth her salt would lure you away for a private interview." Trembling with need, she fumbled with the front fall and slid her hand inside. His stomach tensed to rock hardness under her searching fingers.

At last, at last, she held his pulsing, heavy rod. Her excitement built, set her heart thundering.

"You drive me mad," he groaned, flexing his hips.

She firmed her grip, marveling at his heat and strength. It was like trying to contain some mighty force of nature. "Poor duchess doesn't know what she's missing."

With visible reluctance, he drew her hand away and kissed it. "What happened to my beautiful lady with the sharp tongue?"

"She fell under a rake's spell." She couldn't mistake his hunger. Her confidence surged along with her arousal. Rising on her knees, she ripped his neck cloth away. "Will you take off your coat or will I?"

With gratifying swiftness, he shrugged out of his coat

and tossed it on the floor. He tugged his shirt over his head, ruffling his dark gold hair. He looked like an untidy angel. Except there was more devil than angel in this wicked marquess.

As she stared at his bare chest, her mouth dried with awe and blazing anticipation. She couldn't shift her eyes from the taut expanse of skin scattered with golden hair. She licked her lips and noticed how his feverish attention focused on the betraying movement.

"Take off your trousers," she said in a voice harsh with control. She expected him to object to her commands. But he immediately rose from the bed, tugging off his shoes with more haste than grace before shedding his trousers.

Her heart crashed against her ribs. His nakedness struck her silent. He seemed too beautiful to be human. Too beautiful for the earthy reality of lovemaking.

Inevitably her gaze leveled on the part of him she'd so recently touched. He looked impossibly proportioned, big enough to tear her apart. He was hard and ready for her. Her eyes widened with shock as she watched him grow even larger. No wonder she'd felt invaded in the summerhouse. She raised her eyes to his, expecting him to appear proud, superior, triumphant.

His gaze focused fierce and unwavering on her face. His shoulders heaved with the effort of dragging air into his lungs. At his sides, his hands clenched and unclenched as if he battled the urge to grab her.

With a start, she realized he wasn't basking in victory. Instead he was utterly captive to need. If she was helpless against this magic, so was he.

His unabashed hunger made her burn for the touch of his hands, the weight of his body over her. Once before, she'd known the fierceness of his possession. She ached to know it again. Her breasts swelled against the silk of her chemise. The fine material tormented her sensitive nipples, made her shift restlessly.

Still he didn't touch her. He just stood and let her stare.

Or perhaps he poised in breathless suspense, awaiting her invitation.

"Antonia, for God's sake . . ." he forced out.

Aware she tormented him, she bit her lip. Anticipation made her belly twist and tighten. Hot moisture welled between her legs. She sucked in a breath that hurt and grabbed her shift in shaking hands. Clumsily she wrenched the final covering over her head.

Nicholas's face sharpened with hunger. His expression was so raw, she'd recoil if she didn't feel equal extremity. This was why she'd been unable to resist coming to him tonight, whatever the risk. This passion. This craving. This searing connection.

A dizzying sensation of power flooded her. She shook her hair back from her shoulders and inhaled so her breasts begged for his touch.

She swallowed to moisten her parched throat. She swallowed again and forced out the only words she needed.

"Nicholas, take me."

Chapter Nineteen

ANTONIA'S husky invitation incinerated Ranelaw's restraint.

Swiftly he crossed the room and covered her body with his. His hands closed around her hips. He peppered her throat and shoulders with a rain of kisses more savage than the tempest that rattled the windows. The tempest raged inside him. She stirred him as no woman ever had.

Through weeks of sleepless nights, he'd pictured her nakedness. In life she exceeded every fantasy, beggaring eloquence. She was glorious. Her form ripe and curved, the skin warm and creamy in the flickering candlelight. She promised an empire of pleasure.

He'd devoted more time than he wished to admit to wondering what color her nipples were. Pale pink? Dark rose? Brown? Her nipples were the rich red of summer raspberries. Puckered against her white skin, they were a sight to make a man grateful he was alive.

She protested under his frenzy, half laughing so he knew she didn't mind his eagerness. Through the thunder in his blood, he realized he must be crushing her. He struggled to leash the ravening beast as he raised his head to stare at her. She was flushed with arousal and her lips were lush and full after his rough kisses.

The sight of Antonia's nakedness, the vulnerability in her

eyes, sliced at him with unfamiliar poignancy. He wasn't used to sex having this emotional dimension. He might be supremely confident in the physical realm but this night, this woman, demanded more. A more that he wasn't sure he was capable of delivering.

His hand mortifyingly unsteady, he reached out to stroke one tight peak, then the other. She released a whimper of pleasure and the pale areolas flushed darker pink. He already knew her breasts were deliciously sensitive but seeing her tremble when he touched her pearled nipples blasted arousal through him. And more of that unwelcome emotional need.

Ranelaw was a passionate man. Of course he wanted to possess her body. But every moment that passed bolstered the unwilling recognition that he also sought less tangible treasure from Antonia. Her strength. Her trust. The gift of her bright, passionate spirit.

"Beautiful," he whispered, dipping to kiss one quivering tip.

She arched toward him and her grip on his shoulders tightened. With voluptuous enjoyment, he sucked her nipple between his lips, drawing on it, circling it with his tongue.

He dipped his hand to the feathery curls at the base of her belly, stroking, testing, teasing. He scraped his teeth against her nipple and she rewarded him with a sobbing moan.

The freedom to touch her like this made him burn with satisfaction. She'd led him such a dance. Now she was in his arms. He still hardly credited it. He bit down on her breast before lifting his head.

Last time, he'd made love to her in the dark. This time, he intended to watch every reaction cross her lovely face.

"Don't stop," she begged hoarsely, pushing up into his hand and parting her legs to give him access.

"Never." Touching her was like basking in sunlight. Before this, his life had been so cold. He kissed a random path across the beautiful breasts that had haunted his imagination. "You don't know how much I want you."

"You've got me," she whispered.

If only that were true. Even now, he wasn't sure of her. The urge to claim and keep burgeoned, and for once he didn't try and reason away his possessive urges. Desire blasted reason to ash, revealing the primitive who recognized only passion's dominion.

He slid his fingers along the sleek folds. She released a strangled sound and jerked. Then jerked again when he concentrated on her center. She felt like hot, wet silk. With purposeful slowness, he built her need, using his hand between her legs and his mouth on her breasts.

Her hands dug hard into his head, tangled in his hair, held him closer. Only when her breathing was a tattered staccato did he relent. He trailed his lips across the soft plain of her stomach, then gripped her thighs in both hands and parted her legs.

His belly cramped with excitement.

Avidly he drank in the sight of her sex. Plump, pink, glistening. The sharp scent of her arousal made his head swim. Or perhaps that was the wild pounding of his yearning heart.

Lingeringly he kissed her there, tasting salty desire. She was so primed, within seconds she began to tremble and cry out. He'd never been so attuned to a lover's response. Her rhythmic moans created a delicious counterpoint to his depredations.

He lapped at her and slid a finger into her passage, working in time with the flick of his tongue. On a broken moan, she tightened to keep him. The physical verged into a new realm when he took her in his arms. If he wasn't so aroused, he'd be bloody terrified.

He penetrated deep and felt the precise moment her hold on reality snapped.

Ah, yes . . .

Her sobbing rapture was the sweetest sound in the world. Still he didn't stop. She'd driven him to the verge of madness. He intended to return the favor. He'd pleasure her until she disintegrated. Then he'd make her anew with his name inscribed on each spectacular inch of her.

She would be his. Utterly.

What created this uncontrollable hunger to possess every atom of Antonia? Right now, he was so lost to sensation, he hardly cared.

She still quaked when he set to build another climax. Her fingers speared his hair, tugged hard. He drank of her, used teeth, tongue, lips to summon that wild crescendo.

With shocking swiftness, she tautened into her peak. Her responsiveness astonished him. Flooded him with poignant wonder. Fantasies of having her had tormented him for so long. The reality surpassed his dreams, left him reeling.

He wanted to send her across the barrier again. He wanted her delirious with ecstasy, addicted to him. He wanted her very blood singing his name. The craving to thrust into her threatened to obliterate him, but having her spread out before him like a banquet offered its own satisfaction.

"Nicholas . . ." she begged in a cracked voice, even as the hands she buried in his hair loosened to a languid caress. "Nicholas, wait."

The sound of *Nicholas* on her lips was like music. He'd make her scream his name before he was done. Luxuriously he licked her again, probing the wet, delicate folds. He'd envisioned this moment too long to rush. In Surrey he'd made that fatal mistake and she'd deserted him.

"Nicholas . . ." Her voice faded on a sigh as he tasted her again, relishing her musky flavor. She dug her fingers into his scalp. "Nicholas, please."

Reluctantly he raised his head. She looked feverish and frantic.

"Don't you like it?"

His voice was gravelly. Her essence was rich on his tongue. He wanted more of her. Hell, he always wanted more of her.

"Of course I like it." Irritation burred her answer. She slid up against the headboard, her beautiful breasts rising and falling with each choppy breath. "You know I do."

"Then why stop?"

Her legs cradled his shoulders and her hot scent was more intoxicating than any wine. He could taste her on his lips. Delicious.

"Because . . ." She swallowed and lowered her eyelashes to evade his searching gaze. "You know why."

His voice lowered into persuasion. "Tell me what you want, Antonia. *Tell me.*"

A choked whisper emerged and color surged into her cheeks. "I want you to stop teasing me."

He couldn't help smiling. "You'll have to be more specific."

Her chin lifted and she shot him an annoyed glance under her lashes. "I want . . ."

"Yes?"

"Curse you, Ranelaw," she snapped, staring at him directly out of eyes heavy with arousal. The effect was wildly inflammatory when she stretched naked before him, her full breasts quivering with each unsteady breath and her sex open to his gaze.

His smile broadened. "That's no answer."

"You leave me no pride." She blasted him with another incendiary azure glance. "I want you inside me. I want you to fill me until there's room for nothing else, not thought or guilt or regret. I want you to stop treating me like a toy and accept that here we're equals."

Antonia . . .

Hell and the devil. Any impulse to tease disintegrated in a flare of heat. Her words laid claim to his soul.

Even as he struggled to come to terms with her searing honesty, she continued in the same low voice. "I want you to make the world outside this room disappear. I want you to pound into me so hard, I only feel you, I only know you, I only think of you."

She faltered into silence. She breathed rapidly, unevenly. Her gaze fixed on him, hot as fire. Conflicting emotions flickered across her face.

Vulnerability. Of course. Her frankness left her undefended.

Fear. Courage. Challenge.

Above all, desire.

Slowly he sat up, his eyes not wavering from hers. She made a mockery of his defenses. How ironic to think he'd devoted such effort to conquering her, only to recognize she was in the end the victor.

He wanted her more than he'd ever wanted another woman. Worse, she exerted a pull on his emotions he'd never felt before. And he didn't know how to break this fatal fascination.

"Antonia, I don't deserve you," he said with utter sincerity.

With every moment, this encounter swept him further from the safe harbor of easy lust. He'd always known Antonia would be extraordinary. Now he realized she would mark him so deeply that he'd never be free of her.

Her dark blond eyelashes fluttered down then up again. An uncertain smile curved her lips. "Have I shocked you?"

"No . . ." Then he recognized her candor merited better return than face-saving denial. He leaned over her, supporting himself on his arms. His heart pounded so hard, he thought it must crash from his chest. "Yes."

She tilted her head to meet his eyes. The blue was so clear, he saw all the way to her soul. He'd spoken the truth when he said he didn't deserve her. The tragedy was at some profound level, he wished he did.

"Kiss me, Nicholas."

He obliged. Such passion. Such desire. *Antonia . . .*

When finally he lifted his head, her eyes were brilliant with excitement. Her voice was throaty as she shifted down the bed to lie under him. "Now, Nicholas."

At last . . .

The moment stretched into infinity as Ranelaw angled

his hips and slowly pushed inside Antonia. Immediately he experienced that sense of homecoming. As though in all the turbulent world, this was the place he belonged.

She was taut, trembling, drawing him in. Her face was strained as though, like him, she recognized the importance of this joining.

Even though the need for completion blared in his head like a company of trumpets, he resisted the urge to thrust.

Take her. Take her. Take her.

But the tenderness that lit his passion like the last glow of sunset made him pause, take his time, ensure her pleasure. Beneath his physical hunger lurked a need to cherish this woman, with her spirit and beauty.

She sighed, a shaky exhalation, and shifted to take more of him. She linked her hands behind his neck. "Nicholas, don't play games."

Again the sound of his name pierced him to the bone. Such effortless power she exerted. "I'm trying . . . to demonstrate control," he muttered.

"I don't care," she said roughly, arching with a restless ardor that set his pulse thundering. Her squirming promised to hurtle him over the edge.

He gritted his teeth and bent her knees around his hips. The change in position squeezed the head of his cock. He bit back a tormented groan. And tried to remember why he didn't claim her in one deep lunge. "I do care."

I do care . . .

Brief clarity blasted through the scarlet fog of passion. God save him, he did care about her. As more than a willing bed partner, magnificent as she was in his arms.

He barricaded himself against the unwelcome revelation. Easy when this woman rocketed good intentions to the skies.

Had she even heard his broken, unprecedented confession? He set out to make her forget his foolish words, drown their echo in passion. But whatever he did, the reverence underscoring his every touch declaimed the unwelcome truth.

He cared for her.

Desperate to stifle discomfiting emotion, he inched further. She was hot as a furnace and drenched with desire. Her breath emerged in frantic gusts and her fingernails raked his shoulders. The sting was negligible compared to the agony in his balls as he battled to delay possession. To tease her into pleasure.

Although this didn't feel like anything as trivial as teasing. This union sent the planets spinning from their orbits.

She whimpered and her fingernails dug deeper. He'd emerge from this night as bloody as if he'd fought off an angry tigress.

Oh, yes, she was a tigress. He'd always loved that about her.

His muscles screaming, he made another incremental advance. Her choked whimper combined distress and pleasure. The sound roared through his blood.

More minuscule progression. His vision narrowed to a tunnel. He saw only Antonia. Her skin gleamed with a fine sheen of sweat. Her breasts shook with the shuddering force of each breath. Her hands opened and shut on his shoulders in frantic supplication.

With a clumsiness born of frustration, she twined her legs around his buttocks, forcing him down. Resistance was excruciating, but resist he did.

"Please . . ." she begged in a cracked voice. "Oh, please . . ."

Her unabashed need jolted hunger through him. He couldn't delay much longer. Red lights flashed behind his eyes as he struggled for one last, quaking moment of restraint before he yielded to the whirlwind.

From his depths emerged words he'd never thought to speak to a woman. In a final flash, before he sank into mindless passion, he recognized this was why he shoved her so pitilessly to the brink.

"Say you're mine," he growled in a voice he didn't recognize. "Damn it, say you're mine, Antonia."

She hardly seemed to hear. She'd retreated into sensation. Each breath emerged as a strangled moan and she tossed her head side to side against the pillows. Her lashes fluttered against her cheeks. She looked as though he tortured her.

He rose to his knees and shifted his hands to her hips, hauling her into him without giving her what she wanted. She wriggled, sliding closer with a sinuous strength that tested his last shreds of control.

"Say it," he repeated in that same guttural voice.

"Nicholas . . ." she whispered in helpless pleading. Her hands left his shoulders and closed like shackles around his straining forearms.

"Say it . . ."

She opened her eyes and stared up. Her gaze was opaque. "I . . ."

"Say it, Antonia," he snarled, edging a fraction further. Her muscles contracted as she struggled to draw him deeper. Each tiny movement shot flame through his head, singed his mind.

"I . . ."

Her face was stark with arousal, with longing, with discomfort. He knew what he did tried her to her physical limits. Her nails scored his flesh like knives.

"Say it." For all his pride and determination, he knew he couldn't hold back much longer.

"I . . ."

She surged up and in a conflagration of light, he lost his futile battle. With a broken groan, he buried himself to the hilt. He slumped forward as she closed around him.

As if she never meant to let him go.

She inhaled on a jagged sigh and shifted, her beaded nipples grazing his chest with sweet friction. "I'm yours," she whispered.

The shaken confession etched itself on his skin. He released his breath in a powerful gasp and closed his eyes, seeking triumph.

And found none.

He hadn't won this war between them. Because her admission echoed the words ripping at his heart.

That if she was his, he was hers. Forever.

Chapter Twenty

ANTONIA firmed her hold on Nicholas's sweat-sleeked back and felt the trembling tension in his muscles. She was overwhelmingly conscious of the throbbing, massive invasion of her body. His weight and hard power pinned her beneath him. He held preternaturally still as though her unwilling, broken confession turned him to stone.

Then with a desperation that both thrilled and terrified her, he began to move. The fierce purpose of his thrusts pounded her deep into the mattress and set the bed creaking. It was as though he struggled to hammer them together into a single entity, a pure infinity of passion forged from crackling flame. The wildness of his possession unleashed an answering wildness in her. Taut as a piano wire, she shuddered, her fingers digging into his shoulders. Hot need spiraled higher with every thrust.

His fury quickly tore Antonia from the world and flung her screaming into a fiery heaven. The climax threatened to rend her into tatters. For a long moment, she knew nothing except the dark fire lashing her.

For a blazing eternity, he held her quivering at the extremity of rapture. His hands tightened around her hips, hard enough to bruise, keeping her safe as lightning raged around her. She closed her eyes against blinding light and surrendered.

Through the violent, buffeting storm, she felt Nicholas jerk in uncontrollable release. He groaned and flung his head back, the tendons in his neck standing out as he pumped into her. Hot liquid spurted deep inside her, flooding her womb.

Even as she gradually slipped from the dazzling heights, the radiance remained. When she drifted back to reality, Nicholas was crushing her into the bed, forcing the breath from her lungs. Sticky tears drenched her cheeks and her belly quaked with the aftermath of bliss.

After this, how could she live without him?

Ranelaw buried his head in the curve of Antonia's shoulder. The scent of strenuous sexual fulfillment surrounded him. His blood pulsed in heavy waves. Velvet oblivion beckoned.

In all his life, he'd never felt so good.

Too good to shatter the moment.

He still wandered among the stars, a lost explorer in the wide reaches of sky. He'd always considered himself a connoisseur of the sensual arts. A man who knew all about sex and its pleasures. How wrong he'd been. Hell, before tonight, he'd had no idea.

Eventually he snagged one of the jumbled thoughts drifting through his mind and realized he must be squashing Antonia. She was a tall, strong woman, perfectly formed for a man like him, but even so, he was a dead weight. He braced to slide free of her body, although he loved to rest inside her and feel the soft clasp of her muscles as she descended.

"No," she murmured in drowsy protest when he shifted.

She was rubbing his back in circular movements. His heart skipped a beat every time she stopped and started again. She still had a lamentable ability to affect his pulse. Even now when desire was a slow simmer not a raging forest fire.

"I should move." He didn't budge in case he disrupted those languorous caresses. If he was a cat, he'd purr.

"Not yet."

On a sigh, he decided against arguing. He didn't want to spoil this silent communication flowing like a calm ocean between them.

He knew he surrendered to self-delusion as unrelated to harsh reality as an opium addict's fantasies. But the knowledge couldn't compete with the soft pleasure of lying here with the woman he'd wanted for so long and who at last gave herself to him without demur. Antonia surrounded him. Her hair, her skin, her scent.

Time and necessity blurred into a golden haze. He floated in a pleasurable dream as his body gradually quieted.

He summoned his last ounce of strength to turn his head and place an exhausted kiss on the side of her neck. He clung to the dream a little longer, then forced himself to speak. "I wasn't careful."

Her hands paused in their fiendishly sweet movements and he felt her struggle for breath. Because of his weight or because of what he said?

After a silence, she started to stroke him again. Her voice emerged with a steadiness that surprised him. "There's nothing we can do about it."

He frowned into the soft cushion of lavender-scented hair. That response seemed uncharacteristically fatalistic. He needed to see her face. Her words told him nothing.

At last, reluctantly, stiffly, he rolled off her. As their bodies separated, he stifled a pang of sorrow. For too fleeting an interval, life had been perfect. He wasn't yet ready to relinquish that heaven.

Rising on one elbow, he rested his head on his palm. "In Surrey, I promised to protect you from a child."

With a slight wince, she lifted herself on the pillows and pushed her hair off her face. He imagined she must ache after that untamed mating. He'd used her hard and without mercy. But then he checked more closely and masculine satisfaction swamped any guilt. She looked like a rumpled, well-pleasured goddess.

Her eyes were grave but clear as they leveled upon him. "Neither of us was thinking just now."

Her calmness left him puzzled, mistrustful. He'd expected her to be angry at his carelessness. Hell, he was angry at his carelessness. "There could be repercussions," he said with studied mildness.

A shadow flickered across her face. To his regret, she tugged the sheet up to cover her nakedness. "I . . . I didn't fall pregnant when I was with Johnny," she said in a faltering voice.

Like that, Benton's name ripped a jagged chasm between them.

Ranelaw struggled to say something. Something that wasn't a furious question about how a woman like her could ever imagine herself infatuated with that sapskull.

After a fraught pause, she spoke. "Maybe I'm barren."

And maybe Benton wasn't man enough to get a child on you.

Of course Ranelaw couldn't say that, however his gut twisted with frustrated rage. What right had he to deride Benton? It was the height of hypocrisy to want to murder the cur just for the crime of touching Antonia.

The silence that descended bristled with difficult questions.

Eventually he could no longer endure his clamoring curiosity. As he couldn't endure not touching her. He caught her hand in his, gripping hard. The contact immediately settled the restless brute inside him in a way he didn't want to examine.

He inhaled and voiced the question that had tormented him since he'd discovered she wasn't a virgin.

"Will you tell me about Benton?"

Antonia had dreaded this moment, even as she'd known it must come.

Old misery flooded her. Whenever she contemplated

her youthful sins, shame coiled in her stomach like angry snakes. Tonight was meant to be an occasion of joyous pleasure that she'd remember forever. It wasn't meant to be about her guilty secrets.

The full, disastrous story remained locked in her heart. She'd never really spoken about what had happened when she was a girl. The last person she should ever confide in was a man notorious from one end of the kingdom to the other for his profligate appetites.

She prepared to tell Nicholas to mind his own affairs. To insist she owed him no explanation. To point out such a libertine was in no position to demand an accounting of a lover's past liaisons.

Antonia opened her mouth to give Nicholas the setdown he deserved. Different words emerged. "Johnny was at Oxford with my brother. He came to stay with my family the summer I turned seventeen."

"Benton recognized your beauty from the first, didn't he?" Nicholas's tone was edged with anger—for her or her lover?—but his grasp on her hand conveyed more of that damned tenderness. The tenderness she resented because it made her yearn so fiercely for more.

"He certainly flattered me," she said expressionlessly.

Nicholas withdrew his hand. Immediately she missed his touch. *Poor, pathetic Antonia.*

He rolled to his side again and took up his watchful pose with his head resting on one hand. Displeasure lengthened his mouth. "I'll wager the bastard wrote sonnets enough to paper the Houses of Parliament."

Sour humor edged her voice. "And Brighton Pavilion besides, I should think. He immortalized every inch of me in verse. His villanelle upon my left eyebrow was my favorite."

Her feeble joke didn't lighten Nicholas's expression. "He might be a fool but I can't fault his taste. You're a pearl beyond price. What I find so bizarre is that a woman like you fell for the puling milksop."

A pearl beyond price? She stifled her astonished reaction

to the description. She was less capable of stifling her reaction when he brushed his lips across hers. The fleeting kiss somehow conveyed boundless faith in her. She knew it was illogical—after all, Nicholas hardly provided an example of morality—but she'd been sick with terror that he'd despise her for giving herself to Johnny.

Her hands clenched in the sheet as a tide of longing swamped her. Physically she was helpless against Nicholas, but that was to be expected. He was beautiful and glittering, and no woman with blood in her veins could stay immune. With every moment, she succumbed to a more dangerous craving for the man beneath the spectacular façade. For the erratic gentleness and the humor and what she deceived herself was a profound loneliness hidden even from himself.

The sweetness of his kiss bolstered her to continue her difficult confession. Her voice was somber as she struggled to contain the dark memories. "It was exciting to have such a handsome young man in the house. My life had been secluded and very dull up until then. Johnny was the first gentleman to pay me any attention."

"Benton always set female hearts aflutter." Nicholas's eyes narrowed to an angry ebony gleam. "And of course you imagine you still love the blackguard."

His voice was rough with disapproval. And certainty.

Chapter Twenty-one

"*Don't* be absurd." Outrage made Antonia stiffen against the elaborately carved headboard. With unsteady hands, she clutched the sheet to her bare breasts. Talking about Johnny left her feeling naked, both physically and emotionally, and she hated the vulnerability.

Nicholas shot her a disbelieving look from under his lowered dark brows. "You must have thought you loved him at the time."

"At the time, I was insane," she said flatly.

"Is that your excuse?" He watched her with such concentration, she felt he counted the pores in her skin.

The silence extended, became uncomfortable. Nicholas lay beside her, his gaze fixed on her and his long body tense with displeasure. If he were any man other than the Marquess of Ranelaw, she'd imagine he was jealous. But she was bleakly aware that he didn't care enough about her to feel possessive.

Mustering her courage, she told herself without conviction that she'd survive a confession of her sins. Biting her lip, she stared down to where one hand pleated and smoothed the sheet. She sucked in a shaky breath and made herself continue.

"I was bored, and curious about a wider world I was afraid I'd never see. Johnny descended like a visitation from a god, which given what he's really like contains more than a touch of irony. I was sure a man who wrote reams of poetry must have a great soul." Her tone soured with self-denigration. "I dreamed of loving someone with a great soul. The people in my immediate vicinity only talked about farming and foxhunting."

"You were a romantic."

She winced, although Nicholas hadn't sounded critical. "That was knocked out of me, at least."

Except tragically that was far from the truth.

In spite of the ensuing misery, her dreams hadn't changed much since she was a girl. She still cherished fantasies of everlasting love, even if no respectable man would ever consider marrying her. In the depths of night, she dreamed of a knight in shining armor rescuing her from her barren existence and showing her all the excitement she'd imagined life with Johnny offered.

"Surely someone as smart as you saw through Benton." Nicholas snapped Johnny's name between his sharp white teeth as though it tasted rotten. "Once you get past how the bugger looks, he's not that interesting."

Nicholas's anger reminded her she had good reason to loathe Johnny Benton. But her hatred seemed unimportant compared to the disgrace she'd brought on herself and the pain she'd caused her family.

"He swept me off my feet. He promised to show me the Colosseum by moonlight, the Bay of Naples at sunrise, the temple at Delphi."

"His bed," Nicholas said harshly, his brows drawing together in a frown.

Her lips twisted with acid humor. "He was vague about his physical demands. He kissed me before we eloped, but he was careful not to frighten me until he had me to himself."

"The bastard raped you?" Furious horror darkened Nicholas's expression and his question emerged cutting as a whiplash.

"Good God, no." She grabbed his hand, which had fisted

in the sheets as if to pound Johnny to a pulp. "No, Nicholas. No."

"Not far off," he snarled, his black eyes flashing with savagery.

For all Johnny's legion of sins against her, he'd never forced her. "I always knew Johnny wanted me. I wasn't that green, even as a seventeen-year-old virgin. He didn't hurt me. Or not that way. The most shocking part of it all was that I was sure he'd marry me before he took my maidenhead. I was at least that conventional. And innocent. It's just that the . . . the promise of seeing those places was more of a lure than becoming his lover. He made them sound so marvelous."

"He told you what you wanted to hear," Ranelaw said grimly. The hand under hers was taut with anger.

"Yes, he did. I didn't look beneath the surface. Someone that handsome had to be beautiful inside and out, surely." Derision for young Antonia's stupidity edged her words.

"You're too hard on yourself," Nicholas bit out. "I can guess how the cur pursued you."

She released his hand and resumed playing with the sheet. "Of course you can guess. You're another rake."

He bared his teeth. "I doubt anyone believes I have a beautiful soul."

Once she might have agreed. After the last days, she wasn't so sure. The man who saved her from scandal, who took the care to show her such ecstasy, who fumed on her behalf now, was more heroic than he realized.

"I was a naïve little fool." Her voice frayed with regret. "I thought I'd return in triumph from my adventures, the wife and inspiration to a literary lion."

"I still don't understand why he didn't marry you." Nicholas reached to still her fidgeting. More kindness although she knew he'd scoff if she expressed any gratitude. His touch soothed her restless movements even as rage sharpened his features. "Ten years ago, he wasn't much more than a boy himself, although that's no excuse for what he did.

I still wouldn't say that Benton's hardened in evil." Nicholas paused and she knew he struggled against adding, "Like I am."

Again her foolish heart insisted Nicholas was a better man than he acknowledged. "No, Johnny's not deliberately evil. He's just selfish and weak and convinced the world owes him everything he wants because he's beautiful."

She paused. After all these years, she still cringed to revisit her greatest shame. She drew strength from the clasp of Nicholas's hand. Longstanding humiliation roughened her voice. "He didn't marry me because he retained at least that much honor. He was married already."

Nicholas jerked upright. His grip clenched painfully hard. "The devil, you say. I had no idea."

"Nor did anyone else." She struggled to keep her voice even, although Nicholas must guess she hated revealing this final evidence of her gullibility. "He'd kept an actress as his mistress before going up to Oxford and he'd got a child on her. I'm surprised the woman got him to marry her—coercion must have been involved. Johnny wasn't exactly brave when someone threatened his famous profile."

She paused and moistened a dry mouth. Her idiocy when it came to Johnny's lies still made her want to cringe away from the light. "I don't know what happened to the child. Johnny always claimed ignorance."

Nicholas growled low in his throat. Abruptly he released her and rolled out of bed. Even through her distress, she couldn't help admiring his complete lack of self-consciousness. There was something breathtakingly animal about the marquess.

She watched him prowl in naked magnificence toward the mahogany chest of drawers. Excitement shivered through her when she noticed the bloody marks her nails had left on his back. For ten lonely years passion had been lost to her. For good or ill, she'd rediscovered passion with Nicholas. The experience was so rich, she couldn't regret what they'd shared.

"When did you find out?" With restrained violence, he lifted a decanter of claret from the tray.

She tugged the sheet higher over her breasts and told herself she'd come this far, she was strong enough to complete her sordid story. However painful the last part of her confession.

"My father tracked us to Vicenza within about four weeks. We were living in utter penury." Old humiliation choked her. Through a haze, she watched Nicholas pour two glasses of wine. She drew a shuddering breath and forced herself to go on. "I didn't see Rome by moonlight or the Bay of Naples. The idea that he needed funds before he eloped with his best friend's sister never occurred to Johnny."

Nicholas left his wine on the sideboard while he carried a glass across to her. Sightlessly she stared at it until he took one hand and curled it around the stem. She trembled so badly, the claret threatened to spill. She inhaled and strove for control as Nicholas returned for his glass.

"Useless clodpole." Nicholas's mouth thinned with anger even as she read unstinting compassion for her plight in his black eyes.

Her heart lurched against her chest. She didn't deserve sympathy, but it was sinfully sweet to know he comprehended her grief and anger. She'd never imagined anyone would take her side, least of all this spectacular, profligate man. It was terrifying what his lack of condemnation meant to her.

"Johnny was more disappointed at the collapse of his romantical notions than I." Again she tried to inject a note of sardonic humor into her voice. Again it rang completely false. "I was always a practical creature, or so I discovered when I had to exist on a pittance in a foreign country. I was lucky Johnny didn't whore me to the highest bidder. Although it could have come to that if my father hadn't settled our debts."

Nicholas stood beside the bed and took a mouthful of his wine. Antonia feared she'd gag if she drank. She stared up at Nicholas. A muscle jerked in his cheek and he studied her with unfathomable black eyes.

"Your father wanted you back?"

A bitter laugh escaped. "Now who's being romantic? No, he called me a filthy slut and said I was dead to him." Just speaking the words felt like slicing her skin with razors. "As far as family and neighbors were concerned, I literally was dead. My father put it about that I caught a fever while visiting France with a cousin. When he disowned me, he informed me that my gallant lover was married."

"The sod claims he still loves you." Nicholas's voice dripped disgust. "He went to your family home, but your brother told him you were dead."

She was too inured to Johnny's weakness to be either surprised or angry. How typical that after wrecking her life, he pined artistically for ten years.

"Johnny's just wallowing in the drama." She didn't have to pretend ruthlessness. "No man treats a woman he loves as he treated me."

Nicholas's hands tightened on his glass until the knuckles shone white. "But do you love him?"

Odd, before this she'd never believed Nicholas had much truck with the idea of love. She stared him direct in the eye and spoke with complete certainty. "I don't love Johnny Benton. I didn't love him at the time, although I convinced myself I did. What I loved was the excitement of playing at grand passion." Her voice lowered into self-loathing. "I was stupid to run away with him. I realized my mistake within a couple of days. And it was a mistake I couldn't fix by offering my parents contrition and the promise of better behavior."

Nicholas frowned into his wine. "You were very young."

"Old enough to know better," she bit out. "At least my father prevented a scandal. He kept everything quiet. In all these years, I've never heard a whisper. Not that hushing everything up would have been difficult. Almost nobody outside neighbors and family knew I existed. I didn't go to

school, I had governesses instead. I hadn't been to London.
Goodness, I hadn't been as far as Newcastle."

His regard was searching. "No wonder you felt stifled.
It's cruel to shut a high-spirited, intelligent female away like
a pariah."

"That's very progressive of you," she said with a hint of
cynicism. And surprise. Yet again Nicholas confounded her
easy expectations. She'd never pictured this reprobate as an
advocate of women's rights.

"I have a gaggle of sisters and half sisters. I know the
trouble an inadequately occupied woman can cause. If your
father possessed a modicum of sense, he'd have realized a
dazzling creature like you needed a wider stage."

Her heart stuttered at his swift defense. Still Nicholas
sought to excuse her rashness. And called her a dazzling
creature besides. "Thank you."

He touched her cheek with a glancing caress that she felt
to her toes. "You're welcome, my darling."

He'd called her his darling once before, when he'd kept
her from running headlong into Johnny at the Merriweather
ball. The endearment still set her trembling with yearning.
Before she could summon any response, pleasure, gratitude,
protest, he continued. "Given nobody knew, why didn't your
family take you back?"

"Because I'd rebelled and had to pay the price," she said
bitterly. She swallowed to ease her tight throat. The pain of
her banishment stabbed, even a decade later. "My father
didn't want a headstrong trollop as his daughter."

"So he abandoned you to Benton?" Censure weighted
Nicholas's question.

She shrugged, although she felt anything but indifference
when she remembered that awful day Lord Aveson slammed
into their shabby room in Vicenza. He'd been so determined
to forbid her from coming anywhere near the family again,
he'd undertaken the arduous journey through Italy to tell her
himself. He wanted no doubts in her mind that he'd ever
relent and accept her back at Blaydon Park.

He vastly underestimated his daughter's understanding. Antonia immediately realized when he arrived and addressed her as if she were lower than the dirt beneath his feet that her actions forever severed all links between them. The revelation of Johnny's secret marriage had tolled the final grim note in her grand adventure's death knell.

As long as she lived, she'd never forget the repugnance in her father's face when he surveyed their squalid bower. He'd found her half dressed trying to mend one of Johnny's shirts so he was fit to be seen on the street. Johnny lolled in their tumbled bed as the sun rose toward noon.

"My father flung some money at me and told me not to contact anyone from my former life. He told me . . ." She swallowed again as excruciating recollection surged. "He told me he'd shoot me himself if I dared approach the family."

His face vivid with compassion, Nicholas sat on the bed and took her hand. Immediate warmth flowed into her, combating icy desolation. "But what was to become of you?"

"I doubt he cared."

Nicholas frowned. "What about your mother, your brother? Surely they weren't so inflexible?"

"I'd humbled my father's pride. There was no chance of insinuating myself back into the family." She smiled sadly and returned the clasp of Nicholas's hand. Ridiculous really how his touch eased old hurt. "Without Godfrey Demarest, I don't know what would have become of me."

Abruptly a bristling silence descended. An unfamiliar expression crossed Nicholas's face, replacing compassion and warmth. An expression that lanced a chill through her. She couldn't be sure but it looked like a flash of pure hatred.

Briefly he wasn't the man who had made love to her. He became a stranger. A frightening stranger.

"Nicholas?" she asked uncertainly, tightening her grip on his hand.

"Yes?" He was back to looking like her ardent lover.

"Nothing." She must have imagined the loathing. She

withdrew her hand from his and steeled herself to finish her sorry tale. "Without Johnny's protection, I couldn't stay in Italy. I came back to England."

She quailed to recall the horrors of that journey. She'd been heartbroken, frightened, almost penniless. Only once she left Vicenza did the full implications of her reckless actions sink in. When she ran away with Johnny, she'd told herself she was daring and brave. After her father disowned her, she knew herself for a foolish wanton, at the mercy of any man who looked her way.

This time she couldn't mistake the fury blazing in Nicholas's face. "That bastard Benton could have made sure you were safe."

"My father threatened Johnny with ruin if he set foot in England."

"No excuse. I wish I'd bloody shot the worm."

She'd forgotten what it was to have a champion. "Thank you."

He looked puzzled. "For what?"

Emotion pinched her throat. By admitting how his understanding comforted her poor bruised heart, she made her vulnerability too clear. "For . . . for listening to me. For not saying I deserved what I got. For . . . for standing up for me."

"Damned lot of good it does," he said grimly, snatching her hand and pressing a quick kiss to her palm.

"It's too late to change what happened," she said sadly, even as the flick of his tongue on her skin heated her blood. "My father died without setting eyes on me again."

"Can't you go back now?"

She shook her head. "I promised I wouldn't. I disgraced them, whether the world knows or not. My mother died not long after I eloped. My brother inherited. I'm sure he'd rather preserve the family name than welcome a wayward sister. Where could he say I'd been all this time? Too many questions would arise."

"Questions can be answered," Nicholas said sharply. "Your brother may not even know you're alive."

"Do you think I haven't told myself that? That I haven't longed to see my brother again? But my actions place me beyond forgiveness. I must make my way alone." She blinked away stinging tears and raised her chin. Her voice steadied. "I have a home with the Demarests. Luckily Mr. Demarest recognized me on the packet from Calais and immediately came to my assistance. I owe him my life."

It was pure chance that she'd shared the vessel with her second cousin, who returned from one of his regular forays into the Paris demimonde. Although they'd met only occasionally, he recognized her immediately. The Hilliard coloring made her noticeable, she supposed.

She'd never deceived herself that Demarest's kindness was anything less than a careless act of the moment, and in return she'd devoted years of service to his daughter and his estate. But the prodigal thoughtlessness that so often drove her to distraction meant also that he paid no heed to her disgrace. It had cost him little to offer her shelter, and in return, he'd enjoyed playing the gallant rescuer.

Nonetheless he *had* rescued her, and from a dangerous and hopeless situation. She'd never forget that as long as she lived.

Nicholas stared down at the hand he held, his lashes shadowing his cheekbones. His thumb brushed her skin in a casual caress that set awareness swirling. She couldn't read his expression.

Was she wrong to sense tension in his stillness? He was angry on her behalf. Perhaps that was all it was.

She braced for him to rain down curses on Johnny and her father, although she'd long ago accepted responsibility for her downfall. She'd been fittingly punished, was fortunate her punishment hadn't been worse. To fend off destitution, she might have ended up selling herself. She suppressed a shudder. After Italy, her prospects had been bleak indeed. She'd grown up over those weeks of rough travel. Grown up and recognized her fatal weakness.

Which hadn't deterred her from falling into Nicholas's

bed. A handsome face still incinerated her common sense. Despair knotted her belly even as she clung to Nicholas's hand like a lifeline in a stormy sea.

When he raised his head, his voice was gentle and his black eyes were impossibly deep. "Drink, Antonia."

"I don't want . . ."

"Just a little wine." He extended his own glass to her lips. She took a couple of sips and was surprised when the claret's warmth soothed her tight throat.

He placed his wine on the bedside cabinet and reached forward to stroke his thumb across her cheek. Only then did she realize her face was wet. She'd tried so hard not to cry. Painful memories and, even more, Nicholas's unquestioning partisanship had defeated her.

Leaning forward, he softly pressed his mouth to hers in a kiss more of comfort than passion, although the promise of passion flickered behind the care. He cradled her head in one hand and ran his tongue along the seam until she opened. He tasted of claret and Nicholas. With an unhurried gesture, he took her wine and set the glass near his.

"I've never told anyone else about Johnny," she admitted. Surprisingly she felt lighter after her confession, although nothing could absolve her sins. "Not everything."

"Thank you for telling me." He kissed her again, the warmth balm to her wounded soul.

As she closed her eyes, traitorous tears surged once more. What right had this dissipated roué to rip at her emotions? He didn't pretend to love her. At least Johnny had convinced himself he cared.

Yet when Nicholas kissed her, he cracked her heart wide open.

After tonight, his magical kisses would become a memory. She could hardly bear to think she'd never lie in his arms again. She'd miss much more than his kisses. His touch. His voice. His intelligence. His laughter. And the powerful thrust of his body.

She had a dismal premonition that after leaving him, she'd feel empty until the day she died.

In that moment, she realized there was no similarity between shallow, self-involved Johnny and this man. Nicholas was the lover she'd dreamed of as a young girl, and still dreamed of as a mature woman.

He was the lover she'd waited for all her life.

She kissed him back with all the fervor in her heart. Her hands crept up to encircle his neck.

When he raised his head, they both breathed unsteadily. Her breasts swelled for his touch. She ached for him to take her again, so quickly he'd stirred her desire.

"Make me forget everything but you," she whispered, her lips so close to his that she felt like her breath continued the kiss. She closed her eyes as arousal overwhelmed her. It felt like much more than arousal. It felt like the bond true lovers shared.

"I promise." He flung the sheet from her, then, his gaze unwavering, he stretched out next to her like some reclining Greek god in a sculpture.

A beautiful, strong, *virile* Greek god.

His lips curved upward in appreciation. Unfettered excitement juddered through her. His eyes glittered with anticipation and as she flicked a glance lower, she saw other parts of him expressed anticipation too.

When he noticed the direction of her gaze, his smile turned wicked. "With every moment, I just want you more."

Her heart crashed painfully against her chest. She couldn't bear to hear such things. Not when tonight was all they'd ever have. She had to wrench herself back to reality before she drowned in this perilous bliss.

Desperately she struggled to find words to pierce the joyous abandon enveloping her. "You say that now but I'm sure you'll be glad I'm gone. The way I'm sure you're glad to be rid of every woman you tumble into this bed. Or at least once she's served her purpose."

She should have known she wouldn't shatter his sensual mood so easily. His lips kicked up at the corners. "Your purpose seems to be torment."

He cupped her breast in his powerful hand. She glanced down, and the sight of her pale flesh framed between his long, tanned fingers sent a thrill rippling through her. The self-protective impulse to keep him at a distance faded. They had so little time left.

He kissed the areola, then drew her nipple between his lips, rolling the tip against his tongue, then biting down gently. Her belly contracted with desire. He knew a thousand different ways to touch her. Each left her trembling and needy. She was defenseless against his physical mastery. It was as if he replaced her will with his.

Except today her will and his focused on the same goal. Ecstasy.

She stretched on a rack, caught between these teasing preliminaries and needing him to rush to completion. She moaned and shifted in encouragement. She needed to scotch the unhappy memories of the past. She needed his passion.

She needed . . . him.

He raised his head from her breast, his regard curiously intent. "And you're wrong—I've never brought another woman to this house."

With desire brewing like a summer storm, speaking was difficult. "What . . . what did you say?"

The question ended on a groan as he drew hard on her nipple and squeezed her other breast. From all directions, he assaulted her senses. He battered her with bliss.

"Mmm?"

He didn't sound interested in talking. If he kept suckling her, she wouldn't be interested in talking either. But what he'd said was so astonishing, she knew she must have heard incorrectly.

"You said you didn't bring women here," she forced out.

"Did I?"

With taunting slowness, he slid one hand down to test

her heat. She squirmed and released a strangled sound that combined protest and pleasure. His thumb penetrated her slick folds, then circled.

"Y-you did," she gasped, digging her fingers into his shoulders as need built. Sparks fired behind her eyes. "Nicholas . . ."

"Yes?" He too sounded caught in rising excitement. "Are you sure you want to talk?"

A strangled laugh escaped. "No."

To her regret, he shifted his hand. He raised himself on his arms and stared down, his black eyes brilliant with hunger. "This house is my sanctuary. It's not for an army of hysterical women."

With a shaking hand, she smoothed the lock of dark gold hair that tumbled across his forehead. "Poor you," she said with heavy irony. "Are all your lovers hysterical?"

He turned to skitter a brief kiss across her fingers. Her pulses leaped at the dancing contact. "Inevitably."

"That means I'll be hysterical too."

Another smile tilted his lips. "Probably."

"So why bring me here?"

"Hysterical and inquisitive."

"Yes, well."

"You're not like my other mistresses."

She grabbed a handful of his hair and pulled until he winced. "I'm not your mistress."

"At this moment, nobody would find that assertion remotely convincing." The smile became more pronounced. "You're blushing."

"With annoyance."

He glanced a quelling but incendiary kiss across her lips. "With excitement."

"You're a vain coxcomb." In her own ears, she sounded considerably more breathless than she had before he kissed her, and she hadn't exactly sounded self-possessed then.

It wasn't just his kisses, intoxicating as they were. Unwilling emotion cramped her heart. He'd never brought a woman here. At least in that, she wasn't just another conquest.

"You're more talkative than my other mistresses." His voice roughened as his gaze dwelled on her lips.

"Poor things were probably struck dumb by the size of your conceit."

"By the size of something at any rate." His short laugh did nothing to disguise his determination.

Sweet preliminaries drew to a close. Within moments, he'd slide inside her. Her skin tightened with delicious suspense.

"Do you really want to talk?" he whispered. "Isn't there . . . something else you'd rather do?"

He turned *something* into a salacious invitation to sin. She was so afire, everything seemed an invitation to sin. She really was a hopeless case.

She pulled his hair with less force. "You're a wicked man, Nicholas Challoner."

In unmistakable demand, he pressed his erection into her belly. "My darling Antonia, you don't know the half of it."

Chapter Twenty-two

*R*ANELAW stirred from a restless doze. The candles on the sideboard burned low, the room was hushed as if waiting. Something had disturbed him. Then he heard the sound again. The lark's sweet trill from his garden. The new day dawned.

He lay on his back with a warm, relaxed body curled into his side. Silky hair trailed over his naked chest. A slender arm draped across his belly. He held her close as if even in sleep, he didn't want this woman too far away.

Although he'd never shared this particular bed in this particular room before, he knew exactly where he was and who he was with.

Antonia . . .

Sweet, sweet Antonia.

She'd suffered in the past, his beautiful girl. His gut knotted at how she'd paid for her passionate nature. Listening to her story, he'd burned to pulverize Benton, to horsewhip her narrow-minded father, to slam his fist into her unknown brother's face.

Ranelaw wanted to jump to her defense, spare her every ounce of misery.

This helpless, frustrated drive to protect was agonizingly familiar. He'd struggled with the same futile rage when Demarest ruined Eloise.

The stark truth was that no amount of anger had saved his sister. Nor could it save Antonia from tragically similar circumstances. Ironic that this woman who drew him so powerfully had been betrayed just like his beloved sister.

As if she knew he thought about her, she made a soft, contented sound and cuddled up against him. Her naked breasts flattened into his side and one thigh crooked across his.

Her drowsy murmur was astonishingly arousing. His cock twitched with immediate interest. He was a man who rarely ignored his physical urges, but he didn't immediately slide her legs apart and lose himself in her.

Although the temptation was devilish strong.

Instead he tightened his embrace and stared sightlessly into the shadowy room. His eyes were scratchy with lack of sleep and his body was heavy with pleasurable lassitude.

After her confession, he'd taken her again. In a languorous exploration that had spun molten seconds into hours and sensation into an inferno. Tonight had contained one surprise after another. He'd imagined he'd captain this voyage to ecstasy. Swiftly he'd realized Antonia held the key to unknown and dazzling worlds. She certainly ripped restraint to shreds. Once again, at the crucial moment, he'd lost control and pumped into her. It was as though his body wouldn't forgo that final primitive act of possession.

Much as he prayed no child resulted from his recklessness, how could he regret such transcendent joy? What he shared with Antonia held a dimension that was new, astonishing.

Terrifying . . .

He'd rolled off her, sated, drained to the lees. Then, even though the time allotted was so precious, he'd plummeted into dreamless sleep.

No other lover left him so replete. No other lover swept him to the edge of endurance. No other lover threatened to crack the hard shell he set over his emotions.

Not just when they had sex. And that was the most worrying revelation of all.

Her arm shifted a few inches. The brush of satiny skin on his bare belly heated his blood. Part of him wanted to nudge her awake, to have her again. When she said she could stay until morning, he suspected she meant some uncivilized hour that permitted her to slip unnoticed into Demarest's house. Ranelaw's gorge rose at the prospect of her crawling from his bed back under that bastard's roof.

He wondered with another surge of anger if the cur had ever made advances to her. Demarest was a man of unconstrained appetites and surely he'd long ago recognized Antonia's beauty. Perhaps he'd decided a quick tumble wasn't worth risking the convenience of someone taking responsibility for Cassie. Or perhaps Antonia's connections with her unidentified yet indubitably influential family made him mind his manners. By now, Ranelaw had picked up too many hints to imagine her blood was anything other than blue.

In slumber, her face was calm and beautiful. He battled the impulse to kiss those softly parted lips. The craving to take her set up an urgent throb in his veins, but still he resisted.

Staring at her was a luxury. She lay in profile, her lashes dark blond fans on her cheeks. He dwelled with voluptuous pleasure on details, the slope of her cheekbone, the pink fullness of her mouth. Her skin had a bloom like a ripe peach. A slightly abraded peach where his stubble had chafed her.

Even as satisfaction ripped through him, he knew himself for a barbarian. He'd marked her. There would be traces of his teeth and beard everywhere on her body. On her neck and breasts and thighs. Pleasure flooded him as he remembered tasting her. She'd been delicious. He thirsted to do it again.

Not yet. Although he was achingly aware that every second they lay wrapped in radiant peace was a second closer to parting.

It was unprecedented, disturbing that he wanted a woman to stay. Usually after a conquest, he became impatient for the next lover. And the next.

Antonia made him eager to linger.

Almost surreptitiously, her hand slid from his rib cage toward his navel. She released another husky sigh and pressed closer.

Ranelaw tensed under that seeking touch. The witch tortured him. She buried her face in his side and he felt her breath against his skin. Oddly, that was almost as arousing as the erratic path her hand traced across his body.

For a few seconds, they lay unmoving. Then slowly, oh, so slowly, her hand dipped lower. Lower. His chest rose and fell with every jagged breath. Serenity rapidly sizzled into need.

She verged so close to his aching cock.

"Stop teasing me," he growled, burying his hand in her thick, tangled hair.

She released a husky giggle and nipped him sharply on the flank. A shock of heat made him start. "You knew I was awake."

"Of course I did." Although he'd only just realized. Her meandering caresses had suddenly struck him as too deliberate to be accidental.

"Liar."

She kissed the place she'd bitten and another shudder of arousal shook him. Nothing to compare with the jolt when she slid her palm the few last inches and closed hard around him.

"Damn it, Antonia . . ." he protested in a constricted voice, one hand digging into her hair, the other clenching in the sheet.

"Lie still," she murmured, squeezing him with a steady rhythm that turned his vision to exploding stars.

He closed his eyes and stretched out, releasing her hair. "I'm at your mercy."

Another of those soft laughs. She sounded utterly self-confident. That built his arousal. Hell, just the fact that she breathed built his arousal. She turned him into a complete satyr.

To his regret, she paused after a few heart-stopping caresses and knelt over him, giving him a breathtaking view of her breasts. When his hand cupped one white globe, it was betrayingly unsteady. Her breath snagged, then again when he teased her nipple with his thumb. She had beautiful breasts. He'd already spent an eon exploring them with his mouth. It wasn't time enough.

Would he ever have time enough to get his fill of her? He feared the answer was no.

He wasn't a religious man, but as she bent her head and peppered his chest with nips and licks and heart-stopping kisses, he sent up a prayer of gratitude. He didn't deserve this but, dear Lord, he intended to enjoy it while he could.

She suckled his nipple and any thoughts of a sacred bent disintegrated. He tangled his hand in her hair, feeling her head move as she pleasured him.

Her exploration continued and he gradually realized she'd spent the night storing away everything he'd done to her. Something about that intense focus on his actions made his heart lurch with unfamiliar emotion. Now it seemed she meant to devote the results of that study to his pleasure.

Or torment.

Thoroughly she tasted every inch of his torso. He suffered in gallant silence until she dipped her tongue into his navel. He released a long groan.

"Don't you like it?" she murmured, raising her head and staring at him with curiosity but no pity.

He'd seen the same expression in the farmyard cats when they played with a mouse. Hard to equate this seductive enchantress with the woman who had wept distraught in his arms in the Merriweathers' library. The memory of her distress enlisted a protectiveness that did nothing to ease the pressure in his balls.

"Of course I bloody like it." Talking was difficult when arousal made him light-headed and his cock ached like the very devil.

"Good." She rose with a natural grace that sent his heart smashing against his ribs once more. Her lips took on a triumphant curve as she straddled him.

She was the most beautiful thing he'd ever seen. Her pale hair flowed around her slender shoulders, her breasts jutted in impudent invitation, her long legs framed his hips.

His gaze fell to the dark blond curls between her thighs. He sucked in a shuddering breath redolent of her hot scent and wondered if he'd survive long enough to penetrate the secrets behind that plump delta. Right now he wasn't sure he fell victim to pain or pleasure or a heady mixture of the two. He closed his eyes, but the image of Antonia naked and eager remained burned on his brain.

The effort of keeping still turned his belly hard as stone. Although not as hard as another part of him.

The provocative wench shifted from where he so desperately wanted her. When she knelt over his legs, black agony swept Ranelaw as he realized she wasn't going to take him.

Or not yet.

He closed his eyes and told himself he could endure. He could endure.

If only he believed it. He was a fraction away from dragging her under him. His hands clenched so hard in the sheets, he heard the linen rip. His teeth ground together as he battled not to fuck her like a randy animal.

Slowly, slowly, he regained some threadbare control. Then lost it again in a blast of light as her hand closed around his cock. Another tattered groan escaped and he fought to form words to warn her if she touched him there, he wouldn't last.

He opened his eyes. She stared down at him with an unreadable expression. Then through his daze, he watched incredulous as she bent. The thick fall of her hair tickled his belly.

Surely she wasn't about to . . .

Anticipation held him silent, waiting. With a shaking hand, he pushed her hair away to watch her.

She hesitated.

His balls threatened to explode. Even as he fought not to push her those last few inches, his fingers dug into her hair. He gasped so hard for air, he sounded like he suffocated. He prepared to beg her to move further off. To remove the temptation of those soft, pink, moist lips.

She lowered and sucked the tip of his cock into her mouth.

Antonia heard Nicholas's great inhalation, then nothing, as if he held his breath in suspense. He was quiveringly still. She had no idea if he wanted this or not, but the need to taste him became irresistible.

She closed her lips around the head, his rich flavor flooding her senses, and tentatively sucked.

He shuddered.

With enjoyment or revulsion?

She applied more pressure and Nicholas groaned. His hand fisted in her hair. Her tongue flickered out and she licked him with a slow thoroughness that made heat settle hard and heavy in her belly. The flavor of his skin was stronger here. He tasted warm and virile and salty.

With a surge of determination, she took more of him. He trembled and his breath sawed in and out as if he couldn't get enough air. Her nostrils filled with the heady aromas of fresh male sweat and arousal.

She paused. Wondering if she should stop. Wondering if she could. What she did held a compelling fascination. And there was a searing pleasure in seeing Nicholas helpless under her caresses.

"Hell, Antonia, keep going," he gritted out as though speaking hurt him.

She looked up. His head tipped back against the pillows, the sinews in his neck strained against the skin, and his features were stark with need. Triumph mapped a zigzag path through her. He liked what she did. More than liked it, if his ragged plea was any indication.

Feeling more daring with every second, she took him

again. Imitating the advance and retreat of the act of love, she lifted her head and lowered it again.

She loved the hard slide inside her mouth. Her grip on the base of his rod firmed. She felt she held the source of his life. This final intimacy smashed the few crumbling barriers that remained between them. By tasting him where he was most a man, she staked her possession of him.

Instinct alone guided her. Instinct and the astonishing moments when he'd kissed between her legs. Johnny had once tried to make her do this but she'd been repulsed. Taking Nicholas into her mouth made her toes curl with excitement.

She set up an uncertain rhythm between mouth and hand, testing what drove him to the edge. Easy to tell. His breathing caught and released in unmistakable encouragement. His hand in her hair opened and closed in time with her movements.

Quickly, more quickly than she'd imagined, she discovered the pattern that provided his greatest pleasure. She made a low sound of satisfaction and concentrated on driving him mad.

When he groaned with frustration and his muscles were taut enough to snap, she glanced up. The skin of his face was so tight, she could see the bones beneath.

"Damned . . . witch," he grated out.

A smile curved her lips. Gently she squeezed his sac and kissed the swollen head of his rod with all the welling tenderness in her heart. She felt more than a physical delight in what she did. Performing this act, she offered Nicholas everything she was.

A creamy pearl of liquid oozed out. Delicately, knowing he watched, she licked the drop. His broken groan filled her ears. For a moment, she savored his taste, watching his face, knowing her pleasure in pleasuring him fed his arousal.

Then because she ached to feel him inside her, she rose on her knees and sank down in one smooth movement. She sighed with perfect joy. He filled her, invading her soul as well as her body.

He palmed her breasts, rubbing her sensitive nipples until she trembled. The familiar quivers began in her belly and thighs but she resisted her climax. She wouldn't relinquish this moment until she had to.

Completion hovered too near. She bit her lip and struggled not to move, to extend the searing prelude.

He arched and she clenched, wanting him to stay with her. The effort of holding back became too much. She muffled a sob and at last rose. The glide inside her set off wild bolts of reaction. When she lowered, that immediate feeling of wholeness gripped her.

Dear God, after this, would she ever feel whole again?

No, she wouldn't think of the future. Not now. Now she wanted sensation and the knowledge that Nicholas was completely hers. If only for this moment.

She set an agitated rhythm. He seemed to understand her sudden need for sensual oblivion. His hands tightened on her breasts, driving her ever closer.

It couldn't last. She ascended toward heaven with dizzying velocity. Too soon, the world exploded and she tumbled into flame. Her bones dissolved with rapture just as Nicholas gave a guttural groan and spilled himself. She flailed in vermillion darkness where the only reality was the powerful body claiming hers and her own shuddering reaction.

When she returned trembling to earth, she slumped over Nicholas's chest and her cheeks were wet with tears she hadn't known she shed. Outside the windows, the sky lightened with morning's approach. She snatched a choked breath and told herself her brief folly ended in spectacular style.

The thought offered no consolation.

Chapter Twenty-three

RANELAW lay beneath Antonia and let his heart steady from its wild race. Exhilaration, power, hope rushed through his veins. He felt strong enough to fight demons, battle monsters, ride the gale on a winged horse.

Early light filtered through the window and the candles guttered into puddles of wax. The night was almost over.

This night of miracles.

Antonia stirred. Already he knew what she meant to say. He didn't want to listen. In mute denial, his hands tightened on her back.

"It's morning," she whispered, turning her head and resting her damp cheek on his chest. It seemed a gesture of trust, as though she felt safe in his arms, as though she wanted to stay there. Damn it, he wanted her to stay there too. He was too exhausted for the insidious thought to perturb him as it should.

"The servants are away until tonight. Let's see what they left us for breakfast." What he really meant was *Stay with me.*

"You know I can't." She moved again, her hair a soft caress on his skin. He held her against his body. After brief resistance, she subsided.

"Yes, you can," he said implacably.

She didn't answer. He sucked in a relieved breath and tasted air sharp with sexual satisfaction and the chill of dawn. The fire needed stoking, but he was too contented where he was.

How the mighty had fallen. This beautiful dragon had trampled his pride to dust. The terrifying truth was that in his ramshackle life, he'd never been as happy as he was right now.

She shifted again, and this time managed to roll away and prop herself against the headboard. She drew the sheet over her breasts. He loathed that sheet.

He lifted himself beside her and raised one hand to her soft cheek. "You've been crying."

She gave a choked laugh. "How embarrassing."

Poignant tenderness flooded him. "No."

"Yes."

She brushed back the tumble of silvery hair. When her expression hardened, a grim weight settled in his gut. Her voice even sounded different. Not his willing lover's soft, husky murmurs. She sounded like the martinet who shepherded Cassandra Demarest. He didn't want her to sound like that woman. That woman wouldn't have anything to do with him.

"The household are used to my morning walk. If I'm back before breakfast, nobody will be curious. Any later, questions will arise."

"Let them ask." His hand trailed down the valley between her breasts, pushing the despised sheet down as he went. "Don't go, Antonia."

"I have to."

"Why?"

She frowned. "For a thousand reasons. Mostly because scandal will harm Cassie and her father. I owe them better than that."

How he abhorred hearing her speak of Demarest with gratitude. How he abhorred remembering that his quest for revenge wouldn't just devastate Demarest and Cassie, but Antonia as well.

He shoved the uncomfortable thought away. His revenge

upon Godfrey Demarest was important, but less urgent right now than his need to keep Antonia. He ignored the taunting voice that insisted his two goals were mutually incompatible. The Marquess of Ranelaw lived to reconcile the incompatible. Hadn't he managed to coax the fearsome chaperone Miss Smith into his bed? As a reward, hadn't he just experienced the best sex of his entire worthless life?

He cupped one breast and gently kissed her nipple, feeling it bead under his lips. She was so lusciously sensitive. He raised his head and stared into eyes darkening with arousal. "When can I see you again? Tonight?"

To his dismay, she stiffened and the dazed expression seeped from her beautiful eyes. A twinge of foreboding pierced his physical well-being. Something wasn't right. Something apart from her plans to sneak away from his bed like a criminal.

"I thought you understood," she said in a low voice.

He drew his hand from her breast. He had a bleak premonition he needed to concentrate. "Understand what?"

She swallowed and looked down, plucking at the sheet again. He'd long ago recognized this as a sign of nerves. What in Hades made her so nervous?

"This is all we can have."

Abruptly he sat up and glared at her. "What the blazes does that mean?"

"I can't stay in London. Not if Johnny is back." Her blue eyes swam with tears. At least she didn't look happy about this nonsense. "I'm returning to Somerset. At least in the short term. Mr. Demarest may not continue to employ me now I'm no use as chaperone."

"After last night, do you think I'll let you go?" Ranelaw straddled her, staring into her troubled expression. He caught her shoulders in an implacable grip. "Your wits have gone a-begging."

She met his gaze bravely although he knew his face must be vivid with anger. "Anyone who sees me here would say my wits have indeed gone a-begging."

His hands tensed as something that felt suspiciously like hurt pierced him. "Tell me you don't regret what we did."

She bit her lip. "Why do you care? I'm just one more woman."

After the glories of the night just passed, her bitterness jarred. "You're more than that. Tell me you're not sorry you came to me yesterday."

His heart faltered to a halt when she didn't immediately answer. This turned into a damned nightmare. How was it that only ten minutes ago he'd basked in contentment? Now she ripped him in half.

Just by threatening to leave.

He was right. She was dangerous. Fatally dangerous.

"Antonia?" he asked again, and hoped he didn't sound as needy to her as he did in his own ears.

Still she didn't speak. Instead she studied his face, as if he held the answer to every mystery.

At last she answered, her voice shaking. "No, I don't regret it. I've never known such joy." Her lips twisted into a humorless smile. "No wonder you're famous."

Rage surged at her final comment. "Don't belittle what happened."

She regarded him as if he babbled in a foreign language. "It's only two bodies coming together, Nicholas."

He scowled at her. "Don't be a fool, Antonia. And don't pretend that's all you felt. I want you to stay. I've . . ."

He paused. His profound reaction left him wallowing. Putting what he felt into words tested his limits. He fell back on the safe option. "I want more than you've given me."

Her lips flattened. In disappointment? Or anger or shame? He couldn't say. When his body united with hers, nothing divided them. Communication was perfect. But when they spoke, words only created an unbridgeable abyss between them.

"Well, for once, you're not going to get what you want," she said crisply as though what he said, what he wanted was unimportant. "I have to disappear or there will be an almighty scandal. I can't risk that. For Cassie's sake. And for my brother and Mr. Demarest."

He rarely felt at a loss with a woman. He'd felt at a loss with Antonia over and over again. Never more so than now. She wanted him. He knew that. She was willing to risk her reputation for him, or else why was she here? Surely that indicated her surrender last night was more than a trivial whim.

Yet she was so determined to leave him forever.

He struggled to come up with something to make her reconsider. "What if you're pregnant?"

She arched a cynical eyebrow. "What if I am? What can you do about it?"

With every moment, she moved farther away. He hated it. But apart from slicing open his heart in front of her and letting her trample over the bloody remains, he didn't know what to do.

"I can make provision for the child."

"I'll manage on my own," she said in an uncompromising voice.

He quashed an evocative image of Antonia's beautiful body growing round with his offspring. His childhood had been a nightmare. His parents provided the poorest example of nurture. He'd make the world's worst father. If Antonia bore a baby, her shame would be complete.

Still that image of her glowing and pregnant haunted him.

"Any child wouldn't be just yours, would it?" Hoping he worried unnecessarily, he kept his voice neutral. If he challenged her absurd independence, he risked rousing bitter resistance.

How would she support a baby? Her pride led her wrong.

"Yes, it would." She lifted her chin in a gesture that reminded him of the woman he'd first met. That woman had intrigued him but they'd moved past that now.

Or at least so he'd believed.

He snagged one hand in her hair, holding her face up

as he kissed her hard. It was a kiss to compel cooperation, a travesty of the passionate kisses he'd showered on her through the night. She remained stiff and unyielding beneath his lips.

Eventually she wrenched free and glowered at him. "What does that prove, Nicholas? It's over."

She didn't even sound like she minded, blast her. "Don't say that," he growled, tightening his hand in her hair and staring at her reddened lips.

He'd been rough. He deserved a whipping. But how could she be so calm? When he imagined never seeing her again, he wanted to smash every stick of furniture in this room to splinters.

The anger drained from her expression and she studied him as if she saw all the way to his confused heart. Her shuddering breath wasn't far from a sob. He was unjust to accuse her of lacking feeling.

"What else would you have me do?" Her voice was choked. "Stay in London as your mistress?"

"Yes."

He knew it was impossible. He knew before she shook her head that she'd refuse. But he wanted her with him.

God damn it, he wanted . . . *more.*

"I won't be your mistress."

He spoke with an urgency that welled from the deepest part of him. "I'll be faithful. I'll treat you like a queen. I swear."

With every word, she looked more distressed. "No . . ."

"You'll never want for anything. I'll give you money to set up a life afterward. You'll be yourself at last. Tonight's vibrant, sensual creature, not a dour duenna to other people's children."

"And what if *we* have children?"

He knew she didn't consider his offer seriously. Still he tried. "You can have everything in writing. A house. Allowance. Carriages. Cattle. Support for offspring. My parents' bastards prospered, entered professions."

He'd never offered a woman so much. Never imagined he'd want to stay with a woman long enough to need such arrangements. With Antonia, his interest wasn't the usual fleeting fancy. With Antonia, he plumbed depths he never imagined. He needed more than a few weeks to satisfy this passion.

Perhaps he'd found a woman to hold him for years.

The idea was rash, revolutionary.

His voice lowered into resonant persuasion. The irony was that for once in his misbegotten existence, the desperation was no artifice. She'd opened a new world to him. He couldn't bear to think she slammed that door in his face and threw him back into the cold. Because with grim inevitability he recognized, without her, his existence was deathly cold.

Cold, meaningless, barren.

Her severe expression didn't soften. "They were still bastards."

"We haven't been careful, my darling. You may already carry my bastard."

At the endearment, a shadow crossed her face. He watched her reject it as only another insincere attempt to seduce.

Oh, Antonia, don't you know that with you, these cheap words I've spoken a thousand times are true and not cheap at all?

"Fate couldn't be so cruel," she whispered, then angled her chin as if daring fate to confound her. "I will not have my name bandied across England as another of your conquests. I will not shame my family and friends by becoming a kept woman."

"Is it better to live a lie?" His earlier anger revived. Surely after tonight, she knew what she sacrificed. "Is it better to burn? Because you will burn. You'll yearn night after night in your lonely bed. You'll regret this decision."

"Perhaps." Her gaze remained stony. He wondered where the soft, sensual creature had gone. "But not as much as I'd regret abandoning everything I believe in to become a rake's temporary mistress."

"You can't expect me to let you go." He stroked her jaw.

She stared at him with a stubborn misery that shredded his heart. "There's nothing you can do to keep me."

Actually she was wrong. There was something. Something so shocking, the gossips would chatter about it into the next reign.

His voice turned hoarse. His heart thundered as though he'd run a mile. He felt strangely breathless.

"You could marry me."

Chapter Twenty-four

ANTONIA'S mouth dropped open in shock. The sheet drifted down from numbed fingers. A buzzing set up in her ears.

You could marry me.

So casually Nicholas offered to transform her life.

Yes trembled on her lips but she forced the word back. She'd invite only heartbreak if she married this debauched, arrogant man.

The buzzing in her ears crescendoed. Her sight grew dim and Nicholas's face became watery and indistinct.

"Say something," she heard through the chaos in her head.

A sharp pain in her chest made her realize she'd stopped breathing. She blinked and sucked in a great lungful of air. Still she felt she'd been transported to Cloud Cuckoo Land.

He couldn't have just asked her to marry him. It was beyond the realms of possibility.

Once shock receded, her reaction was anger, sharp, fresh, invigorating. The bastard mocked her. How dare he?

She straightened against the headboard and clutched the sheet to her like a shield. If dressed, she'd storm from this room without another word, but she couldn't quite garner courage to parade about naked.

"How gullible you think me," she said bitterly.

He frowned and lifted his hand from her face. "I don't understand."

She tried not to miss his touch. Ruthlessly she reminded herself that after today, his touch would be forever absent. She ignored the pang that pierced her at that reality.

"At seventeen, I was henwitted enough to tumble for this ruse." Her voice was sour. "I can't blame you for trying."

"Antonia, what are you talking about?" He looked devastated. What an actor he was. "Marriage is the obvious solution. You can stay here without scandal and I get you in my bed."

Her voice developed a sarcastic edge even as she recoiled from the pain his ridiculous offer stirred. "And of course you'll continue to promise marriage until you tire of me, when suddenly you'll suffer loss of memory about the proposal. My father has been dead five years and isn't likely to demand we separate. At least we're spared that operatic moment."

He left the bed in one furious surge and bent over her, his hands braced on the headboard to either side of her. "Do you think I mean to trick you? Really? After all that's happened?"

She quailed at over six feet of outraged male scowling as if he wanted to incinerate her with a single glance. She summoned failing courage. "Rakes promise marriage to smooth their way to seduction."

"Except I've already seduced you." His silky tone didn't hide his anger.

She flushed with chagrin. Her lips felt so stiff, it was as if they were carved from stone. "You don't want to marry me. You don't even know who I am."

A muscle flickered in his cheek and his eyes were flinty. "Then tell me."

It seemed absurd to cling to this one secret, but perhaps because it was the last shred of carefully constructed identity, she refused to reveal her name. "No."

"No, you won't tell me who you are?"

She swallowed. "No, I won't marry you."

Something crossed his face that might have been regret. Of course it wasn't. He didn't feel anything for her beyond lust. London was full of women who could sate his lust. He'd briefly focused on her but his attention would inevitably stray.

She'd fallen for a false romantic dream once and paid a heavy price. She was older now. She knew better than to believe a woman like her could have a happy ending. She definitely knew better than to think a man could change from dissipated rapscallion to faithful husband.

Even if he meant this mad proposal sincerely.

She waited for Nicholas to push the issue, to insist on explanations, dear God, perhaps to seduce her into staying. The tragic truth was she was helpless when he touched her. If he deployed his sexual power to compel consent, he'd succeed.

Instead he turned away with a tight-lipped grimace. "Very well, then."

She flinched at the clipped coldness. She'd never heard him use that tone. It chilled as cruelly as a winter wind.

He prowled to the sideboard. The sun hadn't risen but early morning light flooding through the casement windows meant she saw him with complete clarity. His form vibrated tension and, much as she didn't want to admit it, wounded feelings.

With a sharp gesture that indicated anger, he splashed brandy into a glass and downed it in one gulp. Then he leaned over the sideboard, resting his weight upon hands he flattened on the mahogany top. He lowered his head between his shoulders as though considering uncongenial matters.

Trembling with turbulent emotion, she stared at his taut back. Hungrily her eyes traced the strong shoulders, the tight buttocks, the long, powerful legs.

Antonia blinked away tears. She'd had a night of ecstasy such as few women were privileged to enjoy. That was her ration of pleasure. She'd known that when she accepted Nicholas's invitation. It was greedy to want more.

Greedy and dangerous.

Nicholas wasn't for her, although at moments during the night she'd felt so close to him, it was like meeting the other half of her soul. The feeling merely resulted from sensual bliss, she told herself, although her aching heart refused to believe it.

Her aching heart was no guide. Her aching heart demanded she accept that ludicrous, impractical proposal. Her aching heart insisted Nicholas was genuine when he said he wanted to marry her.

What if he was?

Almost with relief, she turned to the cynical voice.

He's incapable of fidelity. He'll be bored within a month. Even if he drags you before a parson, there's no fairy-tale ending here.

She'd gain nothing from staying, apart from heartache. She'd stored up plenty of that already. She must rise, dress, depart.

Awkwardly, wrapping the sheet around her, she slid from the bed. Her clothes lay scattered across the floor, witness to her abandon. She cast Nicholas a quick glance over her shoulder but he remained unmoving at the sideboard. He was furious and she hated it. This wasn't how she wanted to conclude the most glorious night of her life.

She'd been mistaken about him in so many ways, not least assuming he'd be perfectly willing for her to leave once he got what he wanted. Surely a night's pleasure counted as exactly what he wanted. Not just pleasure, but her complete surrender.

A haze formed in front of her eyes. She blinked. She would *not* cry. If only because Lord Ranelaw had left too many women in tears after a night of rapture. She refused to count as one more.

"What are you doing?" he asked grimly without turning.

She bit back the sob that betrayed her distress. Her pride

was all she had left. It had kept her going through the disastrous elopement, it had shielded her from unwelcome masculine attentions on her journey from Italy, it had sustained her through ten miserable years since. Pride would rescue her now.

"Getting dressed." She struggled for composure. She'd spent years hiding her real self. Surely the skill hadn't deserted her in the space of a night.

He turned and glared, his black eyes like ice. "Don't be ridiculous."

She shivered under that frigid glower and stilled, her shift dangling from one hand, while the other clutched the sheet with shaking desperation. "I told you, I have to go."

She wished to heaven she didn't sound so uncertain. So damned young. He stripped her back to the naïve girl. Except the pain of Johnny's betrayal didn't compare to what she suffered now at the thought of never seeing Nicholas again. That and the knowledge they parted in rancor.

He swept a scornful hand in her direction. "I know what you look like."

She flushed and tugged the sheet tighter. "I know," she mumbled, feeling a fool.

He strode toward her, tall, strong and vibrating with anger. He didn't seem to care that he wore not a scrap of covering. "Then you don't need this."

With one savage movement, he wrenched the sheet away, leaving her bare. "Nicholas, don't," she gasped, automatically pressing her shift to her torso.

"For God's sake . . ." He ran one hand through his already disheveled hair and wheeled toward the window.

She hated when he turned away. She hated that she was so poor-spirited. He didn't force her to act the ninnyhammer. No, the idiocy was all her doing.

It required every scrap of will to straighten and glare at him, although she couldn't bring herself to drop the shift. "I know you're angry."

"Terrifically perceptive, madam," he sniped back, facing her.

He stared at her with implacable dislike. Except now she looked more closely, she realized that under the anger, he was also upset, at least as upset as she was. A flush darkened his slanted cheekbones and that telltale muscle flickered in his cheek.

You could marry me.

The words whispered through her mind. She ignored them. She couldn't marry him. They shared nothing but physical passion. She was wise enough to know that for Nicholas, that was as far as his interest would ever extend.

For her. . .

She stopped as if she'd crashed into a wall. She too felt nothing beyond physical passion. But because she wasn't a renegade libertine, it was natural to ascribe physical passion to more than mere appetite.

Except the pain that sliced her heart felt more serious than appetite. It felt like an emotion that shifted the world. Something profound, eternal, life-changing.

She deceived herself. Sexual attraction drew her and Nicholas together. That was all. Once she no longer saw him, she'd forget him. Like one forgot an irritating itch after scratching.

Even the cynical voice didn't bother contradicting that fatuous prediction.

"Let's not part on a quarrel." Her voice cracked on *part*.

"It's not my choice that we part at all," he snapped.

She stood firm, although she felt like crawling into the corner and crying like a lost child. "I won't trouble you any further," she said dully.

A savage expression crossed his face before hauteur frosted it over. The problem was after last night, she knew him too well to be convinced. She didn't want him to hate her. More than that, she didn't want to hate herself for hurting him. She very much feared she hurt him. Once she'd have scoffed to imagine she was capable of wounding his finer emotions. She'd have scoffed to imagine he had finer emotions.

A better man lurked under the charm and dissipation and manipulation. That better man might never see the light of day. But she knew to the depths of her soul that he existed.

With a disgusted sound, he bent, scooped up her gown, and tossed it on the bed with a gesture eloquent of displeasure. "Here."

He proceeded to ignore her, dressing as if she wasn't there. She watched him with unspeaking anguish before pulling her shift over her head.

Still in that horrible, cutting silence, Antonia hauled on her dress and bundled her cloak around her. The rose silk was crushed and she wore no corset. Her hair tumbled around her face. She prayed she didn't run into any of the more curious servants when she returned. She'd try to put her hair up in the hackney on the way home. Right now, she didn't trust her shaking hands.

As she turned to Nicholas, her eyes were dry. Her despair extended beyond tears.

He was fully clothed but it was too late to erase her knowledge of that long, beautiful body. She knew about the dark gold hair that arrowed down his chest. She knew what it felt like to kiss his hard, arching rib cage. She knew the taste of his sex. She knew the sounds he made when he spilled himself.

Though they'd never meet again, an unbreakable bond united them.

He stared back, his eyes stark with what she didn't want to recognize as longing. She knew this separation couldn't hit him as hard as it hit her. Difficult to believe when she gazed into that austere, tightly controlled face. He looked ten years older than the man who had made love to her all night.

Nervously she licked her lips. His glance flickered to her mouth. She waited for him to say something derisive, but he merely collected his hat and marched toward the bedroom door. He opened it with a flourish that lanced pain through her.

It was an unmistakable act of dismissal. Which surely was what she wanted. Why was it so impossible to take the few necessary steps?

She straightened her spine and sucked in a deep breath. She'd faced the unthinkable before. She'd survived. She'd survive again.

No matter that she felt like she was dying.

Still, her feet were heavier than bricks when she trudged to where Nicholas waited in bristling resentment. Her intention was to sail past, avoid further argument. It might be cowardly, but she verged so close to shattering, she couldn't face another clash.

Of course, when she reached him, she couldn't bear to think this was the last she'd see of him. She hesitated in trembling uncertainty a few inches away.

His expression was shuttered against her as she'd never seen it. Only the flaring black rage in his eyes was alive. She should be utterly terrified. Except she saw past rage to desolation.

Knowing it was a mistake to touch him, she extended an unsteady hand toward his arm. Through his sleeve, that contact burned. Her very skin recognized him as her eternal lover.

He jerked. As if he too felt that current. Then he stood still and trembling.

Her heart lurched in agony. Why did she feel she committed some unforgivable sin leaving him? Surely the unforgivable sin was coming to him in the first place.

She forced her lips to move. "Good-bye, Nicholas."

He frowned and gripped her hand. "I'm coming with you."

Startled, she tried to pull away. Fear surged. He couldn't intend to ignite a scandal, could he? Not over this brief affair. It seemed profligate even for the profligate Marquess of Ranelaw.

Her voice shook with urgency and her electric reaction to his touch. "Haven't you listened?"

His mouth flattened into a grim line. "I heard everything, madam." He tugged her through the door and toward the staircase. She mustered no will to resist. "I'm not leaving you to go home unprotected."

"But you can't just . . ." she said helplessly even as her stupid, traitorous heart rejoiced to squeeze another few moments of his presence from this horrible morning.

He still spoke in that stony voice. "It's early. Nobody will see us."

She flinched. He spoke the final words like a whiplash. She wanted to protest, insist she was perfectly fine alone. But she wasn't so strong.

She looked at him, recognizing that he, too, expected her to object to his escort. With a short nod, she stepped forward.

"Thank you."

Ranelaw easily found a hackney. At his side, Antonia remained locked away in impenetrable silence.

He fought the urge to harangue, demand explanations, insist she changed her mind. He'd never proposed marriage in his life. When the one woman he asked to be his wife dismissed his offer in such a cavalier manner, it stung like the devil.

His pride, which had taken such a battering lately, forbade him from pursuing the subject. He'd asked her to stay, as mistress or wife, and she'd refused.

Well, let the hellcat hang.

Except when he glanced surreptitiously at her, trembling beside him in the shabby coach, he didn't want her to suffer. He wanted to take her in his arms and reassure her that everything would be all right.

Whereas of course everything wouldn't be.

Damn, what if he'd planted a child inside her?

He was blackguard enough to wish he had. Perhaps then she wouldn't be so swift to refuse his proposal.

Let her see how it felt to beg him to save her from disgrace.

Except he knew to his bones she wouldn't ask for help. She was the proudest woman alive. She wouldn't humble herself to her lover, however much the lover longed to rescue her.

They approached the park, and she spoke for the first time since leaving his house. "Please stop here. Nobody will question me if I come from this direction."

"I'll see you home," he said stubbornly, even as part of him insisted if the wench was determined on making her own way, he should bloody well let her.

She turned and studied him, her face set and pale in the shadowy depths of her hood. "It's not necessary."

His jaw hardened. "Yes, it is."

"As you wish," she said in a subdued voice.

"It's not as I wish," he snapped back, tightening his hands into fists on his lap.

"I'm sorry," she said almost soundlessly.

To his shock, she took one clenched hand in hers. He'd thought she'd never again touch him willingly. He'd thought his anger defended him against her.

Wrong on both counts.

Before his pride prevented him, he laced his fingers through hers in a desperate grip. Her touch was like balm to his roiling grief.

He couldn't see her face, the hood shaded her features, but he felt her shaking. He supposed it should console him that she seemed as unhappy as he was.

It didn't.

He knocked sharply on the carriage roof. The vehicle stopped with a lurch and he stepped out, still clutching her hand. He tossed a few coins to the driver and headed across the lawns toward Curzon Street.

The air was sharp on his face and birds sang from the thick greenery. London held a touch of freshness before the day's bustle started. He saw a few horses on Rotten Row, too far away to identify riders or for riders to identify him. Nobody was out walking, although there had been a few early hawkers on the street.

Antonia kept her head down. Nobody would connect her with Cassandra Demarest's dowdy chaperone. Even ashen with sorrow, she looked like a sensual angel this morning.

As they approached the side of Hyde Park nearest the Demarest house, her steps slowed with palpable reluctance. Good God, if she was so desperate to stay, why didn't she say so? He wouldn't cavil if she changed her mind.

Opposite the turning to Curzon Street, they paused under a horse chestnut. He longed to accompany her to her door but that was impossible.

She turned to him. He braced for a curt good-bye. But she stared up with a searching glance as if memorizing his every feature.

Hell, this was like being skinned alive. He wanted to tell her to go, to stop eking out the agony. She was so determined that he held no role in her future. Well, why didn't she rush off to start that wonderful new life? Why not go and leave him behind to lick his wounds?

"Kiss me, Nicholas," she whispered.

"Hell's bells, Antonia," he gritted out. He grabbed her shoulders and stifled the urge to shake sense into her. What did she think she was doing? Surely she knew they were meant to be together.

Her eyes glistened with tears. "Please. I love . . ."

His heart crashed to a halt.

She loved *what*?

Suspense tightened every muscle. He held his breath.

If she loved him. . .

After she sucked in a shuddering breath, she continued in a low, ragged voice. "I love the way you kiss me. You kiss me as if the world would end if you stopped. It makes me feel like the most desirable woman in Creation."

Acrid disappointment flooded him. Although of course

he didn't want her to love him. Love was a worthless, dangerous emotion. He didn't need anyone's love, particularly that of a woman who intended to walk away without a backward glance.

Plenty of other women had claimed to love him. He'd lost count of the hysterical scenes his lovers had staged, and the tantrums inevitably involved declarations of affection.

Antonia didn't stage hysterical scenes.

And Antonia didn't love him. Damn her.

"Only my kisses make you feel like that?" he asked harshly. "I must be losing my touch."

A faint tinge of color marked her cheekbones. "Well, and the other too." Her smile wasn't convincing. "But I'll have to be satisfied with a kiss."

He wouldn't be satisfied with anything except her capitulation. He'd kiss her, all right. He'd kiss her to show her just what she'd be missing. He'd kiss her until she admitted she was wrong to leave.

He didn't hesitate, not wanting to give her time to reconsider. Swiftly, commandingly, he swept her into his arms and swooped down to capture her mouth.

She gave a soft gasp and he took advantage of her parted lips to slide his tongue inside, to taste her so deeply that her essence leached into his bones.

He'd planned on remaining controlled, on punishing her with pleasure. The moment she arched, flung her arms around his neck, opened her mouth, he was lost.

He should have guessed any attempt to subdue her was useless. His hunger was too intense. He'd played power games from the start and he'd never won. Instead he sank into a perfect, dark velvet world where there was nothing but Antonia and the heat of her body and the demands of her mouth.

How could she relinquish this? It was utter madness.

He closed his eyes, pushed back her hood, and buried his hands in her loose tumble of hair. He kissed her as if she was his source of air and life. He clung as long and hard as he could. At this moment, she was his without question. He wouldn't release her until he must.

Eventually she drew away. Slowly, reluctantly, but definitively.

"No . . ." He gave no thought to pride.

"I must go," she said in a broken voice. Instead of turning away, she raised her hand to his face and she searched his features with a searing, intense look that made his heart contract with agonized yearning.

"Then go," he said hoarsely, sliding his hands from her body.

This was unbearable. Laughable to think he'd imagined kissing her might gain him some advantage. He felt like a dog kicked in the ribs by its master.

"Good-bye, Nicholas," she whispered, and started to turn away.

"No, not yet." He grabbed her arm.

By God, he wasn't letting her go like this. No man with blood in his veins would. He'd haul her back to his house and lock her away until she admitted she wanted him as much as he wanted her.

The dazed passion in her expression faded and he caught a flash of fear in her eyes. "It's getting late."

"Kiss me again," he said, although he knew she was set on going. He'd never met a woman with such will. He cursed it to Hades even as he reluctantly admired it.

"You know when you kiss me, I can't think. I have to . . ."

"Antonia?"

The man's voice emerged from another world, so bound up was Ranelaw in this battle.

"What the devil?" He wrenched around to face the familiar figure.

Under his hand, Antonia stood as if turned to marble.

Ranelaw had kept her too long. Or he shouldn't have let her leave his house. She'd been safe there. Here he could do nothing to protect her. The urge to grab his lover and flee across the dew-laden grass was overwhelming.

The interloper didn't glance at Ranelaw. Instead he stared at Antonia as if she were a ghost. The man's voice was strangled. "Antonia, they told me you were dead."

Slowly, as if she approached the block for her beheading, Antonia looked past Ranelaw to the man accosting her.

"Johnny," she said flatly.

Chapter Twenty-five

A decade since she'd left Johnny Benton, and Antonia recognized him immediately. He wasn't the perfect Adonis of her youth but he was still breathtakingly handsome. He made her heart race, although not with excitement. No, her heart pounded with horror. And a futile anger that after all her stratagems, he found her so easily.

"Antonia . . ."

Johnny couldn't move beyond repeating her name. He stared at her as if he didn't believe his eyes. He hardly seemed to notice she was in the company of one of the kingdom's most notorious rakes or that she'd obviously spent the night rolling around Nicholas's bed.

The possibility flitted through her numbed mind that she could claim to be a stranger. Johnny hadn't seen her for ten years and he had it on good authority that she was dead.

One glance at his distraught face and she knew the ruse wouldn't serve. Just like him, she hadn't changed much. Especially this morning when he caught her undisguised. She thought with futile longing of her unbecoming wardrobe and her lace cap and above all, her tinted spectacles, abandoned in her bedroom.

She felt trapped in some horrible fantasy. Her fraught parting from Nicholas split her in two. Now she confronted the man who had ruined her.

Johnny still seemed in a trance. His theatricality was so ingrained, she knew his bewilderment was sincere. At seventeen, she'd imagined his dramatic behavior promised a larger life than the conventional one her father planned. Now it just irritated.

He burst into speech. "I saw your brother when I went to Blaydon Park to find you. Lord Aveson said you'd died in France. When I heard that, I thought my life was over. I've spent ten years wanting you back, desperate to make reparations. And when at last I braved a return to my native land, it was too late." He drew an audible breath and spoke with a wonder that made Antonia flinch. "Now here you are, stepping into the dawn like Eos herself."

Johnny's fondness for mythology clearly hadn't waned. She tried to summon words to placate her former lover, to convince him to keep her secret. If he alerted the world that Lady Antonia Hilliard hadn't died scandal-free across the Channel but was alive in London, the damage would spread to the Demarests, then even further to her brother, Henry.

Johnny frowned. "Speak, Antonia. If only to berate."

She swallowed and stepped away from Nicholas, who loomed at her side in bristling silence. "I don't want to berate you," she said wearily.

That was the wrong thing to say. He looked brighter. "Have you forgiven me? Great passion tempted me to great wickedness. If you've forgiven me, perhaps you'll consider my offer."

"Offer?" she said stupidly, wishing herself anywhere but here.

"Yes." To her dismay, he dropped to his knees. "My wife is dead. I'm free to ask what I should have asked ten years ago."

He paused but Antonia was too horrified to interrupt. He continued in a low, urgent voice. "Antonia Hilliard, my beautiful beloved, will you marry me?"

Nicholas made a disgusted sound. "Get up, you bloody fool. You're making a complete ass of yourself."

Johnny looked as though he awoke from a dream. He blinked in confusion and glanced past Antonia to her companion.

"Ranelaw?" He frowned and she realized he'd been so shocked to see her, he hadn't registered whom she was with.

"Yes," Nicholas bit out between his strong white teeth. He strode forward and dragged Johnny upright with such roughness, the slighter man stumbled.

"Don't hurt him," she found herself protesting even as she stifled a distinct desire to kick her former lover. And her current lover as well.

"You're not taking this milksop seriously?" Nicholas shook Johnny like a terrier shook a rat.

If Antonia needed proof of the contrast between the two men, she had it now. Johnny dangled from Nicholas's fist in picturesque helplessness. Nicholas looked big and commanding.

Fool that she was, something primitive within her had thrilled to Nicholas's grumpy protectiveness. There was no thrill now. Just boundless irritation at the machinations of masculine vanity.

"Put him down," she snapped.

Johnny looked as though he'd lost a sovereign and found sixpence. He was pale and shaking. She couldn't help noticing he retained his beauty even in devastation.

"Antonia, what is this man to you? You haven't . . . you haven't sold yourself, have you?"

She gritted her teeth. "You lost the right to ask me that question after you stole me from my father's house, vowing a lifetime of devotion but omitting to mention you had a wife and child already."

"There was no child, it was a lie," he said quickly. "That woman trapped me into marriage."

"What a prize she got for her trouble," Antonia said, not remotely mollified. "Ranelaw, I said put him down."

"I'd like to smash him against the nearest tree," Nicholas said, still in that grim voice.

"You might like to. But you won't," she responded sharply.

She should be terrified of him but strangely she wasn't. He was furiously angry but she knew him well enough to trust that reason would prevail. His was a much less volatile personality than Johnny's. Nor was he as self-absorbed, for all that he lived for selfish pleasure. There was a degree of self-awareness in the Marquess of Ranelaw that shallow Johnny Benton was incapable of achieving.

There was a strained pause. Then with a contemptuous gesture, Nicholas tossed Johnny aside.

"Good God, man, what do you think you're doing?" Johnny stumbled with a clumsiness she knew would chafe his conceit. Panting with outrage, he glared at Nicholas while remaining judiciously out of reach.

She saw so much now that should have been apparent ten years ago. Even as an inexperienced girl, she should have recognized Johnny's lack of backbone and that his principal ambition was to be the perpetual focus of admiration.

She supposed she had noticed. She just hadn't realized how that reflected on the character of the man she convinced herself she loved.

With an injured air, he straightened his clothing. Unfortunately his pouting displeasure made him look like a handsome trout. The glances he cast both her and Nicholas were sulky and childlike. But of course he was childlike. Clearly that hadn't changed either.

Since leaving Johnny Benton, she'd grown up. He'd remained a petulant boy. A pretty boy, she couldn't help acknowledging, studying his face and his graceful body with a jaundiced eye. At least she hadn't deceived herself about his beauty.

"Antonia, I know you still love me . . ."

She burst into astonished laughter. "Of course I don't still love you."

He stepped closer and grabbed her arms. "It's your pride speaking. Or perhaps your womanly modesty. I can imagine the last years. Your trials are my fault and I'll never again mention what you've been forced to do."

With a savage gesture, Nicholas struck Johnny's hands away from Antonia. "Touch her again, I kill you, whatever she says."

His voice vibrated with fury. She shot him a quelling look. He glared back unrepentant. Actually she was grateful he was here. She'd hate to deal with Johnny alone.

Johnny reacted with wisdom if not gallantry and stepped back. "I'll take you to Devon. We'll be together as we always should have been."

Antonia struggled to overcome a sensation of unreality. "Johnny, it's been ten years."

He raised his hands again, but dropped them the second he encountered Ranelaw's baleful regard. "There hasn't been a moment during those ten years when I haven't loved you. Let's put aside the past. Let me save you from a life of vice and unhappiness."

She smothered another scornful laugh. "You're making a lot of assumptions."

He frowned. "There's no need to lie."

"Damn it, man, she's not your responsibility," Nicholas growled, moving closer to Antonia.

She tried to inject a note of reason. "Johnny, it was better for you to believe I was dead . . ."

"Never," he said fervently.

"Too much time has passed. I'm not the girl you knew."

"She's too bloody good for you. She's always been too bloody good for you," Nicholas interjected.

Antonia glowered at him. "You're not helping."

"I don't intend to." He looked particularly lordly as he surveyed her with arched brows and a contemptuous curl of his lip. "Send the puppy on his way."

"Lord Ranelaw, I protest." Johnny retained his distance.

"The lady may have stooped to share her favors but those days are past. I intend to make an honest woman of her."

Reluctantly Antonia dragged her gaze from Nicholas to Johnny. He wasn't a cruel man. He was stupid and self-centered and vain. But Nicholas was right. Somehow, against all the odds, he'd convinced himself he still loved her.

Her voice was gentle and held a trace of sadness for what had once existed between them, however illusory. "Johnny, what you ask is impossible." She sucked in a deep breath. "Nobody can know I'm alive. Think of the scandal if the whole story comes out."

"I want to marry you," Johnny said doggedly. "That will protect you from calumny."

"I don't want to marry you."

"You'd rather endure Ranelaw's sordid caresses? I can't believe that, Antonia. At heart, you're a virtuous woman."

Heat flooded her cheeks. His description struck particularly false when she'd just spent the night in a rake's arms. "Johnny, it's over. It was over when my father told me you were married. Forget me."

"I'll never forget you. I know you still love me."

"I don't," she said with utter conviction.

Years ago, she'd told herself she'd recovered from her infatuation with Johnny's good looks and romantic mien— and it hadn't been much more than that, God forgive her for what she'd done. This encounter proved how right she'd been. When she surveyed him, no trace of attraction stirred.

Compared to Nicholas, he was uncooked clay.

She went on before Johnny objected. "I haven't been living in sin all these years. I found a respectable position with a good family." She swallowed and spoke as seriously as she could. "Johnny, if my identity becomes known, it will hurt the people who offered me shelter after you abandoned me."

She wasn't above emotional blackmail, not if it ensured Johnny's silence. Although he used to be garrulous in drink.

Nicholas's encounter with him in the tavern indicated he still was. "I want your word as a gentleman that you'll never divulge you've seen me."

Johnny's face flooded with pique as he glanced from her to Nicholas. "You can't expect me to believe you're out at this hour with a man of Ranelaw's reputation and you're not his mistress. For God's sake, you look like you've just crawled from between his sheets. I'm not so wet behind the ears as I used to be, my lady."

"I'll box your blasted ears if you don't show some respect," Nicholas snarled, moving so close behind her that she felt like a mountain was about to tumble down on her head.

"For a man who claims no interest in the lady, you're mighty proprietorial," Johnny sniped back. It was the closest he'd verged to spirit, if one discounted his recklessness in proposing marriage to a woman he hadn't seen in a decade.

"That's it." Nicholas brushed past Antonia and stalked toward Johnny.

"Stop it, both of you!" Antonia was suddenly sick of the whole farrago. She'd grumbled about the boredom of life as Cassie's dowdy chaperone but right now, that dull existence seemed paradise. "I will not have you fighting like a pair of dogs snapping over a bone. It's degrading."

Both men turned to stare at her in shock. It was as if a cart horse had risen to make a maiden speech in the Commons.

"Antonia?" Johnny asked in bewilderment. Nicholas remained silent but the aggression drained from his expression.

"I don't want to hear any more. I'm leaving. You can murder each other in peace then." She leveled a glare upon her first lover. "Johnny, I wouldn't marry you if you were the last man on earth. Once you've considered your proposal with a modicum of sense, you'll be grateful for my refusal."

She faced Nicholas and some of her angry self-righteousness ebbed. Nonetheless she managed a good imitation of a woman who knew what she wanted. "Lord Ranelaw, I appreciate your escort across the park. I bid you good day."

With a swish of her skirts, she left both men standing. At this moment, she heartily consigned every member of the male sex to Hades.

Chapter Twenty-six

*R*ANELAW downed another brandy and just stopped himself flinging the delicate crystal glass into the unlit library grate. The act smacked too much of bloody Benton. The act betrayed too sharply how his belly had cramped with misery when he watched Antonia flounce away to a life sans the wicked Marquess of Ranelaw.

He felt anything but wicked right now. The heartless marquess felt bereft and alone and angry.

Oh, yes, he was angry, with the desperately held anger that kept mortal pain at bay.

Damn Antonia. Damn her, damn her, damn her.

Except the person who suffered the torments of the condemned wasn't the woman who had briefly transformed his life into radiance. It was the selfish, careless rake.

The description rang humiliatingly hollow.

After warning that mongrel Benton to stay away from Antonia, he'd prowled back to his house. To what felt like a thousand hours to fill and not a servant within earshot. He'd planned for Antonia to linger through the day. But she'd left him. Meant to leave him for good, blast her.

This dark, empty room where he'd skulked all day seemed a bitter foretaste of the dark, empty years to come. His hand closed into a fist and he slammed it against the mahogany top of the sideboard, setting the decanters rattling.

Curse the witch. Didn't she realize how precious that sensual delight was? How rare?

He ached for her. His need was throbbing physical pain. The excruciating longing wouldn't subside, no matter how he lambasted Antonia.

The luscious, mysterious Lady Antonia Hilliard, only daughter of the late Earl of Aveson.

When Benton spilled that information, she'd been too flustered to notice the slip. Ranelaw had noticed, and he'd wanted to shake her until her teeth rattled.

Why the blazes was a woman from one of the nation's greatest families playing nursemaid to henwit Cassie Demarest?

Even after Antonia's father disowned her, she must have had relatives or friends to turn to. People to ensure her youthful indiscretion didn't stir a whisper of gossip. People to see she took her rightful place in society. That worm Demarest had offered sanctuary, but in return he'd made her his drudge.

Ranelaw didn't keep track of every blue-blooded family. But the Hilliards were famous, inescapable, their history entwined with the nation's since the Norman Conquest. On their vast estates in wild, remote Northumberland, the Hilliards ruled like princes.

No wonder Antonia had refused his proposal. She probably considered him below her touch.

If she'd been a shred less honorable about her disgrace, Antonia Hilliard would be married with a gaggle of children by now. His gorge rose as he imagined her wed to another man, in bed with another man, carrying another man's baby.

The Hilliards were noted for their riches, their pride, and their Nordic good looks. Good God, he should have realized who she was the instant he saw her unusual coloring. Silvery blonds with pale blue eyes marked the line. Her father, a major political figure until his death, had been a striking giant of a man, like an elegant Viking.

Hell, Ranelaw even knew her brother, Henry. They'd

been at Oxford together, although the fellow was a year younger. Not that they'd run in the same circles. Young Viscount Maskell, Aveson's heir, had been a studious cove, not a dissolute blade like Ranelaw and his cronies.

The late Lord Aveson was a martinet and Ranelaw could easily imagine the old man banishing the girl without a moment's hesitation. But Henry, Henry had been a different sort. Gentle, tolerant, an independent thinker. A man with a scholar's open curiosity, not a tyrant's urge for control. It seemed uncharacteristic of him to consign his only sister to almost certain degradation.

Ranelaw's secretary entered with the post. The staff had returned about an hour ago. The man bowed, obviously surprised to find his employer lurking in the gloom, but he knew better than to comment. After the fellow left, Ranelaw wandered across to the desk and lit a lamp. The usual thick packets from his various estates. Once he'd learned to live with his failed pursuit of Antonia, he might muster interest to open them.

A handful of invitations he didn't bother reading.

A letter from Ireland. . .

His hand closed hard on the paper. He couldn't face Eloise's lying attempts to assuage his conscience. Not tonight.

With bleak clarity, he surveyed his life. Antonia was lost to him. He couldn't lure her back. Not unless he sparked a scandal that destroyed her. Not unless he risked the bond they'd forged through their long night together.

He'd always considered himself a ruthless man. He wasn't quite that ruthless.

Antonia had escaped. He must live with that reality, even if his gut clenched in savage denial.

What was left?

Eloise's letter arriving at this precise moment seemed a message from heaven. Or hell.

He'd started this season seeking vengeance. His craving for Antonia had diluted his resolve.

But no longer.

It was time he pursued overdue justice against Godfrey Demarest. He refused to wallow in self-pity because the woman he desired refused him. Nor would he allow a sneaking compassion for Cassandra to restrain him. She was innocent of her father's sins, but she was too perfect an instrument of revenge for Ranelaw to permit her escape.

Antonia hadn't destroyed him with her desertion, she only made him stronger. Even though he'd never spoken the words aloud, he'd made a solemn vow to his sister when her lover betrayed her twenty years ago. He'd wasted weeks pursuing the foolish illusion that one woman might offer something more profound than fleeting physical pleasure. The only truth he believed in now was that Demarest must pay for Eloise's suffering.

Last night in Antonia's arms, Ranelaw had felt remade, renewed, redeemed. Today he realized he was the same miscreant he'd always been. Or at least he would be, once he came to terms with never seeing Antonia again. He would become that callous, driven man or die trying.

That man lived for vengeance. His will was iron. His heart was stone. His determination was unshakable. That man wouldn't care how he damaged Cassandra Demarest or what anguish he caused Antonia Hilliard. He'd promised Eloise recompense and he'd see she got it.

He crushed the letter as if it were his enemy. He was grimly aware what Cassie's seduction would cost him. He'd always known. By destroying Godfrey Demarest through his daughter, he eternally ended all hope of reconciliation with Antonia.

But he had no hope of reconciliation now. He was realist enough to recognize nothing would reunite them. She'd left him. She intended to stay left.

All that remained was his chance to offer his sister some measure of peace.

Locating Cassie the next night was simple. In spite of Ranelaw's reputation, he had entrée to all the *ton* gatherings. There were two or three likely possibilities, half a dozen more if those proved unfruitful.

At the third ball he visited, he discovered Cassie ensconced in the Merriweather party. Automatically he sought Antonia, although he was stupid to expect her. She wouldn't risk encountering Benton. Bitter disappointment shafted through him before he reminded himself he'd become impervious to regret.

Ignoring the weight in his heart, Ranelaw forced himself to concentrate on the Demarest chit. He'd spent too long panting after her chaperone.

Unfortunately his magic seemed lacking. Though Cassie granted him two dances, a sign of favor in spite of his neglect, he couldn't get her alone. She was popular with the other debutantes and more so with the unmarried males. The prowling wolf found himself frustrated.

The next two evenings, he met the same difficulties. For God's sake, isolating Cassie hadn't been nearly so troublesome when she'd been under Antonia's watchful eye.

No matter. Both he and Cassie attended the fête champêtre that the Sheridans hosted at their mansion on the Thames. The party continued most of the day and was always among the season's most popular events.

Ranelaw arrived at the crowded, happy festivities and quickly ascertained Cassie was present, along with the ubiquitous Merriweathers. His plan today was foolproof and abetted by a well-compensated footman. He might feel like the specter at the feast, but his path was set. He would not deviate from his scheme.

With so many people spread across the substantial grounds, it should be easy to lure the chit away from her friends. His arrangements also offered the added advantage of daylight travel to Hampshire. He was all for making this abduction as convenient as possible. Which spoke volumes for his commitment.

He struggled to no avail to relish the misery Demarest

would suffer when he learned his daughter was irreparably
ruined. Even for a scoundrel who forsook every principle
and lived only for vengeance, compromising Cassie felt
more like duty than pleasure.

"Toni?" Cassie skittered down the narrow path, over-
grown with stalky camellias. They served Ranelaw's nefari-
ous purposes, making this corner dark and unfrequented.
The day was fine and the Sheridans' guests preferred stroll-
ing on the lawns or playing silly giggly games in the famous
maze.

Ranelaw stepped from behind a tall shrub and grabbed
her arm as she threatened to barrel past. "Cassie, she's not
here."

The girl stared at him in consternation as the footman
Ranelaw had bribed entered the untidy shrubbery behind
her. "Your note said she needs to see me. It's urgent."

"I'll take you to her. She doesn't want to be seen." Surreptitiously his hand tightened around her slender arm, although the girl displayed no glimmer of suspicion.

Poor foolish butterfly.

"Is it Mr. Benton?" she asked in a low, urgent voice. "I
hope not."

"I'll let Miss Smith tell you," he said in a reassuring
voice. He was surprised Cassie was so quick to mention
Benton, although he supposed the girl must know about
her cousin's scandalous past. He reached into his coat and
withdrew a notebook and pencil. "You'll need to tell Mrs.
Merriweather you've been called away to a crisis at home."
He didn't want to risk someone rescuing the chit before the
damage was done.

"Oh, you're right. I'd hate her to worry. She's been so
kind."

Cassie's large blue eyes focused on him with a guileless
trust that startled a distant yelp of contrition. He ignored his
conscience and extended the notebook and pencil.

While Cassie scribbled a short note, he tried to stir some

anticipation for what was about to happen. He should be breathless with suspense as his plot poised so near fulfillment.

For four agonizing days, he'd struggled to scotch his turbulent, confused emotions. Eventually thanks to resurgent pride and copious liquor, he'd succeeded. Now he was wrapped inside thick sheets of ice, safely locked in a frigid, gray Arctic where nothing mattered.

He felt nothing.

No guilt. No longing for Antonia. No triumph that his plan succeeded either.

He was some monstrous machine that performed at the twist of a key. He'd operate until someone turned him off. If he'd been capable of satisfaction, he'd welcome his lack of turmoil. The world was much easier to navigate when one became numb to all feeling. He honestly believed he could cut off his hand without a twinge.

"Here." Cassie passed across the notebook. Ranelaw cast his eyes over the message, ripped the page out, folded it, and gave it to the waiting footman.

"For Mrs. Merriweather," he said shortly.

The man bowed and left with impressive swiftness. Considering the coin Ranelaw had poured into his pockets, the fellow should sodding well fly.

"We can't delay." Walking so fast that she had to scurry to keep up, he drew an unresisting Cassie toward the nearby gate. It opened onto a side alley leading between high walls from the street down to the river.

"Poor Toni, it's so unfair," Cassie said breathlessly, as if she addressed someone who gave a damn. "She's sneaking back to Somerset to hide. That vile John Benton should be the one to run away."

"I'm sure," Ranelaw bit out, increasing his already punishing pace. The last thing he wanted was a cozy chat about Antonia Hilliard.

"I wish you'd shoot Mr. Benton," Cassie said, scuttling in his wake.

That attracted even Ranelaw's distracted attention. He came to an abrupt halt and turned toward her. "Pardon?"

Cassie stopped and stared back with a surprisingly hard expression in her fine eyes. "You should shoot Mr. Benton. He acted dishonorably and Toni has nobody else to stand up for her." She paused and frowned. "Apart from me. And I can't challenge a gentleman."

In spite of himself, Ranelaw snorted with dismissive laughter. He opened the gate into the alley. "You're a bloodthirsty creature, aren't you?"

She stood her ground and studied him with a thoughtfulness he didn't appreciate. "I look after the people I love. So does Toni."

"Very commendable," he said dryly, ignoring the pointed comment at the end.

Impatiently he gripped her arm and hauled her toward the street where his coachman waited with a light gig harnessed to his two fastest horses. This was the riskiest part of Ranelaw's plan. In front of the Sheridan mansion, there was a chance someone might see them, but he couldn't turn a carriage in the alley.

Cassie craned her neck, checking the street. "Where's Toni?"

He stepped in front of her to block her view. Or anyone's view of her. "I told you, I'm taking you to her."

The lie emerged so easily that the girl immediately accepted it. He handed Cassie into the carriage, vaulted up beside her and seized the reins. Bob coachman stepped aside and they set off with a clatter of hooves and wheels.

Antonia was in her room packing, when she heard a panicked tattoo on her door.

The interruption didn't surprise her. For four days she'd fielded questions from staff unsettled with news that Antonia had left and Cassie spent what remained of the season with the Merriweathers. The agency servants finished tomorrow. The Somerset staff shut up the house then returned to Bascombe Hailey. Bella remained in London with Cassie.

To ascribe the term *packing* to her activity was an exaggeration. She stood unmoving in the center of the room while her mind picked and prodded at her gnawing unhappiness. She knew she'd done the right thing, leaving Nicholas. She couldn't be his mistress, and life as his wife would be purgatory. But without him, she felt some essential part of her had been amputated. Ordinary activities required an energy and commitment almost impossible to muster.

Blindly she gazed at her open bag on the floor, but she saw only Nicholas's stark expression as he spent himself inside her. She didn't want this image, any image from that night, etched in her brain. But she had a grim suspicion that while she lived, she'd remember. And while she remembered, she'd hunger.

Whoever waited outside knocked again, so forcefully the doorknob rattled. With a heavy sigh, Antonia dropped the shawl she carried into her bag and trudged to the door. Every second was gray misery. She felt a hundred years old and these constant, trivial interruptions strained her to the limit.

To her astonishment, Bella stood outside, wringing her hands and panting as though she'd run a mile.

"Bella?" she asked in shock. "What are you doing here?"

Bella barged in, bumping Antonia against the wall. "It's Cassie." She stopped, gasping for air. "You have to do something."

Sick panic constricted Antonia's chest. "What is it? Is she sick again?"

Dear God, had Cassie suffered a relapse? The girl's strength had returned so quickly, Antonia occasionally forgot how recently she'd hovered at death's door.

The maid slumped against the armoire. Worried, Antonia rushed to pour her a glass of water. She extended it to Bella, who snatched it and gulped a mouthful.

"What's happened?" Terror chilled her blood.

Bella looked up, her eyes glittering with tears. "He's got her. I don't know who else to tell. There's going to be the most awful to-do. Oh, my poor sweeting."

The glass trembled so violently, Antonia grabbed it. "Who's got her?"

Bella glared at her. That at least hadn't changed. "Who do you think? That ruddy bastard Ranelaw."

After all her longing, the name was an arrow aimed directly at Antonia's shredded heart. Before she thought to conceal her reaction, she retreated a shaky step, a trembling hand pressed to her breasts.

"The Marquess of Ranelaw?" she said hesitantly. "You must be mistaken."

"He's been after her from the start. The filthy brute. Now he's taken her."

Oh, Nicholas, Nicholas, tell me it isn't so.

Immediate certainty weighted her belly, tightened her throat. Of course it was so.

Was this wicked act revenge on her for rejecting him? She hadn't thought him so childish.

Or—what a gullible idiot she was—had he wanted Cassie all along?

"Taken her where?" she stammered.

"Who knows? I waited outside the Sheridans', in case my lamb came to grief." Her eyes sharpened with resentment. "For all that we've had our differences, you watch her like an eagle. But you weren't with her this afternoon so I made sure she was safe."

Cassie hadn't been safe. Another layer of guilt to pile on the layers that already threatened to crush Antonia.

She stared blankly at Bella as she struggled to make sense of this. Did Ranelaw intend to marry Cassie? After proposing to Antonia only days ago? Immediately she stifled a surge of searing agony at the recollection. His proposal had been a ruse. Obviously. Cassie was much more eligible. Rich, young, pretty, untainted by scandal. So far, at least.

But Antonia wasn't convinced he meant marriage to Cassie. Even now. She had a grim intuition that he sought the momentary gratification of a night's passion, never mind the damage he did.

The man she'd first thought Nicholas to be might do this terrible thing. The man who had held her through a dark, passionate night was better than this.

Or so she'd imagined.

What a wealth of pain that admission masked. The enormity of his crime beggared description. She battered back the need to curl into a ball and scream out her confused rage.

Damn you, Nicholas, damn you to hell for a faithless liar.

Two men she'd allowed into her bed. Two men had betrayed her.

Later. Later she'd pick up the bleeding remnants of her heart. She'd always known it was dangerous to allow Nicholas close. Only now did she realize how dangerous.

Traitorous, heinous, contemptible villain.

"Bella, tell me what you saw," she snapped.

The maid immediately responded to the voice of authority. The voice, did she but know it, of Lady Antonia Hilliard. She straightened and looked less likely to collapse. "I was in the street across from the mansion. I saw Lord Ranelaw come out of an alley with Cassie. Before I could do anything, he bundled her into a gig and took off like the devil was after him."

"Perhaps he just invited Cassie for a drive," Antonia said, even as she accepted with bleak certainty that Bella's suspicions must be correct.

"That's not how it seemed to me." Bella didn't sound like the harridan who dogged Antonia's life. She sounded like a woman facing disaster. "What are you going to do?"

The lethargy that had infected Antonia for the last four days vanished. With sudden purpose, she whirled away and rifled through her bag.

Her hand finally alighted on the mahogany case holding her dueling pistols, a gift from her father on her sixteenth birthday. A relic of the days when the earl had been proud of his daughter's spirit and independence. "I'm going to fix this."

Chapter Twenty-seven

*R*ANELAW kept the gig traveling too fast through the thick traffic for Cassie to risk jumping out. She remained quiet. His reckless speed as he wove in and out of the other vehicles must make her nervous. The last thing she'd want was to interrupt his concentration and send them both hurtling onto the cobblestones.

When they reached London's outskirts, he maintained the breakneck pace. Something in him responded to the velocity. He had a bizarre fancy that if he went far enough and fast enough, he'd leave his disasters behind.

The idea of flying into nothing was hellishly appealing.

"You're not taking me to Antonia, are you?" Cassie's voice was flat.

"What?"

He kept his eyes on the road although of course he'd heard her, in spite of the wind and the carriage's creaking and the fact that he damned well wanted to postpone this particular conversation as long as possible.

"You're not taking me to Antonia."

She didn't sound like the little airhead he'd danced with. He hated to think of Antonia, but he couldn't help remembering she'd repeatedly told him Cassie was considerably smarter than she pretended.

Too bad. Cassie wasn't as smart as he was. And he was

far enough out of London to have her at his mercy. All the brains in the world wouldn't save her now.

He should rejoice. He'd succeeded with such minimal difficulty, he hardly believed it. God couldn't be on his side, not when his purposes were so wicked. Perhaps the devil seized control of his fate.

Nothing new there.

The area was deserted. Fields lay on either side and deep ditches lined the roadside. If Cassie tried to escape, he'd have no trouble catching her.

He drew the carriage to a stop and turned to her, gripping her arm to make sure she didn't do anything stupid. "No, I'm abducting you."

He braced for hysterics. But she didn't tremble under his hand. Instead she fixed him with a steady and remarkably contemptuous gaze. "You want to marry me? Why not just apply to my father? I'm sure he'd listen. You are, after all, from a noble family."

He released a scornful laugh. "Good God, no. I don't want to marry you. I just want to ruin you."

She reacted with a cool curiosity he couldn't help but admire. "Why?"

He frowned. Strangely he hadn't expected he'd have to explain himself. More strangely, the power seemed to have shifted to this astonishingly composed eighteen-year-old girl who regarded him as if he'd just crawled out from under a rock.

"I'm a rake."

Her lips tightened. "Of course you are. But you don't want me."

Ranelaw looked at Cassie. Really looked for the first time. She appeared neither dazzled nor frightened.

Instead she looked . . . disappointed.

"I've pursued you all season." How was it that he felt at a loss? A few moments ago, he'd been master of his world.

"Yes," she said impatiently. "But you want Toni."

He jerked so sharply that the horses sidled and flung up

their heads. He soothed them as his mind churned with bewilderment.

"Your chaperone?" He tried to sound as if the idea was ludicrous.

Her voice remained calm. "Yes, my chaperone. Lady Antonia Hilliard. As you well know. The woman who makes you light up like a candle. The woman you can hardly take your eyes off, no matter how much sham flirting you do elsewhere."

"I was using her to get to you." He already knew this remarkable young lady wouldn't believe a word. Why should she? She was right. The only woman who interested him was the woman who turned his nights to fire and who had deserted him four days ago.

Cassie raised her eyebrows in open skepticism. "No, you weren't." Her voice developed an edge. "Surely you know this stupid prank puts her forever out of reach. What on earth are you thinking, my lord?"

"She's not for me." A fissure set up in the ice encasing him. He struggled to mend it. He loved that ice. It stopped him feeling. It stopped him yearning. He didn't want to think about losing Antonia. He wanted to think about avenging poor, innocent Eloise.

If he couldn't manage that, he didn't want to think at all.

"Not after this, she's not." Cassie spoke with real passion. "She's perfect for you. And you can restore her rightful standing."

He stared at the girl in shock. Suddenly the whole sequence of encounters with Cassie made bizarre sense. She hadn't been encouraging him. Or at least she'd only encouraged him so Antonia would continue to cavil at his unsuitable interest. "My God, you were matchmaking."

Cassie didn't even have the grace to blush. "I think . . . thought you were the man for her. She's been alone too long. You made her . . . alive."

Blast her, he didn't want to hear about Antonia coming alive. It stirred too many memories. He closed his eyes and automatically tightened his hold on the girl's arm. Not because he feared her escape but because every muscle clenched in denial of the truth she spoke.

"She's not for me," he repeated through stiff lips, and inwardly winced as with a silent scream, a great block of ice crashed from his soul into the murky ocean of his life.

"If you take me back now, she mightn't discover what you've done."

Now his victim proffered advice to save his sorry arse. Worse, a tiny, obscure corner of his soul heeded her.

None of which made him consider changing his mind. Even if he returned Cassie safe and sound, Antonia was still lost to him. He owed allegiance only to his sister. He'd pursue his plan to the end, no matter that his conscience kicked like a wild horse under its first saddle.

He forced himself to lie. "You mistake my interest in your chaperone."

Disdain clouded her face. "If you insist."

He frowned. "You should be afraid. Hell, you should be bloody terrified."

"I could run away," she pointed out with almost scientific detachment. "It's not as if you have an army of henchmen to stop me."

He cast a speaking glance over their surroundings. There was a village a few miles back. Another a few miles ahead. Neither close enough to offer shelter.

"And go where? You have no money. You're wearing silly shoes that will carry you about a hundred yards before they disintegrate. You have no escort. I promise, you're safer with me than with a mob of yokels."

Her lips tightened. "Not if you intend to rape me."

He realized that beneath her bravado, she was frightened. He stifled the unwelcome insight that he turned into the sort of degenerate who pulled wings off flies and set fire to kittens' tails.

At least he could put the Demarest chit's mind at rest on one count. When he'd plotted this abduction, he'd sworn to wring every last ounce of fear and misery from his victim. In recent weeks, his taste for theatrics had waned. "I'm not going to rape you."

"You probably imagine I'm willing," she snapped back. "You have an inflated idea of your attractions, my lord."

Against his will, he smiled. "And you have a sharp tongue for a girl the world considers spun sugar."

She raised her chin. "I'm stronger than I look."

He was still smiling. He began to like Cassie. Which was a massive bloody disaster. While she remained a simpering little cipher, success had hovered within reach.

"I'm pleased to hear it," he said dryly. "I swear you'll return to London as virginal as the day you left. You'll be ruined after a night with me whether I touch you or not."

She didn't look relieved. She looked confused. "I don't understand. If you don't . . ."

She bit her lip and looked away, then met his eyes without wavering. He wished he didn't recognize her bravery. Her voice was artificially even. "If you don't want me in your bed and you don't want to marry me, why do this nonsensical thing?"

He supposed shattering any illusions she held about her weasel of a papa constituted part of his revenge. His hands tightened on the reins. "Because of your father."

Cassie looked more baffled. "My father's in Paris."

"Twenty years ago, your father was my family's guest."

He paused, searching for words. It proved more difficult than he'd imagined to alert this young girl to her sire's sins. He plowed on, hoping the recounting would shore up his purpose. He had a sudden bleak recollection of Antonia telling him a story vilely similar to Eloise's. "He seduced my sister and abandoned her to bear a child."

Stubborn denial darkened Cassie's expression. "I don't believe you."

"It's true."

She shook her head. "My father may be a rake but he's never ruined a girl of good family."

Ranelaw's lips twisted in bitter recollection. "Perhaps I should clarify—Eloise is my father's bastard."

Her jaw tightened. "I'm under no illusions about Papa's weakness for a pretty face, but he's never worried the maids at Bascombe Hailey or the girls in the village. He wouldn't seduce the daughter of his host, whether she was illegitimate or not."

Ranelaw shrugged with genuine indifference. Cassie's fate was sealed whether she believed him about Eloise or not. "Perhaps he's changed his ways since his youth. Perhaps he's become wise enough to pursue his vices well away from home and any unpleasant consequences. Not that he suffered any consequences from what he did to Eloise. All the misery was hers. Your father escaped scot-free." He paused as old anger coiled tight in his belly. "Until now."

"I refuse to believe you," she said stiffly, although the gaze she fixed on him was troubled. He could see that his unhesitating certainty chipped at the girl's trust in her father.

"Your prerogative. It makes no difference in the long run."

Cassie looked increasingly upset. "Yes, it does. You tell me my father is a cad of the worst kind and expect me to accept what you say without proof."

"The proof is surely in my scheme against you. But as I told you—whether you choose to believe me is completely up to you."

Perhaps it was his blatant lack of interest in persuading her to accept his story that finally convinced. Devastation flooded her face. He stifled a surge of unwilling sympathy. He couldn't afford to feel sorry for her, either because of his actions against her or for what she learned about her vile father. As it was, he clung to his vengeance by only the frailest thread.

"If what you say is true, I'm so sorry." Her voice trembled. "Your poor sister. What happened to the baby?"

"Eloise's daughter was born dead."

"Oh." Cassie stared down at her lap, at hands clenching so hard, the knuckles shone white.

Ranelaw braced for a volley of questions, further expressions of doubt about her father's role in the tragedy, but she remained silent. Had fear obliterated her courage at last?

"Cassie?"

After a pause, she glanced up, her big blue eyes swimming with tears. She looked like a woeful young goddess. He felt no shred of sexual attraction, which was both a relief and a worry. He should want to fuck this girl. But his principal reaction was the impulse to hug her and tell her everything would be fine. Positively bloody avuncular.

"That baby was my sister," she choked out.

He frowned. "Yes. Just as it was my sister your father wronged. She's rotted in an Irish convent the last twenty years."

"I'm still not sure I believe you." But Ranelaw could see that at last she did. With a shaking hand, Cassie dashed moisture from her eyes. "If it's true, it was unforgivably wicked of Papa." Her voice strengthened. "But it's not my fault."

He scowled even as his conscience stabbed him yet again. "Your father needs to know how it feels to witness the destruction of someone he loves."

Cassie's glance sharpened. "Did Eloise ask you to avenge her?"

"No."

"Then how do you know she wants this?" she asked urgently. "Surely she wouldn't wish disgrace on another woman, a woman who has never harmed her."

His lips tightened. "She deserves recompense."

To his utter shock, Cassie placed her hand on his arm. His muscles tensed with rejection, but she curled her fingers and clung. "You love her very much, don't you?"

He glanced at her as if she spoke absurdities. "Of course I do."

"She's lucky to have such a brother."

Suspicion rose in his gullet. "Don't think to sweet-talk your way into making me let you go."

"I wouldn't." She looked innocent. Too innocent. She must have some scheme in mind. Although for the life of him, he couldn't imagine what. "I see you're determined."

"I am," he snapped, the declaration ringing hollow.

"You know ruining me won't change anything. It won't bring Eloise's baby back or return her lost years."

How dare the chit try to sway him with logic? "Your father will suffer. It's enough."

Cassie's hand tightened. "Antonia won't forgive you if you go through with this."

He'd almost wavered until she overplayed her hand. A vast black wave of rage swept away any whispers of contrition. The same black rage that had gripped him since Antonia had refused his proposal, then strutted out of his life as if he was only a passing fancy.

"I don't give a rat's arse what Antonia thinks." He lifted the reins, ready to drive on. "It's a good few hours to Hampshire."

The girl had the wisdom to withdraw her hand from his arm. Otherwise he thought he might strike it away. Out of the corner of his eye, he caught bitter regret in her face.

"You're a fool, my lord marquess," she said grimly. "You have a chance at happiness and you're throwing it away for nothing."

His mouth tightened and he whipped the horses to a gallop. He refused to grace her asinine comments with a response.

But no matter how fast he urged his horses toward the coast, he couldn't escape the low voice echoing in his soul. The voice that insisted Cassie's words were bleakly accurate.

Ranelaw stared at the road ahead of him. Recounting Eloise's story to Cassie had revived all the thwarted misery of those events. Now he couldn't help remembering.

He'd felt so bloody helpless, so uselessly young as he'd turned the carriage home after Demarest refused to see his sister. There were repercussions once they reached Keddon Hall. This time their father beat Eloise with an unrestrained savagery that still made Ranelaw's gut heave with nausea. Her terrified screams had echoed through his nightmares for years.

Eloise spent weeks locked away under such tight supervision that her brother only managed to speak to her in snatches. When he did, her lethargy and misery broke his heart. How had his vibrant, laughing sister become this pale ghost with glazed, lifeless eyes? With each day, his rage built. Not just for the spineless Demarest, but also for his sire. He'd never liked or respected his father. Now he actively hated him.

A couple of months after that agonizing London journey, Eloise bore a dead daughter. Ranelaw remained convinced that the marquess's violence had contributed to the child's death.

For days, his sister hovered close to dying herself. Ranelaw tried to break in to see her, but the room remained barred to him. He strove to find out where they buried the child. Even that was denied. He was an eleven-year-old boy, powerless to defy the adults ranged against him. His frustration and anger during those weeks had been so bitter, he could still taste them.

He'd braced to hear that his beloved sister joined her daughter in the hereafter. Nobody told him anything, apart from the fact that Eloise was still alive. He only knew she'd recovered at least some of her strength when the marquess informed him that she'd left the house forever, exiled to a convent in Ireland. Her brother was forbidden any further contact with her.

Nicholas had bowed to his father with a contempt he knew the older man noted, turned on his heel, and promptly stolen a horse to rescue his sister.

His father, for all his moral turpitude, was an intelligent man. Nicholas managed to evade the guards on the family estate. He'd reached the highway before two brawny footmen waylaid him and dragged him, kicking and fighting, back to Keddon Hall and a week's incarceration in the cellars. By then, Eloise was untraceable, no matter how Nicholas schemed and connived to discover her whereabouts.

The next term, Ranelaw broke out of Eton with wild plans to quarter Ireland in search of his sister. This time, he made it as far as Fishguard before his father and his minions caught him and forced him back to house imprisonment at Keddon Hall. No more school for the headstrong young Earl of Gresham. No entertainment of any kind until he went up to Oxford and to nobody's surprise, launched a career of roistering and debauchery that had never abated.

Eloise's name was never spoken in Keddon Hall again. As though her disgrace formed the only blot on the Challoner record, she was erased from family history.

Even confined to Keddon Hall, Ranelaw continued his battle to find her. Eventually he discovered a letter from the convent, but by then, Eloise had transferred to the mother house in France. For the next seven years, war raged in Europe. During the brief, uncertain periods of peace, Ranelaw had no luck contacting his sister.

Then a year after Waterloo, a water-stained letter arrived at Ranelaw's London lodgings. Through the chaos on the Continent, Eloise had survived, converted, and taken her vows back in Ireland.

Under duress, Ranelaw was sure.

He'd immediately written to her, promising to bring her home, but she'd responded with a stubborn insistence that she was better off where she was. He'd written once more, pleading with her to leave the convent, but this time she'd refused in such strong terms he'd never asked again. He guessed shame made her believe she deserved incarceration, just as shame that he'd failed to avenge her kept him from traveling to Ireland and dragging her free.

Her weekly letters since then had been full of the daily minutiae of convent life, tales of the other sisters. Memories of their childhood, always concentrating on the years before

Demarest's visit. All with the warm generosity of spirit Ranelaw remembered.

Every letter split another crack in his heart. Every letter reminded him he'd sworn vengeance on Demarest yet never lifted a finger to achieve it. What a disappointment he'd proven to the one woman who had ever loved him steadfastly and unselfishly.

And now, damn, damn, damn, he was about to turn out a disappointment again.

He bit back a heavy sigh and slowed the horses. Cassie, who had been silent for miles, stiffened and glanced at him with a mixture of dislike and trepidation. "What are you doing?"

His voice was expressionless as he faced the carriage toward London. They hadn't come far. He'd have her back before dark.

"I'm taking you home."

Chapter Twenty-eight

*A*NTONIA bent low over her horse's neck and urged him to greater speed. As if Achilles knew how desperate her mission was, he didn't trouble her with his usual tricks.

Her belly churned with sick guilt. She should have realized Ranelaw would pull some chicanery. He'd even warned her he seduced her to get to her cousin.

Oh, he was fiendishly clever.

And infected with a depth of wickedness she still scarcely credited.

As she raced toward the highway, Antonia was vaguely aware of eyes turning in her direction. A woman riding headlong through London was bound to arouse curiosity. She'd eschewed her disguise. Spectacles distorted her vision and what did she care if people saw her face? She was retreating to Somerset once she'd recovered Cassie.

Ranelaw wouldn't slow his pace until he reached safe haven. If she was right, that was his estate in Hampshire. She'd sent Bella and Thomas, the head groom, together on the road north to Scotland. Just in case Ranelaw intended marriage.

Her deepest instincts told her Ranelaw meant only seduction.

She prayed one of her guesses of route was correct. If

she caught up with Ranelaw before nightfall, she might still prevent disaster.

Common sense insisted Ranelaw could take Cassie anywhere. She might be locked away somewhere in the capital. He might plan to whisk her across to the Continent, beyond reach of family and friends.

At least Antonia was certain that Cassie wasn't in Ranelaw's London house. She'd called there before leaving Town, wasting precious minutes while a supercilious butler insisted His Lordship wasn't home. When she finally gave up, she waited in the street and caught a maid on her way out. After a shilling changed hands, the girl was happy to confirm Ranelaw hadn't been home all afternoon.

As she galloped for the coast, clouds of dust clogged Antonia's nose and mouth, irritated her eyes. She ignored the discomfort and urged Achilles to greater speed.

She hoped Ranelaw didn't steal a willing captive. His tawdry attentions had dazzled Cassie, but surely the girl would resist elopement. Once she'd have been certain, but Cassie had changed so much during this London season, Antonia couldn't be sure she wasn't Ranelaw's coconspirator.

Antonia's lips firmed with determination. It didn't matter whether Cassie went willingly or not. If she had to haul her cousin back to London screaming, she'd do it. Ranelaw's vile scheme wouldn't prevail.

He'd taken her for such a fool. As a crippling tide of personal betrayal rose, she fisted her hands on the reins. Furiously she stifled hurt and outrage. Later she'd berate herself for her part in this disaster. Now she needed to be ice, ready to wrest Cassie from her kidnapper without hesitation.

She'd passed the occasional vehicle, mainly lumbering farm carts or speeding stagecoaches. It was the dead time of the afternoon. In an hour or so, traffic would thicken.

When a light gig approached from the opposite direction, she hardly paid attention, apart from automatically acknowledging the horseflesh. She was her father's daughter that far. Traffic heading for London was of no interest. Her only concern was carriages traveling toward the Hampshire coast.

Only when she was almost upon them did she realize she'd intercepted her quarry. Shock made her rein Achilles in so roughly that he curveted and neighed his displeasure.

Ranelaw must have recognized her much earlier than she recognized him. He already drew the smart little carriage to a halt with a flourish that made her want to murder him.

Right now, everything made her want to murder him.

She tamped down her rage although her belly clenched with the impulse to hurt him as he'd hurt her. She needed control. Above all, she needed to win.

"Lady Antonia," he said with a nonchalance designed to irk. He doffed his hat and bowed as if they met in Hyde Park instead of on this deserted stretch of road. "What a pleasant surprise."

Lady Antonia.

He'd discovered who she was. Dismay gripped her. Although it hardly mattered now, she supposed. As Miss Smith or as the aristocratic if tarnished Lady Antonia Hilliard, she was capable of foiling his plans.

Ignoring Ranelaw, she glanced across to where her cousin huddled against the seat. "Are you unharmed, Cassie?"

The girl managed a shaky smile that conveyed relief and gratitude in equal parts. "Yes."

Briefly Antonia closed her eyes. "Thank God." She slid to the ground and looped the reins over her arm.

"You must have ridden like the devil," Ranelaw remarked in a conversational manner that made her skin prickle with temper. He clearly intended to carry this off in high style. "But of course you're an accomplished horsewoman. Old Aveson's daughter would hardly be anything else."

He sought the advantage by revealing he knew everything. It was too late. After today, he was nothing to her. If he lay bleeding in the street, she'd kick him in the teeth, then walk on.

Without turning her back on the gig, she reached into

her saddlebag and drew out the pair of pistols she'd loaded before leaving London.

"I see you're taking the melodramatic route," Ranelaw said dryly.

He didn't betray a morsel of fear. Of course he wouldn't. She'd been mistaken in so much, but she'd never mistaken his overweening pride. She could shoot him where he sat and he wouldn't utter one word in his own defense.

"Get down," she said in a hard voice, pointing the guns at him.

"Toni, I'm so glad you—" Cassie shifted but Antonia waved her back into her seat.

"Not you. The toad next to you."

Ranelaw's lips curled in a derisive smile, as if she behaved like a troublesome child. "And if I don't, you'll shoot me? Doing it too brown, Antonia."

She cocked the right pistol, her aim perfectly steady on his head. "No court in the land would convict me of your murder."

He didn't budge an inch. "You're taking your woman scorned act to an extreme, my love."

Cassie's gaze sharpened on her. No chance now of hiding that she and Lord Ranelaw had indulged at the least in a flirtation. He'd used her Christian name and the *my love* emerged too naturally. For all that it was a foul lie.

What matter? Let him expose her sins. She didn't care as long as Cassie was safe. "Get down," she repeated.

"Or what?"

"Or I blow your lying face off," she said stonily.

Her heart should be flint when she looked at Ranelaw. That's what she wanted. Why couldn't she achieve it? Anger still twisted her belly and blocked her throat. But as she stared at this tall, powerful man with his glinting dark eyes and ruffled gold hair, her principal emotion was regret.

Not regret that he'd misled her, however much that rankled.

Instead a new, chilling emotion turned her blood to icy

sludge. Briefly he'd made her believe in everything vivid and sweet. Passion and tenderness and laughter.

And it was all false.

Under that beauty lurked vast ugliness. He turned the world to night.

At this moment, she could kill him without a moment's remorse. She regretted that too. Because four days ago, she'd almost convinced herself she loved him.

"You wouldn't," he said with utter certainty.

She didn't bother answering. Instead with cold purpose, she pointed the gun at one of the finials on the seat behind his shoulder and pulled the trigger. A puff of sawdust replaced the delicate scrolled carving.

She jerked with the recoil, her ears ringing. Cassie screamed and cowered away. Achilles tossed his head and neighed, but he was trained to withstand gunfire and he didn't bolt. The carriage horses whinnied and reared in the shafts but settled at a sharp word from Ranelaw.

He didn't move although his shoulders tensed into a straight line. "You missed," he said with another of those devil-may-care grins.

"That was merely a warning," she said coolly. "I'm a crack shot. As you said, Lord Aveson's daughter wouldn't be anything else. And I have a second pistol."

His mouth tightened and she recognized the instant he decided it wasn't worth calling her bluff.

Cassie watched her with round-eyed shock, as if she'd never seen her before. Antonia cast her a faint smile meant to reassure, but the girl's tension didn't subside. "Cassie, hold the reins."

She kept the loaded gun raised as Ranelaw leaped from the carriage with a breathtaking physical ease that, in spite of everything, made her heart lurch. Yet again, she marveled how outer magnificence disguised such corruption.

Keeping the gun leveled at Ranelaw, Antonia moved to tie Achilles behind the gig. She stepped up into the carriage and took the reins from Cassie.

"It's all right. Nobody will even know this happened," she said in a low voice.

Ranelaw regarded her with an unwavering light in his eyes. Once, she would have imagined his expression conveyed admiration. Now she couldn't rely on anything she saw.

Pain battered at her shell of control. After she got Cassie home, she'd yield to disappointment and rage. First she must banish the snake from her Eden.

"Do you indeed mean to shoot me?" Ranelaw asked as if her answer made no difference either way.

She glanced to where he waited. "I should." She paused. Harder with every second to muffle devastation. But she would. She would. "I will if you ever come near Cassie again."

The rogue had the gall to smile. "What about you? Can I come near you?"

Antonia's lips flattened as she battled the urge to scream. "Only if you want a bullet in your black heart, my lord."

Last time they'd been together, she'd called him Nicholas. She wouldn't call him Nicholas again. She wished with all her soul that she'd never met him.

Even through defeat, he retained his confidence. "Won't you leave me the horse? You've made your point."

"You have your life. Be grateful you've kept that much. The long walk is an opportunity to contemplate your sins, my lord. I suggest you start. It will be dark in a few hours."

"Toni, he only took me because Papa ruined his sister," Cassie said urgently.

Antonia's gaze didn't flinch from the man who had held her close through a night of fiery ecstasy. "Your innocence in exchange for his sister's?"

Ranelaw didn't answer. Perhaps he was wise enough to realize any excuse Cassie offered him was no excuse at all.

"His sister had a baby who died," Cassie said. "It's so sad."

Antonia didn't shift her focus from Ranelaw's deceitful face. Her voice was steely. "Even if it's true, it means there's no difference between the Marquess of Ranelaw and Godfrey Demarest. They both destroy anyone who interferes with their selfish pleasure."

Through cold numbness, she felt a distant satisfaction when he paled. She waited for him to argue, but he remained silent.

Nausea rose, soured her mouth. She couldn't bear to look at him any longer. She urged the horses on and bowled down the road without a backward glance.

Ranelaw stood unmoving under the sweltering sun and watched the gig speed away. He was under no illusions that Antonia would relent and return for him. He was under no illusions how close he'd come to a bullet between his eyes.

Dear God, he wished she had shot him.

It would save having to recognize the complete mull he'd made of everything. Only at this moment did he realize just what he'd done, how irretrievably he'd shattered all hope of happiness, how he deserved to stew in his own bitterness for however many empty years the Deity allotted him.

Yes, a bullet would be welcome right now.

Antonia Hilliard was the most magnificent creature he'd ever beheld. There was nobody to match her.

And he, sodding useless fool he was, let her slip through his fingers like a handful of sand on a windy beach.

He'd had glimpses of her quality. She'd fascinated him as no other woman. She'd infuriated and challenged and enticed him until he couldn't think straight. Hell, she'd made him forget the revenge that had occupied his last twenty years.

How stupid he was not to treat her with appropriate caution from the first. How stupid he was not to realize that the plain woman in the ugly dress was his destiny.

He'd never believed in love. He'd never seen much evidence of it. But as he stood, beaten and humiliated for all his jaunty confidence to Antonia's face, he recognized that love did indeed exist.

He'd been madly, hopelessly, inescapably in love with Antonia Hilliard for weeks. Probably from the first moment he'd seen her, when she'd snarled like an angry sheepdog at a wolf. He'd only tumbled more deeply in love since.

She was his beloved, his soul mate, his other half, his fate. All those mawkish, sentimental words people chose to describe that one person who lent the world meaning, who set the heart beating, who gave the sun a reason to shine.

He wasn't a poet, even an inept one like Benton. But he couldn't doubt what he felt.

He loved her.

And she loathed him.

Through a radiant night, she'd offered herself to him with an open joy that made him feel like a god. That in itself should have been clue that this liaison was a universe removed from his usual flirtations.

Now she never wanted to see him again.

That knowledge was a knife twisting in his guts. He closed his eyes and sucked in a shuddering breath as grim truth seeped into his bones.

Never, never, never.

He'd never see Antonia again. She would never cry out as he took her. She would never rest replete in his arms. She would never kiss him. She would never talk to him.

How tragic that the great rake, the Marquess of Ranelaw, found himself mourning the absence of a woman's conversation. She'd taken the rough, unpromising substance of his soul and molded it into something new.

The agony was she wanted nothing to do with her creation.

She was strong and she was adamant, his darling. He'd spent his life coaxing women into doing what they shouldn't. He'd treated those women like children, easily placated with toys like jewels or flattery. He didn't fool himself he'd worm his way back into Antonia's good graces with gifts or charm. Her soul was granite, not wet straw like most of the people he knew.

Of course that was one reason he loved her. Would always love her.

He opened his eyes. The scene was ordinary. That it seemed the image of hell was purely a reflection of the desert in his heart.

The gig was out of sight. They'd reach London before dark and Antonia would ensure Cassie's reputation suffered no damage.

His revenge was in ruins, as it should be.

His love was lost to him. He didn't deserve her.

He supposed he'd survive this. Right now, he didn't much care.

Because he had little option other than to walk or huddle in the ditch and wait for blessed nothingness to descend, he put one foot in front of another.

He had a long hike ahead. As his wise beloved said, it provided opportunity to contemplate his numerous sins.

And what he did next.

That was clear enough. Abject failure made his choice ridiculously simple. A single course of action still lay open. He could perform only one more service for Antonia.

After that, he didn't give a tinker's damn what happened to him.

Chapter Twenty-nine

"*I*T was a wicked thing Lord Ranelaw did," Cassie said in a low voice after they'd covered a number of miles without speaking. When Cassie turned, her eyes weren't glazed with the tears Antonia expected. The girl was pale but composed.

Antonia's hands tightened on the reins. A dull, pounding determination had sustained her since she'd retrieved her cousin. She didn't think beyond the moment. It was as if the harm was so great, she couldn't comprehend its scale.

This blankness wouldn't endure. How could it? But she was mightily thankful that devastation held off, if only briefly.

Her rational mind insisted life would continue. She'd return to her unexciting existence running the Demarest estate, at least until Cassie married and she had to find other employment. Cassie, pray God, was safe from any ill effects from today. Ranelaw would hotfoot it to hell in his own way as he always had.

The world hadn't ended on that dusty highway.

She realized she hadn't answered Cassie. She forced her voice to work. "Yes, wicked."

Another thorny silence descended.

Cassie fiddled with her skirts. "He was bringing me back."

Antonia jerked so the carriage swerved wildly. She fought to control the horses. "What?"

"He was returning to London when you caught us."

Antonia couldn't help remembering Ranelaw hadn't been heading for Hampshire. "That doesn't mean he wouldn't attack you."

"He wasn't going to touch me."

"So he said."

"I believe him." Cassie's jaw adopted a familiar stubborn line.

Antonia's eyebrows arched in disbelief. "The man meant you no good."

"He had reasons."

"Instead of excusing the brute, you should thank heaven I found you in time," Antonia snapped.

"You're too angry to listen to reason," Cassie said evenly.

Antonia tensed her jaw so hard that her teeth ground together. "I'm so angry that it's an effort not turning this gig around and putting a bullet in the handsome marquess's pretty hide."

"He loves you."

A bitter laugh escaped Antonia and her hands tightened on the reins. "Don't be absurd."

"I thought . . . I thought he was the one for you." Cassie's voice was muffled and her gaze darted away from Antonia as if she confessed something shameful.

Antonia wrenched the horses to a jolting stop. "What did you say?"

Cassie looked upset, more upset than since Antonia had rescued her. "He's so strong and handsome and clever. It was clear there was something between you. I thought he'd make you happy."

Bewilderment forced its way up through her suffocating misery. "But he was courting you. You encouraged him."

"Only because if I didn't, you'd have no reason to talk to him."

Antonia released a shuddering sigh, furious with her

cousin, and with Ranelaw for not being the man she'd believed him. Above all she was furious with herself, that the sound of the blackguard's name still flooded her with sinful hankering. "Cassie, I don't know where to start. He's a rake. He's a man without principle as today proves. He's—"

"He's got a spark in his eye and a spring in his step. He looks at you the way my father's stallion looks at his favorite mare."

In spite of everything, Antonia couldn't restrain a horrified gasp of laughter. "Well, that's romantic."

Cassie shrugged. "He's an exciting man."

"He's a scoundrel."

"Perhaps that's why he's exciting. You're woman enough to keep him in line."

Cassie couldn't know how her every word stabbed Antonia like a knife. But then her cousin had no idea quite how foolish her chaperone had been. "Don't be ridiculous. I'm a dowdy spinster past courting age."

This time Cassie laughed. "Now who's being ridiculous? You're beautiful. And you've paid for your indiscretion." Cassie cast her a surprisingly adult look. "He called you his love."

Blast Ranelaw and his indiscreet tongue. Antonia knew she blushed. She hoped Cassie interpreted it as a sign of outrage not embarrassment. "He calls every woman his love."

"He's never said it to me."

Antonia clicked her tongue to the horses to make them walk on. "He was just awaiting his chance."

Cassie's voice lowered. "Antonia, I know you don't want to tell me everything. There's no reason you should. And I'm sorry Lord Ranelaw turned out a disappointment."

A disappointment. Caustic humor leavened Antonia's pain without providing the slightest relief. Yes, that was one way to describe this stabbing agony, she supposed. Her heart wanted to stop after every beat. She felt like she entered an endless, dark tunnel. Her future held no light. Ranelaw's wickedness doused all radiance.

* * *

Evening closed in by the time Antonia drove into the mews behind the Demarest house. She dispatched a groom after Thomas and Bella and arranged for a footman to return Ranelaw's gig. She felt a momentary urge to set fire to the expensive little carriage but she restrained herself. A spiteful, vengeful Valkyrie squirmed in her breast, but she refused to give expression to the screaming virago.

Eventually Cassie had forced her to listen to what Ranelaw had told her about his sister. Her cousin poured out her anger and confusion about her father's misdeeds that long-ago summer.

Antonia desperately wanted to disbelieve what Cassie said. Godfrey Demarest, after all, had come to her rescue at the absolute nadir of her fortunes and had sheltered her since.

But the problem was she knew him well enough to picture him behaving just as Ranelaw had described. He was a careless man, inclined to pursue his passions without forethought. And he was always more than happy if someone else mopped up any unpleasant consequences. She hadn't managed his estate for ten years without discovering his faults in fairly short order.

He was capable of great kindness if it didn't cost him anything in time or effort. But he was also capable of weaseling out of responsibility and leaving others to cope with the ill effects. Nor had she ever deceived herself that he was anything but a man who relentlessly pursued sexual conquest. His frequent absences from Somerset sent him hying for the fleshpots. He made a cursory attempt to hide his penchant for debauchery from his daughter, but even Cassie was aware that when her father was away, he led a life of hedonistic indulgence.

He'd seduced Eloise twenty years ago. If Godfrey Demarest was prodigally irresponsible in middle age after marrying and siring a child, he must have been wild beyond belief in his youth.

Sadly, however much Antonia didn't want to accept Demarest was guilty of seducing Eloise Challoner and abandoning her to suffer the results, something in her immediately acknowledged the truth that spurred Ranelaw to revenge.

Antonia's heart went out to Eloise's sufferings. How could it not, especially as she too had fallen victim to a young man's lies? But as she'd said on that dusty road to Hampshire, Godfrey Demarest's wickedness provided no excuse for Ranelaw to kidnap Cassie.

That she could never forgive. Just as she couldn't forgive Ranelaw for making a commitment to her—in actions rather than words, perhaps, but nonetheless a commitment—then betraying her.

He was dead to her.

Or he would be once she muted her endless ache for him.

What if there's a child?

She quashed the sly, whispering question. A month of Johnny's lovemaking and she hadn't conceived. A night in Lord Ranelaw's arms couldn't plant a baby in her womb. She refused to countenance the possibility.

They entered the house through the garden. "I'm engaged with the Bridesons for the opera." Cassie sounded unenthusiastic as they walked side by side up the dim hallway toward the main staircase.

Hardly surprising the girl flagged. Antonia felt like locking herself in her room and never coming out. And she hadn't been in serious danger, whereas Cassie had held her nerve through a kidnapping.

"I'll send a note saying you're indisposed. I'll also send a note to Mrs. Merriweather saying that the family emergency was a storm in a teacup. She must wonder what crisis stole you away from the party without speaking to her first."

Cassie cast her a grateful glance. "I'd forgotten the Merriweathers."

"We're going to bring you through this without a whisper of scandal." Antonia noted how her cousin's shoulders slumped and weariness weighted her usual light step. "Why not have supper in your room? Then an early night."

Cassie nodded and answered in a lifeless voice. "Thank you. I will."

"I'll come in and sit with you, if you like." Antonia smiled. "I'm proud of you, Cassie."

Cassie looked startled and paused in her progress. "Why? If I hadn't been so eager to promote a match between you and Lord Ranelaw, I wouldn't have been in trouble."

Antonia squeezed the girl's shoulder. "Ranelaw plotted revenge long before he met you, I'm sure. Most girls would have collapsed into hysterics hours ago. You're brave and you're smart and I love you."

"I wasn't brave at all. I was terrified." Tears filled Cassie's eyes and her lips trembled. "I couldn't see it would do any good to show it."

"That's the definition of courage."

"Oh, Antonia, it was awful," Cassie said brokenly and flung herself against Antonia.

Antonia's arms closed around her cousin with fierce protectiveness as Cassie burst into a storm of weeping. Damn Ranelaw for threatening this wonderful girl. The hatred and outrage that she'd held at bay since she'd learned of the abduction surged on a bitter tide.

How she hoped someone somewhere made that snake suffer. Suffer the torments of the damned. She wouldn't be there to witness it but she wished Lord Ranelaw a lifetime of pain and sorrow. She wished him every ill in the world.

Then when he tested the bounds of wretchedness, perhaps the evil he'd perpetrated today would stir a trace of repentance.

Little chance of that, but she found brief pleasure in contemplating Lord Ranelaw's broken heart. The difficulty was that today she'd arrived at the conclusion that he had no heart to break.

"What is this? My two favorite girls hiding in the back reaches of the house?"

Antonia looked up to meet the perennially amused glance of Godfrey Demarest. After learning what he'd done to Ranelaw's sister, there was something nauseating about his ready smiles. In all their years together, she'd never known him to take anything seriously. Once she'd found his unfailing good humor appealing. Now she'd discovered he was just as selfish and destructive as Johnny or Ranelaw. His smiles indicated nothing but shallow self-interest.

"Mr. Demarest, welcome home." Antonia surreptitiously kept Cassie behind her. Cassie was rigid with nerves, although she must know Antonia would never tell her father about the dangers she'd faced today. Neither Cassie nor Antonia would benefit from sharing how reckless they'd been with regard to the disreputable Marquess of Ranelaw.

"Thank you." Demarest looked past her to Cassie. "Tears, my lovely daughter? What is this?"

"Cassie's upset I'm going back to Somerset," Antonia said quickly.

It was an effort to sound natural. She searched her employer's face for proof of irredeemable evil but as with Ranelaw, his appearance didn't reveal his corruption. He looked exactly the same as ever. Middling height, perfectly arranged light brown hair, regular features, twinkling gray eyes.

The urge rose to ask him about Eloise. Perhaps there was some extenuating circumstance that explained his seduction of an innocent girl.

But if she mentioned Ranelaw's sister, she inevitably revealed that her dealings with the marquess had extended far beyond those required of a companion defending her charge against a rake's attentions. She couldn't bear for anyone to know how stupid she'd been, the lunatic risks she'd taken. And for what? A man who wasn't worth a moment's pain. A treacherous man who had dealt her a wound that left her staggering.

"Cassie, you silly puss." Her father opened his arms.

Cassie had always adored her father, no matter how neglectful he was. So it set another crack in Antonia's heart to note the slight hesitation before the girl flew into his embrace with a sob. To Antonia, the emotion seemed extreme for a parent's homecoming, however beloved.

Demarest as usual noticed nothing amiss with his world. Laughing, he returned his daughter's hug before drawing her toward the library, calling Antonia to follow. Then, typical of the man, there was a humorous narrative of his doings in Paris—carefully edited to avoid entanglements with courtesans, Antonia didn't doubt—and the unwrapping of extravagant presents.

He coaxed Cassie to recount her social triumphs. At first the girl was stiff and unnatural, but her father's warmth eventually told. Antonia remained separate from the gaiety, although she'd played a part so long, acting the proud chaperone was no stretch.

When Cassie retired after dinner, Demarest indicated for Antonia to wait. She was tired and pain pounded in her temples. As the night proceeded, fortifying anger ebbed. Instead she was left exhausted and miserable and desperate for privacy so she could release the demons of grief and fury that warred inside her.

But she worked for Godfrey Demarest. More, whatever his sins toward others, she owed him a debt of gratitude she'd never repay. She just prayed he didn't keep her downstairs too long. Her eyes stung from fighting back tears.

"Come into the library for a brandy." Demarest opened the dining room door for her.

From the first, when he'd encountered her alone and terrified on the boat from France, he'd treated her as a lady. She'd always been awake to his flaws: his carelessness, his selfishness, his flagrant womanizing. And after learning how he'd wronged Eloise, she should despise him. But even after today's revelations, it was difficult to maintain a cool distance when his charm embraced her.

It seemed nothing destroyed her weakness for a rake.

"I'm glad you came back," Antonia said, once they both settled in leather chairs before the hearth.

The sheer familiarity offered some comfort to her wounded soul. Mr. Demarest was frequently away, but when he was home, he'd sit after dinner and discuss the day's activities. Again she considered asking him about Eloise, but really, what could he say in his defense? Just as with Ranelaw's kidnapping of Cassie, no excuse could ever be good enough.

Instead she broached the most urgent matter between them. "I wasn't sure what to do. I can leave Cassie with the Merriweathers but I wanted your approval. If you're here, my departure won't cause comment."

"I was appalled when I got your letter. Left Paris as fast as I could. How dare that reprobate Benton show his face in England?"

"My father is no longer a threat," she said dryly. "I imagine Johnny wants to return to social acclaim and the bosom of his family. He's been away for ten years after all." She sipped her brandy. The warmth trickling down her throat felt alien. As the night progressed, she'd grown colder and colder. As if the life slowly seeped out of her.

Damn Ranelaw. He wasn't worth this agony.

"Have you seen him?"

"I met him by chance in the park." Was it only four days ago that she'd left Ranelaw's bed in a sensual daze? She no longer felt like the same woman. "He recognized me."

"You haven't changed from the girl I took into my house, except you've become more beautiful."

Antonia frowned into her glass. Flattery wasn't Demarest's usual conversation. "Johnny's wife is dead. He wants to marry me."

"I hope you sent him to the devil."

"I was too startled to be so succinct, but, yes, I refused. He hasn't changed either." She struggled to keep the conversation going. She felt as though her head were stuffed with wool.

"Do you think he'll spread scandal?"

"His role in the elopement does him no credit. Discretion

might rule. It's still best that I leave Cassie under someone else's supervision. Are you staying?"

"For the moment."

"Good. I'll leave tomorrow."

He rose to lean one arm on the mantelpiece. His eyes fixed on her. "Antonia, there's something I'd like to talk to you about." He sounded unusually serious. "Something I've thought of for a long time."

Oh, no, not today. Grim premonition weighted her belly. Her fingers tightened on her brandy glass. She'd barely dealt with Ranelaw's betrayal. Losing her home as well seemed too cruel, although she'd known this day would come when Cassie entered the marriage market.

Just not so soon.

Demarest stared down at the fire. "I expect Cassie will receive many offers."

"She's beautiful, bright, and rich. Any man would be lucky to take her to wife."

"Serious contenders?"

She shrugged. "Lord Soames seems a suitable match and Cassie likes him." She paused and forced herself to speak the loathed name. The words crammed in her throat but she got them out. "The Marquess of Ranelaw has shown interest."

Demarest didn't react with noticeable guilt. It was difficult to reconcile this urbane gentleman with what she knew of Eloise. But then remorse had never been her cousin's forte.

"I hope you gave that scoundrel short shrift. I'd heard he was sniffing around. Must have decided it's time to set up his nursery. He must be over thirty now."

"Cassie knows what she's about."

Another pause, then Demarest spoke almost idly. "When she marries, what of you?"

Antonia squashed a cowardly impulse to delay this discussion. "She says she wants to take me with her. I suspect her new husband may have different ideas." She swallowed and ventured a hesitant suggestion. "I thought as you're away so much, you might consider allowing me to continue running your estate."

When he shook his head, her heart shrank. Her hand clenched harder around her glass although she struggled for outward composure. Demarest had done so much for her. No reason he must keep her as a charity case forever.

His voice was uncharacteristically somber. "Once Cassie is no longer in residence, that wouldn't be suitable."

Antonia set her glass on the table between the chairs. Her hand shook so badly, the brandy spilled. "You're right." She raised her chin and wondered if she had courage to endure this on top of everything else. "I appreciate all you've done for me and it's been a joy bringing Cassie up. Will you supply me with a reference for another position?" Another position with a family who would indeed treat her as a servant. How would she bear it?

Demarest didn't seem to realize the blow he'd delivered. "If that's what you want."

She frowned. "I can't see an alternative."

His voice was soft and deep. "I could ask you to marry me."

Chapter Thirty

ER mind in turmoil, Antonia retreated to her bedroom. The last days had been too turbulent, too confusing. Shock and disbelief warred in her over Mr. Demarest's proposal. She twisted in a whirlwind. As though she'd split into a hundred different people and she understood none of them.

The drab chaperone. The passionate lover. The woman who rejected Johnny's proposal. The Amazon who rescued Cassie and threatened to shoot Ranelaw.

Among these myriad identities, should she now include Godfrey Demarest's future wife?

Her belly churning, she sank down on the stool before her dressing table. Her body ached as if she'd trudged a hundred miles through a wild storm. Bewildered she stared into the mirror. Apart from two hectic flags of color high on her cheekbones, she was pale. Her eyes were dark and troubled.

Hard to credit, but in the last few days, three men had proposed marriage. When she'd believed herself utterly ineligible.

Of course the only offer she seriously considered was her cousin's. She'd sat astonished and silent while Demarest explained he wanted her to continue running his estate. Basically nothing would change. Except Antonia would regain the status stripped from her after her elopement. She'd have security at last, a place in the world.

Had he planned this ever since he'd discovered her on the packet from France? It seemed unlikely. She knew from her own experience that her cousin rarely looked ahead to consider consequences. Eloise Challoner's tragic story bore out that perception. He was a man who lived for his own convenience, and Antonia continuing to handle his responsibilities would suit his pleasure, she had no doubt.

Did it suit her pleasure?

While Demarest made no pretense that he meant to relinquish his rakish pursuits, he mentioned his hope for children. It was a delicate way of saying he'd come to her bed if she wished, but he wouldn't enforce his husbandly rights.

Her hands formed claws against the mahogany dressing table. She wanted children. She wanted a family. She wanted a home that belonged to her and wasn't the result of casual charity.

Was she willing to accept an unfaithful husband to obtain those things?

Was she willing to overlook her cousin's sins against Eloise Challoner?

Was she willing to accept Godfrey Demarest as her lover?

She closed her eyes and struggled to forget the transcendent joy she'd experienced in Ranelaw's arms. Because when she recalled the joy, she also recalled the betrayal. The agony made her shake and threatened to send her crawling into a dark hole.

No, she must expunge Ranelaw from heart and mind. All the passion. All the lies. All the sinful, seductive delight. All the choking rage. Instead she must decide her next step with her head, not her heart. Her heart never led her right.

Perhaps she and Godfrey Demarest had a chance of happiness. She knew him well, both the bad and the good. There was good in him when he wasn't too lazy or self-interested to ignore the promptings of his conscience.

Neither Demarest nor she expected grand passion. Bascombe Hailey was her home and she already considered Cassie as a sister. Considering her as a daughter would require no effort.

What choice did Antonia have but to accept this proposal?

Most people would say after her lapse, she was fortunate to have any choice. Strict morality insisted she rot in the gutter. Yet now a settled life as a rich man's wife beckoned.

If she stretched out her hand and seized it. . .

Mr. Demarest didn't look surprised when Antonia requested an interview after breakfast. He must know she was perilously short of options if he ceased to employ her.

When she entered the library, Demarest rose from behind his desk and came to meet her. His manner when he ushered her into the room conveyed a hint of the proprietary. Clearly he expected her to say yes to his proposal.

In spite of her exhaustion, Antonia hadn't slept a moment. Dry-eyed and as empty inside as an old nutshell, she'd watched the sun rise over London. Briefly she'd wondered where Ranelaw was, then she ruthlessly blocked curiosity. All night, she'd struggled not to think of him. But the ache in her heart and between her legs reminded her she'd once again given herself to an unworthy man.

She didn't cry. This agony went beyond tears. She'd cried an ocean over Johnny. Ranelaw's betrayal surpassed any pain she'd imagined.

If she meant to marry Godfrey Demarest, better to think of him. But over and over, she had to superimpose his pleasant face over the intense, angular features of the man who could destroy her if she let him. Everything about Ranelaw was fraudulent, especially her memories. There was no sweetness and passion. There was just falsehood and manipulation.

Even knowing that, erasing his image proved hellishly difficult. But she would do it. However long it took. How-

ever many pieces of her soul she had to slice away to achieve
blessed numbness.

Mr. Demarest took her hand and led her to the chair
she'd sat in last night. "You're in fine looks this morning,
my dear."

Antonia bit back a wry laugh. She looked like a hag.
Sleeplessness and anxiety left her pale and drawn. The eyes
she'd met in the mirror were dull and sunken, and a pounding headache took up residence in her temples.

They both sat down. Although she'd requested this meeting, she found it impossible to mention the subject of his
proposal. She'd never before experienced an awkward silence with her cousin. She hoped this wasn't a sign of things
to come. Although of course, if she accepted him, mostly
she'd manage the Somerset estate alone, just as she had
during the last ten years.

How ironic that she now contemplated marriage with a
man who shared so many of her first lover's failings. Like
Johnny, Demarest wasn't deliberately evil. He was just selfish and unwilling to consider the repercussions of what he
did. She should view him as abhorrent, but in the end, she
couldn't hate him. He was a spoiled child, just as Johnny
was.

"Have you thought about what I said?" he asked eventually.

She linked her hands in her lap and stared down at them.
They were surprisingly steady. Despite what she knew about
Demarest and Eloise Challoner, she'd made her choice. The
only choice she could make. She'd live with it.

"Of course."

He must have sensed hesitation because his voice deepened into kindness. The same kindness she'd heard when he
discovered her on the ship from France. It reminded her just
what she owed this man, whatever his sins. "I realize my
offer isn't at all romantical."

She smiled without meeting his eyes. "You and I have
moved beyond the age of being romantical."

The traitorous memory of how romantical she'd felt in Ranelaw's arms swelled like a tidal wave. The effort of damming it back into the darkness where it belonged made her release a shuddering breath not far from a sob. Her armor of calm threatened to disintegrate. But she must do this. She had no alternative.

She felt Demarest studying her. "You've reached a decision?"

Her hands clung to each other so tightly that her fingers set white marks on the flesh. She must speak, but no matter how she tried, the words wouldn't emerge.

Courage, Antonia. Courage.

She raised her head and stared at him, this man she didn't love but who offered hope for her future. He'd committed transgressions just as heinous as those Ranelaw or Johnny Benton had committed, but to her he'd always been kind and generous. She should scorn him for ruining Eloise, but her desperation for a roof over her head was too pressing for her to be overfastidious.

"Mr. Demarest . . ." she began in a faltering voice.

"Godfrey, please, Antonia." He touched her poor tortured hands in silent reproof. "I've asked you so often to use my Christian name. You are, after all, family. Now I hope . . . I pray . . . you'll be more."

She studied his face and realized he wasn't doing this totally to save her from poverty and servitude. His eyes held a light that she couldn't help reading as genuine fondness, and his grip on her hand was eager. This marriage would be no hardship to Godfrey Demarest.

She sucked in a shaky breath. "Godfrey . . ."

There was a scratch at the door, and the butler entered bearing a card on a tray. "Lord Aveson to see you, sir."

Demarest's head rose sharply and he jerked his hand from hers. "Damn it, Eames. I said I wasn't to be disturbed. By anyone." Then he frowned. "Who?"

Lord Aveson. . .

Antonia grabbed the arms of her chair as shock ripped

through her and sent her heart crashing against her ribs. Unlike Demarest, she didn't need to question the name. She'd heard perfectly clearly.

Her brother was here.

Ten years and no word. Now he appeared without warning. After the tumult of the last few days, she couldn't muster strength to confront Henry. It was too much. She felt as though she shattered like glass.

The butler remained oblivious to his explosive announcement. "Lord Aveson, sir. I know you requested privacy but he is most insistent that he see you."

Antonia rose on trembling legs. Dread iced her veins. Flight seemed her only choice. "He can't find me."

"Antonia, you're in my house. No harm will come to you." As Demarest stood, the compassion in his face made her want to accept his marriage proposal in a trice. Before she could speak, he glanced at the impassive butler. "Send him in, Eames."

"Yes, sir." The butler bowed and left.

Suffocating shame closed Antonia's throat. The years vanished and she was once again the humiliated seventeen-year-old her father condemned as a whore. "I can't . . ."

"Yes, you can." Demarest caught her arm to stop her darting toward the door. He used the same voice that had reassured a distraught girl fleeing Italy.

"Let me go. Please." She squirmed to escape but it was too late. When she whirled, her brother stared at her from the doorway with what she immediately interpreted as disgusted disbelief.

"Antonia . . ."

Henry sounded as shocked as she. She shot a pleading look at Demarest, although he couldn't spare her this painful encounter.

Struggling to revive failing courage, she sucked in a deep breath and drew away from Demarest. Yesterday she'd threatened to shoot her lover. Surely today she had the backbone to face her brother, however much the frightened girl cringing inside her longed to disappear. Godfrey Demarest wasn't the strongest man in Creation, but he wouldn't allow her brother to condemn her as a slut and toss her onto the street.

"Lord Aveson," she said faintly, dipping into a curtsy and rising with her chin at a defiant angle.

Henry still didn't move from the doorway. His face was ashen. "Antonia . . ."

He hadn't spared a glance for Demarest. Instead his gaze fixed on her face. To her horror, his blue eyes, twins to those she saw in her mirror every day, shone with tears.

Confusion swamped her false bravado. This wasn't the reaction she expected. "Henry?" she wavered, suddenly unsure whether formality was the best way to greet him.

In spite of her roiling humiliation, she couldn't help staring at him avidly. How she'd missed him. During what had been in many ways a lonely childhood, she'd always looked up to him.

Even after the long separation, he was heartbreakingly familiar. He'd been a gangly youth, only twenty when she ran away, but the years had filled him out. Like all the Hilliards, he was tall and graceful and as blond as a Viking. He looked the image of the father who had cast her aside so callously. The ominous comparison sent a shiver down her backbone.

Except her father would never have betrayed such vulnerability, looked so devastated. Even when he banished his daughter from his life forever.

"He . . . he told me you were dead," Henry said in a hoarse voice. "God forgive me, I believed him."

"I'm not dead," she said stupidly.

Her brain felt full of soggy oatmeal. Nothing made sense. She searched Henry's face for the disdain she deserved. In Vicenza, her father had been so adamant that her mother and brother wanted nothing to do with her.

"What are you doing here?" Demarest asked from behind her. She started at the sound of his voice. She'd forgotten he was in the room.

Henry blinked too as though lost in the fascination of seeing the sister who had disappeared from his life. He didn't shift his gaze from Antonia. "John Benton wrote to say he'd seen my sister in London. I rode down immediately I got the letter."

Antonia realized that her brother was covered in a fine coating of dust and he looked exhausted. Dark circles marked his eyes and he was unshaven and windswept. In the shock of his arrival, she hadn't noticed details.

"But how did you know I was here?"

Had Johnny followed her from the park? Surely he hadn't, if only because Ranelaw would have stopped him. At best, he'd guessed her general direction but not the specific address.

Again Johnny Benton let her down. She'd begged him to conceal the fact that he'd seen her. She should be furious, but after Ranelaw's treachery and Henry's astonishing arrival, this new disappointment from her first lover barely mattered.

"I didn't." Henry looked as bewildered as she felt. "I hoped to enlist Godfrey's help in finding you. I've lost touch with most of my London connections and Godfrey has always known everyone. He seemed the right man to ask."

"She's been with me the whole time," Demarest said. "Since your ass of a father threw her out into the world without a penny to bless herself."

Neither Antonia nor Henry paid him a moment's attention. Instead they stared fixedly at each other as if gauging their next step in this strange, fraught reunion.

"Why should you want to find me?" She stiffened and bitterness sharpened her tone. "To make me swear Lady Antonia Hilliard will stay dead? Ten years ago I promised Papa I wouldn't contact you or Mamma again."

Henry paled under her attack and his face tightened with grief. "I can't blame you for hating me. I'm so sorry for everything."

Sorry?

The word shuddered through her like a physical blow. Henry didn't owe her an apology. It wasn't his fault that she'd eloped with Johnny.

She was vaguely aware of Godfrey Demarest watching her with a concerned expression. Shock held her speechless as she stared at her brother. She desperately tried to understand what he wanted of her. Once she'd been certain he'd never wish to see her again. Now she wasn't nearly so sure.

When she didn't immediately reply, Henry looked troubled. "I hope you'll find it in your heart to forgive me for accepting Father's word when he told us you'd died of a fever in Italy. Even then, I should have realized it was all too convenient. I'm a damned scientist. I know to look more closely at the evidence."

If they'd ever met again, she'd expected him to greet her with outrage and derision, but he didn't sound like he detested her. He sounded as if he regretted her absence, as if he'd missed her all these years as she'd missed him.

Hungrily she searched his face. He was so like their father, except his eyes were kinder and his mouth wasn't set in perpetual judgment upon an inadequate world. Now her brain worked again, she read guilt and unhappiness and astonishment in his expression.

She didn't perceive a shred of condemnation.

Her hands clenched at her sides as uncertainty hammered at her. All this time, had she misjudged Henry? Had she also accepted her father's edict too easily? Should she have plucked up courage to write to her brother after the late earl's death? She'd longed to, if only to share her sorrow now that both their parents were gone.

"Henry, I was sure you'd hate me." Her voice was thready. She folded her arms over her chest to steady her shaking.

"Of course I don't." Henry ventured a step closer. He was close enough for her to see he trembled too. His voice was raw with emotion. "I've mourned your loss the last ten years. I've blamed myself for what happened. I loathed that I introduced Benton into our house. If I'd known what the blackguard intended, I'd have horsewhipped him from the door before letting him come within a foot of my sister."

Hesitantly Henry laid a hand on her arm, as though afraid she'd vanish in a puff of smoke like some magical creature. His face was somber and his voice shook with the power of his feelings. "I can't tell you how happy I am to find you alive."

Antonia quivered under his touch but didn't shift, either forward or away. After the long silence, this swift, unconditional acceptance seemed unreal, untrustworthy. "Are you?"

"Of course." He laughed with what she was surprised to recognize as joy. His voice rang with certainty as he repeated his assertion. "Of course!"

She blinked back hot tears. This still felt like a dream, although she'd long ago relinquished dreams of reconciliation with her family. Of all the possibilities for her future, she hadn't imagined that her brother might find her and offer absolution.

"Really?" she asked unsteadily.

"Really," he said with such a wide smile, she couldn't doubt his sincerity. The smile was heartbreakingly familiar and made him look much younger, for all his physical exhaustion. Briefly he looked like the boy she'd grown up with, not the man he was now.

She wasn't sure who moved first, but suddenly he hugged her and she hugged him. Although she told herself she'd cried enough, she burst into difficult sobs. All her misery and fear and regret united with this unexpected blessing to level her last defenses. For ten years, she'd felt completely alone, yet now it seemed her brother had always loved her.

"I still can't believe it," she said in a choked voice when she eventually drew away. She dashed her hands across her eyes but still tears welled.

"Neither can I." Henry kept his arm around Antonia as he turned toward Demarest, who had moved to stare out the window to give brother and sister some privacy. "Thank you for keeping her safe. Although why in God's name you didn't tell me you had her, I'll never know."

"I was sworn to secrecy." Demarest turned to survey them with a faint smile. "And your father was such a self-righteous prig, if you'll pardon my frankness, I knew he wouldn't relent once he'd disowned her."

"He never admitted the truth, even on his deathbed," Henry said with a trace of anger, his arm tightening around Antonia. "At least that bastard Benton showed a glimmer of conscience and informed me Antonia was alive. When I read his letter, I was terrified to think what my sister had suffered without her family's protection."

"She's had her family's protection," Demarest said with a hint of hauteur.

"I'll always be grateful," Antonia said, even as she couldn't scotch the recognition that Eloise Challoner's fall from grace in similar circumstances to hers had resulted in a much harsher fate.

She couldn't quite place her cousin's mood. While he seemed pleased for her, his manner held an element of reserve. Perhaps he realized that Henry's arrival meant at the very least a delay before Antonia accepted his proposal and his life proceeded as he wished.

Demarest crossed to the sideboard and poured three brandies. "It's early but we all need this."

With an unsteady hand, Antonia accepted the glass. Long ago, she'd smothered the smallest hope of returning to her family. It was too late to make peace with her mother. Her father, she knew, would never have forgiven her.

But her brother was here. More than that, her brother didn't hate her.

The shock left her reeling.

Henry released Antonia and turned to her. "I want you to come home."

Antonia frowned, not sure she'd heard right. "Are you sure? We might spark the scandal Papa was so eager to avoid."

In spite of her doubts, her heart lurched with relief at the prospect of returning to Blaydon Park. To the places she'd loved. To life as Lady Antonia Hilliard.

No more disguises. No more deception.

A new start where she could rise above Ranelaw's treachery. His cruel deceit and irredeemable wickedness had bruised her soul. Even the miracle of Henry's loving welcome couldn't heal that festering injury.

Escaping to Blaydon Park provided a spark of hope. The idea of home would always have beckoned like soft music on a summer's evening. Now she wanted to weep with gratitude at the promise of safe harbor.

Ranelaw would never follow her to Northumberland.

Don't be ridiculous, woman. Ranelaw won't follow you anywhere. Nor do you want him to. He's a liar. He deserves nothing but scorn and hatred.

"If there's a scandal, we'll weather it." Henry drank his brandy as though gossip worried him not one whit. "I've finally found my sister. I'm not giving her up just to silence a few wagging tongues."

It wasn't going to be easy, whatever Henry's confident predictions. Her past mistakes might still poison her future. "Johnny could talk."

"I doubt he will," Demarest said, sipping his brandy. "He might be a fool but even he must realize his actions do him no credit."

"Let him talk," Henry said steadily. "That cad Benton isn't going to dictate my future."

Antonia realized Henry had indeed changed. He'd grown immeasurably stronger. Although he was her senior, she'd been the one to defy their parents, to insist on her own way. He'd always been lost in scholarly pursuits, unworldly, eager to restore peace so he could retire untroubled to the library. His determined expression as he raised his glass to her in a silent salute indicated he'd learned to fight for what he wanted.

She tried to draw courage from his certainty but she felt

battered by the heart-rending events of the last days. She'd lived through a storm of passion, fury, danger, and bitterness. Now a new life stretched ahead. Or perhaps a return to an old life she'd thought barred from her forever.

She felt too much at a loss to be happy, although gratitude for her brother's ready forgiveness warmed her heart. For the first time in so long, she had a genuine choice in what became of her. She hardly believed it. More than that, she belonged to a family again. Perhaps returning home to Northumberland as Antonia Hilliard might knit together the tattered fabric of her heart.

Chapter Thirty-one

*T*HE dawn was pure and fresh, promising hope and a new beginning.

Lies, all lies, Ranelaw knew. He tilted his head to stare into the sky. It was the perfect pale blue of Antonia's eyes.

The memory cut like a honed knife and he briefly closed his eyes in pain. When he opened them, two swans flew overhead. For all his anguish, the sight made his heart leap.

A good day to die.

A better day to wipe Benton from the face of the earth.

Behind him, Thorpe murmured to the doctor. Across the open field, Benton checked his pistols. The man hadn't glanced up when Ranelaw arrived in his stylish curricle drawn by two magnificent grays.

A pity—Ranelaw had taken particular care with his appearance. He refused to face his enemy looking anything but his best. His dark blue superfine coat was new, he wore his favorite waistcoat with its twining ivory Chinese dragons, and he'd had Morecombe shave him to within an inch of his life.

Pun intended.

Tracking Benton down yesterday had proven easy. The man might consider himself a louche bohemian, but he'd been predictable enough to take up residence at the Pulteney Hotel. The duel had been equally simple to maneuver.

Ranelaw had claimed not to like the fellow's waistcoat—the truth as it happened; the maggot dressed like a damned macaroni.

In his hotheaded younger days, Ranelaw had fought several duels. Never killing affairs, although his right arm bore a scar where a bullet had grazed him. Since then he'd kept up his shooting, the way he maintained all the skills of the London gentleman. Only now did he reflect on his life and consider how much time he'd wasted in meaningless pursuits.

What he did this beautiful morning had meaning.

He didn't deceive himself. No matter what happened, Antonia was eternally lost to him. Two women he'd loved and two women he'd failed. Eloise's ruin would go forever unavenged. But today he'd redress the besetting tragedy of Antonia's life.

Benton approached. Ranelaw recognized his second although he couldn't immediately remember the fellow's name. Benton's second and Thorpe stepped aside to discuss arrangements and try to resolve the quarrel without bloodshed.

Ranelaw had no intention of accepting Benton's apology. Even if Benton had something to apologize to his opponent for. Benton owed his apologies to Antonia. But she rightly scorned both his excuses and pathetic proposal.

How Ranelaw loved her proud spirit. He recalled the moment she'd aimed her gun at him two days ago, her hand as steady as an old soldier's. He couldn't think of another woman in Creation with backbone to do that.

He'd waited his whole life to fall in love. At least when that calamity befell him, he'd chosen a female worthy of his devotion.

He wasn't worthy of her. Although he'd remember to his last breath how it had felt to hold her in his arms.

"I never considered you virtue's defender, Ranelaw," Benton said snidely.

Ranelaw arched his eyebrows in a manner designed to

make Benton bristle. "Virtue? I'm shooting you for your sins against fashion, old chap."

Benton's shoulders formed a stiff line and his hands fisted at his sides as if he wanted to punch Ranelaw's supercilious expression. "Any harm is purely the concern of the lady and myself."

Choking fury wedged in Ranelaw's throat. He fought the urge to wring the wretch's neck. "If a lady was involved, I would hope you're gentleman enough not to mention her name."

Benton's lip curled in disdain. Through his anger, Ranelaw was unwillingly impressed—and surprised—at the man's courage. He'd expected the milksop to weep and tremble.

Benton seemed angry rather than afraid. Perhaps Antonia hadn't been so mistaken in her infatuation after all. Whether jealousy fueled Benton's outrage or not, he demonstrated considerably more pluck than he had in Hyde Park. Obscurely Ranelaw was glad. Shooting a sniveling coward wouldn't satisfy the murder in his heart.

The seconds approached and made a final attempt to effect reconciliation. Ranelaw remained strangely divorced from proceedings, as though he observed events on a stage. Automatically he followed the protocol, paced out the distance. Turned. Benton gazed back with steady dislike as he raised his gun.

No, Antonia hadn't been mistaken in her first lover.

Briefly Ranelaw glanced at the sky, aware this was the last time he might see it.

Blue, blue, perfect blue. Antonia's eyes.

There was a sharp report, birds burst squawking from the surrounding trees, Ranelaw felt a burning, blinding pain in his side. He staggered, not immediately connecting the three facts.

And realized Benton had shot him.

Devil take the fellow, he'd never imagined the bastard would muster the nerve.

Blackness edged his vision and each beat of his heart vibrated through his body like a huge drum. He swayed and realized he'd collapse unless he overcame this weakness.

If he fell, he mightn't shoot.

Another failure in a life redundant with failures.

No, it wouldn't be. He'd die accomplishing this one thing. Then he wouldn't make a squeak of complaint when Satan snatched him below.

As if down a long, long tunnel, he was aware of Thorpe rushing forward. His friend said something low and urgent. Through the din in his ears, Ranelaw couldn't make out the words.

He summoned strength to gesture the man away. "No." Anything further was beyond him.

He could do this. He would do this.

Benton stood firm, his gaze unwavering. Slowly, so slowly, Ranelaw lifted his arm. The gun suddenly weighed ten tons. He was shaking and the world approached and retreated in a most alarming fashion. If not for the blazing pain, he'd imagine he was three sheets to the wind on rotgut gin.

He waited for his aim to steady. His attention fixed on his opponent, the man who had seduced and betrayed Antonia and set her on the path to another rake's bed ten years later.

He'd hated Benton with a passion since he learned how the slug had wronged Antonia. The virulence of his loathing should have told him she meant more to him than he was willing to admit.

But self-deception was a way of life for the Marquess of Ranelaw.

No longer.

Benton waited stoically for the bullet. Waited to die. Ranelaw gritted his teeth and forced himself to focus.

As he stared down the barrel of his pistol at the man he'd sworn to kill, he couldn't deny the stark, unpalatable truth.

Johnny Benton was no worse than Ranelaw himself.

In fact, he and Johnny Benton were brothers under the skin. Brothers in iniquity.

He could shoot Benton. He could do it now. But he had no real right to take the fellow's life.

"Ranelaw, for God's sake, let the doctor see to you," Thorpe begged behind him. The voice traveled down that same long tunnel, longer now. As though the world receded further and further away.

He should regret his demise, he supposed. When all he really regretted was not telling Antonia he loved her. She wouldn't care now, but once, once she might have appreciated knowing they shared more than tawdry seduction.

Except there had never been anything tawdry between him and Antonia. Apart from how he'd betrayed her to stay true to his sister.

Life was hellishly complicated. By rights, he should be relieved to relinquish it.

He staggered and felt rather than heard Thorpe leap toward him. "No," he said again.

The agony approached a point where he had difficulty staying upright. He struggled for one last moment of clarity.

Before giving up the ghost, he needed to do something. He stared at Benton. The man's face was set with grim knowledge.

Ranelaw raised his gun, paused to beat back a wave of dizziness.

And fired into the air.

The shot echoed eerily. Blackness surged up to steal the light.

Antonia waited in the hall for Henry to come down from his room so they could leave for Northumberland. Yesterday she and her brother had talked until exhaustion after his hard ride overcame him. She was still nervous about returning to Blaydon Park, but Henry assured her everything would be all right. During the long journey north, they'd come up with some believable story to explain her reappearance.

This morning Cassie was engaged to go shopping with the Merriweathers. Only Antonia and Cassie were aware of the strategy behind the decision to continue with her social activities. If rumors arose about her disappearance from the fête champêtre, her public insouciance would contradict gossip.

At breakfast Cassie had been subdued and a little snappish. Eloise's tragic history still gnawed at her so she'd been unusually sullen with her father, not that he seemed to notice. Antonia's departure left Cassie bereft and unsettled, however glad she was that the rift with Henry was healed. Northumberland was at the other end of the country and it was clear Antonia would never again play the dour and watchful chaperone.

Although Antonia was touched by Cassie's unhappiness at her departure, it had been a relief to consign the girl to her friends. Recent days left Antonia jittery and overwhelmed. She had little patience to spare for a fractious Cassie.

She knew she'd miss her cousin like the very devil, but today she felt drained and listless. She just wanted to flee London without delay. Freedom hovered like a heavenly vision.

Henry descended the stairs at a canter. It was oddly comforting how immediately they'd returned to their easy affection. Hard to believe ten years had passed since they were together. She felt like she'd left him only yesterday.

Demarest followed Henry more slowly. She knew he was happy her brother was restored to her. But she also knew that, for a man whose comfort was his priority, the delay in her answer to his proposal irked. She couldn't keep him waiting long. But she needed to see her childhood home, become Lady Antonia Hilliard again before she decided where her path would take her.

Henry had asked her to become chatelaine of Blaydon Park. That offer would make her father twitch in his grave, she was sure.

Life as Henry's hostess wouldn't be so different from life

in Somerset, except she'd receive all honor due Lady Antonia Hilliard. She'd reclaim her independence, and she'd never again have to deal with lying rakes who broke her heart without a second thought.

Demarest had wanted Henry to stay in London, recover from his journey, reacquaint himself with his sister in a familiar setting. But her brother had always hated Town, and Antonia was eager to return to Blaydon Park. She supposed it was a sign of grudging approval that Demarest lent them his traveling chaise. And fresh clothes for Henry. Her brother had been in such a lather to find her, he hadn't packed any necessities.

She couldn't help wondering about the condition of the estate. The Henry she'd known tended to lose himself in his studies, remaining blithely unaware of practicalities. In a way, this was reassuring. One of the satisfactions of her restricted existence in Somerset was that Mr. Demarest was such a careless landlord, he left all decisions in his absence up to her. But of course she now realized he was careless about everything, including people.

Henry had never been careless, just preoccupied. Which offered her an opportunity to exert a positive influence on Blaydon Park.

She badly needed to feel necessary to someone somewhere.

Whatever choices she made, she'd never marry for love. Passion wounded too deeply. A comfortable, settled life with an older man who made no demands still appealed. The lure of becoming Cassie's stepmother was a strong inducement for accepting Demarest.

Or maybe now she was a woman of means, she wouldn't marry at all.

She couldn't imagine she'd ever return to London. She would remain safely in the country. In the capital, she ran the risk of Johnny causing trouble or someone recognizing her as Cassie Demarest's chaperone.

For so long, she'd been at fate's mercy. Now new opportunities beckoned, offering more than she'd ever imagined. It seemed too good to be true.

She knew it was too good to be true.

No matter. She had to move beyond the pain and illusory joy of the last weeks. Her future mightn't be exciting or romantical, to use Demarest's term. But it was at least secure.

"Are you ready?" Henry asked.

"Yes." She choked back a sob. Which was ridiculous. She refused to cry over losing Ranelaw. He hadn't been hers to lose.

The fact that he didn't merit a moment's regret couldn't change her heart. Her heart was determined to mourn him. And hate him. She hoped he roasted in hell. Even if she wept bitter tears of pity over his damnation.

She abhorred this morass of contradictory emotions. The longing for Northumberland's clean emptiness was an ache in her bones. Perhaps once she was back where she belonged, she'd stop feeling so confused and miserable.

With silent punctiliousness, a footman opened the door to the street. Defiantly she raised her chin. A new life awaited. The Marquess of Ranelaw be damned.

Mr. Demarest pressed her gloved hand with a meaningful gesture. "Please remember what I asked you," he murmured.

"Of course," Antonia replied equally softly.

She hadn't mentioned Demarest's proposal to Henry or Cassie. What would her brother make of such a marriage? Perhaps having finally found her, he'd feel she owed him her complete attention. At least for the foreseeable future.

Another footman opened the coach door. Demarest took her arm with a possessive gesture that only someone as unworldly as Henry would miss. He led her outside.

She was about to step into the carriage when she realized someone ran along the street toward them.

To her astonishment, it was Cassie. Not Cassie in decorous London mode. But Cassie as her boisterous, pink-cheeked country self. The Cassie she'd watched chase stray calves and runaway chickens and flap her arms to frighten birds off sprouting seedlings.

"Antonia!" Several paces behind her, Antonia saw Bella struggle to catch up to her charge, who hurtled down the city street as though she crossed an empty field. "Antonia, wait!"

Cassie must have decided to say good-bye after all. Pleasure briefly warmed her turbulent regret. Mr. Demarest—Godfrey, she supposed she should call him—smiled tolerantly at his daughter's hoydenish ways. Henry stared curiously at his cousin. With her bonnet askew over ruffled fair hair and her face flushed with exertion, she looked breathtakingly pretty.

Cassie raised a trembling hand to her heaving chest and spoke in a wild rush. "Antonia, there was a duel. Ranelaw's been shot. He's like to die."

Like to die...

All Antonia's self-serving lies about looking forward to her new life evaporated in an instant.

To reveal the jagged shards of her heart.

"What?" she stammered, wrenching free of Demarest.

Cassie bent at the waist and struggled for breath. Her words emerged in staccato bursts. "John Benton shot him. This morning. In Richmond."

Through the clamor in her head, she managed an astonished whisper. "Johnny shot Ranelaw?"

How was it possible that *Johnny Benton* had shot *Ranelaw?*

Ranelaw was the lethal one. Benton was as friable as pastry in comparison.

This made no sense. Duels were illegal, a capital offense. If death resulted, the survivor risked prosecution for murder.

Demarest grabbed her arm. "What is all this? What is this scoundrel to you? I thought the cur went after Cassie and you told him to take his filthy attentions elsewhere."

She shook him free and stared aghast at Cassie. "You must be wrong."

Slowly Cassie regained her breath. Heaven knew how far

she'd come. The girl's reaction to hearing the Marquess of Ranelaw was at death's door must have aroused curiosity. It hardly mattered. All Antonia heard, repeated over and over like a tocsin, was *like to die*.

Nightmare images of blood flooded her mind. Ranelaw lying in a pool of red, screaming with agony. She closed her eyes and struggled to prevent her stomach forcing her breakfast back up her throat. How could Ranelaw die? Even when she'd threatened to shoot him, she'd recognized a mere bullet couldn't put paid to that animal vitality.

Yet it seemed a mere bullet promised to do just that. A bullet fired by her effete first lover. The earth popped off its axis and went dancing through space.

Cassie spoke in a jumbled rush. "Suzannah's brother heard at his club. Ranelaw had some quarrel with Benton's waistcoat. Benton's fleeing for the Continent to evade the law. Ranelaw is at home, but they say he won't survive the day."

Henry frowned, his eyes darting between the two women as though he measured volatile chemicals in an experiment. "What is this to my sister? It's interesting gossip, I grant. But surely not worth haring across London to deliver."

Cassie stared at Antonia. "You can't let him die believing you hate him."

"I do hate him," she said flatly, even as she felt her life ended with Ranelaw's.

Cassie's jaw hardened with purpose. "Then I daresay you don't care he's dying."

"I . . . I didn't say that." Dizzy, she grabbed Cassie's hands and squeezed them. She was sinking in horrible sucking quicksand. None of this felt real. Ranelaw couldn't die. She wouldn't let him.

Blindly she released Cassie and whirled toward the waiting carriage. Henry rushed after her. Through her anguish, she heard his angry bewilderment. "What's this about, Antonia? You told me you've spent the last years as Cassie's chaperone. Yet it seems you're on terms of intimacy with a libertine whose reputation is so foul, gossip's reached Northumberland. I knew the marquess at Oxford. He was as wild as a jungle tiger even as a youth."

"Antonia, explain yourself," Demarest insisted from beside Henry.

If she'd been less distraught, the weight of masculine disapproval might have daunted her. As it was, she barely noticed. All that mattered were those grim words, *like to die.*

"I must go to him," she said under her breath, speaking to herself as much as to anyone else. She placed one trembling hand on the coach's door frame.

"Don't be insane, woman," Demarest spluttered behind her. "You can't call on a single man in his home. Particularly a single man of Ranelaw's depraved habits. The fellow's a loose fish."

Antonia turned to respond but fell silent when Cassie glared at her father. Fleetingly the girl looked much older than her eighteen years. Older, wiser, and adamantly unforgiving.

"Don't be a hypocrite, Papa," she said sharply.

"Cassandra Mary Demarest!" he began.

"I know about Eloise Challoner." Antonia had never before heard Cassie use that frigid tone.

"I have no idea what you're talking about," Demarest blustered. But a flush mottled his face and he stepped back as though disowning his role in that old tragedy. If she'd ever doubted that her cousin had ruined Eloise, she doubted no longer.

"Don't lie," Cassie said still in that cutting tone. When she turned to Antonia, her voice softened. "Toni, you must hurry."

Every rule of society, of common sense, insisted Antonia depart London with Henry and never spare Ranelaw another thought. She owed Ranelaw precisely nothing. Over the last two days, she'd almost convinced herself she loathed him.

Of course she didn't.

The truth was as inarguable as the sky above her or the hard pavement beneath her feet. It had been part of her so long, she'd hardly noticed.

She noticed now.

She loved the Marquess of Ranelaw. It didn't matter what sins he'd committed. Nothing changed what she felt.

She hadn't given herself to Nicholas because after ten years of chastity, she suddenly had an itch to scratch. She'd given herself to Nicholas because she loved him more than she'd ever loved anyone.

She couldn't let him die. Nothing—reputation, duty, fear—would stop her seeing him.

"Henry, I'm sorry," she said quickly, her heart thundering with panic. "We must delay our travel. Or you can go without me."

"I don't want to go without you." Her brother looked troubled.

If Nicholas was as close to death as Cassie said, Antonia had no time to make him understand. As though he'd ever understand why his ruined sister, finally on the verge of rehabilitation, was set on ruining herself again. This time for good.

"I'll send a note when I know the situation." Or slink back grieving. She didn't say the words aloud. She refused to countenance the possibility that the man she loved might die. If Nicholas could lure her into his bed, he could do anything. Including survive this ridiculous duel he fought over her. She wasn't green enough to imagine that the identities of the adversaries could be accidental.

Nicholas was a fool. But he was *her* fool. She'd be damned before she relinquished him to the grave.

Demarest scowled and she suddenly wondered if their marriage would have been the arrangement of equals she blithely imagined. Although she could never marry him now, however advantageous the match. She couldn't marry another man when every beat of her heart echoed Ranelaw's name.

"Antonia, be sensible," he said urgently. "Even if the villain survives, he'll only tumble you, then discard you for another bit of muslin."

"I don't care," she said stubbornly.

"You of all women must realize—"

"I don't care," she repeated, and glanced up at Thomas, listening avidly from the driver's box. "Thomas, take me to Grosvenor Square. As fast as you can."

"Yes, my lady." He tipped his hat in her direction.

She leaped into the carriage, slammed the door, and clung tight as the vehicle lurched into movement. It was absurd, but she had the strongest presentiment that if she saw Nicholas in time, he wouldn't die.

She realized she murmured over and over in a low voice. A repetitive plea to heaven. Surely God wouldn't deprive her of her beloved just when she'd discovered she couldn't live without him.

She heard shouting behind her. She paid no attention.

The coach jerked to a halt.

Oh, no, no, no, no, no.

Her heart stuttered with anguished denial. They couldn't stop her now. Demarest might deny her the carriage. In which case she'd find a hackney. Walk if she must.

Good God, she'd crawl across London to convince Nicholas to fight for his life.

At this moment, she didn't care whether he spent the rest of that life with her. All she cared about was that he recovered. That somewhere in the world Nicholas still walked and spoke and laughed. The prospect of him pursuing other women paled to insignificance compared to the horror of losing him altogether.

Her hands clenched in her lap as the door opened and Henry swung in. The fusillade of angry words died on her lips as he landed next to her. "Henry, what are you doing?" she asked blankly.

He wrenched the door shut and knocked on the roof.

The coach resumed its progress with a rattling dash that answered her burning anxiety.

"You could be heading into a difficult spot." Henry smiled, taking one of her hands in silent comfort. "You might like someone at your back."

Chapter Thirty-two

*A*NTONIA braced for an inquisition but Henry remained blessedly quiet as the carriage careered through the thick traffic with a recklessness that in other circumstances would terrify her. As it was, she hardly noticed. She only knew her desperate need to see Nicholas, to offer forgiveness, to beg him to live.

Sightlessly she stared out the window at the packed streets. All she saw was an inner landscape of blood, darkness, and despair.

And unbearable, eternal loss.

She'd wondered whether Cassie's news was accurate. The moment the carriage reached Grosvenor Square, she wondered no longer. Outside Ranelaw House, thick straw lay along the street to muffle traffic. Onlookers massed at the black railings dividing house from footpath.

Tidings of the Marquess of Ranelaw's approaching demise spread. As their coach pulled up, more people joined the crowd. Surprisingly the gathering was subdued, almost respectful.

The arrival of the Demarest coach and the alighting of two people from society's upper echelons, even if two people unknown to the mob, caused a stir. Antonia lowered her head so her bonnet hid her distinctive features. With silent reassurance, Henry took her elbow and effortlessly cleared a path to the two brawny footmen guarding the shallow stairs.

Antonia hadn't prepared to fight her way through curious bystanders or servants determined to preserve their master's privacy. She should have realized that Nicholas's wound would be a public matter. She should have realized, in contrast to her previous visit, that Ranelaw House would be a center of activity.

She had cause to be grateful for Henry's partisan presence. Another sign that he'd matured beyond the callow youth she remembered. His quiet authority, his air of breeding, his refusal to allow mere domestics to bar access to the house countered all opposition. He and Antonia swept inside without revealing their identities.

Fear held her trembling and mute as the door shut, enclosing them in the marble entrance hall. The dull thud held a grimly doom-laden note and the statues loomed against the walls like funerary monuments.

As her belly cramped with the painful, joyful memory of the last time she was here, she dragged in a breath to steady her nerves. What transfiguring passion she'd shared with Nicholas. She was such a willfully blind fool. She should have realized then that she was hopelessly in love with the scapegrace.

To her surprise, Lord Thorpe emerged to greet them. She'd expected a servant, perhaps the supercilious butler who had refused her admission the day of Cassie's abduction. Thorpe had always impressed her as a sensible man. In fact, at first she'd been puzzled that he and Nicholas were friends. For so long, she'd obstinately closed her eyes to any evidence that Nicholas was more than a selfish hedonist.

Cassie had lent her a traveling dress, so she was more fashionably turned out than usual. It was unlikely Thorpe would identify her as Miss Demarest's harridan of a chaperone, although she'd watched him dance and flirt through a multitude of balls.

Thorpe smiled at Henry. "Lord Aveson, I haven't seen you in a dog's age."

Henry removed his hat and bowed. "Lord Thorpe, not since our days at Oxford."

"You were such a swot, I'm surprised you remember me."

Antonia stifled an impatient sigh. What did social niceties matter when Nicholas lay dying?

"Antonia, allow me to introduce Lord Thorpe." Henry turned to her. "My lord, this is my sister, Lady Antonia Hilliard."

Manners forced her to curtsy and extend her hand. Thorpe bowed over it and peered into her face. She watched him struggle to force a wisp of memory to the fore. She hardly cared whether he recognized her, but for Henry's sake, she kept her expression neutral as though she met a stranger.

"What can I help you with?" Thorpe asked once courtesies were complete.

"I want—" Antonia began impetuously but Henry spoke over her.

"My sister is an old friend of Lord Ranelaw's. She's heard about the shooting, of course. We come to inquire after his health."

Antonia stared into Thorpe's face, her heart racing with sudden hope. Perhaps he'd say Nicholas made a miraculous recovery, that the rumors of his precarious grip on life were exaggerated. Her chest clenched painfully tight as sorrow settled on the man's pleasant features.

"They've removed the bullet but he hasn't regained consciousness. The doctors, I regret to say, aren't optimistic."

No! Dear God, no!

Antonia staggered and the light faded. It couldn't be true. It couldn't be. When she returned to awareness, she clutched Henry's arm. She sucked in a shuddering breath as the room slowed from its whirl. Both men stared at her in consternation.

"I'm sorry, Lady Antonia. I had no idea—" Thorpe stopped.

Even through her distress, she saw his dilemma. Any woman who had dealings with Ranelaw couldn't be respectable. Yet she bore an illustrious name and she arrived with her brother as if paying a social call.

"I have to go to him," she said in a low voice to Henry. She managed to stand without support. She couldn't weaken now. Not when the worst lay ahead.

"The doctors insist on no visitors." Thorpe stepped toward her with a regretful expression. "If you leave your direction, I'll make sure you receive word."

When he dies.

The sentence's ending rang clearly, for all that it remained unspoken. With a choked sob, Antonia pushed past Thorpe and darted onto the stairs.

"Lady Antonia! You can't—" Thorpe cried out behind her.

"Let her go," Henry said.

Quickly she glanced behind to see her brother grab the other man's arm. Heaven knew why Henry helped her. She could only be thankful.

Her mind closed to every concern but the blazing need to see Nicholas. She picked up her skirts and dashed to the landing. Knowing her familiarity with the house's layout told its own tale, she turned toward the master's bedroom.

Panting with panic more than exertion, she edged open the door to Nicholas's bedchamber. Outside, it was bright day. Inside this room, it was deepest night. The heavy brocade curtains were drawn so close, not a chink of sunlight invaded. On the sideboard, a lamp was turned down low, the dull light gleaming on a frightening array of bottles and vials. A fire burned in the grate. The air was thick and still, and held the rusty taint of fresh blood.

Cautiously, as though sudden movement might initiate untold catastrophe, she crept inside. A balding, middle-aged man sat at Nicholas's bedside. At her entrance, his head turned toward Antonia and his face filled with dismay.

"Your pardon, madam, but His Lordship's physicians forbid visitors." He rose to his feet.

The man must be a butler or a valet. Easier to banish than a self-important doctor. "You may leave us," she said frostily. "I will watch him."

The man looked flustered. "Madam, I . . ."

She read genuine concern for Nicholas in his face. Her voice softened. "I promise to look after Lord Ranelaw. I'll call the moment there's any change in his condition."

The servant glanced from her to the man lying so still, then back again. She read a dawning understanding in his expression. Fleetingly she wondered just what it was he understood. Then she dismissed her curiosity. All her focus was on Nicholas.

The man bowed. "I'll sit outside the door."

She'd seen off Nicholas's last guardian. Dizzying relief shuddered through her, making her knees wobble. She reached out to grab the back of a chair.

"Th-thank you," she whispered.

"At your service, my lady. My name is Morecombe if you require assistance. I am His Lordship's valet."

She nodded, too overcome with fear and grief to summon an answer. Trembling she clung to the chair while Morecombe left the room. Antonia hardly noticed. Her gaze was fixed on the man bathed in shadow.

She straightened, the pressure in her chest building. With shaking hands, she tugged off her bonnet and dropped it onto the chair. Gingerly she approached the huge bed where for a few precious hours, she'd discovered heaven.

Was that only days ago? She felt like she'd aged twenty years since.

If Nicholas died, she'd never feel young again.

He stretched out on his back, the sheet folded at his waist. His guinea gold hair was dark and matted with sweat. A thick white bandage covered his bare torso. His arms lay straight at his sides and his hands splayed flat upon the mattress.

Her heart slammed to a stop. Dimness frayed her vision and she swayed. A choked whimper escaped.

Dear God, she was too late . . .

Then she noted the almost imperceptible movement of his chest. His unnatural stillness resulted from unconsciousness, not death. She sucked reviving air into aching lungs.

With the clear, seeking regard of newly acknowledged love, she studied him. The commanding nose, the high cheekbones, the dark circles beneath his eyes, the lips pale with pain, for all that he lay as still as the statues downstairs.

It seemed sinfully wrong to see him in this neat, unrumpled bed. He wasn't a restful man. He devoured life, stirred turbulent whirlpools of energy wherever he went.

She couldn't let him go. She didn't care what his doctors said. They were wrong. They must be wrong. Johnny Benton wasn't man enough to destroy her beloved.

With a shaky sigh, she dropped to her knees and reached for one of those frighteningly lifeless hands. His flesh was cold under hers. She bit her lip so hard, she tasted blood.

"Nicholas?" she whispered, as though he merely slept. She knew better. He hovered on the brink of the next world.

She'd felt sick with dread since hearing of the duel. But in this quiet room where he remained stubbornly locked away from her, fear deepened to hopelessness.

Tears welling, she pressed her face against his hand. "Nicholas, oh, Nicholas . . ."

She lifted her head and stared into his face, expressionless as it never was when he was awake. He'd moved too far toward oblivion to hear, but she couldn't silence the desperate words. "How could you do this? Johnny isn't worth one moment of your time. I don't care about Johnny. I told you over and over."

Silence greeted her. And in that pause, something clicked at the back of her mind. She stared into that austere, drawn face and a great wave of revelation washed over her.

Nicholas, you fool. You gallant, misguided fool.

As if he'd explained every step he took toward his calamitous decision, she knew why he'd challenged Johnny. What had made no sense suddenly made perfect sense.

The duel wasn't, as she'd immediately assumed, over petty jealousy.

Of course Nicholas understood that her first lover meant nothing to her now. Nicholas knew her better than anyone else and he knew she no longer loved Benton.

He hadn't set out to eliminate a rival. He was too clever to view Johnny as serious competition for her attentions. Nicholas was also too clever to imagine that after abducting Cassie, he'd inveigle his way back into Antonia's favor by shooting the man she'd eloped with so long ago.

Johnny's death wouldn't promote his suit.

As she looked at him, something struck up an echo in her mind. An echo of a man who kidnapped Cassie to avenge a beloved sister.

Because that remained as the only recompense he could offer to a woman forever lost to him.

Were all Nicholas's sins born from the same quixotic impulse to balance the scales of justice? Was she right about his desperate, ill-judged, but strangely courtly purpose in challenging Johnny?

Was the duel some idiotic attempt to redeem her tarnished honor?

"Oh, Nicholas . . ." she whispered, hardly seeing through her tears.

His gesture seemed so outlandishly romantic. Could she be mistaken? Nicholas Challoner was a wild reprobate. Shallow. Uncaring. Unaffected by the tragedies of others.

Except none of that was true. That might be the impression he strove to maintain, but in their tempestuous dealings, she'd seen more than he wanted the world to discern. He'd revealed a universe of feeling the night she'd spent in this room where he lay so close to death.

The echo became louder, turned into certainty. The duel conveyed an unmistakable air of despairing self-destruction.

His reckless challenge carried the same aura of sacrifice that had marked his kidnapping of Cassie.

He'd acted on behalf of someone he loved.

Someone he loved . . .

Surely not.

Nicholas didn't love her. No matter that his attempt to shoot Johnny indicated he cared for her more than she'd realized.

Her frantic mind continued to arrange facts into new patterns. There was so much she hadn't seen, hadn't reckoned with.

In the end, Nicholas hadn't been able to go through with kidnapping Cassie, had he? Or killing Johnny.

Antonia had long ago recognized that he meant to be considerably more ruthless than he was. If he was truly the conscienceless rake of legend, he'd have seduced her the night he broke into her bedroom. Seduced her, then blackmailed her to get to Cassie.

He'd done neither. Poignant emotion stabbed her as she remembered that night. His treatment of her had demonstrated a piercingly sweet chivalry.

He was flawed, he was occasionally wrong, his intentions toward Cassie, toward her, had been black with wickedness. But in the end, he couldn't bring himself to play the complete villain.

She'd often wondered if he was a better man than she thought. Now she recognized that a reluctant hero skulked inside the Marquess of Ranelaw. A hero she'd fallen in love with, in spite of everything she told herself she believed about him.

Her heart had been wiser than she'd credited, after all.

Antonia drew a shuddering breath and in that instant, forgave him freely and absolutely for how he'd hurt her. She just prayed she got the chance to tell him.

"Nicholas, you're a bigger fool than I thought," she muttered, raising his slack hand and pressing it to her sticky cheek. Her throat was so tight, speaking was painful.

His silence crushed her heart. He'd drifted beyond reach. Horrible certainty burgeoned that she was too late. She'd sit here until his last breath seeped away.

It was too much to bear. She bent her head and sobbed, kissing his hand again and again as though her lips could restore life. She'd forgo all the years remaining to her if Nicholas opened his eyes.

"Don't die. Please don't die. Don't leave me." Then in a burst, shaking with feeling, "I'll do anything you want. I'll be your mistress. As long as you want, as publicly as you want. I can't go on without you. You made me live again."

She paused for a ragged breath. Again she spoke, although she realized he couldn't hear. The words were for her sake. Words she'd never said when she'd so frantically raised barriers against him. Barriers that had crumbled the moment he touched her. And he knew it, the rogue.

Please, God, let him live to know it again.

Her voice vibrated with emotion. "You've won. You won long ago. I surrender unconditionally. No more resistance. No more denials."

He remained utterly still, his face pale and peaceful. The peace jarred. Her beloved wasn't a peaceful man.

Antonia's last hope drained away. Excruciating pain lanced her heart.

Right alongside Nicholas, she died by inches. Because the best part of her died with him. The part she'd struggled against acknowledging because it was too wayward and passionate. The part that transformed her into a creature of light and flame. The part that had loved Nicholas first, although love for him now permeated every cell.

She rose on her knees and kissed his lips. He didn't respond. She couldn't bear this. He always responded to her kisses.

In an unstoppable wave, the last, most agonizing confession escaped. "I love you, Nicholas. I will always love you. You will be in my heart the day I die." Then on a final whisper, "God bless you, my darling. God bless you through eternity."

Still nothing.

She lowered her head to his shoulder and wept as her heart cracked into a thousand pieces.

Antonia's frantic pleas made Ranelaw burn. But he was so damned weak, he could only lie still as a stone while she cried over him as though she loved him.

She loved him.

He'd wandered in from the blackness as he would from a riotous night on the town. Not sure if he'd stay at home or return to his carousing. He'd felt the clasp of Antonia's hand. He'd heard the choked anguish in her voice as she begged him to live.

Had she knocked him out with the poker again? Beautiful, fierce dragon.

Then he'd tumbled back into night. The erratic blackness that pursued him wasn't quiet. It was peopled with his ghosts. His chaotic family. Eloise glaring at him in accusation. Cassie, who had proven so unexpectedly valiant.

Most of all Antonia. Passionate, vital Antonia.

The woman he loved. The woman who loathed him.

It made no sense that she pleaded with him not to leave her. Two days ago, she hadn't cared whether he took another breath.

She loved him . . .

During his unruly career, many women had proclaimed their love. This was the first time the truth of the words speared his heart. This was the first time he wanted to return the vow with the same sincere simplicity.

She was so generous, his darling. More generous than he deserved. More wonderful and lovely and good than any man deserved. Although he'd make bloody sure he lived to see she squandered that bounty on him.

He was just such a conscienceless blackguard.

As awareness gradually returned, a chaos of sensations assailed him. Her sticky tears. The ragged sobs. The tingling memory of her lips on his skin.

His side hurt like hell. Like someone poked him with a red-hot iron. Slowly, imperceptibly, he struggled to lift his arm. The movement tugged on his wound and a low, agonized groan escaped.

She jerked up. Immediately he missed the soft press of her body. "Nicholas?"

He felt her shift. The slightest jarring of the mattress shot pain screaming through him. He didn't care as long as she stayed.

Her voice was choked. "I'll fetch the doctors."

Damn it, he didn't want those quacks. He wanted Antonia. Most of all he wanted Antonia to say she loved him. So he could be sure pain-addled fantasy alone hadn't conjured the declaration.

Thank God, she registered his inarticulate protest. She stayed where she was.

Slowly, as though he hoisted a full-grown oak tree with one hand, he forced his eyelids upward. In the gloom, her face swam into sight. Her cheeks were wet and her eyes were swollen with weeping. He'd never seen anything so beautiful.

"Beauti . . ." he forced from stiff lips.

She misunderstood and rose, disappearing from view. He was too weak to turn his head and watch her. Damn it, he yearned to seize her in his arms, yet he couldn't summon strength to move his little finger. Another growl escaped, this time of frustration.

He listened to the clink of glass across the room then, thank God, she came back. Very gently, she slid a hand under his head and trickled water across his lips. He bit back a stab of agony at the movement. Liquid dribbled over his chin and his gut knotted in humiliation. This wasn't how he wanted her to see him.

"Nicholas, please don't die," she said brokenly, wiping his lips with the sheet.

"How . . ."

Her eyes glowed with a light that looked like love, and the pain in his side receded a mite. She worked magic. "I fought through a wall of monsters to get here, my darling."

My darling?

"Not . . ." He stopped and sucked in a breath, then was sorry when his wound protested the movement of his ribs. "Die . . ."

"If you do, I'll hunt you down in Hades," she said with a determination that reminded him how she'd threatened to shoot him.

It seemed perverse to cherish that memory, but he did. He'd chosen an indomitable woman. Life with her wouldn't be easy but, Lord above, it would be exciting. No milk-and-water miss for his marchioness. He'd marry this virago and sire a dynasty of hellions. The prospect shot tingling life through limbs that moments ago had been fit only for a shroud.

She dripped more water between his parched lips. Eagerly he lapped at the coolness. He was as dry as the bloody Sahara. Dear God, he felt like overweight elephants waltzed all over him. Surely his last bullet wound hadn't been this painful.

He forced another word. "Love . . ."

Through the dimness, he saw her color rise. The pink in her cheeks was delicious. *She was delicious.*

"You were awake for that, were you?"

He tried to tell her with his eyes how he hungered to hear those words once more. She glanced down in sudden shyness, then met his gaze squarely.

"I love you, Nicholas Challoner." The vow emerged steadily, firmly, without demur.

He closed his eyes against stabbing emotion. His eyes burned and his throat constricted. What a blockhead. The Marquess of Ranelaw never cried.

Her hand closed hard around his. "Nicholas, I swear if you die, I'll shoot you myself."

That's my girl.

Still something worried him. "Forgive . . ."

Her hand tightened. Strength and vigor flowed into him, making him feel a hundred times stronger.

"I forgive you for snatching Cassie. I even understand why you did it. You're misguided, of course, but not beyond redemption."

If he'd had possession of all his faculties, he'd laugh. Misguided? Yes, that was one way to describe his sins. She turned his rash, dangerous quest for vengeance into a mere peccadillo.

"Not shoot . . ." Good God, he hurtled toward recovery. He managed two words consecutively.

Her lips curved in a misty smile. "I won't shoot you today, at least."

"Risk here . . ."

She shrugged. "I couldn't let you die."

"Not die." A long pause while the pain in his side scaled giddy heights. "Live."

Dizziness distorted his vision. Two sentences clearly sapped his strength. His last words emerged as a hoarse whisper. "With . . . you."

"Yes."

She pressed a fervent kiss to his knuckles. Then she leaned forward and brushed her lips across his. His overflowing heart leaped at that fleeting contact.

Through the pounding in his head, he wondered what she made of his last statement. He suspected she pictured an arrangement considerably less binding than the one he had in mind.

Bad luck for her.

There would be times, he knew, when she'd be sorry he'd claimed her. That didn't mean he'd ever set her free. She'd had her chance to escape and she hadn't taken it.

He struggled to muster fading strength. She needed to know she was his forever.

"As . . . wife."

She'd tame the dissolute rake into a respectable married man. He could hardly wait.

"Nicholas . . ." she said in a faint voice, although she didn't withdraw her hand. "Don't make promises you'll regret when you're more yourself."

Did she but know it, he was more himself now than he'd ever been. Through the discordant symphony of pain, he squeezed her hand. He probably managed little more than a tiny shift of his fingers, but in his imagination, he grabbed her hand with all the purpose in his soul.

"Marry." A cold sweat broke out. His wound hurt like a hundred demons prodded him with pitchforks. His vision turned hazy. He struggled to focus on her face.

He was accounted a brave man but the truth was he just hadn't cared. At this moment, he cared more than life. He needed every ounce of courage to speak.

"Love . . . you." Pain crescendoed with cymbals and trumpets and drums. "Marry . . . me."

Blackness swelled, strong and inexorable as the tide. He couldn't resist its power. Before the dark swallowed him, he heard her speak. Over the stormy rush of blood in his ears, over the thundering agony in his side.

"Yes, Nicholas, I'll marry you."

Good.

He was almost sure he didn't speak the word aloud. But her hand firmed on his in silent acknowledgment. His Antonia held him fast against death. If need be, she'd drag him screaming back to life.

She was his life.

Epilogue

*T*HE convent's parlor was no more welcoming than its gray granite exterior. The only concession to comfort was a small fire in the mean little grate, although the warmth hardly penetrated the winter cold. No flowers or cushions softened the room. The sole decoration was a plain wooden crucifix above the door.

Shivering, Antonia sank onto one of the oak chairs ranged against the wall. She watched her husband pace the flagstone floor like a cantankerous tiger.

Nicholas bristled with hostile edginess. All day he'd been in an odd mood. Longer than that, since the moment she'd convinced him to undertake this journey. Last night when they'd made love, he'd been wild and desperate, almost as wild and desperate as during their first time in the summerhouse. Wicked creature that she was, his unrestrained hunger had thrilled her to the bone.

"They won't let her see us," he said grimly, pausing near one of the tiny barred windows on the far side of the room. It was an overcast day and the cold light shone stark on his moody expression.

"It's not an enclosed order, Nicholas. The sisters are allowed visitors," she said steadily, as she'd said a hundred times before. "Eloise wrote that she was delighted you were coming to the convent."

His lips set in a discontented line and he folded his arms over his powerful chest. He stared out the window. "Well, why isn't she here?"

Antonia smiled at his spiky agitation. It still astonished her to recall her first impressions of this man as someone impervious to emotion, self-absorbed, vain, careless. That shallow assessment was laughably far from the truth.

Six months of marriage had taught her that, if anything, he felt too strongly. He was intimate with few people, but once someone joined that inner circle, Nicholas pledged his complete loyalty. And with that loyalty came vulnerability. When he'd said he loved her, she'd been unaware what a powerful commitment he made to her.

She was strong enough to flourish in the blasting furnace of Nicholas's love. How ironic to remember she'd rejected his original proposal because she'd doubted his fidelity. He loved her with a concentrated ferocity that made her feel the most cherished woman in the world.

"We're earlier than we said we'd be." A good three quarters of an hour.

The convent dominated an isolated glen on the Connemara coast. The nearest town offering suitable accommodation was an hour and a half away. The late marquess had clearly decided to place his daughter beyond reach of temptation.

On the way here today, Antonia had thought Nicholas would get out and seize the reins himself, he'd been so impatient with their driver. Even though the roads were rough and muddy and the way traversed steep hills that tested the horses.

He turned to face her and her brief amusement died. She caught the raw emotions on his face. Hope. Fear. Self-disgust. Yearning. Uncertainty in a man so rarely unsure of himself. "Should we have come?"

"Yes." She spoke with conviction. Eloise's ruin and banishment constituted the defining upheaval in Nicholas's life. He needed to make peace with the past.

They'd been rapturously happy since marrying by special license a few days after he regained consciousness—partly to save the scandal of her presence in his house. But Eloise's fate still weighed on his conscience.

Once she'd scoffed to imagine he possessed a conscience.

He began pacing again. She laced her fingers together in her lap and prayed with all her might that today's meeting had a happy outcome.

As so often these days, her mind strayed to another happy outcome. One hand inched to brush her belly in silent greeting to the child resting there. The child Nicholas had no idea existed.

If he knew, he'd have delayed this difficult winter journey or left her behind. And she couldn't let him endure this fraught reunion without her.

She hadn't worried about traveling. She was as strong as a horse. But she suspected Nicholas would prove a doting and protective parent. Once he knew she was pregnant, her itinerary wouldn't include excursions across the Irish Sea.

Watching him prowl about the room, she wondered what he'd say when she told him about the baby. She hoped he'd be pleased, but he described his own childhood so coldly, she couldn't be sure. Even if he was happy about the news, he'd be furious she'd embarked on this arduous journey while carrying his child.

It had been an interesting six months. Lusty certainly. She'd expected that. Her husband's voracious appetite was familiar. Before his wound was completely healed, he'd debauched her all over his house. At first she'd fretted that sexual activity might slow his recovery, but he'd regained his health with astonishing speed.

Their six months together had delivered myriad surprises too. Passionate clashes as two strong characters established how to live together—it only occurred to her after they married what little time they'd actually spent in each other's company without making love. Clashes followed by even more passionate reconciliations.

A tiny smile touched the corners of her mouth as she recalled those incendiary unions. Then she chided herself for carnal thoughts in this sacred place.

When Lord Aveson's sister appeared seemingly out of thin air and married the Marquess of Ranelaw so precipitately, there had been talk, much of it vicious. Luckily nobody connected Lady Antonia Hilliard, newly returned from a long sojourn in Italy, and the dragon Miss Smith, doyenne of chaperones.

Safe in Nicholas's arms in his rambling manor house, she hadn't cared what poison the *ton* spread. She was happier than any woman had a right to be. If the gossips guessed her joy, they'd be jealous as well as curious and spiteful.

Henry had quickly reconciled himself to the marriage. He expected people to tolerate his scholarly eccentricities and in return he rarely passed negative judgment on others. Late in the summer Antonia and Nicholas had spent a month at Blaydon Park and she'd been touched to note the growing friendship between her husband and her brother.

Returning to Northumberland had been a bittersweet experience. Marriage and ten years away meant that the old house no longer felt like home. She'd enjoyed revisiting childhood haunts but felt no yen to live there again.

Blaydon Park belonged to yesterday. Tomorrow was all Nicholas. And the baby who arrived late spring or early summer. With hopefully more children to come. The big house on the cliffs called out to her to fill it with laughter. She'd garnered enough to know Keddon Hall badly needed an infusion of happiness.

The door opened and a tall woman entered with a purposeful step. Antonia was so busy watching Nicholas's face, she barely paid attention to Eloise. Ready to leap to his defense, she rose. Although why she imagined he needed defending, she wasn't sure.

Fleeting regret shadowed his eyes, then he smiled at Eloise with a surpassing tenderness that made Antonia's heart somersault. Yet again, she recognized what a remarkable man fate had placed in her path when the Marquess of Ranelaw decided to ruin Cassandra Demarest.

She'd wondered if he'd be stiff or distant with his sister, but he surged forward to take Eloise's hands with an open affection Antonia couldn't mistake. "Eloise, I don't know why I waited so long." He kissed her on the cheek.

"Neither do I." The woman's voice was low and musical. With instinctive grace, she untangled her hands from Nicholas's and turned to Antonia.

Without introduction, she'd still guess the nun's identity. Eloise shared Nicholas's black eyes and striking, elegant features. A wimple covered her hair, but even in her shapeless garments, it was clear the young Eloise Challoner would have been beautiful enough to set the world alight. In her late thirties, she was still breathtakingly lovely.

She smiled with the charm Nicholas shared. "You must be the new Lady Ranelaw."

Antonia dipped into a curtsy. "Yes, Sister Eloise. Although please call me Antonia."

"So pretty. And my name is Sister Mary Therese. Nicholas is the only person who calls me Eloise these many years."

Inevitably Eloise's attention reverted to her brother. "Thank you for bringing your wife to see me." She gestured to the hard chairs against the wall. Nicholas's lordly manner must be a family characteristic. "Tell me everything. Your letters left much to be desired, brother mine."

Antonia's dangerous, rakish beloved looked sheepish. She hid a smile as she sat. Nicholas hesitated, then took his place beside her.

At first conversation dwelled upon childhood memories, brothers and sisters and their families, changes to the estate, how his life altered with marriage. Antonia learned more about the widespread Challoner clan in this one afternoon than she'd managed to ferret out of Nicholas in six months.

She hid another smile at his expurgated version of events leading to his wedding.

A novice delivered a tea tray and afternoon wended toward evening. Inevitably the atmosphere became more somber. Nicholas caught his sister's hands in an urgent grip. "Let me take you away, Eloise. Antonia is happy for you to live with us. Or we'll set you up in your own establishment if that's what you prefer."

Eloise frowned, not seeming to understand. "For a visit, do you mean?"

"No, permanently, of course."

She looked puzzled. "Why on earth would I leave?"

"I know you're unhappy."

She tried and failed to pull free. Antonia had noticed her discomfort with physical contact, perhaps part of her training as a religious. For the first time, the façade of calm cracked and bewilderment edged Eloise's tone. "For eleven years I've told you how content I am."

"I know you sought to reconcile me to your incarceration."

To Antonia's surprise, Eloise released a hearty laugh. "Nicholas, you're still a romantic. You were such a brave, intense boy, determined to protect the people you loved. I always admired that and hoped you didn't grow out of it."

Antonia glanced at her husband, wondering how he took this assessment. It seemed his sister saw him much as she did. How could Antonia condemn his chivalrous streak? She knew he'd die for her. Good God, he almost had.

He glowered at his sister. "You don't need to lie anymore, Eloise."

"I've taken my vows."

"Under duress. I'm sure allowance can be made."

Eloise still smiled. "I didn't take my vows under duress. I took my vows because what happened when I was eighteen delivered me to my destiny." This time she managed to pull her hands free. The act seemed symbolic to Antonia, as if she claimed a space Nicholas couldn't share.

"But Father exiled you against your will." Nicholas looked strangely bereft.

In silent support, Antonia took one of his hands. His fingers laced through hers with a swiftness that betrayed how difficult he found this conversation. He'd spent most of his life certain that Eloise was a prisoner. It must be a painful shock to discover his mistake, much as she knew he didn't wish his sister unhappy.

"Of course I was miserable when I arrived. Miserable and ashamed because I'd sinned and I knew it." She paused and for the first time, regret laced her voice. "My wickedness led to my baby's death. For twenty years I've prayed for God's mercy and offered penance for what I did."

For an agonizing moment, the tiny ghost of Eloise's lost daughter hovered in the silent air. Eloise looked pale and sad while Nicholas vibrated with outraged sorrow. Antonia's grip on his hand tightened.

"That bastard Demarest seduced you," Nicholas eventually said through gritted teeth.

Antonia squeezed his hand to remind him where they were. Since her marriage, she'd seen neither Cassie nor Mr. Demarest. In any just world, Demarest should suffer for ruining Eloise, but he continued as he always had. Perhaps rescuing Antonia counted in his favor in the universal balance.

Antonia still cherished hope that she and Cassie might resume their closeness. They wrote regularly but her father had forbidden Cassie to accept Antonia's invitations to Keddon Hall.

Finally Cassie had summoned courage to ask her father about Eloise, but he'd snapped her down and refused to discuss it. He'd blamed Antonia and her new husband for putting ridiculous fancies into his daughter's head. Antonia was well aware how Godfrey Demarest reacted when he was caught wrong-footed, and this anger was typical.

Cassie had confided that she was unsure she'd ever surmount the coldness that now existed between her and her father. So perhaps there was justice after all. Losing his daughter's unconditional love, Godfrey Demarest paid in some measure for his misdeeds.

Eloise drew her serenity around her like a cloak. "I long ago forgave him."

"I didn't," Nicholas snapped. "I never will."

A bell tolled in the distance. With the grace that invested her every movement, Eloise stood. There was a composed strength about Sister Mary Therese that made Antonia immediately accept that this woman had no quarrel with her circumstances.

Eloise's glance at Nicholas conveyed a wealth of love and a stubbornness that Antonia had long ago recognized as a Challoner trait. "I'm sorry. Both that you've come here under a misapprehension and that our meeting was so short. I must prepare for Vespers. If you don't leave soon, you'll be on those awful roads after dark. I don't recommend that."

Nicholas and Antonia stood too. "It's been wonderful to meet you," Antonia said. Beside her, Nicholas was taut with emotion.

Anger? Disappointment? Surprise?

A flash of a smile from Eloise. Again Antonia thought how beautiful she was. "If you're staying in the area, I'd love to welcome you back tomorrow and show you our farm. I've instituted some improvements I think you'll find interesting."

Nicholas inhaled and Antonia tensed for his answer. If this meeting ended in bitterness, she'd hate herself. Her husband needed to absolve himself of his part in Eloise's fate.

His response emerged steadily and with a warmth she couldn't mistake. "I'd like that very much."

Antonia released a relieved breath. It was going to be all right.

Eloise bowed her head as if acknowledging a victory. "Shall we say ten tomorrow? You're welcome to join us for Mass and a simple meal at midday."

* * *

As their shabby coach retreated from the convent, Nicholas remained quiet. Antonia didn't intrude upon his meditations. Difficult to meet a beloved sister after twenty years. More difficult still to come to terms with reality after so many false assumptions.

Only once the convent was well behind them did he release a shuddering sigh and turn to her. With a desperation she felt to her bones, he dragged her into his arms, crushing her tight against the carriage's jolting. She closed her eyes and slid her arms around his waist. Her heart overflowed with love and the longing to stanch his wounds.

For several miles, they remained wrapped in wordless communion. Slowly the shaking tension drained from his body. She tightened her hold, knowing he drew strength from her steadfast love.

Eventually he kissed the side of her neck. She shivered with immediate response.

"I want you." His velvety murmur set anticipation humming in her veins.

Reluctantly she pulled away until her arms loosely encircled him. The interior of the ancient carriage they'd hired in Clifden was dim, but there was enough light to illuminate the hunger in his face. Over the last six months, she'd learned to recognize this expression.

Her lips twitched. "When we get back . . ."

His eyes glinted with sensual purpose. "No, I want you now."

He sounded ruthless and determined. Excitement rippled through her. "But we're in a carriage."

A wicked smile curled his lips. "I haven't debauched you in a carriage."

She blushed. "Actually you have. In your gig in the woods at Keddon. I got a kink in my neck."

Amusement flickered without dissipating the intensity of his desire. "I don't recall you complaining."

As if he'd heard consent, he inched her skirts up. The

trailing heat of his hand on her stockinged leg shot another quivering thrill through her. She caught his hand as it reached the bare skin above her garter. "So you do remember we've made love in a carriage."

"A gig. Not a carriage."

"Do you intend to tumble me in every possible location, my lord?"

He scattered nibbling kisses up her throat and his answer was muffled against her skin. "A man needs a hobby."

She bit back an unsteady laugh. "Anything to keep you occupied and out of trouble."

"Very wifely, my love."

His hand escaped her admonitory grasp and continued up under the leg of her drawers. Then he stopped, curse him. So close to where she wanted him. After six months, she knew he liked to tease.

"I'll arrive in Clifden looking the veriest hoyden." She liked to tease too.

"How else would the veriest hoyden look?" he asked with a sly look.

She arched her eyebrows. "Very droll."

"I promise the jokes will improve if you sit on my lap."

"They'd better." As a sign of acquiescence, she removed her bonnet. Because of course she wanted him too. She'd succor him against the world's harshness. As he said, *very wifely.*

The road was pitted and winding and the carriage's springs were at least thirty years old. Clambering across him, she nearly lost her balance. Cursing under her breath, she grabbed his shoulders and rested her knees on the worn seat on either side of him. Even when his hands circled her waist, her position felt precarious.

She stopped worrying about falling when he stretched up to kiss her. She tasted hunger. More, she tasted the turbulent emotion of the last hours. She wasn't surprised. His lighthearted act was just that, an act.

Love surged in a great wave. She'd use her body to heal the gash in his heart. She'd give him her soul for his plaything. She'd do anything for him.

She kissed him back with every ounce of love she felt. His lips lured her into a magical world where only Nicholas and his touch existed. Until the carriage lurched into a pothole and she nearly toppled into the well between the seats.

She laughed breathlessly as she tightened her grip on his shoulders. "This seems a dangerous occupation."

"Love is always dangerous," he said softly, and cupped her breasts with exactly the pressure she liked.

With pregnancy, her breasts were particularly sensitive. Under layers of wool and linen, her nipples tightened. Liquid pooled between her thighs and she shifted restlessly against his legs.

He groaned into her lips, kissing her again. "Hold on."

She leaned in, brushing her breasts over his chest. The clothing that separated them created unbearable frustration. So quickly he'd stirred her need. He slid his hand through the opening in her drawers and stroked deeply. Stifling a moan, she closed her eyes.

He tugged his breeches open and shifted her so she bore down on the hard pressure. She lifted slightly, delaying the moment of joining.

He buried his face in her neck and she felt his breath, hot and moist, on her skin. She braced against the carriage's sway and sank down.

Immediately there was that sensation of completion that became more profound with every union. He groaned her name and began to move. He wasn't leisurely or gentle. She didn't want him to be. There was something primitive and free about taking him like this as their carriage rattled along the wild Irish coast.

The vehicle's jolting made his thrusts uncharacteristically clumsy but she didn't care. She rose and fell with abandon, clenching handfuls of his coat. It was like riding a runaway horse. Exciting. Reckless. Dangerous.

Just like her husband.

As she shattered into climax, heat flooded her womb and he released a broken sigh. His hands gripped her waist with painful force. She closed around him, draining every last drop of love.

The tension leached from his body as she still quivered around him. She closed her eyes and crumpled upon his chest, feeling the uneven rise and fall as he fought for air.

"I love you," she whispered, her hand resting over his heart with weary tenderness.

She felt him kiss the top of her head. With a satisfied sigh, he settled into the corner so she draped across him. She felt utterly safe and utterly loved.

How strange to think that less than a year ago, she'd been convinced she'd stand alone all her life. Fate had chosen a crooked path for her, a path fraught with unhappiness and difficulty, but she couldn't argue with the final destination.

Nicholas was her heart and always would be.

She listened as his breathing slowed, relishing his strong embrace, drinking in the musky scent of their lovemaking. He rested his chin on her head. She was half asleep, somnolent with physical satiation. The days of traveling had exhausted her.

So far she'd escaped morning sickness, but her body made her aware it was changing. She'd also suffered broken nights, fretting about the meeting between Eloise and Nicholas. Today had been so tremendously important to him. She'd prayed when it was over, he'd find peace.

"When are you going to tell me?" he murmured so low she hardly heard over the carriage's creak.

"Hmm?" She snuggled closer. He was so warm and with night approaching, the winter air grew colder.

Without releasing her, he reached across to open the blinds. Faint laughter edged his voice. "You heard me."

Very reluctantly, she pushed herself up to see his face in the evening's fading light. "Tell you what?" she asked sulkily although of course she knew.

He studied her with the same seriousness she devoted to him. "About the baby, of course."

She stiffened. "You know," she said flatly, placing one hand on his chest, partly for balance, partly because she needed to touch him at this moment when the secret new life inside her ceased to be a secret.

His lips quirked. "My darling, we've shared a bedroom for six months. Of course I know. I'm guessing we'll christen a son or a daughter in six months or so."

Relief flooded her that he didn't sound angry. But did that mean he was pleased? Oh, dear God, let him be happy about the child.

Her hands fisted in his shirt and she spoke in an unsteady voice. "Why did you let me come on this trip, then?"

"Ah, that's it." His black eyes glinted with dawning comprehension. "Would you have stayed behind if I'd asked?"

"I promised to obey."

He snorted derisively. "I've seen little indication you took that promise seriously."

"If you'd insisted, I would . . ."

She paused at the skeptical lift of his eyebrow. "All right, if you'd insisted, I *might* have agreed."

"Really?"

"No," she admitted, and circled her palm in an apologetic caress, feeling the steady, powerful thud of his heart. "Do you mind?"

She caught the hint of a smile. "About the baby or about you accompanying me to Ireland?"

"Either." She paused. "Both."

"Neither."

Joy flooded her. Her lips turned up in an irresistible smile although she didn't move closer. "So are you glad?"

"Yes." Then as if to make sure she didn't misunderstand, "About both. About everything. Most of all that I had the remarkable good sense to marry you, Lady Ranelaw."

She recognized the light in his black eyes as a joy to equal her own. With a tenderness that pierced her heart, he cradled her jaw. He touched her as though she were fragile as glass, strong as steel. He touched her as though she contained his whole world.

"I'm glad too." She heard the betraying croak in her voice. "Now say something provoking before I bawl all over you like a lost calf."

He stroked her face in gentle reproof. "You leave me speechless. I find myself all out of provoking remarks, my beloved."

She rounded her eyes in theatrical shock. "Good God, I don't believe it."

"Believe it." His kiss felt like an act of worship. Her throat closed with poignant emotion and she blinked back tears. His voice dropped so deep, she had to strain to hear it. "In fact, there's only one thing I want to say, dearest Antonia."

She stared mistily into his glowing eyes, her heart brimming with so much love, she thought it must surely burst. "What's that?" she whispered.

"I love you and I always will."

He smiled as if she were more precious than all the jewels on the earth. She managed a wobbly smile back, while tears inevitably won the battle.

"My wonderful Nicholas, that's just perfect."

COMING JUNE 2011

The Sins of Viscount Sutherland

By Samantha James

TURN THE PAGE FOR A SNEAK PEEK . . .

*If Claire Ashcroft could take a knife to
Viscount Grayson Sutherland, first hero of
the Lords of Sheffield Square, she would.
He's the man who killed her older brother
in a duel, indirectly causing the death
of her heartbroken father. Claire doesn't
have a sword to avenge her family, but she
does have her feminine wiles. She plans
to go to London, passing herself off as
a widow, and make Gray fall for her . . .*

$\mathcal{I}T$ was time to let the night play out.

To one who might look on, Claire Ashcroft was the very essence of aplomb. Of composure. Indeed, one never would have guessed the churning need for vengeance that seared her soul. Knowing her nemesis was near tied her stomach in knots.

He stood near the edge of the ballroom, a figure clad in black—a fitting color for the man. His jacket was stretched taut over wide, muscled shoulders; nary a wrinkle was visible. He stood tall and powerful, like a pillar from ancient Greece. His height was such that he seemed to stretch clear to the ceiling. He embodied power. Confidence.

Her eyes slid over his profile. She couldn't deny he was arrestingly handsome to the eye. His hair was black as coal, cropped short. High cheekbones slanted above a square jawline. He was clean-shaven, but his jaw was faintly shadowed. It spun through her mind that he must doubtless shave twice each day.

His was a pose most formidable, yet his pose was indolently careless. His expression was impenetrable.

Claire sucked in a breath. The sight of him made her shiver.

His gaze roamed the room, an almost lazy perusal. She sensed boredom. She sensed cynicism. A distance that was almost icy set him apart. And then he turned—

Their eyes locked, for one long, nerve-shattering moment.

So this was Viscount Grayson Sutherland.

The blackguard who had killed her brother. The man who had changed her life forever.

A strange sensation slid up her spine. He stared at her

through pale blue eyes—or were they a crystal gray? She didn't know which. And now his examination of her had turned no less than fierce. A hundred feelings went through her in that instant. It was as if everything else in the world stood still.

The sheer physicality of the man was . . . Claire struggled for the proper word. Formidable. Almost frightening. She wasn't prepared for it. It was as if his eyes—were they a pale blue or a silvery gray?—sliced into her. A tremor shook her, a shiver that was almost violent.

A hand touched her elbow. "Claire?"

It was Penelope. Dear, sweet Penelope who had paved the way for her reception into Society. Her dearest friend in all the world, Penelope Grove—her name had changed from Robertson when she wed Theodore Grove.

The two of them had attended finishing school together. Penelope was a year older. They were an odd-looking pair, the two of them. Penelope was as delicate as fine china, her demeanor tiny, her features angelic. Claire was half a head taller than Penelope, her limbs long and spare. To Claire, her proportions always seemed out of kilter.

She and Penelope had become acquainted in a rather unusual way. Claire had always felt odd duck out. She was taller than most girls and, indeed, many boys. Little wonder that she'd start finishing school feeling the outsider. She was aware she was the brunt of amusement for several older girls. She had been a bit awkward, the subject of many a joke. She pretended it didn't hurt, but it did. Outside one day in the schoolyard, she saw an older girl named Ramona deliberately push Penelope into a puddle. The front of Penelope's gown and face was spattered with mud. Claire saw tears in her eyes—and saw red. She helped Penelope to her feet and turned to Ramona.

A moment later Ramona was seated on her bum in the middle of the puddle. She burst into tears.

Oh, what satisfaction there had been!

Ramona teased neither of them from that day onward.

And, well, Claire hadn't been dismissed, though only because of her parents' intervention.

She and Penelope had become the best of friends. To be sure, it was Penelope who had taught her there was more to being a lady than anything she'd learned in school.

And Claire was no longer graceless. No longer sensitive to her height. She'd grown into a tall, striking woman who earned many an admiring glance. Her carriage was one of pride and grace, her limbs were long and elegant. But on the verge of a come-out, her mother's unexpected illness took the family back to Wildewood, back to the country—all but Oliver. Claire remained at home to nurse her mother through her illness, a lung infection that had been long and difficult. There was neither the time nor the inclination to return to the current of Society. It all seemed so shallow and insipid after those months at her mother's side.

Then came the stunning blow of Oliver's death.

No, she thought. Not his death—

His murder.

"Are you ready?" Penelope's gaze held hers. One hand rested on the small rise of her belly. Covered by lace and pleats and ribbons, her condition was hardly apparent.

Claire frowned. "Are you all right? The baby—"

"Is merely reminding me of his presence. He moves often now, particularly when I wish to sleep."

Penelope was convinced she carried a boy.

"And as for you, Claire—" Penelope raised her brows— "I would feel better if you told me. Are you ready?"

Claire took a deep breath. She nodded.

"I . . . am ready." Did she sound convincing?

It would seem not. Penelope looked at her closely. "There's still time to change your mind, Claire."

Claire's chin came up. It had taken great care and planning to get to this point. She couldn't have done it without Penelope. Dear, sweet Penelope, whose husband Theo was in the Peninsula fighting that upstart Corsican. It was Penelope's most ardent hope that Theo would be home in time for the birth of their baby.

She suspected that if Theo were here, he might not have approved. But Penelope's help had been immeasurable. Invaluable. Penelope had helped her find lodging, a small, comfortable house—oh, and so many things!

At first Penelope shook her head. "I've seen him at parties, Claire, and he is not a man you should associate with. He is more often foxed than not. He gambles to excess. And where women are concerned—"

"I'm aware of his reputation," Claire had said quietly. "Indeed, I am counting on it."

"Why? How can you gain satisfaction?"

"You won't approve, Pen."

"I won't help you unless I know."

At times Penelope could be stubborn.

"Very well, then. Given the viscount's predilection for the ladies, it's my hope I can use it to my advantage."

Penelope's apprehension was clear. "How?"

Despite her married state, Penelope could also be decidedly innocent. Claire remained silent, while dawning awareness spread over Penelope's face.

"Claire, no! You cannot—"

"Make him fall in love with me?"

Pen's mouth still formed an 'O' of astonishment.

Claire sought to explain. "It's all I can think to do." She was silent for a moment. "Perhaps I am a fool," she said softly. "But I will never rest easy until I make him hurt. I must have some measure of satisfaction. I must at least *try.*"

Claire had reached out and squeezed Penelope's hand. "I beg of you, help me, my dearest friend. I've been away from Society for a long time." Penelope was the daughter of a viscount. "You can take me places where I could not otherwise go. Places where he will be present. You can show me to Society once more."

"Claire, the man is the worst kind of scoundrel."

Penelope's expression was pained. She took a long breath, torn, it seemed. Yet she knew there would be no changing Claire's mind. "Very well, then," she conceded. You are my friend and I will help you."

Claire reached out to hug her. "I know I could count on you, dear. I knew it."

And with Penelope's introduction, the doors to Society had opened. There was Lady Belfield, at whose home Claire had attended tea the other afternoon. And there was Lady Sumpter, whose fete she had attended only last night. And now she was here, at Lady Blakely's ball—her first—in the hope that the viscount would be here.

"No." Claire was adamant. "I won't change my mind, so please do not try to sway me."

"I worry for you," Penelope confided. "I do not want you hurt again."

"He can hurt me no more than he already has." Bitterness seeped through her soul, like slow poison. "He robbed me of my brother. He robbed me of the last of my family." She took a long, steadying breath. "It's time, Pen. Time to make myself known to Grayson Sutherland as your widowed cousin, Claire Westfield, visiting from the country."

Her gaze softened as she beheld Penelope's worry. "Thank you, Pen. No matter what happens, I thank you."

"I would never abandon my greatest friend in all the world." Penelope squeezed Claire's fingers.

Claire smiled slightly. This was it, she thought. The time had come. Was it a fool's errand she undertook? Panic flared, leaving her breathless for an instant. What if the viscount discovered her intention? Her plan to lure him under her spell—to make him fall in love with her—then cruelly dismiss him as if he were nothing.

As Oliver had been nothing to him, she reminded herself. *No, she thought. No.* He couldn't possibly. She wouldn't fail. It was just as she'd told Penelope. She wanted this too much. And she and Penelope had been scrupulously careful, painstakingly anticipating every detail.

In those days following Oliver's death, nearly every thought was of Sutherland, and every thought of him consumed her. If she could take a pistol and shoot the blackguard the way he'd shot Oliver, she would. But she was a woman. She hated the helplessness lent her by her sex.

At night she paced, unable to sleep. Thoughts twisted every which way in her mind. There had to be a way to make him pay. There *had* to be.

And perhaps there was. Claire could not say precisely when it occurred to her. Perhaps she was not as powerless as she thought. After all, his reputation was scandalous. It was said no man dared cross him. No woman could resist him. Her own reputation was of no consequence. By God, perhaps she could use the cur's hedonism to her advantage.

So it was that her plan was set in motion. Her intent? To make Viscount Grayson Sutherland pant after her while holding the cur at bay, only to ultimately turn him away. Only a year ago she would have been horrified at herself. Spitefulness was not her way. Malice was not her way. But if she could wound him in some way—strip him of his pride perhaps—it would give her at least some measure of satisfaction. The cost to herself was of no consequence, none at all.

All she had to do was play her part.

Perhaps Penelope sensed her sudden self-doubt. "You're beautiful, Claire. Every man here has eyes for you."

It was only one man Claire was concerned with.

Beside her, Penelope sucked in a breath. "He's here, Claire. Near the dance floor. Next to the man in gray pinstripes, the Duke of Braddock. Sutherland wears black—"

"I see him." An odd sensation seized hold of Claire. Her voice was faint. She sounded so strange as she heard herself speak.

Pen's eyes searched her face. "Are you certain you want to do this?"

Claire's eyes darkened. "I must," she said fervently. "I must." Determination swept away all fear.

"You must be careful," warned Penelope. "Watch yourself. And watch him."

Adamant as she was, in truth Claire was terrified. But she disguised whatever fears she had. This was too important. Indeed, it consumed her entire being.

Her gaze returned to the man who stood across the polished parquet floor. Hatred spilled through her. Lodged in her breast was dark resolve.

This man had robbed Oliver of his life's blood. Robbed him of all that life's journey should have held.

Oh, yes, Viscount Grayson Sutherland would pay, she vowed. He would pay for Oliver Ashcroft's murder.

She would see to it.

It was time to begin in earnest. Time to put her plan in motion.

By heaven, the game was on.

Two men stood next to each other on the fringes of the ballroom. One possessed hair as dark as blackened ink, the other but a shade lighter. When standing, they were evenly matched in height and build. The pair had been friends since attending Eton together. And now here they were, two of the so-called four Lords of Sheffield Square.

They were womanizers, all, but the duke was indeed a particularly coveted prize. Despite his horrid reputation, matchmaking mamas steered their daughters toward Clive Fielding, Duke of Braddock, eager to gain the prize of marrying a rich, handsome duke. It seemed they would overlook his reputation.

Which quite suited Viscount Grayson Sutherland. Many a miss thrilled to a glance from the viscount, but their matchmaking mamas were quite horrified. They shooed their daughters far distant. Gray cared not that his manner was called beastly. It didn't matter to him in the slightest that he was not considered a "suitable" match. Once . . . once he had been a coveted prize indeed—

So much had changed since then, for now with the

women he sought out—and the women who sought him out—there existed a mutual understanding. Each sought the carnal pleasures of the flesh, no more, no less.

All sought amusement in the arms of a woman.

And now two male gazes had fastened appreciable eyes on the woman who stood near the edge of the dance floor. A beauty he'd never seen before.

Gray couldn't take his eyes from the lovely lady in pale green silk. Her hair was a rich chestnut, gathered in a chignon that set off the slim length of her neck. The sweep of her shoulders rose bare and creamy and silky above her neckline. He watched as the woman raised a hand to tuck back a stray hair that had escaped from her chignon. He caught the flash of gold. A ring.

On her right hand.

One corner of his mouth curled up. His eyes flickered in satisfaction.

Clive followed the direction of Gray's regard.

"The lady has captured your attention, I see."

A smile creased Gray's lips. She had indeed.

"I don't believe I've ever seen her," said Clive.

"Nor have I," Gray murmured. He hadn't yet taken his eyes off the lady. "I believe she warrants closer examination."

"Well, then, if you do not take the first step," Clive said softly, "then I shall.

"I think not, my friend. You have a weakness for blondes. And I should hate to see us quarrel over a woman."

"Ah, never that," Clive said with an arch of one black brow. He paused. "Well, man, what are you waiting for?"

"Indeed."

He advanced. Halfway across the room, he felt a hand on his arm. Glancing down, he saw that it was his mother who waylaid him.

He stopped and gave a low bow. "Mama."

Despite her fragile demeanor, her pale-perfect complexion, Charlotte Sutherland could be an intimidating presence.

Still strikingly attractive, her hair was dark as her son's, shot through with only a smattering of gray.

Vivid blue eyes the color of his flashed. "I know your intention, Gray. I saw you and Clive eyeing that young woman." She waved a hand toward where the lady stood.

HIS MOTHER WAS NOTHING IF NOT DIRECT.

She pulled him to an outside wall. "She is young, Gray, too young for you."

"What," he drawled, "have I joined the realm of the ancients at the age of three-and-thirty?"

"I will not countenance your ruination of that woman."

One black brow climbed high. "I but admire a woman who has been blessed with nature's beauty. And you don't seem to have noticed, Mama, but that woman is a widow. She wears her ring on her right hand, but I would wager she's broken many a man's heart before she ever wed."

"Where are the rest of your profligate friends?"

"Ah. I assume you mean the duke?"

"You know very well of whom I speak. Yes, the duke. And of course the earl and the marquess." Her mouth compressed. "Where has the duke gone?"

Her gaze swung wide before coming to rest again on her son. "Is he finding his entertainment for the night? Every young miss in London should be on guard. I'm well aware of his so-called 'extraordinary' prowess in the bedroom. He is as heartless as he is handsome!" Charlotte's mouth turned down. "And let us not forget the earl and the marquess. I daresay the ball is too tame for their tastes?"

She referred to Bramwell Leighton, Earl of Greystone, and Lucian Tremaine, Marquess of Blackthorne. They were not present this night—

Indeed, they *had* proclaimed tonight's ball . . . insipid.

"Mama, I'm sure I have no idea of their whereabouts tonight. Why do you dislike them so?"

"I'm well aware the duke is known for his so-called performance in the boudoir." Charlotte rapped her fan sharply on his hand. "I do not deny the earl is a man of remarkable good looks, but the knave considers himself quite irresistible, doesn't he? As for the marquess, I'm quite aware of the last affair hosted by the man—an orgy!" She sniffed her disapproval.

"Mama! I am shocked that you know of such a thing. And here I feared your tender ears."

Charlotte's lips were pinched in disapproval. "I am not ignorant of all that goes on in the *ton*. I know of your scandalous reputations, Gray, the four of you. The Lords of Sheffield Square—bah! You are the rogues of Sheffield Square."

"I shall be sure to tell them when next I see them."

"Are you so proud of it, then? Perhaps your efforts would be better put to good use if you sought to save your good name. You haven't been to Brightwood in months. Why, perhaps years!"

"Two," he said coolly. "It's been two years. And I have done my duty with regard to the family estates."

"Have you? There is dignity inherent in our name and your title, Gray. But now, all the world knows of your . . . liaisons."

"Mama, I do not set out to seduce and discard."

"Gray! I know it's in you to love again. Why do you disdain it?"

He stiffened.

"Tell me, Gray. Have you had any kind of lasting relationship since Li—"

"Pray do not speak to me of Lily." His jaw might have been hewn in stone. What his mother said was true. He offered his heart to no one, nor would he. God knew, he had nothing left to give. And what he wouldn't give to forget!

But ever present was the guilt he knew would haunt him forever.

"I do not want a lasting relationship, Mama. I will never marry again. Any woman with whom I am involved expects no more of me than I of her. If you wish me to be blunt, Mama, all we share is a mutual passion—"

"Passion!" Charlotte snapped her fan shut. "Is that what

you tell yourself, Gray? Is that how you excuse yourself? You leave her bed and you feel nothing. You sate your lust—"

"Ah, forgive me, Mama. But you are right. I misspoke. 'Lust' is indeed the better word. I merely thought you might find 'passion' more palatable."

"By heaven, if we were alone, I would box your ears!"

"Mama," he drawled, "I assure you, my women, as you call them, are well-satisfied."

"Do not mock me, Grayson Sutherland."

"Do I distress you, Mama? It was you who began this conversation."

Something passed over Charlotte Sutherland's face. "What has happened to you? How can you be so cold? You have changed so much!"

She was right, Gray acknowledged. He had changed. He'd closed off a part of himself tight against the world. Against himself. Once, his life had been so very different. But now he was empty inside. There were too many shadows. Too many memories. Too much heartache.

That life was gone. He could never reclaim it.

How could he have been so blind?

It was that which tormented him. His mouth twisted in self-deprecation. Whom did he fool? Not his mother. Not Clive. Always, the pain remained. It never left him, no matter how he tried to close it away. And he did try to close it off. With drink. With women. But his pain left him in bondage. It put him in bondage to the past. And no matter how hard he tried, it never left. Why couldn't he be numb inside?

In that instant, he resented his mother—resented her fiercely!—for making him feel like this.

"Gray! Oh, dearest! Where is the man you once were? I don't understand—"

"Precisely," he said with lips that barely moved. "You do not understand."

"Then help me. Help me to understand! I want you to be

happy. Oh, Gray, I know you lost what was so precious to you—"

Gray's tone was brittle. "I pray you, Mama, cease this lecture."

Charlotte's gaze turned as icy as his. "You use cynicism to mask your pain, Gray. That I do understand, so you do not fool me. I know better." She drew herself up to her full height. "Now, I shall take my leave."

Gray cupped her elbow. "May I have a footman call your coach for you?"

"You may consider me old, but I remain quite capable."

With his mother gone, Gray's gaze returned to the woman who had captured his attention. She was still there, standing by an ivory pillar. He found her intriguingly contrary. She was tall, but there was a delicate air about her. Slender, but he sensed a woman of fire on the inside. He found himself gripped by raw, physical desire. He imagined her naked.

Her legs, he had already noted, would be slim and long, long enough to wrap around his waist. The thought made his rod swell. And beneath the neckline of her gown, her breasts promised an enticing fullness. He imagined what they looked like, smoother porcelain flesh filling his palm. A dark stab of desire settled in his gut. The prospect of finding her beneath him, his legs parting her wide as he settled over her, made his rod tighten; he relished the idea of finding out for himself. And when he did, he would pleasure her again and then again.

Her profile was exquisite as well, small, perfect nose and long-lashed eyes. She turned his way then, and Gray sucked in a breath. Christ, she was beautiful. His reaction was immediate. Intense. Once again his eyes slid over her.

She did not shirk. She did not flinch from his scrutiny. Indeed, the chit evaluated him with an appraisal just as bold as his.

Precisely the response Claire wanted.